THE
HEART
OF A
LIFE

DAVID ILLSLEY

CRANTHORPE
—MILLNER—

Copyright © David Illsley (2022)

The right of David Illsley to be identified as author of this work has been asserted by him in accordance with section 77 and 78 of the Copyright, Designs and Patents Act 1988.

All rights reserved. No part of this publication may be reproduced, stored in a retrieval system, or transmitted in any form or by any means, electronic, mechanical, photocopying, recording, or otherwise, without the prior permission of the publishers.

Any person who commits any unauthorised act in relation to this publication may be liable to criminal prosecution and civil claims for damages.

This book is a work of fiction. Names, characters, places and incidents are either products of the author's imagination or are used fictitiously. Any resemblance to actual events or locales or persons, living or dead, is entirely coincidental.

First published by Cranthorpe Millner Publishers (2022)

ISBN 978-1-80378-100-6 (Paperback)

www.cranthorpemillner.com

Cranthorpe Millner Publishers

Prologue

Spain, 1936

This was the night for the taking of sides. It was almost time; there was just too much hate in the air, and the waiting was all but done. The boy smothered the shared cigarette, then crawled side by side with his friend to the very lip of the cave and gazed down and across to the heat-bleached valleys below, his shirt chalked and grey as the worn stone walls of their lair. Beneath their feet, quiet beneath the dust, and facing east, lay the shallow rock-cut tombs of two warriors, brothers, incised by the chisels and tears of grieving tribesmen long since cold. The boy could not know this of course, and spat. In the distance a column of soldiers lumbered darkly along the pale straight road, the nimbus of dust they wore above them rising as terrifying testament to their strength.

The pair observed in silence as every few minutes, and for no sane reason, a high-explosive shell was hurled high into the dying twilight sky, causing the egrets to scoot surf-white from the backs of the bulls with the tick-rich hides. Each blast wave seemed to shimmer over the slopes, dragging fear in its wake; it was almost as though they could see its morbid shape as it peeled across the swaying fields of wheat, leaving a momentary hush about the world as it passed.

The first boy seemed indifferent to the performance and rolled onto his side to study the profile of his friend against the dusk. Grass stalks skewered him through his shirt; dimly he was aware of the slick movement of insects, of the rumour of hidden things which bite; he did not seem to care.

"Seriously?" he asked at last. "You want us to go and fight for that lot? Is that all that bothers you? Your blisters and your boots?"

His companion smiled back at him, his starved eyes vast in the gloaming. "Yep. That and food. And girls. I told you a thousand times. The proper army will give us boots. Don't look at me like that. Look at the state of us! Arms like sticks, and my skin's still green from all that bastard unripe corn."

The first boy waited, frowning.

"Face it," his friend said at last. "It's here, it's happening. One way or the other, tonight we've got to choose. No matter what, it has to be tonight."

Ahead of them General Franco and the Army of Africa streamed slowly towards the town which his enemies had sworn to defend, and the two boys, along with tens of thousands like them, men and women spread out right across the land, were trying desperately to decide which flag to support. These people were neither fickle nor passive nor irresolute, but in the end this fratricidal war had come to them, not the other way around, and now they felt unjustly ambushed and stunned by the imminence of combat.

Just hours earlier, back in the town, had you seen them, you would not have doubted the boys' commitment to the left-wing cause – the Republican cause, that is: the cause of people sick of rule by priest and king, and of those who wanted no more than the lawful continuation of the recently elected Republic. Beguiled by the passion of the speaker, by the poet, by the intensity of the crowd, and the optimism of so many deadbeats like themselves with nothing left to lose, they had chanted and sung like true believers. The town itself had been a furnace. Despite the shade of the cathedral walls, it had been dementedly hot beneath the makeshift canopy, and rank with the stink of the hungry and unwashed, yet still dark enough for them to see the sparks which sang from the blacksmith's metal-hungry grinding wheel. The boys had studied his tremendous hands as he toiled, feeling their own sense of invulnerability swell in tune with the honing of their blades. They had accepted them reverently as the giant returned them, heads bent like altar boys, then stepped back into the sunlight to join the line of thin and soft-cheeked lads.

Daggers, old swords, a pruning knife, an axe; their edges whet by hope and stone, all shone war-proof in the mad and brutal heat. Young men, sharp steel, a common cause: they felt themselves immortal.

But then another stolen *fino* at the bar, another oath. And the two of them had crept away to climb the bell tower, to take stock just one last time.

"Go!" a swaying, self-appointed captain had brayed, waving his cutlass. "See the view!"

Still it felt like trespassing. The winding stairs were limed with the shit of countless birds; they had to duck to miss the beams, and each tread buckled and creaked with the weight of so much time. Halfway up, and rope cobwebs guarded the window which looked down onto the pretty patio. Pushing them aside they saw again the stack of six dead priests that lay in the middle, next to the fountain. They'd seen them earlier with the crowd, and jeered along with the others; up here, alone, the sight was vile and strangely more upsetting. A solitary dog circled the now untended pile and stopped to lap from a puddle of blood. The younger boy flinched and looked away; if he'd had his gun, he would have shot it. Instead, he took from his pocket the delicate marble hand of a saint, his trophy from that morning's pyramid of shattered effigies, and flung it in disgust at the creature. He missed, though watched in satisfaction as it detonated, and four centuries of fine sculpture exploded into nothingness.

Towards the top, the stairs gave way to a ladder, whose handrail was worn and grooved by centuries of God- and vertigo- fearing fingers. Up close the bells were monstrous. The boy reached out to touch one, his inquisitive fingertips determined and quick as those of a surgeon, then he struck it hard with the hilt of his knife. The power of the dull gun-metal boom shocked them deeply, continuing to reverberate long, long after the initial blow. To mask his fear the boy had snarled and stared out across to the hilltops; it was then that he had first seen the frightening column of dust.

"Let's get higher," they had said to each other as the bell still sang. "Up to the hills." Perhaps they could see the soldiers better from there, perhaps they could slide in behind them, count them, join them, even. "Let's get ourselves back to our cave."

And so they had left the sanctuary of the cathedral, excited and afraid, and still crazed by indecision.

All that was then. Now they watched as the column of men and dust came closer, and felt the fear grow.

"Let us never leave this cave," the younger one said. "Let us stay and ..."

But his friend suddenly raised a finger to his lips, then turned and stepped out alone, and down the blackening slope, for at last he understood, and knew that it was time.

Chapter One

Central London, 2010

Jess sensed the cold shriek of stone on steel as it wound itself up through the floor of the car, writhing up through the pedal, and into the soles of her feet. Concentrating hard, she edged the car forward, desperate that they would rise above whatever obstacle was holding them down. Sharp voices outside and inside the car, and even inside her own head, seemed to be screeching in unison with the howl of hurt metal.

Despite herself she looked up into the eyes of the policeman who stared down at her from the pavement.

"Maybe back her up a bit, love," he suggested patronisingly, and she revved the engine hard and threw the car into reverse. A small crowd had gathered to watch. Nothing to see here: just a car parked illegally outside a toyshop, caught on the kerb and blocking the pedestrian traffic at nine o'clock on a busy London morning. Inside the people carrier the three children were still squabbling, whilst their spaced-out mother in the passenger seat ransacked her bag for cigarettes.

Jess turned around and barked at the children to be quiet, just for a moment, please. As usual they ignored her, continuing to bicker as if she were not even there.

"I told you we couldn't just stop here," she said accusingly to the woman in the passenger seat, who turned her vacant, beatific smile towards her. Earlier that morning, during the regular sugar-fuelled breakfast rampage, the children had argued yet again, with the twins insisting that they should have the same crayons as their brother. To her dismay, Jess had been told to drive them all back to the same expensive shop on their way to school, for the sake of peace. Poor, spoiled kids, was this the best the grown-ups could do for them?

She looked at them again, then stared out through the windscreen. It was an oddly quiet moment. Stillness filled her, and the world outside seemed to be drifting by beyond, as if she were no longer part of it. Across the street, she watched as an old woman shuffled slowly between the cars, oblivious to the danger. Her hat was too large, and she carried flowers. She paused as she reached the far pavement, then disappeared through a gate in the hedge, followed by a stooped old man in faded pinstripes, he too with a small bouquet of pink carnations. Jess saw everything very clearly.

The desire to speak came out of nowhere.

"Your husband," she said quietly, "he's not done anything … illegal, not quite, but the way he behaves around me … it just can't go on. I can't put up with it much more."

It had been building slowly, slowly over weeks. As if in slow motion she observed the tanned, elegant hand of her companion as it reached towards the ash tray, a Marlborough Light balanced between long crimson fingernails. The ash tray was full to overflowing, and suddenly the car was filled with the odious stench of months-old tar and nicotine.

"God, how boring. Not another one. It doesn't bother me, you know. Not anymore."

If she had to be precise, then that was the exact moment. That was when Jess knew that she could no longer accept the disdain, the casual bullying, the scoldings and the abuse. She suddenly became aware that she was no longer angry, she was just indifferent.

The policeman had at that moment turned his back to remonstrate with someone on the pavement. Without thinking, Jess opened the car door, stepped out, and keeping her head down, slipped out into the scrum of the crowd. She expected shouting, someone to grab her, but it was as if she were invisible, and a few seconds later the flux of pedestrians guided her round the corner and out of sight. She kept on walking; an automaton guided by the will of the masses behind her. For good measure she pulled up the hood of her raincoat, though by now she knew it was no longer necessary: she was free.

She followed the throng as it moved inexorably towards the waiting throat of the underground, and at the last minute dodged sideways into the comparative calm of a newsagents. Looking absently at the rack of magazines for inspiration, she eventually selected an *El Pais* newspaper to keep up her Spanish, and a packet of mints. As she went to pay, she caught sight of the half-familiar profile of a woman on the monitor behind the till; it took her a moment to realise that she was looking at an image of herself, caught on the security cameras.

As she stepped once more onto the pavement, she was hit by a mixture of guilt and exultation. She shouldn't have left them like that, it was irresponsible. But they deserved it, after all the things they'd said, the things they had and hadn't done. Especially him, with his new, crude expectations. She wondered now why she had been able to stand it for so long. Truth was, they had abused her good intentions, taken her for granted, and she felt ... abraded, that was it, sanded down, the interesting parts of her life worn away to nothingness by routine and this exploitative servitude.

This was not a part of the city that Jess knew well. A double-decker bus hissed to a standstill beside her, and on impulse she stepped aboard and climbed the stairs. Why not? She was free. It felt liberating, intoxicating almost, and she gazed about her in tourist-like wonder as the bus stop-started its way along the busy street. After a while the bus stopped altogether, and to much groaning amongst the passengers, the driver switched off the engine. Ahead they could see a long line of angry cars, and in the far distance the dismal sight of traffic lights. It was already starting to get warm, and the man next to her struggled to open the hinged window above them. As she stared past him she noticed the church next door, soot-stained, dark and incongruously old beside the modern glass buildings to either side. Joining the people who had decided it would be quicker to walk, she descended the stairs and looked up at the spire of this timeworn building she would not normally have noticed. It looked oddly inviting.

The intimidating oak doors rumbled on their hinges as they closed behind her, instantly numbing the clamour of the city. There must have been a wedding recently, for the scent of flowers clung to the air; she breathed in the reassuring perfume of dust, hymn books and wood-stain, and began to relax. It was warm here too, and the intensity of the light that streamed through the stained-glass windows left her spellbound. Sanctuary, that's the word. She isn't religious, but she does appreciate the silent mystery of churches, and she gazed about her, charmed and at peace, until a young priest, stooped already with the weight of ostentatious piety, glided down the aisle towards her. He moved so serenely that she wondered for a second if beneath his cassock he was wearing those kids' trainers with the wheels embedded in the heels. But then he ruined it: smiling at her benevolently, he began his approach. Could he not see? She didn't want redemption; she just wanted to be on her own.

Abruptly she rose to her feet and strode back through the great doors, blinking in the sunlight and astounded by the disharmony of life outside. Reluctant to return immediately to this hubbub, she turned into the relative quiet of the overgrown cemetery behind the church, and sat self-consciously on one of the graffiti-covered benches. In the corner she noticed a discarded syringe; there was litter everywhere, and what little was left of a Styrofoam box of chips was being attacked energetically by a seagull. Opposite her, two drunks with implausibly posh accents were discussing the football. One caught her eye and offered her a swig from his bottle. She declined with a smile, which she realised he might well mis-read. It was time for her to go.

The traffic was moving again. She had forgotten how hungry she was, and walked briskly down the high street, trying not to think about the fumes. She preferred to steer clear of the major global chains, but knew her resolve would be tested this morning if she smelled roasting coffee. She needn't have worried, for the first place she came to was a small French patisserie. Perfect. The barista, noticing the *El Pais* under her arm, told her that she was from Madrid, and they chatted companionably until the next customers arrived. Jess loved the coffee, the croissants, and the opportunity to speak Spanish again. As she left she picked up a card which advertised a Spanish conversation class. *Why not*, she thought to herself: it's not as if she won't have time on her hands.

The day stretched long and emptily ahead of her. At the end of the road there was a tube station, and as she studied the map she realised that with just one change she could be on the Hammersmith line, and out to Mile End, and that she could go to see Duncan.

Poor Duncan. She hadn't really known him that well, he was just a half-familiar face amongst hundreds in her final year. But later, by chance, they happened to have been on the same Protest March, and it was he whose head had stopped the brick that some National Front moron had lobbed in the name of Queen and country, and who still lay almost lifeless in the Coma Unit. A group of his friends and family took turns to visit him now and then. Some would read to him, others played music. Ex-teammates read the reports from the County Championship, for as well as being a brilliant linguist he had been a gifted cricketer and for a while on the books at Middlesex. It was such a bloody waste, everyone said. But to her it was more than that. It was senseless, it was evil, and it represented all the hate and absurdity of twenty first century Britain.

But her mood had lifted by the time she got to the hospital. A busker was entertaining a small crowd at the entrance to the tube, and as she ran up the final flight of stairs she found she was still whistling along to the tune of *Summer Holiday*, a song which she detested.

She went past Reception and straight up to the ward. A nurse with a familiar face was standing behind the desk, fussing over a maze of charts, and she smiled at her.

"I know it's out of visiting hours," she began politely, "but would it be okay if I slipped in for a while to see Duncan?"

The nurse's smile vanished. She stepped from behind her desk and laid a hand on Jess's shoulder.

"Did no one tell you?" she asked softly in her Scottish accent. "Did you not hear? Poor boy ... he's gone. He passed away last week. Poor wee man. Will you not sit down? Will you have some tea?"

But Jess was backing out, moving away. She had to be alone to absorb this. No. Not Duncan. Why had nobody told her? She felt the tightness in her throat as she ran down the corridor. She gulped at the water from the tap in the Ladies, then stared at her reflection in the mirror. Outside, at the top of the steps, away from the antiseptic haze, she peered at the people coming into the hospital. *Who else among them would be going home with bad news*? she wondered. She saw that the sun was shining. She heard the strangled tune of an ice cream van, then watched it as it parked across the road. She struggled to remember Duncan's surname. Had she ever known it? Could you mourn for someone you never really knew?

She walked slowly down the steps and back towards the tube. Mercifully, the busker was gone. How did you deal with a sadness like this, this weird half-grieving for a half-stranger? She turned left, through the gates of a litter-strewn park, and waited for the tears to come. They didn't. Instead she perched on a bench and mused on the everyday shitness of life, and on all of the unshed tears that remained, until two small ice-cream spattered children joined her on her bench.

"Will you hold our kitten, miss? Will you help? We're trying to feed him some of this lolly and he keeps scratching us."

She took the creature gratefully. It was a cute little beast and to help these guileless kids was a service even she could render in her worthless frame of mind. *Small steps*, she thought, *small steps*, and stifled an obscenity as its tiny claws raked across her wrist.

Chapter Two

2010

Maria, living in London, had gone years without speaking a word of Spanish. Only in her worst dreams would she cry out in those strange, perplexing sounds of her mother tongue, her husband Tom told her, and in those times he would waken her gently. He wasn't the least bit interested in the learning of languages, in fact he found it strangely beneath him, and although in her eyes it did him no great credit, she had respected this lack of curiosity.

And in many ways it was better that way. In fact, it was probably the only way. Long before she met Tom, she had arrived in exile as a refugee from the Spanish Civil War in 1937, carrying no more than a sea-goer's kitbag and a shattered heart. In essence it was a simple story, like all the best ones. She and the man she loved had been separated against their will by people and circumstance, and she no longer knew where or whether he still drew breath.

His absence became the fulcrum of her existence. Her days seemed meaningless; the night skies tamed of their blaze. The simple act of waking was a trial. With him, her life for too short a time had shimmered and burned with an almost unendurable intensity, and now it lay lank, reduced, like the cold, lacklustre film on a London puddle. Once, in a different life, a robin had sat for them on the handle of a spade, an offering from Cupid sent to charm them; after a few days alone in England another had posed on her doorsill, this time the gift of a toxic God. "*Petirrojo,*" she had whispered to it, and the melody of the word in her mouth had all but dropped her to her knees in sadness. It scared her, even the sound of Spanish was becoming unholy to her.

At first, working in London at the hospital where she had volunteered as a non-qualified though much-needed nurse during the Blitz, she had come to know several compatriots, and they would chat away in the quiet hours, such as there were, but slowly they had all drifted apart. So many like her were simultaneously desperate for news of home, and equally terrified of receiving any. And so it was that she entered a strange form of benighted half-life, in which the ignorance and not knowing, although tortuous, was grotesquely preferable to the certainty of something dreadful.

Thus were her nights possessed by the most appalling anxiety and doubt, for she had identified several possibilities, each as horrible to contemplate as the next. Perhaps he was wounded, maimed, unable to move. Or he was dead. Or he had met and fallen in love with another girl. Or the vile possibility, the worst almost, so painful that she couldn't look it full in the face, was that she herself had been duped, that all the time he had been deceiving her with the enemy. A spy. The only other possibility that remained was that he was imprisoned. And this last, though terrible, was the least repugnant. It was the one thing she could cling to, the one last fragment of hope, and as the months dragged on to years, the one thing that gave her the strength to go on. In her innermost secret self she kept it hidden and aflame, as in a casket, a tiny shard of belief; her predicament was that if she considered it too long, it burned her.

All this while, almost by chance, she had begun to re-invent her life in an exclusively English-speaking environment. She was a quick and confident learner, and enjoyed the process. As the war ended, so did her real interest in nursing; it was all very well her doing her duty by the smashed up soldiers who came back from the fighting, but it was beyond her to stay longer on the wards once they began to fill with ailing civilians. However, she enjoyed the sense of caring, and was intrigued by the ambitious promises now being made by the left-leaning British politicians, and so seized her chance when offered a job as a temporary clerk in the incipient National Health Service.

At some level it was an unconscious, yet clinical decision to move on, to walk away from the past, away from Spain, away from him. The process almost tore her apart. Without any real confidante, or counsel, she was able – just - to divert herself with work through the daytime, but the dank, sleepless, dream-scarred English nights had become unbearable. She had somehow to become a new person: her old self was just too crushed by the weight of memory, the spirit of it too mutilated, and she had to let go.

And this new persona needed the habits and props to go with a new life: she allowed herself to get close to Tom, she studied hard, and within a few years she had a small pile of certificates to her name, and, eventually, a wedding ring. Later she took a position as Office Manager in a branch of one of the newly-formed Oxfam shops. She and Tom went to concerts in the evening, for walks in the park. To the outsider she was a modern, respected, and, yes, happy young woman.

To the outsider; she obsessed about this figure. As a foreigner, she would always have a trace of the outsider clinging to her skirts, that was normal, she knew that. The problem, in the darkest days, was that she was never completely sure if she was an outsider even within her own marriage, an impostor, a play actor. Or whether Tom, with his battle-damaged leg, and war-damaged heart, was likewise a character in their own home-spun drama, that they were both impersonators. Oh, there were times when they were good together, happy together, but she was so often left with the sense that things between them were somehow ... *diluted*, that was it. She had always been candid about her past, as, she hoped, had Tom. Right at the start he'd told her about Marjorie, his fiancée, and how desolate he'd been when she had died in the Coventry air raid, but his was a different kind of anguish, she thought privately. Quite naturally, his was underpinned by a sense of survivor's guilt, and a generalised rage against the universe, which he fought valiantly to control.

But there was something else too, he had once tried inarticulately to tell her. It was somehow that all the energy of his life had been compressed into those few, incandescent months of the war with Bomber Command, when he knew that his life might end at any moment. Nothing that happened afterwards could ever compete with the intensity of that time. He didn't enjoy the war, he had said, he was scared all the time. And he had never wanted to kill anyone; he didn't hate the Germans, he didn't hate anyone, he just wanted not to be killed, and to protect his fellow airmen, whom, in a macho, reticent kind of way, he confessed, he had loved and grieved over. It was as if he had reached the crescendo of his life too soon, and was now sauntering through the epilogue. And this Maria had recognised and understood, and – paradoxically – had therefore begun to love him slightly differently.

But at this deep, meaningful level they spoke very little. It wasn't just that this was post-war England, when few men of her acquaintance would ever admit to owning feelings, let alone have the tools to describe them, but it was likewise a failure on her part. At first she blamed it on an internalised mistrust of her abilities in English as a means to communicate intimate emotions, but then, as her English improved, she came almost to resent any attempt at probing. She understood that this reluctance was wrong at so many levels, but wished nonetheless to keep a part of herself secret. She had opened her heart to just one man, and to do so again would be an act of betrayal.

And so she and Tom had muddled along together all those years quite happily, each timidly conscious of the other's dull pain, but friends, true friends. Eventually she reached a plateau of relative serenity, and that, she knew, was the limit of her ambition. From time to time some memory would still stir the demons in her dreams, and for days afterwards she would listen to the gnawings deep inside that told her she wasn't living the life she was supposed to lead. But she understood too that hers was a life that was more than tolerable, and so she and Tom had leaned upon one another as they made their way past middle age, until he had died suddenly in 1989. And even after his death she had spoken hardly any Spanish until the incident in the park, near Highbury, many years later.

"You need to calm down, my lovely," she had heard the flustered policeman say to the girl. "I can't understand a word you're saying, slow down, tell me again." But the young woman was by now hysterical, shouting, pulling him by the arm, cursing in the deep-flavoured tones of Castille. Without thinking Maria grabbed her by the shoulders, assessed the situation, and translated swiftly to the man in uniform. In the end, it was over in minutes; the little boy was found far from the pond, gazing at a poster of colourful ice creams on the wall of the café.

And that would have been that, had the woman not insisted on buying her coffee and cake, and on conversation. Slowly Maria felt the Spanish words come back to her. It was if she could taste them in her mouth, flowing back like the flavour of a long-lost childhood recipe; her tongue heavy and clumsy with the effort.

Alone, on the walk back home, she practises these half-forgotten sounds, teasing out the trills of the long Spanish 'r', enjoying the melody and cadence of a language she had left so long submerged . Hesitatingly, like a mad woman, she describes aloud the things around her: the trees, the big red bus, the shadow of the streetlight; softly she begins to sing the tune of a half-remembered nursery rhyme, but stops when it starts to make her cry.

There is a newspaper kiosk close to her home, and on a whim she buys for the first time a copy of *Hola* magazine, and reads aloud to herself in the kitchen. She has no interest in the stories, nor the celebrities who grace its pages, but in the revelation provided by the language itself. A similar thing had happened once before, she recalls, alone in an Italian restaurant, when the unexpected taste of simple olive oil, poured over rough bread, had illuminated a deep buried memory like someone pulling back a curtain. But now the Spanish sounds she makes are at once exotic and commonplace, and she is fascinated as they tumble from her as though from the lips of a stranger.

She crosses to Tom's room, aware that the memories that now embrace her are far older than the dust that covers his desk. Beneath it there is a tape recorder. He used to get up at dawn, and she would sit silent as he tried to record the birdsong. Now she reads aloud the review of a new action movie, and sits down as she presses the play button to consider the sound of her own voice. She listens to the shape of the words, her voice deeper than she would have expected. The Spanish harmonies seem to reflect something of her which she knows to be there, but cannot see, like a mirror of sound that allows her to see behind her, around her.

Thinking this, she drags the machine over to the full length mirror on the dresser and watches captivated as she mimes her own voice to the silent image in front. A long string of beads lies on the table, which she wraps unconsciously around her neck. The room is quiet beyond quiet, wrapped in half-light and the familiar, musty perfume of her old clothes and mothballs. It's a strange performance, but she sees, she hears, the past, as it drags her back to meet it. And then she feels him. She will always swear she feels his presence behind her, and turns to look for him, and then, as she swivels, shocked, in the darkened ebony corner of the mirror, she sees his face.

Chapter Three

London, 2010

Jess had promised herself that she would go, just to try it, but by lunchtime the appeal of the Spanish conversation club was waning. She had a slight headache, and it was beginning to rain. She would buy a sandwich at the deli down the road, and watch her video instead. But then Lynn, the flatmate, had arrived back breathless with Handsome Boyfriend Number Three, and the idea of hearing them having noisy afternoon sex as she watched *Casablanca* in the room next door was simply too much to bear.

And so it was that an hour later she arrived damp and forlorn at the grand old rooms above the pub in Hackney, and pressed the doorbell with no real sense of excitement. Any thoughts she may have had that the gathering would be sober and earnest were instantly dismissed. Her spirits lifted immediately. There was food, and there was drink, mostly wine, and she had forgotten how exuberant the Spanish could be, and just how loud. There must have been around thirty people present, but it seemed like more.

She gave her name to the two English girls who seemed to be the organisers, handed over the two pound fee that made her a member, and was introduced to a group of people her age. It was fun. Some of them wanted genuinely to study Spanish, some wanted English conversation classes, and others, most in fact, just wanted to relax in the warmth of a Spanish environment.

Jess was amongst the last to leave. By the door an old lady was saying her goodbyes. Jess had noticed her earlier, clearly the oldest person in the room, sitting serene and comfortable beneath a tartan blanket as people drifted across to chat with her. Jess had been too shy to approach her then, without an introduction, but now offered her arm to help her down the steep stairs.

They talk easily on the way down, and linger for a while in the imposing, tiled entrance hall. As Jess opens the door they see that it is raining hard. Lights from the shops opposite reflect blackly in the road, which hisses with the weight of passing cars. A silvered, sleet-covered jumble of umbrellas side-step and mumble their apologies on the pavement, and even at this distance it's as if Jess can feel the slow, wet presence of the Thames so far away.

"Pissing it down!" says the old lady cheerfully. "That's one of the first English expressions I ever learned."

Jess laughs aloud. "Pub?" she asks, pointing to the door to their right.

"Pub," the old lady agrees. "That was one of the other things I first learned!"

Arm-in-arm they enter the Fox and Hounds. It is quiet, and the bartender, a hard-bitten skinhead with an Irish accent, smiles warmly at the old lady, and greets her by name.

"So you're Maria ... I'm Jess," she says as they sit down by the window. There are cups and glasses left over from the previous drinkers, but they are lured to this table by its proximity to an enormous cast-iron radiator.

"I know," Maria says, "I asked, I saw you." Jess is taken aback by this information, and strangely pleased.

"Sugar," says Maria for no apparent reason. "Sugar for my bones!" She reaches across to a discarded cup and saucer, lifts a half-open sachet and waves it in the air. "It's what it used to say on the sugar packets in Spain. Complete nonsense of course. Couldn't say it these days, they'd be prosecuted. Our cook used to say it every morning at breakfast, made us laugh. Our cook ... I don't mean we had a cook, I was a maid, a kitchen help ... I was poor."

Jess waits patiently for more. "Go on," she says when it isn't forthcoming, "I'm intrigued."

Old Maria looks at her. "It's a long story, most of it dull, really, you don't want to ..."

But Jess cuts her off. "Oh but I do," she says, "I do. And it's wet outside. How better to spend a long evening than in the pub, with a new friend, learning Spanish. And it's all history, you'll tell it all in the past tense, I can practise all those irregular verb endings!"

Maria sighs. She's strangely nervous, but energised. "It's mostly boring. I've not told my story, not to anyone, not the full story, not for such a long, long time." She drifts off for a moment. "You don't want to know."

Jess squeezes her hand. "Try me," she pleads. "If it gets boring I'll stop you, promise." She waits, and for a moment the old lady looks so sad that she thinks she may have overstepped the mark. "Sorry," she says, "have I upset you?"

"*Cariño*," she says. "Not at all. I just don't ... I just don't know where to begin. Sometimes the past is so alive to me, so real, more real than today ... and other times it seems so far away that it's like it didn't really happen. I was somebody else, so it's not a story that has a beginning and an end; life's not like that, not mine anyway."

Jess stares at her, and nods. She understands, in a way. "Tell me how you got to England then, how's that?" she asks gently after a while. "If you want to ..."

Maria sits back in her chair. She doesn't know quite why, but she feels a stillness in the presence of this young girl; she reminds her of someone, though she can't think who. It will do her good to try to remember again. She begins with the journey from Spain. She doesn't explain how she got there, nor what happened during the voyage, just that she had travelled in great discomfort.

"I didn't know where we were, to be honest. Turns out it was Portsmouth. As the ship sailed in, all I could see were the shiny black roofs of little houses, it must have been raining, and the sea was brown. It was funny, the only sea I'd ever seen was the Mediterranean; I thought all the seas were blue!"

Jess smiles in solidarity. She can picture her, cold and confused. In her imagination she sees her as some young Penelope Cruz, dragged uncomprehending from the warmth of Castille to the chill grey sleet of the English coast.

"I was lucky. I knew people, or, that is, I had somewhere to go. It was around the time of the Kindertransport, you know, all those trains that brought in the poor Jewish children, trying to get away from the Nazis. I wasn't a Jew, or a child, but there were people – probably still *are* people, because the British are great like that – people who cared about what was going on in Europe, and who wanted to help. I really felt it, a warmth, somehow ..." She pauses. "A warmth in the people, I mean, not in the weather ... I was so fucking cold, so often." She glances up, wickedly, wondering if she would shock. Jess is delighted.

"And the people who I was to stay with had sent a car. I'd hardly ever been in a car before. All that way ..."

They had ordered sandwiches, and Jess observes her quietly as they eat. She can see that she is thinking hard, putting her thoughts in order. Hesitantly she begins to paint a picture of the journey, of the big house and its occupants. Jess listens entranced as she describes her friendship with one of the daughters, a woman in her 20s, who after a month or so had broken both legs in a car crash. Maria had looked after her, had fed her and changed her, and in doing so had developed a talent for nursing, whilst the woman, by teaching English to Maria, had discovered her interest in education.

"It's funny the way that things sometimes turn out like that, as if they should ..."

Her voice tails away. Jess can't leave it alone.

"And then what happened?" she asks.

"What happened? Well, what always happens ... things just happen, don't you think? I just bumped along, carried along on the tide of events, like everyone else. When I look back, I don't think we have much choice really, not as much as we think, anyway. An expression in English that's always troubled me is that people say that they come to a decision, but in my experience it's usually it's the other way round: a decision comes to you, at least the big ones." She looks a little tired, as if she means to stop there.

"So you don't believe in free will then?" Jess regrets this instantly; it sounds pompous. She shouldn't be showing off with this lovely old lady as if she were still some pretentious undergraduate.

But not for the first time, Maria surprises her, and puts her gently in her place. "No free will? No, I didn't say that, not exactly. We do have it, a little, but not in the way you might think. Sometimes, people may have the illusion of control, but they don't, not really ... but where we do have jurisdiction, all of us, is in our reaction to things, the way we respond to events, especially tragic ones ... we always know, deep down, even if we pretend otherwise, that there's a right way and a wrong way to react. And that's where our free will resides, in the way that we answer the questions that life asks of us."

Jess is astonished by the clarity and wisdom of the old lady. "I'm not sure," she says eventually, timidly, "but I think that's roughly what Albert Camus said, more or less, the French, I mean Algerian writer; we studied him at university, he had this ..."

But if she had been surprised by the old lady before, the next revelation stuns her.

"Camus! I fancied him! For a while I had a real crush ... I thought he looked like a Spaniard, an Andalucían! And guess what: I met him once, or at least I saw him close up. I'd gone with Tom to Paris, with his business. It was 1957, and he'd just won his Nobel prize. Camus, that is, not Tom, and we were in this fancy restaurant, being schmoozed by Tom's colleagues, and he walked in. With a woman, Maria Casares, I think she was called, not his wife, and the restaurant just kind of went quiet ... no one said anything, but we all knew it was him, he was a presence. They just sat down at a table, and we carried on."

Jess is dumbfounded by this story, by Maria's consistent ability to astonish her. "And in the middle of dinner I got up to go to the bathroom, and as I walked past his table he looked up and smiled at me. Me! " She looks distant for a second, reliving the moment, and Jess, perhaps seeing a glimpse of the beautiful young woman she must once have been, suffers a strange pang of jealousy. What a life she must have led.

There is a faraway look in Maria's eyes as she goes on. "And the oddest thing is, the cruellest, I suppose, is that we never know, we never really know, whether we've made the right choice or the wrong one, even if we're brave and go the hard way." She leaves this hanging in the air, and before Jess has a chance to pursue it, the waitress comes to clear away their plates, and Maria announces that it is time for her to go.

Chapter Four

London, 2010

Over the following few months an unlikely friendship began to build between Jess and the old lady. Each week they would meet at the Spanish conversation club, where they would both do the rounds and chat and mix with the other members, and Jess especially was happy to develop this new network of hispanophile acquaintances. But what she most looked forward to was the small routine that had quickly been established, when towards the end of the session she would seek out Maria at her table, and they would talk intensely, just the two of them. It was as if the others in the room had learned to leave them alone.

First, Maria would reach across and take hold gently of Jess's wrists, then scrutinise her face with undisguised curiosity. It was never made clear just what it was she sought, but Jess was content to endure this strange analysis. After a while, satisfied, she would mumble indistinctly to herself, and bombard her with questions. Jess always took her time to answer carefully, partly as a courtesy to Maria who listened so attentively, but also because she found it useful to organise her thoughts, as if in self-justification.

In return, Jess would quiz her about her early life in Spain, for she found it utterly fascinating to try to comprehend the profound changes to which her elderly friend had born witness. This was someone who had been raised in complete penury, whose siblings had perished of malnutrition, who had withstood the vicissitudes of a young woman in a semi-feudal Spain, who as a child had worn shoes whose soles were cut from car tyres, who was weaned on the milk of donkeys, and yet who now ordered books on the internet, and who had developed a late-life passion for sushi. It was an enigmatic story, at once remote and yet vividly accessible when related in the first person by its protagonist, and Jess thought her own life mundane in comparison.

And always, skulking cold and brutish behind the enigma, lay the sadness and mystery of what had happened to her during the Spanish Civil War. Jess learned quickly not to push her on this. If Maria happened of her own accord to be reminded of some episode or grievance, then she would discuss it openly, no matter how harrowing these reminiscences might seem. If, however, she was quizzed overtly over some detail, then it always seemed to trigger the same reaction – one of stubborn silence. Much later, when they had come to know each other better, Maria tried to explain that it was as though there were a metaphorical door which separated her current consciousness from memories too painful to bear. If on occasion she was feeling strong enough she would open it a chink and contemplate the past on her terms; if on the other hand this door were forced ajar by the clumsiness of another, then she could easily become swamped by bitterness, rage and regret.

There was still fury there too, and the courage to go with it. Jess saw it at first hand one grey winter afternoon when they travelled together to the Jubilee Gardens, close to the London Eye, to the monument to the 526 British volunteers of the International Brigade who had been killed in the defence of liberty in Spain. Every year Maria and a small group of survivors gathered there to mark the death of Franco, who had died in November 1975, and that morning a journalist from the *Guardian* was to deliver a short commentary.

Maria seemed cheerful, not subdued.

"It wasn't that long ago, you know. You like David Bowie? The previous week he was Number One with *Space Oddity.*"

Jess smiled to herself. She liked these references, these little markers that gave her the framework to consolidate her understanding of the past. She thought of them as the straight edges of the jigsaw puzzle of history, the gettable pieces that helped to make sense of the whole.

"It was a strange day," she went on. "I wanted to rejoice that the old bastard Franco was gone, but I was kind of crushed to hear about it. At first it didn't sink in. We had a party alright, and danced and celebrated, but for me at least it was a bit of an anti-climax. I think I'd been expecting some kind of an end-of-an-era, defining moment where we would all acquire instant closure. But it didn't feel like that, not really. It was more like the day that the scab came off the wound; we knew that the healing was happening, but there was still all the scarring to deal with."

Jess was about to comment on this image when the speaker stepped up onto a table and the crowd grew quiet. He was good. He began by reminding his audience that the volunteers of the International Brigade had disregarded their own Government's advice not to travel to Spain, and that as a consequence many had died unnecessarily in a war they could not win. On one level therefore, it was true: at least from a simple, hateful perspective, these people were losers. But that was the glib, facile version, and the view taken only by the vindictive and the ignorant. He paused to let this sink in. He was a clever orator, and as she glanced around her, Jess was pleased to see that he already had his audience eating out of his hand. For a while they listened in silence.

"And so even from a purely military point of view," he concluded, "their efforts were effective." His voice had risen and was plainly audible above the roar of the city.

"But consider this too: these brave, ill-fated volunteers whose unburied bones still cover the hot dry slopes of Castille were but kin and cousin to those lunatic, lion-hearted sons of England who sailed out so magnificently from Kent just three years later to save the day at Dunkirk. It was the same spirit of selflessness and defiance that lifted the hearts of the Partisans and the Resistance, and which inspired the Poles and the Free French to take their places in the cockpits of the Spitfires as they took on the same fascist enemy – against all odds – in the Battle of Britain.

"And so, let me finish by saying this: romantic, dishevelled and disorganised as they were, the courage and conviction of the Brigadistas is beyond dispute. For many of us their sacrifice and ambition is still a source of inspiration, for what they brought, if nothing more, was *hope*.

"And perhaps this should be their legacy, that although those brave and law-loving, idealistic boys and girls, the gallant carriers of hope, may have bled and died on the battlefields, the flame they carried, the flame of hope itself, did not." By now the man was hoarse, and visibly moved. "Thank you."

The applause began before he stepped down from the podium. Jess blinked away a tear, and was about to speak when suddenly she jumped as a beer can came flying through the air and landed close by.

Maria sighed. "Oh well. Here they come again. The angry wasps have discovered the picnic and want to spoil it for everyone."

A small group of bored, right-wing teenagers had seen what was happening and had swaggered over with their cropped heads and grubby Union Jack tee-shirts and were trying to provoke the listeners.

"The living, breathing proof of British exceptionalism, eh," said an American voice from behind them. Jess turned to look, and noticed that many of the younger members of their own crowd were moving out to confront the aggressors.

"This might get a bit ugly," she whispered to Maria. "Let's move away a little bit."

"What? And give in to these skinny *hijos de puta?* No thanks. I had enough of that years ago. I can't hurt them, but they'll have to hurt me if they want me to move." She spoke in a loud, clear voice and several bystanders heard her. Instinctively they moved to form a protective circle around this frail old woman, and others joined them. "*No pasarán!*" cried someone, and they began to walk towards the intruders.

Fortunately there were police on hand to prevent any serious violence. This was the centre of tourist London, and the security forces were present in numbers as a consequence of a recent terrorist threat. Other than some jostling and the usual shouted obscenities no damage was done.

"That went well," said Maria. "Good to know that the old fire-in-the-belly is still there."

But Jess found that she was trembling and that there was a lump in her throat. This mixture of courage and fragility was intoxicating, but it left her anxious, not so much for herself as for Maria.

It was their sixth outing together, and the more she learned of Maria's astonishing life, the more she came to admire her, and the more she feared for her. Each time, they took a taxi to their destination and Maria refused all possibility of a wheelchair. It wasn't out of pride, she said, nor stubbornness, but was more a determination to remain independent as long as she possibly could, and besides, her doctor had said that it was good for her. She walked with a stick, and moved carefully, but even so, Jess remained perturbed as they tapped their way along the busy pavements, and tried to maintain a surreptitious vigilance. That morning it had been especially difficult, first with all the skateboarders on the Embankment, and now worse, on the ramps leading onto the ferry.

"Stop worrying," she told her. "I crossed this river at night in the Blitz when the sky was full of Luftwaffe planes. You could see the flames of the burning buildings reflected in the water. Now *that* was scary. There had been so many people wounded in Battersea that they took a dozen off-duty nurses to treat them on the spot. The bridges were all blocked, so they took us across in this little, tiny boat. If I can survive that I'm hardly going to fuss over this!"

They had settled together at the back of the modern ferry, and studied the churning, coffee-stained waters of the Thames.

"Who said I'm worrying?" Jess answered, and pulled a face. Between the wind and the roar of the engine it was too loud to talk and they sat in happy silence for the ten minute trip across to the Tate.

As the vessel bumped into the rubber fenders on the opposite pier, Jess could feel the weight of Maria's scrutiny.

"I know who it is," said Maria as they shuffled off on the opposite bank, "I know who you remind me of: Becky! It was the water that made me remember. I'll tell you about her some time."

Jess was about to quiz her, but the wake from an enormous ship caused the pontoon bridge to shudder so that Maria wobbled, and she had to grab her by the shoulders, and the moment passed. Instead they made their way slowly down Millbank as Maria explained her reactions to the film they had seen the previous night. The plan was for them to have lunch at the Rex Whistler restaurant inside the Tate Museum.

"My treat," Maria had insisted. "I know it's a bit decadent, but I love it here, and when you get to my age you take whatever small pleasures you can, even when it's a guilty, bourgeois one like this." She gazed in contemplation at the elegant murals which stretched all across the long wall. "And me: born a peasant girl! Sometimes it's still hard to absorb. Do you think it's hypocritical of me?"

"Not at all. You deserve it. It's me that's the parasite. Now, about that chocolate mousse …"

They were the amongst the last to leave, and when they walked outside the light was already fading. A determined wind blew cold across the river, testing the few remaining leaves that clung to the trees and whipping those that failed into the gutters. The two women huddled in the lee of a great beech tree as they waited for a taxi, unsettled by the change in atmosphere, but alert enough still to wonder at the beauty of the coming night, as one by one the keepers of the great buildings all around switched on their lamps to fill the city sky with light.

"I love this free show," said Maria as she clambered into the car when at last one came. "And you take care now, okay. See you on Thursday!"

Jess waved fondly as the taxi accelerated away, then turned to make her way back home. She was tired but wanted to walk off some of that lovely lunch, so hunched her shoulders and marched into the teeth of the wind, her head down, towards the lights of Tower Bridge, and trying to imagine what it would be like to see the reflected lights of wartime fires burning blackly on the water.

The following Thursday she had made a mental note to ask Maria more about her memories of the Blitz, but to her surprise she wasn't there to take her usual seat in the room above the pub.

"First one that she's missed in ages," said Sandra, the club secretary. "She's not answering her landline and doesn't have a mobile. But listen: Michael lives near enough, so he's agreed to look in on her tonight. I'll call you tomorrow if anything's wrong."

Jess had an odd sense of foreboding which in the end proved justified. Maria had fallen at home and was now in the hospital in Kingston. She closed the file she had been working on and was there within the hour.

To her relief, Maria was sitting up in bed and talking to a doctor.

"It could have been worse," the doctor told her. "She's broken her ankle. A clean break which we've set, but she'll need to be in plaster for at least six weeks, perhaps more, and then a fairly lengthy period of physio. Does she live alone?"

Jess looked at Maria who had been following the conversation.

"Not anymore," said Jess after a pause. "She has a new live-in helper."

After the doctor had gone she sat carefully at the side of the bed, and the two of them held hands.

"Well that's interesting. You just decided that there and then, didn't you? You didn't plan to be my helper. They're the best kind of decisions ... sometimes. You can back out if you want, I won't keep you to it. Think it through a bit."

Jess could think of plenty of reasons why it wasn't a good idea, and what her friends and her mum would say.

"No," she said. "It's just feels like it's the right thing to do."

"You can have the spare room. I'll pay you, we can-"

"No thanks. I don't want any payment. Maybe you can let me live rent-free for a while, but I'll need to keep doing this job, at least part time, and working from home. That's a condition." She held up hand to forbid any further protest. "Deal?"

Maria sighed. "Deal," she said. "But I'll be avenged, you mark my words.

Jess went out to get more information from the doctors. Maria stared after her as she left, then focussed through the window outside where she could see sparrows feeding from a bird-table. She was so tired. She couldn't keep awake. *The right thing to do,* she muttered to herself as her eyelids closed. *The right thing to do.*

When Jess came back ten minutes later it looked to her as though her new patient was smiling in her sleep. Softly she pulled the blanket to cover her bare arm, slid the newspaper she had been reading onto the bedside table, and tiptoed outside.

"All good?" asked the duty nurse in the corridor.

"All good," she replied. "All good," and walked out into the teeming grey rain of West London.

Chapter Five

2010

Jess had just returned from a weekend trip to see her mother in Canterbury. The visit had not gone well, despite their best intentions. They hadn't argued, not as such, but her mother's apparent inability to empathise always left her feeling deflated. It was maddening: she knew her mother cared deeply for her, but her concern always seemed to manifest itself in the form of clumsy, worthy advice, or worse, in those throwaway, judgemental opinions which by accident or design seemed to wound her the most. On the train home she had cried in frustration.

Nor had she slept well, but a lazy morning in the rambling old house in the company of Maria had improved her spirits. The two of them were now talking outside in the sunshine, on the grandiose terrace of a café on the edge of Wimbledon Common. It had been a year since she had moved in to Maria's home and the trip to the café had become a regular treat for the two of them, one they both look forward to.

Yes, her mother means well, Jess says, she knows that. But still it riles her to be told over and over that she is wasting time, wasting her life and an expensive education, that she can't go on forever *treading water.* It's not even as though she's treading bloody water, Jess continues. That at least implies that there's some degree of control, a plan of sorts. But she doesn't feel any sense of control; it's more that she is being driven down a river, dragged along by the current, from time to time crashing into the riverbanks where for a while she clings to the roots of some plant before letting go and being pulled back into the stream.

"It's fine when you're young, like you," her companion advises. "*Le bateau ivre* and all that; the drunken ship."

Jess looks at her, perplexed.

"Rimbaud, Arthur Rimbaud. The French poet. He depicts exactly the sensations you just described.

Jess smiles to herself. At times it seems to her that she's talking to a gifted teenager, rather than an enfeebled geriatric. And she loves that Maria listens properly, supportively, rather than forever challenging her.

"We studied him," Maria goes on. "I tried to do a degree with the Open University in French. Gave it up. Too many essays, too many deadlines. A lot of it was ... I don't know ... but for example, *Le bateau ivre* is one of those poems that everyone agrees is a great work of art, though honestly, I've never understood why. Maybe it's because much of it doesn't make that much sense to me, though I do like one of the underlying notions, this idea that we're hauled along by unseen forces."

Just then two joggers trundle by in unflattering Lycra, the man looking enviously at the cake on their table.

"A bit like all that," Maria goes on, dismissing the joggers with a wave of her hand. "I know that exercise, running, is wonderful, but I just don't *understand* it!"

Jess laughs aloud, happy to be teased, for she knows that Maria worries about her when she does her long runs across the Common, often at dusk. But it's not something that she would relinquish lightly, because she loves the discipline, the routine, and that hard-fought-for sense of physical well-being.

"Well don't worry," she says, "I won't be running this week. I'm exhausted. And listen: when I say I'm not in control that's got nothing to do with my being here with you. You're better now and I know I can leave whenever I want. I'm here with you by choice."

The previous month she had taken yet another temporary post, this time in the administration department of a catering company. It was a boring desk job, but it paid the bills, and there were lots of young people around, mostly European, and she enjoyed the atmosphere. But that week, due to sickness and cock ups, the company had found itself vastly under-staffed for a prestigious event at a National Trust property, and Jess had responded to the call for emergency kitchen workers. What this meant in practice was clearing tables, getting shouted at by irritable, over-worked chefs, and hours of relentless washing up. Her hands were red and sore after so much soapy water.

"Look at them!" she complains to Maria. "It feels as if they're sun-burned."

Maria gently takes her hands and begins to examine them.

"I know," she says thoughtfully. "It hurts. Mine were like that for years. I didn't know it at the time, but a woman's hands are important. When they're soft, manicured, it's part of your make up, almost. I never went in for all the manicure, the nail painting, but nice hands are … I don't know, a luxury, at least when you've abused them for so long."

Jess stays quiet, giving her time to go on.

"I was in service, as they used to say. My mother too, for a while. They'd been farmers, peasant farmers on an estate, and suddenly the

Depression came, then drought, and all the land dried up, so that many of them had to leave the countryside and go off to find work in the cities. Often it was factories for the men, domestic service in the homes of the rich for the women. There was no shame, it was just what you did ..."

As usual, Jess is captivated.

"It was a big house. Two big houses, in fact, first in Madrid, and then Toledo. The family I worked for were canny, well-connected, they could see what was coming, and so almost right at the beginning of the war, when it was all becoming a bit too precarious for the rich, they moved out practically overnight to an even bigger place in Toledo. They were military, the family I mean, real traditionalists."

There is a dreamy, far-away look in her eyes now. Jess knows that if she's lucky these memories will continue to pour out from her unchecked and the details she can question later, so she stays silent.

"There was always the scent of linseed oil. They used it on the furniture. And starch. There was a laundry downstairs; you don't really see starch anymore, but they used it on all the bed linen. They looked after me, mothered me really, not the owners, not them, but the other staff, the cook, the other servants. There was a boy my age. Lots of candles too, religious ones. The windows all had shutters, it was one of my jobs to go from room to room, opening them all up. I'd walk into one room and it would be so dark I could barely see; my eyes would adjust to the blackness and then boom! I'd throw open another one to be blinded. I must have spent a lot of my youth groping around in the gloom ... In the afternoon I had to do it all over again, especially in the summer, you had to make sure the sun didn't shine directly on to the carpets and the tapestries. She'd kill you if you forgot. They used to make me miss supper some times. It was always quiet in the house, compared with the outside: in the street there were always people yelling, arguing, selling things, horses, lots of horses …"

Maria still hasn't touched her cake. "Why am I telling you this?"

Jess holds up her hands. "Overwork," she smiles, "though it sounds like you were overworked a lot more than I ever was; I'm embarrassed!"

"No. It was just a different kind of work, different expectations. And you know what? I was mostly happy there. I could come and go a fair bit, I went out, did mischief. I played a lot with the owner's son, the younger son. I tried to get on with the daughter too, she was only a year older than me, but she didn't like me. She was more like her mother. Some people are born snobs, that's a fact. But there was ping pong, hide and seek, all that kind of stuff. I remember, we went to the park once, with a kite, a huge blue and yellow kite, I can see it now. I was so scared it would lift me away, and so scared I would let it go and the boys would shout at me. But the washing up, yes, they had these great white plates, heavy, and every kind of glass … wine, sherry, brandy, they taught me all of them, they let me lay the table if there weren't guests. And the clothes, my God! They had these great chunks of lime or something that they threw in with the laundry; if you didn't rinse your hands straight away it would take your skin off. In the winter we'd all have these red blotches, flaking skin between our fingers, that was awful."

She takes a mouthful of cake, as if the effort of recollection has tired her.

"But mostly – mostly – despite the hard work I'd say that I was happy. Everyone these days wants to know if you're *happy* to be doing something. It wasn't quite like that before; we just got on with stuff. But to be fair, in the beginning, I was, well, not *un*happy."

"In the beginning? And then what happened?"

"What happened?" She looks sad. "What happened is that they sent me away. To a different house. A different master."

Chapter Six

Madrid, 1933

Maria was barely thirteen when she left her village in the sierras outside Madrid, just one more casualty of the droughts and the Great Depression which laid waste to so much of rural Spain in the early 1930s. In a sense she was lucky, for through a friend she found a position as a servant in a great house in the city. She had few rights and few prospects, but – up to a point – her employers were fair, and she had food. After the first months of predictable homesickness and weeping, she began to settle in; she made friends, she began to explore the city and its ways, and in general exhibited all the curiosity for life of any other adolescent. For a good two years she was, for want of a better word, contented.

But her life was less stable than she had begun to imagine, and subject to the caprice of her superiors. In her state of virtual thraldom she was a commodity. Devotees of Hollywood Westerns may perhaps recognise the word *peon,* an unskilled worker; what they may not know is that it also means pawn, as in chess, and for good reason.

The rich man was a distant relative and had come to her employers' house at the end of spring. He had smiled at Maria, who had shied away and hidden in the kitchen with the cook. But there must have been something about her which pleased him, for the following day a letter arrived, which politely requested that her employers might spare her in order to take up a position at his own residence. There was nothing particularly unusual about this, and non-specialist staff were often traded, as it were, between households with little or no concern for their opinions. Like pawns. If the man had need of her, then he should have her; no doubt at some point the favour would be returned. Meanwhile, although there was general agreement that she was a good and conscientious worker, the lady of the house had lately become suspicious of the bond that was evidently forming between the girl and her youngest son. Nothing good could come of it. Besides, the boy was away at the military academy and only home at weekends; it could do no harm to get rid of her for a while. The decision was made.

The new house was large, built over several stories, with tall balconies set high above a fashionable part of the city. If you looked hard from the street you could see that the windows on the very top floor were much lower than those below; it would be uncomfortably hot up there in the months of Summer with those cramped ceilings - this is where the servants lived. Many years later the building would be converted to a luxury bijou hotel, the top floor transformed into a splendid swimming pool, its history forgotten.

The man who owned the building had lived there as a boy, had been born there in fact, as had his father. The man was a very senior civil servant, whose wife had left him. Given the conventions of the day this had provided a significant shock to his career and to his standing, but he had survived. His wife had even taken their daughters with her, back to her parents in their ancestral home in Bilbao. People said that she was a clever woman, though perhaps too modern for her own good. Within a couple of years the man's reputation had begun to recover, and the scandal died away, as these things do.

By 1933, half of the rooms in this grand building stood empty. For a house of such size there were few staff, no more than a half dozen. This in itself was perhaps surprising, for there was widespread unemployment across the country, due not just to the incompetence of successive governments, but likewise to the concussive effects of the Wall Street crash and its aftermath years later. People were hungry, desperate, and wages correspondingly low. For a wealthy bureaucrat it would have been little burden to add to the small number on the payroll, but, for whatever reason, his servants were few.

Amongst the people in the *barrio*, the local neighbourhood, it was always understood by an invisible bush telegraph which masters were fair, and therefore popular, and those who were not. The man in the half-empty house fell into the latter category. Maria had expected not to like him, and she didn't. She hadn't liked him when he had first set eyes on her a month earlier, at her first house, with Lucas and Jacob and the others, and she didn't like him now.

In truth she conceded that he was not loathsome to look at, but she loathed him nonetheless. For the first few months, nothing happened; he barely spoke to her. She got on with her work, and adjusted as best she could to her changed circumstances. Her duties were often onerous, but no more so than in her previous job. It was more that her new colleagues seemed old to her, and dull. Often she would go back to the old house to see her ex-workmates, and they seemed happy by comparison.

Had she lowered her guard? For months afterwards she would ask herself that question. She had been warned. Even the gentle cook had cautioned her to stay safe, to quit the half-empty house if necessary. She herself had seen it coming. She saw the way he looked at her sometimes. She sensed in him that base, ugly need. She was young, inexperienced, but still some primitive intuition warned her of the even more primitive, malignant nature of his intentions. She made sure never to be alone with him. She even stole a knife from the kitchen, sharpened it in secret, and hid it under a rug in the corner of her room; she was ready to use it.

That morning she was happy. Later she would remember that she had been singing to herself. Every other Tuesday there was a street market in their *barrio*, and all the staff were allowed the morning off; this was what allowed her to go to her class.

The house was quiet. She assumed that she was alone, that the master had gone off early to his office, as he always did. She was in the library, for there was a word in the dictionary that she wanted to look up, a word that Jacob had used.

She remembers every detail. The letters were tiny, her face close to the musky page, her mouth twitching slightly as a finger traced its way alphabetically down the index. There had been a noise, perhaps the faint scraping of a chair, or the creak of a wooden parquet tile; a tiny noise, a warning, so that she just had time to lift her head.

Before he hit her, she felt for one long, horrifying moment the fat, meaty weight of his hand on the back of her neck. The blow when it came was a calculated punch to her temple. She blacked out. And then the awfulness began.

Chapter Seven

Wimbledon, 2011

The doorbell rang just before nine, and Jess skipped downstairs, mouth half full of toast, hoping she would be about to take delivery of her new books. Wiping the last crumbs from her lips as she opened the door, she was convinced that the large brown envelope in the Postman's hand was for her, and so was doubly disappointed when she saw that it was for her landlady. The package was certified, and she had signed for it wordlessly.

"It's for you, Maria," she called, going to the living room and tapping quickly on the door before entering. The old lady was sitting in her chair, peering at that morning's *Guardian*. Jess was glad to see her looking so well and alert; she knew how badly broken bones can affect people of her age, and her fall a year ago had given them both a fright. Her plaster had long been removed, and, stubbornly independent, she still hobbled around in some pain, with the effort showing in her face.

But this morning there is colour in her cheeks, and she's smiling.

"Arsenal won!" she says. "I always look, even now, they were Tom's team, you know." Jess smiles back at her, pleased that her cheeriness seems unforced. She crosses the room and reaches up to draw the curtains properly, standing on tip toe to do so.

"These are such high ceilings," she complains, but looks admiringly at the well-proportioned living room; it looks even bigger now that she has been able to clean out so much of the clutter to allow Maria to move around more easily. The charity shops in Wimbledon must have done pretty well out of her, she muses. She notices a squirrel that has dared to cross the lawn and climbed up to feast on the bird table, and bangs hard on the window.

When she turns she sees that Maria is struggling to open the jiffy bag on her knee.

"Let me get you the scissors," Jess says. "Those things are like leather." She crosses the room and returns with a letter-opener. "There. Best I could do." She knows that Maria doesn't like to be mollycoddled, and turns away before she has chance to remonstrate. "We need some milk. I'm just popping out to the shops. I'll make us some tea."

As she walks down the road to the corner shop she reflects how strange it is that she has grown so effortlessly into this role of unofficial carer. She still works three days a week in the office at the caterers, but much of the rest of the time she spends with Maria, and doesn't resent it in the least. The rent she pays is minimal, so she still earns enough to pay for her gym membership, where she swims, and on Fridays plays volleyball. She knows that her friends – and especially her mum – are mildly anxious that she should start out on a proper career, and ideally meet someone, but for herself it has become an oddly stable existence, and she is, simply, happy. It was obvious that her unusual circumstances were not going to last forever, but in the meantime she was going to enjoy it whilst she could. With this in mind she called in at the deli and bought two chocolate croissants for them to share, then sprinted all the way home to burn off a few compensatory calories.

There is no reply as she calls out her greeting. Assuming that the old lady must have fallen back to sleep, as she often she does, she tiptoes back to make sure that the window in her room is properly closed.

The sight almost knocks the breath out of her. Maria is half standing, crouched with her hands on the back of the sofa, white-faced, her mouth opening and closing stupidly, gasping for air. Jess runs to her, pulls her upright, gets her to sit down, all the while thinking what she must do for a heart attack, for a stroke.

"I'll call the doctor, you ..."

But Maria shakes her head. "Just water," she gasps, pointing at a glass on the table.

Jess's hands are trembling as she hands it to her.

"It's just these," Maria says, and points to her feet. Jess looks down at the floor, where there is a scattering of pale blue, tell-tale airmail envelopes.

Jess squeezes her hand. "Bad news?"

"No ... I don't know ... I ... these are *my* letters. I mean, I wrote them, I sent them, a lifetime ago. And they've come back ..."

Jess is not sure how to respond. Gently she gets her old friend to sit next to her on the sofa, and gathers up the letters. She stares at the faded lettering. "Par Avion," she says. "Is that your writing?" Maria nods. "And this?" She holds up a typed sheet of A4.

"No. That's from an American. A doctor. Imagine that. What a story ... it explains how they survived, the letters that is, and how they got here. See what you think."

Jess reads and re-reads the mysterious text, trying to make sense of what it might mean.

"But these are your letters? I mean, you actually wrote them all those years ago?"

Maria nods. She appears to be recovering from the initial shock.

"I did. It was me. Or a version of me. Can we have more than one version, do you think? I think so."

Jess holds up one of the envelopes and looks at the spidery writing. "To Captain Jacob Hernandez del Rio. Toledo." She looks intently at the old lady, trying to imagine what it would have been like to have known her as a young woman. "Some kind of a boyfriend, maybe?" She waits. "You could tell me a bit if you wanted … I'd love to know."

Maria looks at her. She has never told anyone. To Tom she had given an honest though limited account of having had to flee Spain, and the serious boyfriend who had disappeared, but for both their sakes she had spared him the details. Perhaps it was time, finally, to share some her secret. Perhaps the return of her letters was a sign. It wouldn't hurt, not after all this time.

"It's a long story. Actually no, it was never going to be a long story. It was a short story, really. Too short. But it's the very heart of my life."

She gazes unseeing into the distance.

"If it's too painful for you …" Jess says softly, but Maria ignores her.

"I – we – were so young then. We got caught up in the War, the Spanish Civil war. Things too big for us to control. I managed to get out through Gibraltar. But he … he didn't … his name was Jacob …" As she says his name aloud a sob forms in her voice, forcing her to swallow. Jess squeezes her papery hand. "Jacob didn't manage it. I left so much of me there, with him. I didn't know it at the time, but I did. And I wrote to him for years, hoping, begging, praying that I'd get an answer. And these are *my* letters to him, come back to me. I didn't know what to do. It's not like today, with emails and everything. I just wrote to his family in Toledo, hoping he'd get them somehow. Stupid, really. It feels like I'm dreaming."

She holds one of the envelopes to her chest, in wonder. Jess collects the others from the floor.

"There," she says. "I've put them all in order from the postmarks on the back. You can read them back in sequence."

Maria stares at her. She isn't sure if she is strong enough. The old clock ticks loudly in the corner of the room. Time stops.

"Or I could read them with you, if you wanted," says Jess eventually. "I mean, I don't want to be nosy or anything, but if it would help …"

Maria looks at her, then back at the envelopes. "Please," she says at last, a whisper, "please read them to me."

Jess crosses the room to allow the light from the window to illuminate the faded writing, and reverently opens the first envelope.

"You sure?" she asks.

Maria leans forward in her chair, concentrating hard. "Let's get it over with," she says, and closes her eyes.

Gibraltar. October 1937

Dear Jacob,

God knows I hope you get this. I'm here in Gibraltar, safe for the moment. It was an adventure getting here, and I missed you terribly. I still do. The British have been kind to me, and were more than interested in the letters that I brought them. It makes me feel so guilty to think about all that you did for me, but your courage was worth it. I'm not sure how long I can stay here, but at least I'm comfortable and well fed. I think I must have picked up an infection somewhere because I keep being sick: are you all right? I hope so. There's a woman who looks after me, and every day I ask her if there's any news of you. Every time someone knocks on my door I pray that it's you. Sometimes I go down to the frontier and stare back into Spain, and each time I think I spy you walking to meet me. I'll have to stop doing this: it's killing me. It's been almost two months since I saw you and I ache to hold you again.

Come quickly. I miss you.

Maria

Gibraltar November 1937

At last leaving tomorrow. I was supposed to go two weeks ago but something came up, a little adventure – I'll tell you about it when I see you. Your cousins finally answered and I'm going to go to their house. I'm not sure if they assume that you'll be there as well. God, I hope so. I'm a bit scared about the journey. I pray every night that you'll be here before then. I have this dream where we're on a boat looking out at the sea, with you standing behind me, your hands holding tight to my waist, and we're sailing out towards this desert island. Can we do that some time?

I wish I knew where you are. Wherever it is, stay safe.

I love you. xxx

Leamington Spa, January 1938

I made it. I'm here, at your relatives' place in Leamington. The journey was awful – there was a storm and everyone got sick, but I met some kind people and they helped me to make my way here. Your aunt is so like your father, but a bit less scary. Your cousins are lovely. Olivia is a communist (I didn't know you could be when you're rich, but she is – both!). One of her best friends died as a volunteer fighting for the Brigadistas somewhere in the north. She took me to a Trades Union meeting where they were collecting money for our cause and I spoke up to thank them – in Spanish of course, with Olivia translating. At the end everyone sang the Internationale and I got all tearful. I like Philippa too, though she's a bit more serious. She's just as beautiful, but she's darker and has the exact same eyes as you. I just kept staring at her, I couldn't help it even though I knew it was making her uncomfortable. In the end I had to tell her. I'm not sure if she's pleased!

On Christmas Eve they took me with them to the Cathedral at Coventry. I didn't have much choice. As you know, it's not my thing, but I had to admit it was very pretty with all the lights and the singing. It's a special place, and it's been there since forever. There must have been millions of prayers said there over the years, and I imagine my own little one must be lost there amongst all the others. But I hope not. You can probably guess who and what I was praying for.

There is so much more news I want to share with you, but that will have to wait until we're together again.

Until then,

I love you. xxx

London, October 1938

They say I can't come back to Spain. I feel like a traitor. They say it's too dangerous, illegal. I don't have a passport. I went with Olivia and asked around to see if I can join the Brigadistas, but no one can tell me much. Somebody told me they would only take men. What could I do anyway? I feel useless. And frightened. I'm scared that something might have happened to you. I have this terrible fear that you might have gone back to your family and your regiment. I would understand it if you did, though I'd never, ever forgive you. A girl from Cordoba that I met asked me whether you might be a spy. I wanted to hit her. I said it wasn't true, it couldn't possibly be true, but all the same I had this little doubt. It's not true, is it? Of course not – you *feel* these things, so I know it can't be true. Other Spanish in London keep telling us the news. It's heart-breaking to hear about all the disharmony in Barcelona. Even if only half of the stories are true it's still a calamity. The British are making life hard for anyone trying to get to Spain. They're running scared of both Hitler and Stalin and still don't want to get involved in case they upset either one. That includes even bastard Franco. According to the newspapers, the British have some interests in West Africa, and they're worried that if he wins he might make life difficult for them there. I don't know any more. I keep thinking that I could try and make a run for it, jump on the boat to France, then the train to Barcelona. It probably wouldn't work ... but if I did, and at the same time you finally managed to get to England ... then what would we do? I'm going to be patient, and wait for you here, just as long as it takes. I'm scared your mother is reading my letters, but what else can I try? Get yourself to Gibraltar, or France, or anywhere ... get yourself to me!

I love you.

Maria.

London, September 1939

Dear Jacob,

Here we go again. Just as the war in Spain comes to an end, another one begins, exactly five months later. April first to September first.

Five months! That's the gestation period of a goat. Paco told us that, remember? And now I'm trapped in this one. War seems to pursue me. I can't believe we let that son of a bitch Franco get the better of us. When I think of what he's done, what he's still capable of doing, it makes my blood run cold. And Hitler is stronger, and worse, they say. No one is quite sure whether Britain can stand up to him. I'm scared.

They won't let me fight in the war. Not proper fighting. I want in my dreams to be like La Passionara, or like the Russian girls, and fight with guns. But it's not to be. Not at least until they get to England and we have to fight them in the cities, like in Madrid. In that case I'll get myself a gun somehow, and won't die happy until I've killed a Nazi. I cannot believe how much I hate the fascists. Those people have wrecked my life. Until then I will remain a nurse. Did I tell you? I told them I was a nurse in Spain, and everyone now is too busy to check up on me. Already the wards are beginning to fill up with wounded men from France, Belgium, Poland. You know what? I hate it. All the suffering, the broken bodies, the poisonous smells, the grief. At night I lay awake and curse the world for all the horror there is in it. But I have to do something, any tiny thing; it's my small way of fighting back. And you know what else? Every time some poor, maimed soldier gets bundled in under a sheet, his face hidden, I think of you, laying cold, in pain and unattended in some far-off clinic, and another nurse, like me, coming to your aid, stifling her revulsion at your wounds, and being kind and gentle to you. It's the only way I cope.

But let's not think of that. What else? Ah, another thing: remember the Russian who used to lead the groups in Madrid? My contact? The one who in a sense got us into all this? Him. You were jealous of him, I think, even though he was a homosexual. Is a homosexual, in fact, and living in London! He has to keep it quiet. One of the other girls in the Asociación de Españoles, who works as a translator, told me that she had seen him purely by chance in Regent's Park, of all places. At first he was terrified to be recognised. He had had to flee Madrid in a hurry, just after we did, as the network had been exposed and betrayed. I wonder who it was? At first he went back to Russia, but now he has a job at the University in Cambridge. Something to do with art. He's invited me to tea some time, but I don't think I'll go.

I've been doing a lot of reading. Even the classics. You know how long Penelope had to wait for Odysseus? Twenty years. Twenty! *Madre mia*! Don't make me wait that long, please!

I love you.

Maria x

London, September 1940

I'm scared, Jacob. Hitler's planes fill the skies above London and have almost brought England to her knees. There are bombs every night, here in the city, killing so many people, so many you wouldn't believe. They're fighting back, the English, out of desperation, but it's tough. I see these tiny English planes go out, Spitfires they're called, to fight the Nazis, and it lifts my heart as well as breaks it, because you just know that so many of them won't be coming home. But they have given us just a fraction of hope, these brave, stupid English pilots, and I haven't had that feeling for so long, not since Jubar. You know they're out-numbered, you know the chances are small because the enemy is just so strong, but still there's that small possibility that these evil people can be defeated against the odds.

And I keep thinking: if, against the odds, with courage and strength and patience, the war against the Nazis can be won, then maybe, maybe, we can win too, you and I, after all this time, four years, we too can win, against the odds.

If we don't find each other, I don't know what I'll do.

I love you.

Maria.

London, July 1943

Maybe, possibly, the tide has turned. Could it really be? I almost daren't dream. Some say the allies are winning back ground, after all this time. I don't know if you're keeping up with the news. My Spanish friends tell me that Franco lies a lot. Well, we knew that. But the British and the Americans are pushing into Europe, and maybe, please God, soon into Spain as well and then we can be together again. I know it's been six years but I love you, I miss you so much. You told me that London was cold and grey, and I didn't listen, but you were right. Much of the time I'm miserable. I worry about the war, and I worry about you. I know a lot of the comrades ended up in France. There are such terrible stories. I saw the *Pathé* newsreels about the Spanish refugees on the beach in camps, near Perpignan, men so thin, in rags. And the prisons. I can't bear to think about you tied up somewhere. When I see the suffering that goes on elsewhere I try to remind myself to be thankful for the little that I have. But I can't. The little that I have just doesn't compensate for all that I have lost. Inside me there burns a flame of rage and resentment that I think will never burn out. I'm twenty-seven, and I've been at war for seven years. Seven fucking years. No wonder I'm angry at the world. Come back and save me, Jacob. Please.

I love you.
Maria.

London, November 1944

I want to tell you about a horse. It's a sad little story but I'll tell you anyway. A brown horse, who used to be in the races until he got too old. There isn't much green around here, where I live in London, so sometimes, when I finish on time or if I'm not too tired, I walk the long way home, just to see some countryside. There aren't many flowers, but a lot of vegetables – everybody's trying to grow a little bit because of the war and Hitler keeps bombing the ships that come in with food from faraway. But there are still some fields, all green and soggy, with hedges all around that are filled with birds, and I like to stand by the wooden gate, to smell the grass and the countryside. It doesn't smell like home; I think the grass in Spain must be different, but at least it's fresh there, and quiet, and I talked to this horse, and tried to give myself some peace to think about things. Maybe it's because I'm less busy at the hospital now, but I seem to think more; I've got so much to think about.

I used to imagine how much I'd like to ride that horse with you, to go riding some place where all you can see is endless brown fields and hills and the snow-topped mountains in the distance. Remember that place near Linares, where we stopped the extra days? I was so happy then. Something happened there. I was in love with you before, but whilst we were there in that little house this strange feeling filled me up and I just kind of knew that you would be part of my life until I die. I never liked all that sentimental shit, so it was difficult for me to tell you. But I think you felt it too.

I want so much to go back to that place. I've dreamed about it. I used to feed the brown horse bits of grass I'd picked for him over the fence, feel his warm breath on my hand, and tell him how one day I'd take him there and we'd go riding again. But we can't. There was a bomb. Bombs. They said they must have been aiming for the warehouses at the docks, and missed them in the fog. They're miles away. It doesn't make sense. You can see three enormous craters in the field, all in a row. First they filled with water, and now they're frozen over. Nobody can go near, because they think there may be others, deadly, unexploded in the soft earth. But another bomb hit the stables, smashed up the building and killed all the horses. My horse too. I was so sad. You can't imagine how sad. I've seen so many terrible things in the hospital, seen so many young men die it breaks my heart. But this was worse. I don't understand why. It was just so pointless, so cruel, it somehow got under my skin and I can't stop thinking about it. Sorry if it's a sad story, but I thought that if I could share it with you then it might not be so bad.

Please write. I'm so lonely. I don't know what to do. Jacob, it's been so long, so long ...

But still, against the odds, I love you.

Maria

London, August 1946

I've found someone else. Or rather, someone else found me. God help me. I can't believe I'm writing this. Already I've started this letter six times and it's killing me. I swore to myself I'm going to send it tonight like this and not change anything. I can't tell you any other way. I'm so mixed up. I'm so sorry. I don't know where you are, I don't know if you are even alive or dead. I'm frightened. I love you so much. Remember I used to have such grown up talks with the others in the group in Madrid? One girl, Marta, asked us once if it is possible to love two people at once. She's dead. We teased her. But you can. I do. I love two men. There. I've said it. His name is Tom. He's brave and he's kind and he reminds me of you and he needs someone too. I know you will never forgive me, but know this, my darling, that every night, every single night for eight years, before going to sleep I've thought about you and I pray for you. And I will always do this, no matter what, always, forever. I see your face sometimes in my dreams and I don't want to wake up. You were my first and my best love and without you I feel incomplete. I can never ever tell him this but in a way I'm like Tom. He lost a foot in the war, he is mutilated, and I am too, because without you I have a part of me that is missing. Maybe this is the thing with Tom: we are cripples who balance each other out.

Oh Jacob I am so bitter, so angry with this world that I cannot be with you. I'm torn and tormented and inside I rage, rage till I weep. You are my best, best love and I love you so much and I can't tell you how I really want to die some times when I think I will never hold you again. I'm crying now. I can't breathe. I'm thinking of your smile on that train and I want to kiss your face again, just one more time, oh please, if only. It's fading. Not the memory, not that, but your face, you're so far away and I don't know where. You were my friend, my handsome lovely perfect friend. Oh Jacob, Jacob. I just have to let you go. I can't ever take away our past but I need to amputate our future. My love. Be safe. I'm sorry I've betrayed you. Betrayed us. This is the most desperate night of my life. I don't know. I can't ... I just can't go on. I will not write again. Not ever. I love you.

Adieu.

Maria

That final *adieu* stands out livid, like a scar from a wound, and Jess is shaking as she hands the fragile paper back to Maria. Tears are trailing down her aged, powdered face like ski tracks in the snow. The clock has stopped. Jess watches fascinated as dust motes dance in the slanted morning sunlight. Maria rocks back in her chair, once, twice and at the third attempt pulls herself upright and shuffles across to the fireplace, and gently lays face down the faded photograph of Tom and his brothers-in-arms on the steps of their Lancaster Bomber.

"I never told him, you know," she says softly. "Not everything, not the whole truth. But he knew, I think, and it made us both sad. The not telling."

They sit there mute for a while, strangely connected yet awkward together, until the cat pushes gently at the door. "I think perhaps I should make us some tea," says Maria, as at the same time Jess asks, "What happened to Jacob?"

"I don't know," comes the reply. "I just don't know. At first I couldn't ask, and well, and then I just grew too afraid and I just didn't dare ask. No one knew, you see, no one, it was just our little story. No one. And now you."

She pulls herself to her feet, confused and misty-eyed. "Imagine: the heart of my life ... and I don't even know what happened to him. Isn't that cruel ..." And with that she moves slowly off towards the kitchen, old leather slippers slap slap slapping softly on the threadbare carpet, her tiny cautious steps adding to the riot of dust; an accompaniment to Jess' now unrestrained weeping.

Chapter Eight

The Park, Madrid, 1927

The little boy stands with his forehead pressed tight against the trunk of a tree, hands above his head. He can feel the deep sway of it as it is pulled this way and that by the wind in the great branches far above, whilst around him, other children stand with their arms in the air, trying to catch the leaves as they swirl out madly from the cloudless autumn sky. In his left fist he clutches the folded penknife that his brother had given him; it is his favourite possession.

The boy's eyes are screwed shut, and his lips move silently as slowly he counts out the numbers. He knows that if can just get to fifty then things will be fine. An observer might think that he is a diligent participant in a game of hide and seek; the dedicated catcher amongst friends. But that observer would be wrong, for the boy is not counting out to measure time, but to give himself time to take control of his emotions.

At last he stops, takes a deep breath and turns around to survey the people in the park. Gingerly he puts his hand down the back of his leg and with his fingers begins to explore the welts that are already starting to form. Three. Three slit-cane slashes striped across his calf.

The pain is very great, but what torments him is not so much the brutality of the beating, but the fear of very public disgrace and humiliation.

The boy does not know this, but in the glass pavilion across the park, his father is staring into a cracked mirror, hating himself. He grips the grimy pewter taps so tightly that his fingernails are white with the effort; there will be bruising on the palm of his hand tomorrow. Christ knows, he did not want to beat his younger son. Every time he looks at the boy he surprises himself with the love and tenderness he feels. So much so it is not quite manly. But he had to do it. It will be for the better, eventually. If Jacob wants to be a soldier, another officer, then he needs to accept the importance of discipline. Rank carries its obligations. Giving orders, taking orders unconditionally, there cannot be any compromise. Without that simple discipline the military is nothing, the boy knows that.

The father straightens his tie and goes to re-join the others in the café. Outside the sun continues to shine, and the grandees of Madrid society stroll in style about the manicured gardens. Rakish young men call to each other from within their carriages, the voices of the boaters carry loud across the lake, toffee-sellers yell out the sweetness of their wares, and he watches diffidently as two slim woman with matching silk parasols turn into the lane by the boats.

Across the park he sees the retreating backs of his wife and young son as they begin their walk home. She holds her head high, quick steps. She too will be angry at this minor disgrace, and may not even speak to the boy until the following day. He can picture the frown, the tight thin lips, ill-set against her pretty face.

The boy almost has to run to keep up with his mother, and the water squelches in his shoes after the fall in the lake. He is convinced there must be leeches sucking at his toes, but fear of his mother's wrath keeps him tap-tapping at her side.

"Don't be cross, Mama, please don't be cross," he pleads, but she refuses even to look down at him.

As they're about to cross the boulevard that separates the park from the city, a policeman canters towards them and compels them to wait. To their left they watch as a small cavalcade of carriages advances towards them, the sunlight flashing from the helmets of the outriders on their huge, caparisoned horses. It is Miguel Primo de Rivera himself, the policeman explains. The boy's mother draws herself up to her full height. This is the Dictator, a man beloved – for now – of the wealthy, the Church and the military, who rules the land with a hand, as he puts it, of *paternal conservatism*. The mother stares adoringly after the procession as it passes.

"Now that," she says, "is a great man."

The boy knows nothing of the great man, nor cares, but he is relieved that his mother at last has spoken, and her mood seems to have lifted. She slows her pace to his and smiles at him.

"Your father knows him," she says. "A little, anyway. He was at the military academy with your grandfather, imagine that. *Your* academy, in Toledo, if you study hard."

"I will, Mama," he says dutifully, but his attention has been drawn to a large motorbike that growls its way towards them. Now *that*, he thinks to himself, is a great machine. Mercifully the flavour of the day has been restored, and they wander back slowly to the house, where cake will be waiting.

Chapter Nine

On a beach, Galicia, Spain, 1929

Black; a torpedo shape lumped hard against the silver light, lying there all wrong. That's what he'd seen first, at least that's how he'd remember it, even years later.

The two boys, lithe and awash with life, had set out early, almost before the night was done, reeling cold-ankle deep in the tired surf of low tide. Each carried a spade, and from time to time vaulted suddenly aside to beat the crinkled sand in order to stun the creatures that lay beneath. A furious digging followed, too quick almost to breathe, as raw fingers scrabbled to snare the odious lugworms which would be the anglers' bait that day. The boys were happy. The bucket filled quickly, slick with the vile coilings of their quarry, some pulsing red, others already beginning their slow dying, snot-yellow green against the grey metal. Jacob put in a hand, fighting nausea, as if to feel the ugliness, to test himself against their foulness, then yelled, before flinging one into the face of his companion.

Like beasts they tussled laughing in the tiny waves, their tallness throwing long early-morning shadows down the slab of empty beach. Shrieking, they thought of nothing but their play and their excitement, the innocent power of twelve-year-olds skimming them further and further from home without apparent effort. Then suddenly – at once, together – they noticed it and stared: a seal, thought Tino, and shushed his friend. No. Bigger. A whale even? Against the sun they could just make out the crude, dark barrel of the shape which broke the loneliness of the deserted Atlantic shore. They would stalk it. They crouched instinctively, born hunters, concentrating, alert.

They moved slowly, closer, closer, unable to believe they could get so near, a little afraid now. Was it trapped, stranded, hurt? Tino, six months older, led the way. Suddenly he threw one hand across his mouth, the other, a split second later, behind him – palm up, as if to warn his friend. But too late.

It's as if he'd been kicked. Senses bludgeoned, Jacob found himself staring into the blackening swollen maw of a human corpse as it bobbed grotesquely on the turning tide, one dead hand outstretched on the sand as if to claw its way back towards the land. A crab scuttled out from a trouser leg; Tino thought he saw meat in its pincers, and feared he might wet himself.

They backed away, shocked to silence, standing close.

"We need to get someone," said Tino. "I'll wait here. You run – get my dad." Jacob looked unsure. "We can't leave him – he might float away. Go on, just go, I'll be fine."

Tino watched as his friend sprinted away, refusing to turn seaward, swallowing and swallowing in an effort to drive spit to his desiccated throat, unable to bring himself to look at the reason for his appalling solitude, not even when the water rose, and with a softly sickening thud the dead hand tapped him on the foot.

Help eventually came. His father and two other men, who tied a rope around the body as Tino's father wrapped an arm about each boy and led them quickly away. An hour later a solemn crowd had assembled on the foreshore waiting for the arrival of a policeman. The corpse lay covered with a piece of faded sailcloth; a girl stood by with a pile of stones which from time to time she threw at a ravenous-looking dog.

"They're good boys, brave boys," the Sergeant had said through his moustache, and the onlookers had all nodded in agreement. And that was that. Matter-of-factness descended on the story, if story it were. This was, after all, the *Costa de la Muerte*, where few fishermen ever learned to swim, to avoid prolonging the agonies of drowning, and it did not do to mention these things.

"I heard about your ... *adventure* on the beach this morning," was all his mother had said at dinner. "Are you alright, darling?"

"Fine," he had answered, as his father just stared and said not a word on the matter. Imagine that! Nothing.

That night he said his prayers twice before sliding into bed, then lay horribly awake, knees curled against the salted coastal dampness of the sheets, fearful of the dreams which might assail him. Eventually he could stand it no more. "Can I get in with you?" he had whispered timidly in the small hours as he slipped into his brother's bedroom. Lucas, fourteen, and more gentle than his brusqueness might imply, moved up and hugged Jacob tightly without saying a word.

And that was that. He slept well. He would never forget the incident, though in the end more than a decade would pass before he ever spoke of it again.

Chapter Ten

London, June 2011

Jess was glowing by the time she came out of the gym. A gut-busting spin class followed by a long and thought-free swim were exactly what she had needed to restore her after three long days hunched over a screen at the office. As she left she paid over the odds for a squeezed orange juice, and as she counted her change couldn't help but compare it to the nectar-like drinks she had enjoyed as a student in Granada, which in her mind's eye were not only a vitaminized taste of heaven, but had cost her next to nothing.

But the thought did nothing to dampen her spirits. It was a glorious London morning as she bent to unlock her bike, and she felt uplifted. She could see the sun glinting on the glass towers in the far-off city, and everywhere was the faint childhood smell of warm tarmac. A ladybird had settled on her handlebars, and she carried it cautiously to the bluebells which grew in clumps around the base of the chestnut trees at the edge of the car park. The day was properly warm, she realised, wishing that she had worn shorts.

She sped down the road and across on to Wimbledon Common, weaving between the joggers, the people with prams, the people with sticks, recklessly alive with the rush of this clean June day. She continued to race until she had to brake hard at a crossroads to give way to a pack of horses, whose black-jacketed riders sat prim and upright, a vision of another century. By now she was sweating, and decided to dawdle; she had nothing to rush for. She stopped at the sports pavilion and looked at the forthcoming fixtures. A woman she knew vaguely peered over her shoulder, and they chatted briefly. Further on she stopped once more to watch two squirrels chasing round a tree, then paused again to stare at a schoolboy cricket match. She had no clue as to what was happening, but they looked very fine in their bright white kit, and the timeless scene had a certain mesmerising charm. After a while, and for no apparent reason, the players all clapped politely and began to walk off as a man with an antique-looking lawn-mower trundled out to meet them. Mystified, Jess cycled off towards the row of shops. She would try to get hold of some decent bread and the ingredients for a salad for their lunch.

She sensed the ambulance before she saw it. The blue lights flashed brilliantly despite the midday sun, and somehow, even at this distance, she was overcome with the dreadful certainty that it was there for Maria. She got off her bike and pushed it the last few steps, leaving it propped against the neighbour's privet hedge. The back doors of the ambulance were wide open. It was empty, sterile, frightening, and Jess was horribly aware of her heart thudding inside the walls of her chest.

Although the garden gate was open it seemed to act as a barrier to guard against the small knot of people who stood whispering on the pavement. Jess pushed past them and into the house. She seemed to absorb everything in an instant. Four men were gathered in the living room. One was talking into his phone; another was writing on a clipboard. She saw the stretcher. Saw the faded leather slippers protruding towards her. Saw the familiar rings on the hand that dangled unmoving from the stiff white cloth. She began to reach out to take it, to help, but was stopped by the gaze of the man on the phone, who shook his head at her. The face of the person on the stretcher was covered by a sheet. She watched as her own hand moved involuntarily towards the pillow, aware that the man on the phone was trying to tell her something. She had to do this.

She peeled back the shroud as if in a dream. Maria's eyes were closed, but her mouth was open, with a white trail of saliva running down her throat, down her neck. Instinctively Jess began to wipe it with the sheet. She was conscious that people were talking, conscious that she herself was suddenly shouting. Why hadn't they told her? Why hadn't they come sooner? What was the point of the personal alarm, the panic button, if nobody came in time? Why wasn't anybody doing anything?

Later, when at last she had come to her senses and begun to calm down, she was ashamed of her reaction. The panic button had worked. In fact the ambulance crew had been miraculously close by, and had reached Maria only seven minutes after the alarm call was sent. But it was too late. If it was any consolation – and it was – then she needed to know that Maria had died almost instantly, like a light going out.

That night Jess took the train back into London and slept at the house of her friend, Beth. Beth had lost a brother at Christmas, and the two girls talked and grieved and drank until late.

The following day, sad and hungover, she packed up her few belongings and tiptoed out before Beth was awake. She would call her later. She was going home. She didn't know the rules, didn't know the law or whatever good form might dictate, but Maria's house was her home, and she was going back there until further notice, until they chucked her out. It was weird, and it was scary. But it felt like the right thing to do.

Chapter Eleven

Jess receives some news, London, May 2012

She almost hadn't gone. Would they have made an effort to track her down, if she just hadn't bothered to show up? It was only at the last second that she had decided to go along, and this out of boredom as much as anything else, together with the realisation that the office with the large brass plaque was so close to the bus stop. Had it been the other side of town she would almost certainly have ignored them. The voice on the phone had after all been fairly obnoxious, the man as fawning as he was insistent. She'd found it hard not to be rude, and had arrived at their grand offices in a rebellious mood, in jeans and a faded Sex Pistols tee shirt. She had brought her credit cards too, and some cash, for she suspected that she might end up shelling out for something on behalf of poor old Maria, at least until some relative pitched up to sort things out. If no one arrived she could always reimburse herself by getting rid of the telly or something on eBay.

As it was there was nothing much to dislike; they all seemed normal, friendly people doing their normal jobs. The buxom lady in heavy make-up on reception disarmed her from the first by pointing to her chest and telling her, "I saw that lot … must of been what, about 1977, I reckon. Hackney Empire. Loved it …" before trailing off and looking momentarily beyond Jess and into the absent pale punk faces of boyfriends past, eventually ushering her through to a too-warm waiting room artlessly besprinkled with potted cacti and lifestyle magazines.

She didn't wait long. The door opened and she was shown upstairs to the office of Mr James. He was courteous, efficient, and cut straight to the point. So clear and precise, in fact, that she had difficulty at first in understanding.

It was hers, all hers. The whole house.

Yes, there might be some tax she needs to pay on it as it's a very valuable property, but it's hers.

It's hers even if there were other claimants because, in his lawyer-speak, the 'terms of the will are categorical'.

She was in shock.

"You alright, my lovely?" asked the lady at reception as she came back down. " You don't look that great. Want some tea?"

But no, no thanks; it wasn't tea she needed, it was time alone, and fresh air.

All afternoon she tried to replay the full conversation in her head. She walked out across Wimbledon Common, head down into the stiffening breeze, unaware of the joggers and dog-walkers that surrounded her, unconcerned by the drizzle, crossing and re-crossing the central woodland in the gathering gloom. Haltingly she was able to assimilate the news, to take in the implications not only for herself, but also for the significance it had for her knowledge of Maria. And this was more troubling, for if Jess was truly the heiress, she who had known Maria for little more than a year, then what this suggested was that her benefactor had been more alone, more forsaken, more irreducibly single, than she had ever properly imagined. Poor woman; how gutsy she must have been to face such detachment, and just how deeply sad she must have been, for so long.

That evening she phoned her mother for the first time in a month. They talked of this and that, good-natured but guarded as ever, until Jess felt able at last to break the news of her legacy. Her mother of course was at once stunned and delighted, and wanted immediately to know about plans, about values. Jess understood that this reaction was perfectly normal, but still it somehow vexed her, this lack of compassion, of understanding, and she felt herself becoming tense. She forced herself to stay calm, and there was a brief silence. Then, from completely out of the blue, she blurted, "It means I will have to go to Spain for a while." She hadn't known she was going to say that; she hadn't planned it.

"When?" asked her mother.

"Soon," she'd answered confidently. "I guess pretty soon."

Later she wandered unhurriedly around the large house, *her* house, abstractedly picking up plates, books, knick-knacks, caressing things, as if trying with blind fingertips to gauge the history and relevance of all that heart-breaking clutter. For a long time she held in her hand a chunky copper band, staring past it, abstracted, only dimly aware of the dust-free ring it had left behind on the dresser, and next to this, a small key.

It was still raining when, after midnight, she opened all the windows, feeling guilty, hoping to lose some of the palpable scent of *oldness* that permeated the whole building. It was time to go to bed, she knew, and made her way upstairs to her old room. The door to Maria's bedroom faced her on the landing, still closed, challenging her. So far she had avoided setting foot there. It wasn't as though she was scared, it just seemed too private, too intimate, for her to feel comfortable. Tomorrow, she thought, tomorrow. But then, knowing that she probably wouldn't be able to sleep anyway, she pushed down on the worn steel handle, and stepped inside.

It was tidy within, tidier than elsewhere. Her eyes swept the elegant, empty, clean-topped tables that stood by the bed. Two wardrobes, a mirror, a dressing table, a desk, an oak chest. She was tired. This should be easy to sort out in the morning. She turned to leave, but on impulse opened the top drawer of the desk. She lifted out a beige cashmere sweater which she recognised, a silk scarf, a pair of pyjamas, and then spied, half-hidden in the corner, the irresistible side of a mahogany jewel case, about the size of a shoe box.

It was locked, but she guessed exactly where the key was. She had to wait for a minute to go back downstairs, to allow her curiosity to build until it was strong enough to overcome her feelings of trespass and guilt. With a strong sense of déjà vu she took the box with her to the living room. She located and used the key she had seen earlier, and was not in the least surprised when the lock opened easily. Inside she saw papers, documents, certificates. At the top of the pile was an envelope with four small photographs of Maria, taken recently. Jess gazed fondly at the familiar face, which stared defiantly at the camera, dignified, in full make-up. Glancing at the date on the back she saw that they had been taken just the previous month. Passport photos. So, she had been going to get the new passport after all. Jess began to sob. For months they had talked on and off about their travelling to Madrid together, and nothing had ever come of it. Jess hadn't thought that she was serious, but now, too late, she realised that she just hadn't listened properly. She'd let her down. As if to add insult to injury she stared helplessly at the application form. Next-of-kin: Jessica O'Donnell.

It was too much to bear. She would go through the rest of the box in the morning. Beneath the forms she could see the worn edges of the airmail envelopes that she had read at Christmas, the letters that had moved her so much, and which contained as many questions as they did answers. No, not now ...

But then, just as she was about to close the box, she saw him. It was funny: he looked exactly how she would have imagined. A slight smile, high cheeks, dark Spanish eyes, raven black hair, even in the pallid sepia portrait. No wonder Maria had loved him. The picture was faded, ragged, held in a carefully folded page of a glossy magazine. In fact it was last month's *Marie Claire.* so, the old girl had checked him out recently. She smiled to herself, and studied the photo for a long, long time before finally going to bed.

By the time she had climbed the steps to her room she was slightly breathless. Breathless not from fatigue, but from carrying the weight of knowledge that she was about to do something both offbeat and necessary, something based on pictures taken many dejected decades apart.

Spain. She'd already told her mother. Perhaps deep down she had known it all along. And she would do it, she promised herself as she climbed into bed. She would go alone. And if, God willing, there was a way to discover what had happened to Jacob, then for Maria's sake she would find it.

Chapter Twelve

Paris, 2012

The letters, together with a pile of other documents, had been found at a house in Madrid, whose owner, an old lady, had died a few years previously. They had very nearly been destroyed, but almost at the last minute someone remembered the cousin in America who had asked about the family tree, and the whole lot had eventually been crated off to the States. This cousin, one Doctor Katherine Miller, when working her way through this pile of paperwork, had in turn come across the small stash of envelopes, held together by a time-eaten elastic band which had snapped as soon as she touched it. Those that she read were obviously personal and emotionally charged, and moreover not specifically relevant to her subject. There was a return address – Royal Leamington Spa – the pomposity of which amused her, and so, on a whim, she had put them all in a jiffy bag and sent them back across the Atlantic. Miraculously the same family not only lived at this same address, but because of their devotion to exchanging Christmas cards, also knew Maria's current whereabouts.

And so it was that the letters had found their back to the hands of their creator, thanks to the diligence and caprice of a hitherto unknown relative, and now Jess had a burning curiosity to discover more about the American who had made it all happen.

It had been Jess's idea for them to meet. The American had said that she would be in Paris for a conference, and Jess had volunteered straight away to travel across the Channel to see her in person. It just seemed better somehow. After all that she had heard about Jacob she was intrigued to be meeting this woman who claimed to be his great niece.

She still had an hour before their meeting. Her first coffee at breakfast had been so wonderful that she had ordered a second, and then a third later on in the gardens of the Tuileries, and now her head was hurting. She walked slowly down the Rue Faubourg St. Honoré to kill time, browsing in the fabulous shop windows. She wasn't much of a fashionista, but even she recognised most of the famous names. On impulse she stepped through a gilt mirrored door and into the cool, carpeted hall of a well-known designer boutique. She wished she hadn't bothered: outside in the street she had felt pretty good in her tee shirt and Levi 501s. Now, confronted by the high cheek-boned, short-skirted assistant who appeared mysteriously before her, she felt incurably shabby, acutely aware of the scuffs on her shoes and unmanicured nails. With all the nonchalance she could muster she brushed away the attentions of this catwalk shop girl, and walked courageously to inspect a beautiful Karl Lagerfeld dress that lay spotlit in the corner. Jesus Christ. It cost more than her car. The absurdity made her smile.

"I might come back tomorrow," she lied, and shot out into the car-filled, soot-flavoured street.

Ten minutes later she walked through the revolving door of the hotel where they were to meet, and peered around the near-empty lobby until she spotted her.

"Kathy …?" she asked timidly. The woman she'd approached put down her *Washington Post*, and smiled broadly as she stood, arms open wide.

"Jess! So lovely to meet you." She was tall, with strikingly blue eyes and cropped white hair that contrasted with the black polo neck she wore. As they embraced Jess discerned a familiar scent.

"Chanel?" she asked.

"Bang on! You some kind of expert or something?"

Jess laughed. "No: it's all my mother ever wears, that's all."

"Ah. Old lady perfume then, eh?"

"Not at all. Au contraire, as they say here. Timeless, I'd say. Classy …"

They both grin; they like each other already.

"Can I be rude and ask if we can go some place to get dinner? I am sooo hungry," Kathy asks. "I've been at this Symposium all day and the food on offer was trash; you can't come all the way to Paris and feed on sandwiches. Come on, my treat – they give me an allowance."

They take a taxi to a bistro recommended by a colleague, and fall into easy conversation. Kathy explains that she is a mining engineer based in Los Angeles, but who spends much of her time in Latin America. By the time that dessert arrives they are talking like old friends.

"And so it was that connection really, the Argentinian connection, that first sparked my curiosity," said Kathy. "I'm not a Nazi hunter or anything like that, God, no, but I was doing a lot of consultancy work down there with the gas companies. See, like anyone else I'm fascinated by my family tree, so when I heard that my own mysterious great grandad had pitched up there, I followed it up a little bit. None of the Spanish family in Madrid knew what had happened to him, or at least weren't saying. Talk about a black sheep! But anyway, for one reason or another I had a lot of spare time in Buenos Aires, and you know, I just poked around a little bit, asked a few questions. And to be honest, your old friend Jacob wasn't really part of the equation, he was more of a footnote, shall we say, at least for me. I was only interested in my side, and at first just wasn't too bothered by Jacob's father, who'd done all those terrible things."

Jess has opened a notebook and is scribbling away, trying to keep up.

"I say terrible," Kathy continued, "but you know, these days what he did wouldn't be so bad. Wrong, yeah, but not terrible. I don't think we really do the whole family disgrace thing anymore, do we?"

"Better talk to my mum about that, I think," said Jess wryly.

"But in those days ... and from that background, I guess it must have looked pretty bad. He was a soldier you see, through and through, like his daddy before him, and had his boys in the military too. He must have been unhappy a long time, that's my guess. And then something happened, I'm still not sure what, that must really have shocked him. I always suspected it was family stuff, but whatever it was just sent him off the rails. And then this opportunity came, and he took it."

"Opportunity?"

"To go to South America, some kind of liaison officer with the Germans. He spoke a bit of German, see, they'd sent him off to school again to learn some. It sounds like he was a born schmoozer, and he made pals with some very senior people when they were running the Condor Legion in the Spanish war. They liked him, is all, and they trusted him, old school kinda guy, good breeding."

"But what were the Germans doing in South America?"

"Good question. I'm still not sure. Some trade: steel, oil, that kind of thing. Hitler even had these insane plans to invade the States, so perhaps it was to make some kind of a base there. But there were others too, wise old German heads, who could see what might happen if it all went wrong – which it did, of course – and they wanted to lay the foundations for a back door, an escape route. All completely secret, needless to say, but in the end they needed it. God knows how many Nazis escaped to Chile, Argentina, Brazil, and so on, but it was a lot. Even now there are people, Israelis mostly, who still go looking for them. But they'd had it all worked out, got to hand it to them, the Germans, they had a contingency plan, and I reckon my old great grandad had a bit-part to play, at least before it all went wrong …"

"Went wrong?"

"Well no-one had been aware of Jacob's father's … problems. Not even him. Dependency issues, I think we'd call it these days. But basically he was a bit of a drunk. And a drug addict. And a womaniser too. He wasn't quite fifty when he got to Argentina, clean as a whistle, but five years later he was dead. He hadn't exactly had a sheltered life up to then, he'd been to war, fought in Morocco and so on, but I think it was very much a … *constricted* life. That's it, constricted. And when he got the chance, boy! He just let rip!"

She smiled apologetically. "I know: I shouldn't admire him, but it's such a cool story. By the end he was a sad man, a wreck, but along the way, those last few mad years, he'd had a ball. In his heart he must have been a pirate like his ancestors, a buccaneer type, full of rum and fornication, on one long, last raid. Talk about a fall from grace. He ended up living with a hooker from Montevideo, the pair of them off their heads on opium. In a letter he claims to have smoked it with Jean Cocteau in New York. I mean, him! A Francoist Colonel! Shit, I'm glad I got all my daddy's genes, not my mom's – me, I'm a very responsible person … mostly." She added this mischievously, and smiled at Jess through her brandy glass.

"But that, I'm afraid, is where the trail goes cold, at least where Jacob is concerned. I just didn't get any further, sorry. There's a hint somewhere, some reference to someone close to him who goes AWOL that really bugged him, you know? Maybe that was Jacob? I think from what you've told me that it probably was. I'll send you all the stuff I've got, if you want. There's a ton of it, mind."

Jess was thinking how much it would have amazed and amused old Maria to have known these strange details. The way she had described him, Jacob's father had been a strict and dour traditionalist. Could it really be the same person?

"The family in Madrid, they seem cool," Kathy went on. "You could go there. You never know, just snippets here and there, it helps to build up a picture. Ask for the regimental records, could you try there ...?"

"I'm going," said Jess. "It's already arranged. Next week. I wanted to meet you first. Fancy coming along for the ride?" she added on a whim.

"Me?" Kathy looked surprised. "I'd love to, really, but didn't I tell you? In two days I'm back to LA, and then I take up this contract in Sydney. Three years in Australia! I can't wait!"

Jess shrugged. "Too bad ... you could have been my sidekick. Same kind of work?"

"Not this time. This is mostly teaching. It will give me more time for you know ... living."

Jess raised an eyebrow.

"You know ... surfing ... sex, drugs, and rock and roll and all that ... it's in the blood, like old Carlos ..."

Jess looked at her, not quite sure if she was joking. She must be sixty at least.

"Go girl!" she said. "You put me to shame."

"And I'll let you know, promise, if anything else comes up. My cousin in Madrid was going to ask around about Jacob's mother. She doesn't come across as the most charismatic kind of person, but, you never know, still waters run deep and all that. Besides, nearly everyone else who got through that crazy war had something remarkable happen to them, so it wouldn't surprise me at all if even she had some story to surprise us. I'll fill you in on any new family secrets."

Jess put away her notebook and yawned. Kathy looked at her watch.

"Not quite midnight. Shall we find us a nightclub?"

For a second Jess was dumbfounded. How was it that she kept meeting these energetic women far older than she?

Kathy smiled at her. "Only joking, don't worry. I'm an old lady now, I need my beauty sleep."

Even as she said it Jess was sure she could sense a glint of mischief in her eye. Was she trying to test her? It made no difference. She was so tired. Some other time, perhaps.

And yet later, alone in her taxi, revived by the cold night air and gazing out at the lights of the city as she sped home to her hotel, she still could not shake the feeling that somehow she might be missing out. For some reason it woke in her a memory of boarding school, and of the disquiet shaped by the thought that the rest of her family had been sharing fun in her absence.

She chastised herself. It was wrong to be so maudlin. This was Paris. Paris! She stared at a couple as they embraced beneath the arches of the Rue de Rivoli, and asked her driver for a cigarette.

Chapter Thirteen

On holiday once more, Galicia, Northwest Spain, Summer 1931

Slumbering, dragging himself from dreams, he thought for a moment that he was still on the train.

They had caught the Santiago Express from Madrid, and eventually, after bouncing around the station, the buffet car and the corridors, zinging with the thrill of a last day of term, he had finally fallen asleep on the exhausted grey sheets of his couchette, mesmerised by the shafts of light that had flickered intermittently through the curtains as they chugged their way past insentient townships in the night.

And now there's light here too, glimmering on the ceiling, an insubstantial burst of brightness spreading out like a fan just out of reach above him, so that all tiredness vanishes as he realises where he is. Here, in his uncle's house, where late morning sunlight reflected off the wet pavements outside, projecting upwards through the angled slats of the shutters, creating pixie swords, as he'd always called them, on the hard, white plaster. At last: Galicia. And adventure. Just north of here is Finisterre, the End Of The World as the Romans knew it. He is ecstatic to be back again.

What time is it? He pulls impatiently on the fastening and yanked open the window. He is half-blinded as light streams in, but almost from memory he can see across the rose garden to the pebbled beach, and beyond that to the crinkled, scintillating swell of the ocean. He stretches, lifts himself tall to lean out as a great leonine yawn takes him, and he drinks in again and again the salt sea taste of the breeze, settling himself to the day with deep gulps of recollection.

On the shoreline a silhouette stands clean against the light, looking seawards. Surely not? Already? Can't be ... But the figure moves, bends athletically to pick up a stone, and sends it skimming with unmistakeable grace into the waves. Tino!

Unmindful of the drop, Jacob pulls himself into the frame of the window and with barely a downwards glance leaps down into the flowerbed, and runs shoeless across the cool, damp lawn. It is an old house, built sturdily on a rising promontory to protect it from high seas, and he has to slow himself as he picks up speed on the steep slope. He races over the stones, veers past a rock-pool, skips over a rusting anchor, and onto the hard ridges of the sand, which is left crenulated by the retreating tides.

"Tino!" he calls. The figure turns, stares, takes a step towards him then pauses. Jacob slows, his face a rictus of joy and shyness. The two boys hesitate; it's been a long time. Just a few steps separate them. They are momentarily held in check by the opposing boyhood forces of reticence and delight. But in an instant Tino whoops, bounds towards him and suddenly they are in each other's arms, shouting, laughing, unburdened and alive, whirling ankle-deep in the summer-warm waves.

A year has passed since they have seen each other. Words swarm staccato from their agitated faces likes bees released from a hive, though neither really listens to the other, since they each know with the perfect conviction of all small boys that chat and conversation belong to the world of grown-ups, and instead they splash and shriek and chase seagulls just -

"-like gibbons!" says his mother, who is watching with his elder brother from the bay window. "He hasn't even had breakfast! He's not even dressed! You must go out and get him, Lucas. Go now."

Lucas is not in the least intimidated by his mother, but at seventeen he understands her well enough to know that she is acutely sensitive to all hint of social impropriety, and that the whole first day might so easily be soured by her rage and indignation. He is fond of his lively little brother and doesn't want to see him in trouble, and besides, he hopes himself to escape for a while in the evening to see the girls in the dance hall in town, and as such is determined to keep the familial waters as unruffled as possible. Poor Papa, he thinks as he strides down the path; small wonder he spends so much time at the club. But he regrets this act of filial disloyalty, and turns to wave.

The two boys have their faces to the sea and are unaware of his approach. Lucas ducks quietly for cover behind a small sand hill and calculates the distance between them. As he moves he catches the eye of the other boy and, putting his finger to his lips, scuttles forwards and kneels silently behind his brother. This unrehearsed manoeuvre works perfectly, and as Tino shoves him hard in the chest the astonished Jacob rolls theatrically unhurt onto his back in the sand. In the space of a second his face turns from shock to anger to giggles, and the three dissolve into boisterous teenage guffaws until Lucas remembers his mission, tries to recapture his composure and ushers them back towards the house.

"You coming in for hot chocolate?" he asks.

Tino seems suddenly reticent, and mumbles an excuse. He waits at the edge of the lawn as the two brothers disappear arm-in-arm into the house, then turns and walks slowly away, his slim shoulders throwing almost no shadow on the noonday shore. Then, on impulse he whirls around, some sixth sense telling him that he is pursued, and steels himself for the brothers to leap at him, grinning. But he finds instead that he is smiling into the gimlet eyes of their mother, poised behind the glass. He gives her an embarrassed half wave; she does not move.

Later that day, she advises her sons not to have anything to do with *that boy Faustino*. It wasn't that he was a bad 'un, just that his family were, well, *a bit off*.

"I thought his old man was a teacher?" said Lucas mildly.

" Yes, he is, *at the university*," she replied meaningfully. But Jacob isn't listening.

The next day he and Tino are taking the boat across to the island. They'd planned it last time but had had to abandon it because of the weather. He'd been thinking about this little adventure for almost a year, and wasn't going to be put off this time just because his friend's dad was, what did she say, a teacher? So what? Whatever could she mean?

It is barely light as he creeps from the house the next morning. A lustreless gun-metal sea glowers beyond the sand dunes, indivisible from the greys of the lightening dawn. Jacob stops to tie up his coat, and contemplates the sigh of the placid tide as it hisses its retreat over the shingle. The air is rank with the tang of seaweed. A blanket of gulls covers the edge of the beach, which, furious and yelping, take wing as he approaches, scaring him a little. Relieved, he sees marching towards him the slender figure of Tino, who is burdened by the weight of the sack he carries over his shoulder.

The pair greet each other with a smile and a timid handshake. Tino fumbles in the bag and extracts a still-warm loaf wrapped within a muslin cloth. They eat as they walk, heading towards the creek which serves as anchorage for a number of small vessels. It is guarded by a lonely heron who only deigns to heft her ungainly wings at the last instant of their arrival. As she becomes air-borne, Jacob notices how her upward flight is reflected in the spreading V-shape of droplets which pattern the glassy black surface of the water beneath.

They arrive at a cluster of sailing craft moored to a row of barnacle-clad oak columns standing upright in the reeds. The *Vigo Seal* lies shyly by herself at the back, even more weather-worn than her neighbours. Tino insists again that they are definitely allowed to take her out, that she belongs to a group of his father's friends, that she is what they call a "collective" boat, to be shared freely. What he doesn't say is that she must only be used with the express consent of the others, consent which he has declined to request. For his part, Jacob chooses not to divulge that he is forbidden not only from going out to sea, but prohibited too from spending time with his present companion. In truth at this point neither boy was overly troubled by this lack of full disclosure.

Giddy with the scent of adventure they hurl the bag aboard and cast off, pausing only to check the oars and kick out at the fat black rat which they find sleeping under the mouldy furled sail. The sun rises weakly at their backs, half covered by thin strips of torn cloud, mottled and pink as the tongue of an exhausted hound .. There is not a breath of wind. Around them nothing moves; the morning is limp, inert, and for those who know the temper of the ocean, dangerously silent. But the boys are blind to all this, powered as they are by an inner vivacity and zest that disdains all circumspection. Instead they pull on the oars and row, and laugh, and row some more ...

Until they stop, study their softly blistering hands, and heaving on the sail, look around in vain for the breeze which will push them onwards. Puzzled, they gaze at the oily sea, each waiting for the other to give advice. When Jacob then spies the first heavy splotch which shatters the glass of the surface, he thinks stupidly it must be the heron they had seen earlier, and gapes upwards, amazed beyond words that it should be raining. Together they scan the blackening horizon, and together they slowly realise both the folly of their enterprise and the depth of their predicament.

They pick up their oars and row, heading back towards land, any land. But the sea is rising, and the swell and the current combine to push them ever further westwards, beyond the haven of the bay and out towards the open ocean. The rain has made them cold, and they shiver, their bravura only just keeping the lid on a growing sense of panic. In their anxiety to push harder they lose the rhythm and theirs paddles collide with a wet thwack, and this time, instead of smiling, they glare at each other.

Jacob is sure he can hear thunder, but realises with incredulity it is the noise of an engine. Tino has heard it too. A fishing boat. They stand and wave and scream. Will the pilot see them? Of course he will. He's been watching them all morning, astounded and enraged that such fools exist as will set out to sea when all the signs that God provides are laid out so plain to read. Idiots. He didn't want to come, didn't want to help, but he'd lost a brother to the sea and he wasn't going to sit around and watch boys drown, not like this, even if they were fools.

"Not really a rescue, not really," he says later to Jacob's parents. "Weren't more than a mile out, they were. It got a bit brutish late morning, but we were home and dry by then. They might have made it back by themselves even. Don't be hard on 'em, sir. They're good lads, just a bit wet about the ears."

He leaves, declining all offer of reward. He has saved them once, and has tried to save them again with his words.

But the damage is done. His mother is more than angry, she is outraged. He is in deep, deep trouble. His holiday is over. He will be watched, there will be curfews. Jacob knows deep down that his friendship with Tino is finished, perhaps forever.

Two weeks pass. He spends his time clambering over rock pools, dangling baited hooks into the briny dark ponds left by the retreating tide; he catches shrimps for their dinner, he swims, he reads; he's bored. He's angry at Mama for being so strict, angry at Tino for not coming back, and most of all, he's angry at himself for allowing all this to happen.

Once or twice, during siesta time, he sneaks over to the fishing village to find Tino, but he's never known exactly where Tino lives. It has always been something of a mystery. His parents have warned him that this place is completely off-limits, that it is not properly safe, even. Tino himself has always been annoyingly vague about it, waving his hand dismissively, so often that Jacob has learned no longer to question him about it.

But each time he flunks it: as he approaches he becomes unnerved. With every step he can feel his confidence draining into the wet sand of the seashore, and slinks back towards home before anyone can speak to him. The second time, he's desolate: he sees men sitting cross-legged as they mend their torn nets in the afternoon sun, who nod to him. He sees lines of octopus drying on the upturned hulls of the blue and white skiffs as they await the return of the tide. A pannier-laden mule stands resignedly in the shade of a windblown pine, twitching its great ears to ease its fly-tormented brow. Two girls, sisters maybe, are struggling to fly a kite in the slack breeze, and an old woman in black lifts tiny bellows to the flames of a fire on which silver sardines the size of his hand are beginning to blister in the heat. A younger woman, the age of his mother perhaps, is asleep on a canvas chair, a book propped open on her lap. It is a scene of calm; he senses no hostility. Kind-eyed, the old lady smiles at him through corrugated cheeks and motions at him to come and eat. But no, he can barely mumble his thanks, and instead shakes his head, turns tail and flees home, the imaginary jeers of Tino ringing in his ears as he sprints down to the sea, footprints melting in the surf.

At dinner that evening, Lucas asks if he would like to accompany him to town, for a lemonade down in the port. Jacob knows full well that he's just a pawn in the offer, and that what his brother really wants is the chance to have a smoke and a chat to fellows his age, and possibly to beg a ride on one of the new motorbikes they'd seen there on a previous jaunt, but he's flattered nonetheless and agrees willingly to go. He can't stand the idea of another long evening trapped in the house with their mother, and besides, although Lucas never tires of teasing him, and has developed other interests (girls, mostly), he knows that the pair of them are still close and will get along just fine. Although he'd never admit it, either, he's proud to be seen out and about with his confident sibling and the six-year age gap means he's still too young to want to step out of his shadow.

The housekeeper and their mother watch as their silhouettes disappear into the summer sunset. Lucas, tall, loping, debonair, whilst little Jacob has his face tilted upwards, chattering, a head full of questions, half running to keep up.

"They're such good boys, you know; they'll be fine," says the older woman encouragingly. But Mama just shrugs, and turns away as the boys move out of sight.

"What I want to know though," Jacob is asking at the same time, "is why I can't go to the village. What's wrong with it? Why are they all so cross?

"Because you were a naughty boy, naughty!" replies Lucas and playfully makes to swipe him.

"No, but really why? I mean really, stop messing about!"

Lucas glances down at him, sees that he's serious. "Grown up stuff," he sighs. "Boring stuff." He ruffles his hair. But then recognises the stubborn look on his face, and blows out his cheeks in exasperation. "Look. It's just some ideas that they have, that's all. They're ... liberals, and socialists and things like that. I don't know ... to be honest I don't really understand it all, it's just that they're not like *us*, that's all. Half of the village is fine, the old ones that is, they're just people, but the other half, the ones that come for the summer, they're well, they're *modern,* and read books, the women too, and have all kinds of fancy notions about how the world must change, and now they have this so-called commune in the summer, and do you know, I came back late the other evening and they were all up talking well after midnight, with a bonfire on the beach. And," he adds with a flourish, to give weight to his speech, "they don't like going to church!"

"But you don't like going to church either," says Jacob mildly. "Who does?"

Lucas shakes his head and walks on.

They continue in silence for a few steps, until Jacob asks the question he's been burning to ask.

"What about Tino's family, then? Are they modern?"

Lucas whistles silently through his teeth. "Ah," he says eventually, "here's the thing: look, I like your chum Tino, he's a good lad. But it does sound like his old man is a bit of a rotter. He's a teacher at the university in Salamanca. They say he knows Unamuno, and hangs around with a lot of foreigners ..."

Jacob is mystified. Who or what on earth is Unamuno?

"But we hang around with a lot of foreigners too. Papa is always off with the Italians, the Germans, the British cousins …"

Lucas ignores him. "And it sounds like his mother was a bit of a trouble-maker, too, another *radical;* deserved what was coming to her."

Jacob stops suddenly. He realises that Tino has never mentioned his mother, not once. "What do you mean, *was?* What happened?"

Lucas stops too. His voice softens.

"It was a long time ago, he must have been very small, a toddler. I don't remember, I heard about it from someone, don't know who …"

But Lucas is only half listening. Poor old Tino.

"… there was some kind of terrible accident involving a police horse. She was on one of those processions with a lot of other rebel types, asking for votes for women or something, yes, that's right, and had gone to listen to a speech by … hang on … Clara Campoamor, that's her, up in Bilbao, and there was a bit of a scuffle and a stampede and a few were hurt and she, poor woman, got killed, that's all."

"But I still don't understand," says Jacob. "Why should that matter to me and Tino? It's not fair."

Lucas groans. He's losing patience. Perhaps he's already said too much.

"Like I said, short-arse, it's grown up stuff. But listen: if it were up to me I'd let you play with him no bother, but it's not. Funnily enough, I saw his old man last week, down in the port, didn't know who he was at first, thought he was a fisherman, and we chatted for a bit about sharks, of all things. He told me that the orcas they see sometimes round the Cies Islands are a good thing after all, because they drive the tuna fish inshore for us … seemed to know what he was talking about, that's for sure, quite interesting really … a gentle sort of chap … skinny legs. But anyway, I mentioned this to Mama the same evening and she was absolutely furious! Know that thing she does when she gets really mad, goes white, those lines down the side of her cheeks? Well, she did all that, went really quiet and told me I should know better. Me!"

Jacob smiles slightly; he likes it that Lucas is still not too big to be yelled at; it makes them partners in crime.

"What did you say? What did you do?"

"Went out. What can you do? She'd calmed down by the morning."

Lucas looks around. He hears the crickets in the trees warming up for a night of song, sees a first star gleaming in the iridescent evening sky.

"Come on," he says. "We're late. But I tell you this: if you've got any sense at all, any, then you'll keep away from that stupid village. And Tino."

With this he breaks into a run, and Jacob has no choice but to follow.

In their absence a letter has been delivered to the house.

Señora,

Forgive me for my boldness in writing to you now and for taking up your valuable time.

May I be brief: I am not so foolish as to believe that circumstances will ever allow us to become friends, but at the same time I see no good reason as to why we should remain enemies. However, I respect your situation. Though if between us we are still unable to reach any form of truce, then I beg of you at least that our sons be allowed to play together unimpeded. It seems to me quite wrong that we should allow our own differences to affect the happiness of the coming generation. For their sake, could we not exercise some tolerance?

Respectfully,

Faustino Benavente

Jacob's mother grimaces as she scrutinises the elegant copperplate handwriting for a second time. The envelope bore no stamp; it had been delivered by hand and pushed under their door during the night. She crosses the room and puts it on the fire. She watches the letter as it fuses with the red hot coals of the kitchen stove, and resumes her breakfast.

Chapter Fourteen

A trip to England, 1932

The boys' mother had not at first been keen when she'd heard the news that they were planning to visit their cousins in England: it was tiresome having to make all the arrangements to move such a large household. Her husband, or rather some junior officer, would organise the tickets and the transport and feel therefore that he'd done his share, without ever fully realising what a trial it would be to make sure that all the trunks were adequately packed, as well as the long lists of instructions she would need to leave in their absence for the staff.

Still, now that she was on board she was as excited as the rest of the family. She felt a flush of pride as she watched her husband and sons. Even though today they were not in uniform they looked elegant and handsome in their smartly-tailored suits. She wondered what the English girls would make of Lucas, and indeed, what he would make of them.

A bell rang out, the ship's siren blows, startling her, and the old ship groaned, shuddered, cursed as she heaved herself seawards; all the while the shrill seagulls of Santander screeched their furious farewells. The passengers, landlubbers all, staggered nonplussed and heavy-footed about the sloping deck, excited and as quivery as the ship herself, salted lips tightening against the cold as they moved out beyond the arms of the harbour.

The sun shone weakly, barely strong enough to leave a shadow, and as she looked back to land she could see the remains of the spring snow on the mountains behind the port. It was lovely, she thought, but as they turned into open water the smoke and soot from the two great funnels began to blow back into their faces, and she turned to go indoors. She struggled for an instant to push against the heavy teak doors, and was pleased as Jacob reached from behind her, considerate and courteous, to lend a hand. He was a kind boy, she reflected. With his face now so close to hers she was able to observe the soft bristle about his jaw, and beneath the cologne she thought she could still detect the faint aroma of the child she had once held so dearly. He squeezed her arm affectionately, shyly, and smiled. This one too would break hearts, she thought to herself.

The family dined that night at a large mahogany table with the captain and a handful of rich or high-bred guests. To Jacob's relief the ocean was calm; he had been anxious since Lucas had described the effects of sea-sickness and had no wish to let anyone down. Their father was garrulous, drinking too much, recounting again his heroic exploits as a young officer in the colonies as his two sons exchanged embarrassed glances. At nine o'clock his mother and the other ladies withdrew, leaving the menfolk to their brandy and cigars. Jacob was at the age where he too might have been expected to take his leave, and was therefore proud and pleased when his father invited him to stay. He would be less pleased in the middle of the night as a half-amused elder brother held onto his shoulders in the bathroom as the effects of tobacco and spirits on an innocent constitution followed the natural course of events. The next day, pale and ashamed, he took nothing but water and rice, and was relieved when the steward announced at last that they could see the coast of England.

Against all prediction, the weather in the harbour at Portsmouth was sunny and bright. At this distance it could still be Spain, thought Jacob, though this opinion changed swiftly the moment they went ashore and were confronted by a world whose language and smells seemed utterly alien to him. They were met by a uniformed chauffeur. The cousins, who were industrialists in the midlands, were evidently wealthy, for the car they sent was very grand.

The journey took all day. To begin with, Jacob was fascinated by the novelty of it all, by the neat rows of houses each with their little garden, by the strangeness of driving on the left, by the symmetrical fields filled with cows and sheep. At lunchtime they stopped at a pub with a strange straw roof just outside Oxford. It was gloomy inside, and the ceiling was too low for Lucas to stand up properly. They were given a strange chicken soup, creamy, not like the soups he was used to, and then shared an over-cooked slab of beef which Jacob found difficult to chew. Only good manners and the furtive scowls of his mother allowed him to get to the end of the meal without protest.

The rest of the journey went by in some discomfort, and Jacob was hugely relieved when at last they reached their destination. He stretched in the car like a cat, rolled his shoulders, yawned, then stood blinking in the poor evening sunlight as he took in his new surroundings. They had parked on the gravel driveway of an imposing villa-type house in the suburbs of Leamington Spa, and a woman was bustling down the steps to meet them. It was his aunt Leonara, whom he barely recognised, for he had seen her just once when she had been in Madrid several years earlier.

She was smiling and looked pleased to see them, although she greeted them all with a formal handshake, even his father, her own brother. They spoke Spanish together, though something about her dress, her speech, her whole manner, was strangely foreign – was English, no doubt. After all, she'd lived here more than half her life and now had an English family.

The house is huge. Leonara's husband, their uncle Richard, owns steel mills in Coventry, just up the road.

"They're rich," Lucas had told him on board the ship, "and the mum's a bit of a snob, but they're alright really. I can't wait to see the girls again, because last time I saw them, when I was your age, they were seriously pretty!"

Jacob had groaned at this. Lucas was so predictable, so boring these days. It was all about stupid girls.

But he was right, Jacob now sees. His two cousins are waiting for them in the lobby, one blonde, one dark, and even he can see that they are pretty.

They approach each other warily. The boys' mother notices how Lucas straightens his back and looks taller, whilst Jacob seems to shrink into himself with shyness, so that the height difference between them is exaggerated. For a moment there is mild social confusion, as no-one quite knows whether they should all shake hands or kiss, Spanish-style, on either cheek, until their father embraces his sister and pulls everyone in together for a warm and unexpected family hug, even tall, pale Uncle Richard

Jacob is delighted by dinner that night. They eat salad, chorizo, and a dish of salt cod, followed by rice pudding: he could be at home! He's seated next to Olivia, the blonde, younger sister, who is relaxed and funny and makes him laugh out loud as she teases her father. He can't believe how bold and knowledgeable about everything she is, she seems just like a proper grown up, though she's only eighteen, not that much older than he is.

Perhaps it's the English way, he wonders, not only to challenge but to defy her father; he doubts he could ever do the same in their household in Madrid, he'd be sent to bed: and she is just a girl! Strange.

The evening is not completely free of tension, however. He could tell that Olivia had gone too far when her mother snapped at her for some comment she had made about her support for the feminists, and Olivia had pouted later when her father had been dismissive about the English Prime Minister Ramsay MacDonald. And this had led to a proper row.

"But Daddy," she had said in her almost perfect Spanish, "you can't just keep pretending that a lot of the steel your factory makes isn't going to end up killing people, it's just so unreasonable to say otherwise. We're not all innocents. We know full well that tons of it is going to the companies that make tanks, and here we have Uncle Carlos, who no doubt wants to transport a load more over for the army in Spain ... do you not have enough steel in Spain, Uncle?," she had asked sweetly.

"That's enough, Olivia!" her mother had shouted. "Enough! Either keep your filthy politics away from the table, or leave us, do you hear?"

At that she had backed down. She didn't exactly apologise, but had smiled at everyone, nodding in gratitude to her sister Philippa who had skilfully managed to change the subject, giving Jacob the impression that his cousins were no strangers to these disagreements. A sense of truce and calm ensued, and the rest of the evening passed off without further commotion.

Next morning they attend a concert in the park. It's cold, though the sun shines meekly as they amble down the boulevard and past the grand houses which line the centre of the town. People go about their business, dodging in and out of shop doorways, encumbered with parcels, baskets, umbrellas, each dodging horse-droppings, dodging each other's eyes, watchful of the steady line of carts and cars that rule the roadways. A policeman mounted on a grey mare nods to Uncle Richard, as Lucas gawks at a teashop window crammed with cakes, and a young priest cranes his neck to get a better look at Olivia. It's a familiar, run-of-the-mill, Saturday morning, though for Jacob it's a voyage, it is pure adventure, and his mother tries to stay close to restrain his wide-eyed curiosity.

They pause at the wrought-iron gates that mark the entrance to the Jephson Gardens. Two men are trying to tie a banner to the top of the railings, whilst park officials are attempting to stop them. One blows a whistle, but, disinterested, Jacob and his family wander on, eager to get to the bandstand, chatting easily now, the cousins mocking them as they mangle the few words of English they are endeavouring to teach them.

They stroll noisily past the water lilies and the carp-filled ponds, then grow quiet as they arrive at the strange, covered platform in the centre of the park, and settle down on the folding metal seats which are provided. In Madrid the waiting crowd would be boisterous still, but here the people seemed more patient, certainly more calm. Lucas and Jacob have no idea what will happen next. They are hoping for modern music, American perhaps, some Jazz or Swing, and are therefore bewildered when a large brass band begins to belt out tunes quite alien to them.

Between songs a young woman arrives at their side, leans down and whispers something to Olivia. Jacob, realising that she has nowhere to sit, stands and offers her his seat. She smiles at him, though her uniformed companion glares at Lucas, who stares him down.

Too polite to admit it, the boys are nonetheless relieved when the music at last comes to an end. They join in the polite applause, each silently praying that there won't be an encore, and are grateful when Philippa hastens them towards the tearooms.

Later, benumbed by jam and scones, they saunter slowly back along the sunlit paths. It's a genteel, sedate kind of crowd, says their father, exactly the kind of smart, stout-hearted people they might meet back home in the Retiro park, late on some Sunday afternoon.

But then, quite suddenly, as they reach the gates that lead out into the town, they become aware of a distinct change in the mood of the crowd. The way ahead is partly blocked by people gathered on the footpath, and they have to struggle to get past.

"Oh no, not again!" says Aunt Leonara. "It's those bloody troublemakers, making a nuisance of themselves."

Jacob stands on tiptoe, trying to see what's happening. He won't know this until later when Uncle Richard explains it at home, but they have bumped into one of the Hunger Marches. Ever since the Great Depression there have been people whose homes and livelihoods have been lost who are desperate to find food, and who seek to express their grievances through largely peaceful protest.

Though not always peaceful. The marchers, tired, hungry and desperate, attract much public sympathy, but at the same time are something of a magnet for the cruel mockery of troublemakers with too much time on their hands. Jacob watches as a knot of men argue with the leaders at the head of the parade, preventing them from moving forwards. Behind them a press is developing as those at the back of the march continue to advance, unaware of the impasse ahead. The bowler–hatted man at the front digs his heels in, tries to hold his ground, but the weight of the people behind is too great, and he topples forward, grabbing the lapels of his antagonist to stop himself from falling. For a moment the two men grapple with each other, swearing, with henchmen either side looking more and more incensed. Able to go neither forwards nor back, the marchers spill sideways, mixing with the onlookers. Instinctively Jacob steps in front of his mother, and watches as a woman pops from the crowd and bumps into Lucas who is shielding Philippa.

But it is little more than a skirmish. There is no real menace or venom to the fight, and to the sound of police whistles it peters out as quickly as it had begun. The bystanders have been forced off the footpaths and onto the lawns, trampling crocus and daffodils in the process. The march is moving on. Aunt Leonara is outraged. By her side the uniformed man who earlier had glared at Lucas is shouting insults at the backs of the marchers, fist raised to the sky.

"Scum!" he yells. "Vermin! Get back to-"

But then, this astonishing thing: suddenly Olivia appears in front of him, red lips drawn to a bitter tight line. "Stop it!" she shouts. "Just stop it, Gus!"

He just sneers and moves to go round her, when suddenly she slaps him, hard, so that they all turn and stare.

"These are not vermin, you simpleton! These are decent folk just down on their luck, that's all. Just let them be."

Gus is holding his hand to his cheek. In the baffled silence that follows, Olivia spins on her pumps and runs after the departing marchers. At their tail a flat-capped, underfed youth holds a tin pail intended for alms. Heads turn as they hear the unambiguous jangle of coins from her purse being emptied into its empty mouth. As an afterthought she stoops and plants a kiss on the boy's startled cheek, then meanders smiling back to her family.

Jacob is enthralled. How can anyone so clever, so good-looking, be so kind to these awful people? Did she do that just to provoke her parents, to show off, or does she really care?

Olivia, who by now seems to have recovered her composure, begins to giggle and points at Jacob's feet. He looks down; there, amongst the boot-crushed shrubs, he realises he is standing on a dismembered wooden sign.

"We'll make a rebel of you yet!" his pretty cousin laughs.

"Keep Off The Grass," the sign commands. It is written in English, and, like much of this day's confusing events, it means nothing to him.

Chapter Fifteen

Après le déluge, Madrid, 1933

Maria's world was shattered by the assault. For three days she lay curled up in her blankets, feeling like she wanted to die. A girl she knew had got word to the cook at her old place of work, who had taken her to her own brother's house on the outskirts of the city. This saved her.

There was blood on her pillow where her ear was torn. One eye was too swollen to open. The bruising on her ribs was so bad that it was hard for her to breathe. They refused to give her a mirror, even after she begged for one, and at night they sat with her as she slept, to hold her when she woke from nightmares, screaming.

"If that was a horse, they'd shoot it," she heard one man say.

In the end it was too much, and it was decided that they had no choice but to take her back to her village in the Sierras. None of her family remained, but the people there would take care of one of their own; that was the way of things.

When she was able to stand they dressed her and sent her off in the company of a knife-sharpener to walk the hundred kilometres home. She barely spoke, not on the journey nor when she reached her village.

The women there knew exactly what had happened when they saw her. They took turns to bathe and feed her.

For a month she lived alone amongst the ghosts of her childhood. Gradually the cuts and weals grew less, at least on the outside, and she took to taking short walks to get water from the fountain in the company of the teacher's wife. But still she spoke little, and the women grew afraid that she might be permanently damaged.

One morning her luck changed. A distant aunt was passing through the village on her return to Granada with her husband, and hurried to see her. The woman, Carmen, was shocked: not only was the family resemblance so strong, but so too the familiar confusion and apathy in the poor girl's behaviour. No one knew this, not even her husband, but Carmen had suffered the same fate not three decades earlier; she was convinced that this was the reason why she and Paco had never been able to have children of their own.

She took charge. No one was given much alternative. Carmen was a force of nature and within a few days the three of them were rattling south on the train out of Madrid. Maria was still in a daze. Things just seemed to be happening around her, beyond her control, and she endured her existence in a state of constant anxiety. Eventually she allowed herself to be led from the train to a horse-drawn carriage, and then to a mule. Their destination was a village tucked high in the Sierra Nevada, reached only by a dirt road first put there by the Romans. They climbed high across a mountain pass, breaking through the clouds into sunshine, before descending to the time-locked townlets of the Alpujarras.

Jubar. The village was tiny, just 300 souls. To her it felt like an island, floating in the vast green seas of the mountains. He couldn't touch her here. Slowly she began to feel safe.

Over time, bit by bit in the warmth of the southern sun and the kindliness of people, she started to thaw. She worked hard in the fields and won the respect of the neighbours. Weeding, sowing, threshing, picking corn, fetching wood: she did what she was told and grew strong. In the evenings she talked with Paco and Carmen. In his youth, Paco had been a tailor. Although his eyesight was now poor, he could still, with Carmen's help, cut cloth, and he made her skirts and a deep blue robe. By the spring her smile and with it her good looks had returned, and at the fiesta, boys from other villages stared at her and asked her shyly to dance with them.

But it was always a time of healing, and when the healing was done it was time to move on. One night after harvest they were standing after supper in front of the church; a wall of symmetrical sheaves of grass lay propped side by side, drying out, their greenness mixing with the gold of sunset to turn the dusk to bronze, Maria smiling sadly.

"I'll miss all this," she said, sweeping her hands across the dying horizon. "And you, and all you've done for me."

"You don't have to, you could stay, you could ..." Carmen stopped herself. "I know," she said. "You have to go. I didn't know how to tell you. You need to get back; I understand, I do. All this is wonderful, but it's not enough for you, is it? It's not your fault, or ours, it's just the way it is. You need books, people, ideas. And we need people like you to go out and change the world for us."

Maria hugged her, and together they watched the final sliver of the sun slide behind the hills. As they walked home, slipping into acceptance of her departure, Carmen explained that Guillermo, another cousin, was a barrel maker and could give her a job in Madrid. It was soon settled, and by the time they reached home the plan was firmly made.

And that was that. Just a week later Carmen and Paco stood at the edge of the village to wave their last goodbyes to the mule train which would take her back to the station at Guadix.

And so it was that Maria ended up back in the city. The road to full recovery was slow, and longer than the road from Jubar, but within a few weeks she again felt comfortable in her new surroundings. Guillermo was a big, foul-mouthed man who drank too much, but he was fair and she felt she could trust him. The work was dull, sweeping up the endless mess from the saws and spokeshaves, but she felt safe sleeping in the family home, and she could come and go as she pleased. She made new friends, met up with some old ones. And it was then that she found Jacob again. He was completely unsuitable for her, of course: a boy soldier, a toff, a scion of a rich and upper-class family. And yet … he listened to her. He made her laugh. Despite everything, she liked him.

It was about this time that she ran into Isobel. Isobel had been a maid at the house when Maria had first arrived, and they had become friends. But she had left hurriedly to marry the handsome coach driver at the National Opera, and she and Maria had drifted apart.

One day they bumped into each other by chance at the market.

"He left me," Isobel says simply. "I don't really hold a grudge. I thought I was pregnant, I really did. My monthlies stopped and everything. He did the decent thing, offered to marry me and all, and so I went and told everyone we were getting hitched in Salamanca. That's where he's from, so off we go, and the next thing I'm bleeding again. I couldn't believe it. But no baby, no wedding. I was so ashamed. I stayed up there for ages, got a job sweeping floors at the university."

Maria leans into her, holds her tight. "He was off like a shot. Can't really blame him, not really. And it's probably for the best – he's a good-looking sod, but thick as two short planks. And arrogant. I don't think we would have lasted long! And my dad absolutely *hated* him! It was ages ago …"

They walk along slowly, giggling arm in arm, until Isobel stops abruptly by a low metal door that is wedged between two taller buildings. "Listen," she says seriously, "I bet you'll like this. Have you got time? Wait here." She looks around quickly, then ducks beneath the door. Five minutes later she reappears, and motions to Maria to follow her inside. "It's my *group*," she whispers breathlessly. "He says you can come in. Don't say anything unless he asks you."

It is Maria's first contact with the communists, and she is mesmerised. A tall thin man in a suit leads a class of around ten students. Some take notes, others fidget, one gazes out of the window. Maria concentrates fiercely on what the man is saying. She cannot understand everything he says, but some of the sentences she hears affect her and go to her core as music sometimes does. Images, thoughts, concepts; expressions that clarify and put into simple words so many of the ideas that have swirled around inside her head for so long. At the end of the class she begs Isobel to introduce her.

The man smiles at her. "I watched you listening. Well done, Isa. I think we have a convert."

"You can't convert me," Maria says. "I have nothing to convert from."

"In that case let's call you a new believer instead. No! Not even that, as you may have believed already, to follow your logic. Let's just call you a *believer,* though you may not have known it. Or perhaps you did …" He looks thoughtful. "Perhaps you already had the seed, the germ. My textbooks just provided the water."

This chance encounter opens up a new world. New people, new ideas, new possibilities. Over the next few weeks she returns to the classroom, and each time goes home burning with excitement. One day she is asked to take a message in an envelope to a comrade at the Bullring; another time she and Isobel follow a man in the park to his home, to be certain of his address. For the first time in her life she begins to develop a miniscule, delicate sense of purpose. Could there be more to her life, she begins to wonder, than just fetching and carrying, attending to the wealthy? Could they really challenge injustice, intolerance and poverty? She had thought it was ludicrous. And yet now a tiny spark, a glimmer of hope, had been lit in her, and they, *the group,* were breathing on the flame.

Chapter Sixteen

The Bull Ring, Toledo, 1936

Even in the shade the heat is oppressive. Someone says it's 40 degrees. Jacob's shirt clings to his back and his whole body seems constricted; he feels as if he's suffocating under the weight of cigar smoke and the fumes of the improperly combusted petrol of the taxis that lumber past every few seconds. He regrets the wine he'd drunk with lunch. The shop across the street folds up its shutters and suddenly sunlight from the display window is reflected under the restaurant canopy directly onto his little group, who curse and weave their heads against the unwelcome glare. The air is slick with the haze of frying fish, and the percussive slaps of boastful braying voices resound like bullets and add to his incipient headache. A raucous waiter, impervious to the pandemonium, bellows at Jacob to ask if he'd like to order food, but the very thought revolts him. Instead he orders a large glass of water, with plenty of ice, and retreats to the gloomy interior of the bar where a venerable bamboo fan turns languidly, as ineffectual as the fly traps on the counter.

However, removed from the tumult and incandescence outside, his spirits begin to recover. On the opposite wall hangs a poster which advertises the fight they are shortly to attend. Six bulls from a distinguished breeder, and three eminent *toreadors* whose mission it will be to slay them. In the distance he can now hear the rumble of the gathering crowd, and he feels the familiar churning in the pit of his stomach as his excitement grows. His headache is gone, he realises, and walks outside to the terrace to re-join his family.

He steps through a coruscating wall of light and clamour, re-energised, allowing himself to be carried along by the tide of imminent drama. They move with the throng towards the imposing bullring, from whose many arched windows people are calling and waving, trying ludicrously to attract the attentions of individuals amongst the swarm beneath. With so many people, so much life, so much anticipation, there is a sense of disorder. He catches the eye of a young woman who walks towards him and holds her gaze for an exploratory second, but she turns and speaks into the ear of the man by her side and moves away. There is colour everywhere, and woodsmoke from the fires of the street vendors who sell cold beer and blood-red chorizo sausage. There is an odd tension in the air.

Soon they are within the shadow of the building, and the din seems to ease with each step that takes them closer to the stone entranceway, as though the hordes are awed by its monumental, temple-like presence. This is the quieter side of the arena, where his family always sits; the shaded part, the expensive part. With patrician authority his father now shakes the hand of the man at the turnstile, who opens the gate obligingly. It is cool within, and their footsteps echo along the vaulted corridor that encircles the arena.

His mother is slightly breathless as they climb the stone steps, and Jacob holds her hand as they emerge once more into the ruckus of the crowd. She sits heavily on the bench and pulls a delicate pearl-studded fan from the bag at her side. The bullring is divided into *sol y sombra,* sun and shade, with tickets priced accordingly, but even here in the shade the afternoon is warm.

"Glad I'm not over there with that pestilential lot," she says unkindly. "Imagine what it must be like to sit and roast all day in the sun like that. You would hate it, Jacob, you've no idea."

But in fact he does know exactly what it's like to suffer for hours under the merciless sun. In truth though, suffer wasn't the right word, for he hadn't suffered at all, not that day, because he'd been with Maria. Now when he thinks about it, they'd just had fun, and neither had mentioned the sun at all. Not that he would dare mention any of this to his mother. Imagine: her son, being seen *en publico* with a house maid! He shudders.

Even though it was a year ago now, he recalls every detail. It had begun as a dare, almost, an unstated dare, that he should go with her to the fight. When they were much younger they'd just been playmates, just children thrown together. Then she'd gone away and he hadn't seen her again until they were both sixteen, when he'd returned on holiday to find her working once more for his family. At first there had been a natural tension between them, and he had felt hugely conflicted. It was wrong to befriend someone below his station, but something about her seemed to transcend this notional hierarchy, and if anything she was the one given to haughtiness. As well as her sharp wit she was obviously, visibly, a woman, and he often found himself tongue-tied in her presence. But then he'd met her that time outside the park gates by chance, and for once unobserved and off-duty, things between them had thawed. When she'd suggested they go together to the bull-fight he had jumped at the chance.

They had arrived early. Maria for some reason had presented a docket that had permitted them to enter the gates through which the carters would later pass with horses to drag the carcasses of the bulls to the butchery. For the moment it was still calm inside the cavernous outer halls, reverential almost, as they passed the stables, the hospital and the small private chapel. Inside was a bullfighter, on his knees. "I wonder what he's praying for?" she had whispered. "For glory? Or to be not killed or scared or hurt?" With naïve forcefulness he'd suggested that if it were the latter then he ought perhaps to look for a different job, to which she'd answered seriously that for many it wasn't a job at all, but a calling, "Like a priest or a soldier, or something in between. They inspire us, do violence on our behalf, are wounded for us." How did she know these things?

"Is that why you like it so much then, this glory?"

"No," she replied. "I hate it. Hate the whole stupid lot of it."

He was confused. "So, why do you -"

"Just to see all these brave, handsome men," she taunted, smiling, but seeing the crestfallen look he was unable to hide, had continued, "It's not that, silly, I only come here to leave the messages ..."

"Messages?"

She laughed. "Nothing for your tender ears. Girl things. *Love* things. Billets doux." He blushed. "You've not met my friend, have you? She is so pretty. Much prettier than me!"

"Impossible," he blurted out, then stopped himself, blushing again. She had looked at him strangely, before leading him out in search of a drink before the bars became too crowded.

The fight itself had turned out to be a largely lacklustre affair, and he and Maria had joked and talked easily throughout. He'd felt a lightness as he'd walked home that evening; he'd been effortlessly relaxed and happy all day in the company of a pretty girl whom he liked, and who seemed to like him back in return. Two other clandestine meetings had followed before he had been forced to return to the barracks, and each occasion had left him with that same sense of levity. That was why he was now so disconcerted. He'd been eager to see her on his leave-of-absence, and sought her out at the first opportunity, but she seemed always to be busy, and when he did manage finally to manufacture an excuse to be alone with her she had seemed sullen and distant, reluctant to talk. On another occasion he'd caught her looking at him with a more gentle expression, but when he approached she had fled. He felt oddly bruised by the experience.

But all that had been a year ago, and now his mind was on other, bigger things. As a junior officer he was not privy to secret intelligence, but every whisper, every rumour, every conversation seemed only to confirm that something was stirring, something important. It was seventeen years since the Revolution in poor old Russia, and now it looked like the Bolsheviks were trying to stir up discontent in France and here in Spain. Well, let them try. He didn't know exactly what they wanted, nor what they represented, but if his family and his regiment were against them, then so was he. Today he was hoping to speak to Mathias, an old friend who worked for the government, in an attempt to tease out some more concrete news. He knew that as an old-school bullfighting *aficionado* Mathias would almost certainly be in attendance at such an important fight, and Jacob had sent a message to suggest that they should meet at 8 pm at the members-only bar.

In the meantime he begins to suffer again in the heat. To his right his mother continues to fan herself, faintly red-faced and perspiring. He longs to take off his jacket, to sit shirt-sleeved like the tide of people opposite, but knows that he's forbidden by a strict societal rule that's as unbending as the sturdy oak wall that runs around the perimeter of the arena. To add to the drama some self-styled Lord of Misrule on the terraces above them has a bugle, which he plays so badly it hurts the ears.

It is shortly before 6 pm, and people at last are beginning to take up their seats. The superintendent and his entourage make their way slowly up the steps towards the gallery from which they will preside. Nothing will happen until they are perfectly ready and the signal is given. The crowd understands this need for formality. Jacob finds it fascinating that the ritual of the ceremony can force order so effortlessly, how such a choreographed sequence can calm and yet arouse simultaneously. It dawns on him that he himself is part of the troupe, they all are, each of them a fragmentary bit-part actor, an extra, in the play. Perhaps this is why the drama is so compelling. He feels pleased with himself at his insight; he will share it later with Maria, she'll understand … but then he remembers, and the thought sours. Damned girl.

At last. The strident music of pent-up bugles blares, and the great doors swing open. The three toreadores enter, preening and cocksure, milking the applause as they scan the sea of faces for their best girls. They strut on their silken pumps to the area in front of the presidential bench and bow theatrically; Jacob wonders whether one of them could be the fellow they had seen praying that time. Behind this leading triumvirate come a less arrogant group of picadores, and the horse-handlers struggling to keep hold of the reins of their wide-eyed snorting charges. Everyone is playing their part, following the script, spectators included.

But suddenly there is a bang. From nowhere. Shouting. The whoosh and detonation of a rocket. Horses paw the air. Confusion. What the hell is this? Shrieking. People, dozens, no hundreds, are leaping the barriers and running on to the arena. Stupefaction turns to shock. His mother mouths a question mutely, white-faced. The interlopers begin to sit down as they reach the centre, many back-to back. Slowly realisation dawns: some kind of protest, a demonstration, a reactionary liberal riot. But then what's this? Policemen. Or soldiers? Streaming across the sand in formation. The officer in the lead has his sword raised. He stops, but waving his weapon he urges his comrades forward. So he's a soldier; Jacob recognises the technique from cadet school.

The soldiers reach the seated intruders and begin to attack, mercilessly, methodically; they are well trained. Many of the protesters stand up and begin to fight back. The men stand up ... by Christ there are women there too! Jacob watches in amazement. It is hopeless. The uniformed men are armed with clubs, some wear pistols, not yet drawn. The group of trespassers realise the game is up and begin to scatter, fleeing back to the stands. He sees that many are unable to rise, laying broken on the ground.

Jacob feels bilious. He watches as a girl darts out from the carnage and makes a break towards the fence, raven hair free and flowing out behind, sprinting away from her pursuer. There is something familiar about her gait. No, surely not. The man is gaining on her. It can't be. His stomach lurches. Please no. But she falls. He sees a baton raised, poised, and Jacob suddenly finds himself running, bursting over the benches towards her, careless of the people now staring at him. He vaults the barrier, careens across the sand. He is screaming but it doesn't feel like it's coming from him. He watches in horror as the baton crashes down again on the helpless form crumpled on the ground, and as at last he reaches her, he hears the obscene sound of splintering bone.

"Stop!" he howls. "You'll kill her." The attacker pauses, looks up, grins, and for a moment Jacob thinks he will have to fight him, but he backs away, looking malevolently around for more pickings.

Jacob's heart is pounding and time around him stops as he drops to his knees and puts a hand on the bloodied black hair. Gently he turns over the unconscious body. She's heavy, so heavy, and her hair in his fingers is hot from the sun. He sees that her teeth are smashed and that one eye is swollen horribly, grotesquely, but *God, oh sweet Jesus, thank you, God* it's not her. He starts to breathe again and looks around with pure loathing for the khaki-clad thug, but he has moved on.

He is bewildered. The girl beneath him moans. She'll live. He turns, and to his left he sees a figure he recognises. Mathias. He's sobbing, enraged.

"Fucking idiots! Fucking sons of whores!" He stares at Jacob. "It wasn't meant to be like this. Savages. I told them. Use minimal force. No martyrs. The fucking liberal press will fucking love all this …"

Understanding is dawning on Jacob. An informant, a tip off; they'd been waiting for them. They gaze around them at the wounded bodies.

"Is this all really worth it?" says Mathias.

They stare at each other. Is it?

Jacob makes his way slowly back to where his family are sitting. His mother has regained her composure and is murmuring to her neighbour. Their afternoon has been ruined, completely ruined. She stares at Jacob, but says nothing. He sits down next to her, takes off his jacket, and folds it neatly on the back of the chair in front of him. He leans forward and holds his head in his hands, to hide the tears.

Chapter Seventeen

Madrid, 19ʰ May 1935

The thin walls of the makeshift office do little to stem the sounds of the city outside. The constant chatter and thrum of many voices talking, the whistle of the tram, the thump and clatter of the brewer's barrel as it's dropped and rolled down the teeming pavement, the wail of a crying child.

It's better this way. No one sees them, no one cares. Despite the noise the Russian continues to speak softly, and the eight young people lean forward in their chairs, move closer, struggle to hear him. Yes, it's better this way, hidden in plain sight, with his students, his acolytes, so desperate to hear, so desperate to learn.

He pauses in the middle of his little speech and gazes at them, at their keen, dirty, intelligent faces. What will become of them, what will they achieve? Are they all wasting each other's time? He dare not contemplate this.

His eyes rest on Maria at the back. She's what, seventeen? Eighteen? A real beauty, even he can see that. And she's clever too, so committed, so *engagée* in their cause. Big almond eyes – her forebears could be Berbers, maybe. If he were younger, if he were made differently ... but no. He holds her gaze now for a fraction too long. At the end of the class she'll come up to him and ask a question, a real, substantial question that means something to her, and he'll have to make an effort to provide an answer that will satisfy her. He likes her; they could perhaps be friends, despite the age gap. He will have to tell her though.

He glances at his watch. Not long now. At five o'clock he's meeting Miguel, his new friend, at the British club for cocktails. Dinner later, perhaps, and afterwards ... well, who knows? He sighs, and with difficulty brings his attention to bear on the political theories of Lenin, *Vladimir Ilyich Ulyanov*. He knows his students adore it when he pronounces the names of their heroes so effortlessly well in his native Russian accent.

The girl, Maria, is still looking at him.

Of the eight already identified, she is the one, he's sure of that now. She has all the attributes, and the flame of belief burns strongly in her. She will be an asset. In the morning he will pass her name to the team, and she will be made useful.

But she may have to go back into service, back to the family who first sent her away. He knows about the assault. Swine. His colleagues in the party will be able to manage her re-insertion, of that he is sure. But – with the bruises she carries inside – will she have the courage and strength to perform?

He looks at her again. She's strong, but is she strong enough? He decides that if she is so damaged that she has to turn them down, then he'll kill the man who hurt her.

Whichever. A satisfactory outcome either way, he concludes.

Chapter Eighteen

Toledo, 1936

The armoured car pulled up outside the house, so large it almost blocked the road to traffic. Jacob needed to collect certain maps from the family library, and told the men to stay by the vehicle as he hurried inside. His mother was out, and the place was consequently filled with the shouts of the staff as they went about their business without their usual solemnity. The smell of baking bread drifted up from the kitchen and he pursued it downstairs; if there was enough he would share it with his soldiers.

He clumped along the basement corridor, then stopped suddenly, the nails on his boots screeching on the polished floor. The door to the old games room was open, and there, looking over her shoulder at him, stood Maria. She had only been back with them for two months, but somehow, his home seemed brighter and more welcoming, and he found himself spending more time there than was strictly necessary.

She was standing by the window. Next to her was their old table tennis table, folded and propped against the wall, gathering dust.

"Hey," she said, smiling. "You busy?"

"Too busy for table tennis, if that's what you mean."

He saw that her fingers were trembling as she struggled to pull down the rusted catch at the top of the shutter on the window. He reached up behind her to help, standing close, and put his hand over hers. Innocently. They pulled together, but still the thing would not move, and so, afraid of crushing her fingers beneath his, he pushed her gently away, and tugged harder. Even then it remained jammed, and he stood on a chair to get more leverage. With one last heave it flew open with a splintering noise, so suddenly that he almost lost his balance and she had to steady him as he landed. They were both laughing. There was a cobweb in his hair and she reached to brush it away. As her hand brushed his cheek he had to catch his breath. The light which flooded the room fell first on her lovely face, and for a second he stared at her, transfixed, but had to look away, as if he were not worthy, and scared that she might read his thoughts, for he was imagining just what it would feel like to press his lips to hers. He wanted to speak but the words felt heavy and would not leave his throat. She was watching him with a curious expression.

"Sir!" boomed a voice down the corridor. "We're late. We have to go now! The men are waiting."

The spell was broken; he found his voice.

"Listen," he said, "I've got leave tomorrow. The whole day off. Any chance you might, I mean, if you're not busy, would you … perhaps we could go for a walk in the park or something."

She pulled a face. "Not tomorrow. It's all arranged: I'm going strawberry picking." She thought for a minute. "Come, if you want. Wear old clothes – not your uniform. It'll be fun. Bet you wouldn't dare!"

"Sir!" came the soldier's voice again.

Jacob looked at her.

"Six o'clock tomorrow morning. At the station. That too early for you?" She was taunting him.

"On my way, Sergeant!" he shouted. "We'll see," he told her, and smiled before turning and marching back the way he came. He had forgotten about the bread.

The following day Jacob woke at dawn, eager for the adventure to begin. The invitation was a challenge and he wasn't going to shirk it. He chose an old shirt from the bottom drawer and for the first time in weeks set out into the streets in civilian clothes.

By six o'clock the station was already busy. The previous day Madrid had been tense, weighed down by protests, propaganda and the arrests of prominent politicians, but this morning was an escape, a holiday, a chance for young people to pretend for a while that all was well, and there was a defiant carnival atmosphere amongst the young people as they boarded the train to take them out to the strawberry fields.

Maria was waiting as planned by the main entrance. Jacob spotted her at once and was relieved as she detached herself from a group of girls and came strolling across to meet him.

"You made it," she said. "I wasn't sure you'd really want to be here amongst all the great unwashed."

He smiled, familiar with her teasing. "I'm here for the fruit, not the proletariat."

Pressure from the gathered crowd compelled them towards the train, and soon they were clattering their way beyond the suburbs and out into the open country south of the city. Talking was effortless. He told her about his journey to England, about his cousins there, the flat, ordered fields. She in turn described a trip she had once made to Valencia. They both agreed that they wanted to see New York. It was easy, inconsequential conversation; they were happy.

She taught him how to pick the fat fruit without damaging the plant, and the two of them worked side by side, their wooden crates filling fast as they laboured along the rows with other laughing strangers. The mood of the pickers was good: they were free of the confines of the city, the sun shone, and although they worked for only a few pesetas, it was better than nothing.

It was more tiring than he had imagined. By the time they stopped to rest at midday his fingers were sore and his back ached.

Maria lay with her head propped on one elbow and studied him. At the start of the day she had felt more keenly the differences between them. Even in his oldest clothes he still had the whitest shirt amongst them, and she had been conscious of the stares they had attracted. Now, victim of the dirt and the sweat and the dust, this shirt acted as a form of camouflage, allowing him to blend in with the others. For a while she allowed her mind to play with the idea that they could be like this all the time, trying to imagine what it would be like to spend a week like this on the land, to sleep out under the stars, to ... no! she had to stop it. There were just too many barriers; it was stupid to daydream. She tightened her lips and looked away.

One of the overseers shouted that it was time to begin the midday checking-in. People around them rose and stretched, then began to form into lines to have the contents of their baskets weighed on a huge brass scale. Courteous to a fault, Jacob allowed several women to join the queue ahead of him, almost losing sight of Maria in the process. She turned and laughed when she saw him, and beckoned him forward. He shook his head. He was in no hurry.

Maria stood to one side to wait after she had had her produce weighed. She felt strangely protective towards Jacob in what for him was an alien environment, and wanted also to observe the man operating the weighing scale. She expected to be swindled, this was normal, and she and the others would in turn eat and carry away as much fruit as they could reasonably handle. That was the way of things. But she was intrigued to see just how much he would cheat them.

The girl in front of Jacob could only have been about twelve, Maria guessed. She was pretty, but had the pale, gaunt face of the undernourished, and struggled under the weight of the two crates she carried. One of those poor girls who actually needed the money, Maria decided, and watched as her turn came.

"Give us a kiss, lovely!" the man leered.

The girl smiled uncomfortably as he reached down to lift the cases from her.

"You've been busy!" he said before weighing them. "Must be a good five kilos in each of these."

"Ten. At least ten. You can tell just by looking at them."

"Doubt it," said the man, shaking his head. "Let's have a little look, shall we?"

He took his time, ostentatiously weighing the first basket.

"There! What did I tell you? A shade over five."

The girl's lip trembled.

"It must be more. It must be. I've got my little brother to feed."

"You calling me a liar, sweetheart?"

"Yes. No! Sorry! I mean, the scales must be wrong. There's twelve kilos there, I'm sure."

The man's mouth twisted.

"Well there ain't now," he said, and tipped half of the contents to the floor.

The girl sobbed and dropped to her knees, scrambling to rescue what she could. Maria was about to speak but Jacob stepped in front her.

"Here," he said to the girl. "Take mine."

She looked up, unsure what to do.

The man growled. "This is none of your business, sunshine. Piss off." He took a step forward, and people around them began to back away. Jacob stood his ground, but clenched his fists and balanced on the balls of his feet, ready to spring.

"It is my business now," he said. The man hesitated. He took in the wide shoulders and fearless expression and realised that this was someone he could not cow with empty threats.

"Enrique!" he shouted. "Trouble over here!"

Out of the corner of her eye, Maria was aware of a big man coming towards them. Without warning she threw herself at Jacob, and pulled him backwards, almost toppling him.

"They've got shotguns, you moron. Let's go!" She pulled at him with surprising strength and he had no option but to follow. The small crowd behind them parted to allow them through, then closed ranks again as though by instinct.

They ran for a few minutes then stopped, breathless, on the edge of a small stream.

"They won't follow us. The people would rob them. They chased us off so at least their honour's intact." She was breathing hard, half laughing, but stopped when she saw his expression.

"I'm an officer in the King's Army, for God's sake. I do not run away." With that he turned and began to sprint back towards the pickers.

"Jacob!" she screamed, and as she did so he turned and came charging back towards her.

"But nor do I abandon a damsel in distress." Laughing, he raised her hand to his lips and made a mock bow.

"That's not funny. Those guys are mean. You saw it with the girl. They'd shoot you for fun and probably get away with it."

"They wouldn't, you know. Not with me. My family would be all over them; they'd hang. Justice and all that."

Maria shook her head. "Justice? What justice? You're right: if they harmed you then they might have to pay for it, you with your rank and your connections. But if they hurt the girl, what then? Who's going to come after them then?"

"The police, of course."

"Police? Don't give me that. The police can be bought, threatened, dissuaded. They've all got cousins and brothers in the underworld. Some might be alright, but ... you know what? It seems to me that the main job for the police is to protect people like *you* from people like *us.*"

That stung him. He looked up, almost as if expecting to see a cloud now covering the sun. All day he'd tried his best to play down the differences between them. Not for the first time, he was confused. Was he now to be punished for standing up for the little girl? He saw a rock in the middle of the stream, and with a great leap launched himself towards it, using it as a steppingstone to get to the other side. For a while they walked in silence, the water between them.

"I'm sorry," she said eventually. "Perhaps that was unfair." She stopped, holding out both hands to him, but the gap here was too wide, the stream too deep. "It's just that it makes me so angry, and so sad. You have justice in your heart. I can see it so plainly. That's what makes it all so absurd." She stamped her foot. "You have this sense of fairness, you're a good person, a good man, and yet you still walk along the wrong side of the river."

"The *other* side of the river, let's call it. I'm sick to death of all these *wrongs* and *rights*. It's just different ways of seeing things." Despite himself he was becoming angry. "Don't take us for fools. Just because I'm in the army doesn't make me stupid. I can see the way your friends look at me. It's not easy. People on the right just want to preserve what's ours. Can't you see that that's a noble thing, a fine thing? This government wants to take away all of those things that make us Spanish. Our traditions, our values, our way of life. Most people think ..."

"Stop! Most people? Most people? We've just had an election, for Christ's sake, a free and fair election, and *most people* voted to change your precious way of life." She looked at him in despair. "That's what frightens me, it really does. You genuinely think that we stole the election. Or somehow that the election was unfair, or that democracy itself, the will of the people, is just not a proper way to govern."

"Not so. It's more that your grand coalition of all the lefties, the modernisers, you all want different things. You're too divided, it's chaos. You wait and see. It's as if you've got this great lovely liberal choir, with Spain as the Cathedral, but you're all singing different hymns."

She looked at him. It was partly true. "Well, at least we're singing together. Better than us. You and me. We're friends and we can't even sing a bloody duet."

That stopped him. She was right, he thought to himself, he was a moron. Why should he want to score points from the person he most liked in the world? It was like a sickness afflicting them all, this desire to quarrel. In a panic he looked around for something to distract them. Perhaps she was thinking the same thing, for suddenly she began to run, pointing ahead of them to an old wooden bridge.

"Race you!" she yelled, and he set off in grateful pursuit.

They arrived together. On each side three steps raised the structure in case of high water. They climbed, looked across at each other and burst into laughter: the bridge was rotten; green moss grew across the supporting struts and through a wide hole in the planks they could see the stream running faster beneath them.

"If we were looking for some crummy symbolism ..." she said. "After you, mi Capitan."

"Not at all. After you ... Comrade."

They smiled at each other across the broken bridge.

"Together?"

"Together."

They met in the middle. The bridge held. For the rest of his life he knew he should have kissed her then, but something held him back. Instead they stayed there talking, dropping flowers into the current and watching them float away to nothingness.

Eventually they heard voices in the distance and knew it was time to make their way home. They sat close together on the train and talked in half whispers. It was a strange, melancholy journey. Although Maria was more sure than ever of his affection, the closer they came to the city, the more she felt the polarising pull of the forces that would drive them apart. She grew quiet. "Oil and water," the cook had said to her so many times. "Oil and water, they just don't mix." She knew that. She had always known it. And she knew too the strength of her commitment to the people. That was who she was, that was her sacred pledge, her vow. Even if she had to break both their hearts. She could barely look at him.

"The stream," she said softly, as much to herself as to Jacob. "And the bridge. If only it were all so simple."

The station was crowded. Hand in hand they stood facing each other beside the newspaper sellers. "Time for Action!" read one of the headlines. confinity

Neither of them knew what to say.

"Jacob. I'm sorry. I've got to go," she eventually managed to whisper, and squeezed his hand tight before stepping back into the crowd. Then, before he had the chance to speak, she skipped back and kissed him, softly, quickly, and melted away again, keeping her head down.

His throat was dry. He ached just to hold her. His eyes followed her as she walked away, her long skirt swishing in the dust, and the very air around him seemed to darken as she left.

Chapter Nineteen

The Battle of Jarama, Spain, February 13th 1937

Will, the schoolteacher, could not stop the trembling in him.

The gun in his hand felt cold, felt ugly. And he feared it. No that wasn't quite it: he loathed it. But just now it was all he had to keep his life intact, his and those of his comrades, and he gripped it tight, fingernails hard against the polished black stock.

Just ten weeks earlier he'd joked in a letter to Katherine from the so-called training camp that he'd fallen in love again, in love with his gun that is, since for the first time in his life he'd felt completely purposeful, and strangely valiant too, and the gun seemed to him to be the embodiment of this sense of commitment and power. How fickle his loyalties. He wondered if she'd ever got that letter, or those after, or the one he now planned to write, and he tried to imagine her profile as she read against the gentle light of a Kent mid-morning, brow puckered slightly, smiling from time to time at his wit and observation, hair falling softly over one side of her lovely face, missing him. He forced himself to hold onto the image, but his legs still shook and he pressed his feet hard against the soft clay of the trench, boots still spattered in blood and vomit.

The man to his left looked sad and defeated, half lost in the smoke, caught by the smell of cordite and the evil thud of the mortars. He could have been crying. On his right was Wintringham: pale, handsome and frail, and the only true soldier amongst them. The others looked to him for light, he was their candle, their beacon, this intense, self-righteous officer, and he at least seemed moderately calm amid the mayhem. Night after night he'd told them that they'd no idea how many men they were facing, nor when an attack might come, but that this in itself was a good thing, since if they were in the dark about their opponents' strengths, then probably so too were the enemy. They were holding them down, he said, delaying the advance like a proper army. It wasn't just about killing people, it was about holding the line, about tactics, and they were to be proud of what they were doing. And they believed him.

That same evening he'd marched them back, *marched*, those 140 lunatics, back into this loathsome inferno, from the relative safety of the higher ground, back to the front line, marching so that the damned spotters in the Condor Legion planes that drifted from time to time above them might think they were well-rested reinforcements, rather than the half dead scarecrows who were all that now remained to protect the vital gap in the road linking Madrid with Valencia. There were rumours that the Front to their left had already fallen, which if true meant that he and his companions in the XV International Brigade could now expect the full fury of the *Regulares*, the terrifying, knife-wielding veterans from Morocco. He shuddered. Knives. Jesus. How could it have come to this, that he, a pacifist, a hunger-marcher, a teacher, could be holed up on this freezing February morning in Spain, fighting for his life against Moroccan Fascists? Katherine had been right all along: his ideals of justice and idealism would lead him into deep, deep trouble, and here it was, in spades.

In the foreground he could see the river as it twisted elegantly towards the village, the wind blowing ripples across the silvered surface in the winter sunlight; it shone bright against the grey green foothills, which in turn stood out against the ethereal white-capped crests of the high sierras, floating beneath that kind of truly blue sky that you could never see in England. It was beautiful, he had to admit, despite the unfolding pain and horror. He watched idly as a trio of planes melted into a cloud, observing as they re-emerged how the shadows they cast went scudding up the far hillside, effortless and untiring. For some reason they brought to his mind a memory of his dog, who could run forever up the green chalk hills of home. How old was he now?

On the opposite side of the valley, watching unknown through their precision-made field glasses, stood General Varela, commander of the Fascist battalions, alongside a smart young man who was his acting aide-de-camp. The general smiled.

"Got the bastards trapped, son. You watch: like shooting rats in a barrel."

Will swallowed, though said nothing.

Back with the volunteers, Wintringham was now screaming for them to take cover, the first to realise – too late – that the inoffensive small planes had wheeled quickly and were now heading straight towards them, vicious yellow bursts spitting from the wing–mounted cannon. Worse, the planes were speeding *along* the trench, not towards it. Their own heavy guns were pointing south, thus useless against this lateral attack, and those men who found themselves too far from a fox hole had utterly no protection. It was butchery. With crushing sadness he saw the torn-up body of gentle Caudwell, the poet, fall twisted and broken against the trench wall.

Part deafened by the roar of the engines, stunned by fear and rage, the teacher moved dream-like towards his captain, who was pointing behind him. As he turned, no longer reminded of his dog, no longer cradling the soft memory of Katherine, he saw half a dozen of the enemy struggling to mount a heavy machine gun on a raised outcrop to his left. The captain had already realised that this was a coordinated attack, and he took in its significance in a moment. They were now terribly exposed from both sides, and as soon as the big gun opened fire they would be slaughtered. He turned again towards his companions, his brothers-in-arms, and felt an inexpressible love for them, for their bravery, for their youth, their hopefulness. He was suddenly calm. This happened in battle sometimes, he had heard. He knew he could avert this catastrophe. In his heart he knew he could stop them, and he would, armed with conviction and loathing. The world stood still as he charged. He saw two men fall, then a third as he hurled himself behind a shattered tree stump for protection. He pulled the pin from a grenade, counted to three, then charged again, bellowing as he threw. As he died, shot simultaneously in throat and head, he remembered throwing a cricket ball for Ted, his dog, who he'd just worked out would now be six, and in his prime.

On the opposite hill, Jacob gasped and put down his binoculars.

"Did you see that, sir? That man of theirs just stopped them single-handedly! That was -" But the general cut him off.

"Forget it. That's not bravery, that's fanaticism pure and simple. Those poor fools are just brainwashed commie cannon fodder. They're depraved and they're scum. They're vermin. Now move on!"

Nevertheless, as they continued to watch the progress of the battle it soon became clear that the expected breakthrough had failed to materialise, and the enemy line still held. By now it was late afternoon and the sun was low in the sky. The general was about to signal to call off the offensive to allow his troops to re-group for the morning, when suddenly they heard the unmistakeable whine and crump of an incoming shell. This really wasn't part of the plan; the dreadful Reds were supposed to be on the run. More shellbursts followed, the earth beneath them bucking with the impact; red hot shrapnel slewed from the sky and ignited a canvas tent; a fragment sliced through the leg of a lieutenant whose blood jetted in an arc onto the charts beside him.

"Where the fuck did that come from?" yelled the general, who was crouching on all fours in the mud.

Jacob had remained standing, and was surveying the valley beneath them. For years he had wondered how he would react when he first came under fire, and he was determined to control the fear that now came roiling up from deep inside.

"There's a big gun, possibly two, on the far side, sir. 155 millimetres," he said, sounding calmer than he actually felt. "And at least a dozen tanks, T-26s moving out from the East. We're right at the edge of their range. But it's definitely a counter-attack. We need to move you, sir."

Just then they looked up to see the outline of two planes speeding towards them.

"Not ours, I'm afraid, sir," the young man said, and hauled the general roughly to his feet and behind the protective trunk of an ancient tree. Another shell exploded, close enough to the low-flying planes for their wings to leap violently with the shock wave it produced, though not close enough to divert them from their mission.

Moments earlier, Jacob had noticed the two horses tethered peacefully to the stump of a tree. Transfixed, he watched them again as now they rose and writhed and raked at the air with their terrified forelegs. Against the setting sun he could see them only in silhouette, distorted black cut-outs like the shadow puppets he'd seen as a boy, silent beneath the roar of the engines.

Around him people were going to ground in the fox holes and slit trenches which had been dug the previous week, finding whatever protection the earth would afford. A strange quiet fell upon them as the planes raced away. There was sporadic shouting, and the muffled groans and moans and prayers from the wounded, but the sound that dominated the blood-soaked field came from the poor horses. Once, at a hunt years earlier, Jacob had heard the screams of a half-killed hare, and the noise had turned his blood to ice. Now he watched as the planes banked, and realising they were about to return, took a deep breath and began to sprint towards the horses, ignoring the calls to take cover.

The air was awash with the sickening smell of charred flesh, for burning cinders had peppered the animals' hides. As he reached them he took in the flared nostrils, the red raw terror in their eyes, and thought for a second he would be unable to avoid the wicked iron-clad hooves that reared above him. He saw too that they were held by a single stout rope, and dived to the floor and began to hack at it with his knife, expecting at any moment to be stunned by an equestrian kick or republican bomb. Thank God for Toledo steel, he thought at last, as the rope parted and the terrified beasts surged away on a tide of animal panic.

Exposed, flat out on the ground, he cushioned his head in his arms and trembled as the planes flew past, the world around him ablaze with the heat of their destruction. He twisted his face to free his mouth of the mud that had lodged there, and noticed a tiny white crocus, right by him. Moving his head to focus, he stared in wonder at a patient line of ants each waiting its turn to climb it, unperturbed, going about their business in the midst of all this fury. He made a note to remember; he knew who would enjoy this story. Eventually, sensing the engines' long diminuendo, and panting with fear and relief, he climbed to his feet, and began to make his way back towards his post.

General Varela glared at him. "I thought we'd lost you then," he barked. "For a horse! A bloody horse, Jacob, you bloody idiot."

Jacob mumbled an apology, and kept his eyes down; he could see the mud-stains on the general's knees.

No one mentioned the incident at mess that night. Better that way, Jacob thought; he didn't want his rashness to get him into trouble. Had he done the right thing? He still wasn't sure. He hoped he wouldn't dream about the horses. One of his fellow cadets at the academy used to have nightmares, and would wake them all with his shrieking. They had teased him mercilessly.

That night as he lay in his cot he thought of the sacrifice of that brave man of the International Brigade, and of how an individual had helped slow the advance of a whole company. He thought too of Varela's casual use of that word *vermin*. He remembered how his uncle had used it in England that time, and how his lovely cousin Olivia had then defied him. He was disconcerted, somehow. Of course the enemy were wrong, because they were, well, the enemy, that much was clear, but that night he felt strangely as if he were seeing the world through murky water. He felt too that he needed someone to share this with. He didn't have any doubts, not as such, more that he needed someone to reinforce his clarity. Yes, he'd do this when he got back to Toledo, he'd discuss it with his father, or Lucas if he were there. Though as finally he drifted off to sleep he thought he might also share this with Maria. They'd always understood each other; she would sort him out.

Minutes later, as the other officers returned, sated and bruised after their day of killing, they found him sleeping with a curious smile on his face. Naturally their first thought was to tumble him out of bed and onto the cold, hard floor; but, seeing the strange gentleness about him, they left him to his reverie, and went quiet to their bunks, soothed by their own benevolence.

Chapter Twenty

Jacob visits his brother Lucas, Seville, 1937

The old truck grinds to a halt in the shade of a clutch of towering poplars. Ahead, the road stretches infinitely across the rolling rich hills of Andalucía. For a moment Jacob watches the wind as it blows towards them, bending the supple green grass in the fields as it passes. Then he jumps down and pulls back the tarpaulin, beneath which a dozen soldiers lay sprawled, red-faced in the heat. The stink of so much un-soaped humanity makes him gag, and he steps back laughing as he shouts out the order to dismount.

The men are happy. They are from Seville, and after weeks away from home they have been rewarded with a short period of leave. They are not a lovely bunch, thinks Jacob, as he watches them desecrate the meadow with their needs, but still he smiles, entertained by the clownish, imaginative vulgarity of their language. He is happy too: he has an order to procure more cavalry from the well-heeled ranches of the south, and has used the journey as a pretext to see Lucas. His brother has been in Seville almost since Christmas, and Jacob is anxious to catch up with him.

It is dark by the time the lorry finally rolls into town, and Jacob is sick of it. The cabin reeks of vomit, he is plastered with dust, he is thirsty and his head hurts. He instructs the Corporal to register at the barracks, then sets off on foot to the hotel where he has agreed to meet Lucas. The cool night air revives him. He plunges his head into a fountain and stares up at the stars as he combs his hair with his fingers. Someone nearby sings mournfully to his guitar through an open window: a love song, probably; a gypsy boy pining for his lost girl. He thinks of Maria, as he does so often these days. Is she *his girl*?

The war seems suddenly far away as he walks into the lobby of the hotel. He leaves his kitbag with a porter, and heads straight for the bar. Lucas is sitting by himself at a table in the corner. Jacob studies him unobserved for a moment. He realises it is unusual to see him alone like this, normally he would be the centre of attention within a group of boisterous men, or just as often, women. He steals up behind him.

"Guess who?" he asks as he puts his hands over his brother's eyes.

"Bette Davis?" he replies. "I recognise your soft hands."

The brothers embrace and order cold beer, talking fast, gathering news. Food arrives, the best Jacob has seen in weeks. Lucas is now a major, and commands the staff with a natural ease of authority. By the end of dinner he is in a reflective mood, sombre almost, and talks openly about the progress of the war.

"It's taking longer than we hoped, if I'm honest. The Reds are holding out all over the place, and we're stretched, even with the Italians and the Germans. Bloody militias. If you'd asked me six months ago I would have said it would be all over by now. I'm meeting some of them with Father at home next week ... did you know? Germans, I mean. The old boy has quite a connection with them."

A waiter returns and offers brandy. As they drink, Lucas becomes more serious. "The army – our army – the *proper* army, we're all still holding together. The old regimental units, I mean, the old guys, we're still real soldiers, but …" He pauses as a civilian couple walk past their table. "But some, a lot, of these new people, the late-comers, are just … savages! Brutes!"

Jacob's mind goes back to the soldiers he had travelled with that day.

"And not just the men, the goons, I mean, but the officers as well …"

This is not like Lucas, but Jacob knows exactly what he means. He too has seen things which do little credit to the regiment. It is dangerous talk, disloyal.

"Remember old Valverde? Did he ever teach you?" Jacob asks. "Very old school. *Sense of a soldier's honour* and all that."

"He did. A real old fart. I think he sailed with Columbus, didn't he?"

The brothers laugh, but then Lucas returns to his subject. "Ever since Badajoz, last year, he was there, and afterwards, the killings, the executions in the Bullring, it got so out of hand. There was a … frenzy … there was just no order. And other things too … I know the Reds are evil bastards, but there are plenty on our side too who … I can only ever say this to you, little brother, don't tell Father, but sometimes … I'm ashamed."

Jacob takes a deep breath. His brother is right, he knows, but this kind of opinion could get them into such hot water. Just then a waitress arrives to clear the table. Jacob thanks her politely, and she smiles at him, then turns to smile again as she walks away, plates in hand.

"I saw that!" says Lucas. "You dog! You have a conquest there."

Despite himself Jacob grins, and blushes as the girl comes back.

Lucas grins too, enjoying his brother's discomfort. "Well?" he asks. "What are you waiting for?"

As the waitress walks away, Jacob looks at the floor. Later he will wonder if it was the brandy talking, or if he had said it just to shut his brother up. "I've found someone," he says, " I ... erm ... I have a girl ..."

Lucas claps his hands, loudly enough that people turn and stare.

"Bravo!" he shouts. "Anyone I know?"

Jacob hesitates. "It's complicated," he begins, "she's not from our ... that is, she ... she ... I like her ..." He flounders for a minute, then plunges on. " Maria," he says at last. "Our Maria, the maid."

Lucas's eyes widen. He purses his lips, whistles through his teeth.

"You said it," he says after a while, slowly. "You said it: she's not in our class." He lets this sink in, then grins. "She's far too good for you, sunshine, out of your league completely! Not your class at all; bet she won't even look at you. Man! She's lovely!"

He claps his hands again, delighted. "I knew, you know. Known it for ages. The way you two look at each other. It's sickening."

The brothers smile at each other, the mood completely shifted.

"Does Mother know?" Lucas asks mischievously. "I'll tell her next week if you want."

"Don't you bloody dare!" says his brother, and cocks an imaginary gun.

They finish another brandy, and climb the grand stairway to find their lodgings. They are sharing a bedroom. Jacob is immensely pleased that he's managed to tell someone. It somehow makes it more real. And he is so relieved that Lucas seems pleased for him. If – no – when he tells his parents he will need all the support available, and if he can tell Lucas then he can tell anyone ... even Maria herself! In the coming days he will begin to doubt again, but tonight, fuelled by brandy and his brother's optimism, he knows for sure that his feelings for her are reciprocated. He remembers again their last farewell, when she had held him so delicately; their lips had touched, featherlight, modest, unacknowledged. And it wasn't an accident, a clumsiness, he was sure. She had kissed him.

"Me and you, brother: just like old times," he says happily as he climbs into his narrow single bed. But Lucas is already snoring.

Chapter Twenty-One

Toledo, 1937

In the park, alone, Maria re-read the letter. The Russian had handed it to her at the end of the last meeting, and it gave her strength. She liked his odd, quixotic, exotic use of words. He had travelled, met great people, and – as intended – it encouraged her to think that clever, educated people were there at her side.

Your face had gone cold. The fire in your belly gone away. I thought for a while that they had broken you. It happens, you know, even to the finest. For some the fire is extinguished forever. I saw it: I was your age in Moscow when the Revolution began. Men crushed, the spirit in them snapped, the truest of women destroyed by pain and fear. You see it in the dead-eyed stares, brave souls dragging behind them the remains of dreams, shamed by failure, the hunger in them gone.

Others recover. In some deep and secret space they keep the spark alive. Are they the lucky ones? I do not know. This fire is a wondrous thing, a noble thing, a gift, and yet so often it scorches the carrier as much as those around. So when I saw you slowly waking back to life

... I confess inside I said a little prayer of thanks to someone, anyone. Somehow in you I had matched the ambition in your desire for change with the success of the struggle to which we now commit. I did not dare to see you beaten, since strangely you personify the larger fight. And when I see the determination in you, and your predicament, I weep with pride and rage.

I came to your country to set the place alight. It is, I still must think, a worthy aim to want to rid the world of tyranny and tyrants. But some nights sleep no longer comes easy to me, since I know that risk and retribution fall more heavily on the shoulders of my comrades than on mine. And it pains me beyond words to ask so much of those with least to give.

And you are back amongst us! Fuelled by what I do not care. Revenge? Faith? Destiny? Love?? As to the reason I remain indifferent; I care only that you have survived your terrible episode, and hope that your memories of that vile man will have begun to fade. Don't be ashamed; I discovered what had happened. I would have had him killed, you know, if you hadn't come back to us. I almost did. It would have been a messy business, dangerous. It's always a mistake to get personal in these affairs, but there are limits. It would at least have soothed something in my stupid soul. You are my talisman!

It cannot be easy for you in that house of those rich swine in Toledo, and I do not ask you lightly. But three officers living under the same roof, and well-connected ones at that, and the chance of having a clever, steadfast mole to watch them! This is an opportunity we would be foolish not to take.

They are on exceptionally good terms with the Germans, the father especially. He seems to have developed a peculiar friendship with one of their Generals, and a taste for Prussian brandy. From time to time we know that there are parties at their house. No debauchery – you remember the mother, don't you! But influential people gather there, and we need a sharp mind to tell us who these people are, and a clever pair of ears to listen out for any gems of information.

Will you do this for me? For us? Will you do it for yourself?

There will be instructions later, but remember this: anything you retrieve you must give in person to Kyriagin, and to no one else, unless you hear that this is no longer possible. In that case, take it to the British in Gibraltar; we have a friend there who will know what to do.

Bon courage.

Chapter Twenty-Two

Jacob receives a gift from his brother, Seville, 1937

Jacob wakes groggily, head throbbing, mouth caulked with the unforgiving taste of yesterday's brandy. His brother looks pale, and in the morning light Jacob sees the dark rings beneath his eyes, the tell-tale sign of long term tiredness, not just the fee for a single evening's celebration. Neither mentions the indiscretions of the night before. They take turns to pour water over each other's heads from the long-necked pitchers which are provided for the purpose, wincing from the cold. Lucas has an early appointment and has to leave first, but they agree to meet for lunch.

"And don't be late," he says on his way out. "I have a surprise for you."

Jacob reads for a while, then reports to the barracks near the bullring. Once his paperwork is completed, he asks a corporal for directions to his rendezvous with Lucas. Despite listening carefully to these instructions, he is soon disoriented in the narrow maze-like streets of the old quarter, and twice has to stop to ask the way. A man now points to the pale dome of the Church of Santa Maria la Blanca, which they can see rising above the rooftops in the distance.

"It's in the little square just opposite that church, sir," says the man. "Good coffee."

Jacob, still coming to terms with the excesses of the previous night, had skipped breakfast, and quickens his pace at the thought of something to eat. He is intrigued too about the mention of a surprise, and daydreaming slightly. As he rounds the next corner he becomes aware of shouting, then sees that a group of people have come together in the plaza.

He gathers his wits instantly. Amid the noise a man is lying half naked on the ground, surrounded by a yelling mob of men who are kicking him. A woman runs screaming from an adjacent door, and flails at the backs of the attackers. To his horror, Jacob watches as one of them turns and strikes her hard across the face with a short piece of wood. To the side, two Guardia Civil officers are chatting unconcernedly.

"What the hell's going on?" Jacob yells at them. For a split second they ignore him, but seeing the captain's pips on his uniform, the older one salutes.

"Communist, sir. Something like that. These men found him."

"Well stop them!" Jacob says angrily.

"Shouldn't really get involved, sir. This lot are mad, and when their blood's up, and they find one of these guilty sons of bitches, it's better to let them have their way."

Jacob looks at him open-mouthed. Behind the two policemen a priest is surveying the scene, smiling slightly.

"But ... how do you know he's guilty?"

The officer shrugs. "They usually are, sir, mostly. The crowd are usually right."

Just then Jacob sees agony on the face of the man as a heavy boot crashes into his ribs.

"Stop this, stop!" screams Jacob and pushes his way into the aggressors. For a moment they hesitate, then continue their assault. Jacob is used to being obeyed. He pulls his heavy pistol from the holster and fires twice into the air. The shot reverberates around the tight-packed square and instantly stops the attack. In the silence they hear the victim whimper. Jacob draws his gun in an arc around the men, daring them to challenge his authority.

"What the hell is going on here? Are you savages or what? Who's in charge?" Jacob is breathless with rage.

"This piece of shit is a teacher," says one of the men. "He's a communist, and he's been teaching his filth to our kids! Innocent, God-fearing kids."

The men murmur and nod their heads in agreement. Jacob is confused, outnumbered, an outsider.

"Even so," he manages, "even so ..."

"I think we can take over now, sir." It is the older Guardia Civil. "Perhaps it's better if we take it from here ... Thank you, sir." Jacob looks at him gratefully.

"Yes, yes ..." he stammers, and begins to back away. He sees that the woman has managed to crawl over to the man, and she now half-kneels, cradling his head in her lap, their blood puddling together in the cracks between the paving stones. Jacob remembers the white marble *Pietà* he had seen in the Cathedral in Leon. The priest now stares at him as he retreats, and with raised fingers makes the sign of the cross in benediction.

Jacob still feels sick as he walks into the café. Lucas has yet to get there, and he sits brooding in the corner, trying to make sense of what he had just witnessed. Had he done the right thing, should he have stayed, or was he just being stupid? Slowly, in the warmth of the bar, cheered guiltily by a hot slice of bread and sweet coffee, he begins to unwind. It was all so complicated, he reminds himself; it wasn't his job to figure things out, he was a soldier, a man of action, not a philosopher. An aching, Maria-shaped splinter of doubt remained snagged in his conscience, but little by little, two coffees later, he was re-made, and decides not to mention the incident.

The roar of a powerful motor shakes the bar just as Jacob stood to go to the bathroom. The noise subsides, replaced by the deep throb of an engine at idle. Startled, Jacob and the other patrons look up to see Lucas wheeling through the door, in full uniform, arms outstretched.

"I'm going flying!" he yells, flapping his arms, grinning. "And you, little bro', you're gonna love this! Look!"

He pulls Jacob to his feet and drags him outside. Four young boys, who stand admiringly around a gleaming black motorbike, scuttle away at their approach. Lucas leans across to the throttle and guns the engine, which responds with a threatening roar, and pushes a button to silence the beast.

"A Royal Enfield ..." whispers Jacob. "Is it the *Bullet*?"

Lucas nods. "It is," he says. "Trouble is, it's not mine. It belongs to my dispatch rider."

Jacob runs his hand enviously along the sleek, smooth curves of the machine, and tries to see his face in the chrome.

"Eh?" he says after a moment, "You're cavalry. You don't have dispatch riders."

"Well, I have one now. He's a bit thick, a bit ugly, a bit slow on the uptake sometimes, but ..."

Understanding slides across his brother's face. "How ...?"

"Let's just say it was a gift to a grateful nation. Let's leave it at that, shall we. A rich *socialist* acquaintance of mine, who claims he won it at Poker from a British captain in Gibraltar ... he insisted I take it.

You know, war effort and all that."

Jacob sits astride the machine and kicks it into life. "Seriously?" he asks. "Can I ride it?"

"All the way to Toledo, baby bro'. It's got to be registered properly with HQ. Got to play it by the book, more or less. I know you hated the journey down, so I recorded it as a new acquisition, the property of your regiment back home. By tomorrow you should have all the documents."

Jacob cautiously revs the bike, inches forward. People turn their heads and stare as he rides down the street. It's insanely noisy; he's worried he might scare the horses, but by the time he returns to Lucas he's grinning wildly.

Later, after a hurried lunch, they set off together to the aerodrome. Lucas is equally excited by the prospect of his first flight. He is to travel with General Mola, who, Lucas says, is the only one capable of standing up to Franco, but who is also a terrible snob. They ride all the way up to the aircraft, the bike bucking across the sun-browned turf. To Jacob, the plane seems tiny, and the canvas fuselage incredibly flimsy, though the exhilarated Lucas insists it is invulnerable. This exact conversation will come back to haunt them both just one month later, when they read in the newspapers of the death of Mola, whose flight had crashed in the mountains of the Basque country.

Jacob stays in Seville for almost a week. When he's not sleeping at the barracks, he motors between the city and the coast, happily shattering the peace of various grand *haciendas* in his quest for more horses. The army requires them, he repeats again and again to reluctant ranch owners, who each seem to have a string of excuses. In the cool of their vast, adobe-walled homes these stylish Andalucían aristocrats show such little willingness to make even the smallest of sacrifices that by the end of the week Jacob is sick of them. "*I sometimes wonder if they even deserve our support ...*" he begins a report to his commanding officer. But he destroys it: that kind of opinion could so easily come back to bite him.

On his final morning he packs his belongings into the two saddle bags he has adapted from a mule's pack pannier which he had bought in Carmona. The fine weather has broken, and in the night it had rained steadily. Immediately after he leaves he is forced to give way to a military convoy at the cross roads. As he waits, he recognises the priest he had seen on the day of the disturbance. There is something strangely menacing about the man's face. Seeing his opportunity, Jacob accelerates as fast as he dare, aims for a large puddle, and spatters the cleric in dark red mud.

People turn and stare at the crazy soldier who hollers his delight as he barrels down the unpaved street. Jacob doesn't care. He's happy: he has a fast bike; he's twenty-one, and he's going home, going home at last to see his girl. As he comes to the edge of the city he sees the long straight road ahead of him, and accelerates again, pushing the heavy machine to its very limits.

Chapter Twenty-Three

Back to the barracks, 1937

The purloined Enfield motorbike might have been powerful and fast, but still it took Jacob the best part of two days to get from Seville to Toledo. It rained the whole time. Everywhere there were mud-stuck convoys to negotiate, endless patrols at which he must identify himself, and even when he saw open road the surface was treacherous enough that he had to crawl at what seemed like the pace of a mule. Eventually, despite his eagerness to get home, he was forced to spend the night close to the small town of Palma del Rio, where tensions ran high after months of constant blood-letting. He'd heard some of the stories, and decided that if even only a tenth of the rumours were true then it would forever be a place of nightmare, recrimination and guilt, with each side accused by the other of the most unspeakable atrocities.

His hands were beginning to cramp with cold, and his eyes sore from the muck thrown up from the road; worse, the motor had started to splutter in dissent at the ceaseless drenching, and he was growing increasingly anxious at the very real prospect of having to sleep out in this grey and inhospitable country. As such, when told by a dripping sentry that the road ahead was blocked, he offered minimum protest, and went as directed to the sanctuary of the officers' billet, a rather grand building as it transpired, for the army had just appropriated the house of a local merchant, whose sons, both teachers, had died fighting for the republicans. The place was large, comfortable, and above all, dry; the poor foot soldiers sheltering outside in their tents and beneath ineffectual tarpaulins eyed Jacob with ill-disguised resentment.

"If you think our lot look miserable, you should see the prisoners," said a young cavalryman, pointing over his shoulder. Through the gloom Jacob could just make out a courtyard surrounded by clumsily erected barbed wire fencing. He peered into the dissolving light, trying to make sense of the cavalryman's words. Indistinct figures, phantoms, pale faces reared in and out of focus in the grey swirling of the mist, and for some reason Jacob was reminded of that play he had been dragged along to see, so long ago now, the Greek one, a tragedy, with all the pallid sheet-clad actors whirling through the smoke and hanging curtains on the stage.

He could not help himself. Pulling a blanket over his head he walked slowly towards the prisoners, who stood huddled in nothing but pants and vests as the rain spattered down. A hollow-eyed ghost his own age stared back at him through the makeshift fence. Neither man spoke. In shame Jacob removed the blanket from his head, and reaching through the wire, handed it to him. The man ignored him. As Jacob withdrew his hand he pricked it on the barbed wire, and accidentally dropped the blanket at the prisoner's feet. The man bent down, so starved that as he stooped to pick it up, Jacob could see his shoulder blades, ribs, pelvis, all working together, as though tied together by twine. With visible effort he pushed the sodden bundle back through the fence and it landed with a tired splash at Jacob's feet.

"Long live the Revolution!" said the man in a feeble cry, and for a second Jacob thought he saw the shadow of a smile. They continued to stare at each other until Jacob clicked his heels and saluted, before walking back subdued towards the comfort and warmth of the requisitioned villa.

"Don't let it get to you, brother," said a lieutenant who had been observing this exchange. "They'd do the same to us if they could. There by the grace of God and all that."

Jacob shook his head. "I know," he said, "but still it's …"

He was distracted from his thoughts by the arrival of two porters and the shouting that accompanied them. A door had been torn from its hinges to make a tray big enough to hold several loaves, a pile of plates and, in the middle, a vast copper vessel wreathed in a cloud of fragrant steam.

"It's more bucket than tureen," said a clipped voice beside Jacob, "but if it's anything like last night then it's going to be fucking gorgeous. That chef chappie deserves a medal. Let's get in there!"

Jacob stood back and was last to be served, well aware of the juxtaposition between the comforts that lay inside the house and out, yet none too principled to hold back when his turn came. The man was right: it was gorgeous, especially when you hadn't eaten all day, and by the time that dessert came round Jacob had pushed all unsettling images of the penitentiary to the back of his mind.

Later, bone weary, he was shown to a room kept warm by a small coal fire and the presence of three other snoring, farting officers. Dismayed by the stench he nonetheless slept soundly, waking long after dawn.

"Any chance of coffee?" he said sleepily the next morning to a man being shaved in a chair in the corridor, and followed his nose and the man's fat thumb towards a canteen that had been set up in a manger outside. The day was bitter cold, though at least the clouds had gone, revealing the purplish rain-stained contours of the hills all around. A stubbled, sad-eyed private handed him an elegant teacup, and Jacob whistled.

"Bone china," he said. "Nothing but the best, eh?"

The man shrugged. "Wait till you taste it, then we'll see. The cup might be fine, but it still tastes like otter piss. At least ours does."

Jacob smiled and wandered out towards the garden to inspect the temporary gaol. It was, he reflected, the first time he had been able to stand so intimately close to one of the enemy. He recalled the sad face of the man to whom he had offered the blanket, and wondered if he might dare speak to him. What he had sensed in him was not outright hostility so much as a muted dignity, and despite himself he had to admire the fellow's courage. And that unexpected faint smile, he remembered, and the reproach and acceptance that it bore within it; that response too was strangely likable. It came to Jacob suddenly that in other times, in another world, had they not been set apart by the colour of their uniforms, then he might even have sought out the company of this random, enigmatic stranger. Perhaps, who knew, they had been born just days and a few kilometres apart. The knowledge unsettled him, and for a second he had to remind himself of just why these people were his foes. He would ask him where he was from, he decided, and despite whatever convention or prohibition might now exist, he would try to talk to him.

To his astonishment the yard was empty, the prisoners gone. Pools of water still stood on the sodden earth, some red the colour of blood. In the middle was a single soldier's boot, pathetically alone, and as the breeze rose the puddles rippled as though shaken by some secret life within them.

Jacob looked about him. Tilled terracing and well-tended orchards disappeared far above into scrubland, and above that, in the distance, dense forest. He cocked his head, concentrating. Was that gunfire? There, deep in the high valley. Who could be up there? He couldn't be certain, not with the birdsong and the soughing of the wind in the grasses. Yet there it was again, still so faint as to be ambiguous, the almost childish rattle of a light machine gun. He waited for answering fire, but none came. He walked closer, puzzled, desperate to be sure, right up to the wire fence. His foot caught on something as he moved along the perimeter, causing him to stumble slightly. When he looked he realised that it was the blanket from the night before, trampled, half-buried, the same colour as the stinking mud. It made an obscene sucking gurgle as he released it slowly from the ground, and as he stood there, listening for more shots, he unconsciously held it out to one side to prevent the foul water from dripping onto his already dirty boots. He waited, pensive, detached, his coffee grown cold, until behind him he suddenly heard an unmistakeable click, and he instinctively dropped the sopping blanket.

"Man, that's gonna be a beauty," said the woman holding the camera. Her voice was foreign, heavily accented.

"You look like a bullfighter like that, trailing your cape, waiting for the kill. Just your silhouette, menacing. Really hope there's enough light, it's kinda gloomy here." She held out a hand, and he took it uncertainly.

"Gerta," she said. "I hope you don't mind. I'm with Robert, over there, trying to get images for a magazine."

He didn't mind, not really. She had startled him from a kind of trance, and now he looked at her, embarrassed, trying to make sense of this sudden turn of events. It were as if he had been on the edge of discovering something important, and now he could feel it slipping through his fingers, and the more he tried to hold on to this unformed notion, the more it sped away from him. It felt so absurd that he almost laughed. On another day he might have stopped to talk to her, but her curious presence was a barrier to the still nebulous thoughts that had just now so nearly congealed, and he apologised and walked away. It was too late, he realised, and whatever discovery he might otherwise have made was now gone from him. He smiled ruefully. Perhaps if it were important the idea would come back to him some day.

"Hey soldier!" he heard her shout after him. "Hey Matador! You forgot your cape!"

"Keep it," he yelled over his shoulder. "A gift from Franco's army."

Matador. Her use of the word annoyed him. In Spanish it means "killer", as well as bullfighter. Perhaps she had touched a nerve. Also, he mused, an earlier, more zealous, more conscientious version of himself would never have been so cavalier with army equipment, not even for a humble blanket; it was the principle that counted, not the value. Was he changing? He walked on away from the photographer, staring around at the remnants of the broken town. There had been such terrible violence here. What was left of the main street was cratered with shell blast. Many of the terracotta-tiled roofs were holed by mortar fire; the whole wall of a shop had been peeled back to reveal the contents like those of a doll's house; the sails of an old windmill sank sickeningly to one side, and the two smashed windows of the house opposite seemed to regard him with the eyes of a blind man.

With a jolt he realised that he did not even know who was responsible. Was this the work of the Republican Army, or his own? He was so sickened that he didn't even want to ask. He shivered, a ghost running over his grave, as his father would have said. It felt like a signal; this was not a good place, and all he now wanted to do was to get himself free.

Less than an hour later his saddle bags were strapped to the bike, and he was speeding away from the town without once looking back. He passed the photographer, who beckoned for him to stop. He ignored her, and instead accelerated as hard as he dared, feeling better by the second, the cold air sluicing through him and shocking him awake.

The morning's doubts and fears drained from his shoulders and lay suddenly scattered by the wayside. A farmer saw him and raised a defiant fist in greeting. Jacob waved back. A fist, a salute, even a finger ... it didn't seem to matter just now. After the first few miles he could already feel the aches all over his body, and he was slithery with the gunk and mire of a thousand horse-shit spattered puddles. But none of this mattered as he roared into the next bend. He was going home.

Chapter Twenty-Four

Jacob hears news of an old friend, Toledo, 1937

Jacob had finally arrived back in Toledo just before sunset, thrilled and exhausted, and had slept solidly for almost twelve hours.

He was sorry to see the bike go. Despite the stiffness in his legs and shoulders he had grown fond of the noisy machine on their adventure from Seville, and he patted its saddle as if it were a horse as it was wheeled away by an army mechanic. It felt good to be back at the barracks. The sun was already warm on his back, and he was soothed by the distant rhythmic stomp of boots on the parade ground and the irritated shouts of the drill sergeant. In the lull between the yells he was aware of the droning of the flies which swarmed about the straw in the stables, and of the screech of the swifts which came in turn to hunt them.

His brother had summoned him with a note to meet at the mess at 10.00h. Jacob saw him standing alone at the end of the trestle bar, and ran the last few steps arms outstretched, gliding in like an aeroplane.

"Well?" he asked. "How was it?"

"Incredible, nothing like it." Lucas was grinning broadly. He may have been a full army major in his mid-twenties, but for that moment, alone with his brother, he was a little boy again, still glowing with excitement. "It took us just over an hour. It's the future, you wait and see. But God, it's loud! And you get shaken all over the place. I thought I might puke, but that could have been the cigar smoke and the stink of kerosene. Scared? Me? Well, maybe a bit, but I wasn't going to show it, not with that lot. I was glad when we landed ... the ground felt so ... I don't know, so solid. Does that make sense? When all this is over I'll find a way for us to fly somewhere; you'll love it!"

Jacob was delighted by his brother's candour and exuberance. They talked easily, and he could see that Lucas was amused by his descriptions of the mud and hold-ups on the road. For some reason he decided not to mention his encounter with the prisoners, although he remained troubled by the episode. Slowly, however, the conversation became less light-hearted.

"It's going to take ages, you know. The Reds have really dug in at Madrid, and short of blasting them out and killing tens of thousands there's not much more we can do but keep them encircled. Mola says a year, minimum, and if the French or the English get involved it could get really messy for us. He – Mola – says it's curious that they haven't been more pro-active. You know they have this so-called untouchable pact with the League of Nations which swears that none of the Europeans will intervene, but it's now an open secret that the Italians and the Germans are fighting here, so it wouldn't be any great surprise if that lot joined in too. After all, the French are our neighbours, and the Brits will usually fight anybody for fun. There's a bit of a theory that Spain could end up as one enormous battleground, a bit like Belgium did twenty years ago. That would be interesting ..."

Jacob smiled. "Let's hope it doesn't come to that. Wouldn't want to fight our English cousins, would we?"

The mess hall had begun to fill up, and Lucas nodded to a man in the far corner. The brothers' moment of intimacy was coming to an end.

"There was something else I wanted to tell you," said Lucas. " I didn't want you to find out for yourself, and you to think I'd been hiding it from you."

Jacob held his breath.

"Maybe it doesn't matter anymore; it was years ago. But remember your friend, Tino, the son of those neighbours at the holiday home near Vigo? Course you do, you two were thick as thieves. Anyway, he's been picked up by the police here. God knows what he was doing, but no doubt it was something subversive."

Jacob was staring at his brother, his mouth dry.

"I saw his picture in the papers a couple of years back," Lucas continues. "A bullfight. Think you might even have been there, no? The anarchists had planned some kind of disturbance but the cops had been tipped off and were lying in wait. There were photos the following day. I recognised his face and it really bugged me because at first I couldn't place him; it didn't come to me for days. But as I say, it looks like he's been up to his old tricks and now he's been nabbed and is banged up in the military jail, poor bugger."

Jacob was no longer listening. Out of the blue he'd been assailed by a pin-sharp memory of his friend Tino's laughing face, a snapshot frozen in time: a beach, a boy, white teeth, black hair falling across his eyes, his thinly muscled arm arrested in mid-throw, bound by pearls of seawater. From which part of his consciousness had this entombed recollection so quickly leapt? Jacob felt nauseated and tried to keep his voice steady. "How did you hear?" he asked.

"Mama. It annoyed me; she sounded kind of triumphant, in that told-you-so kind of way. That's why I thought I should warn you. You know what she's like."

Jacob did know, only too well, and he felt again the stirrings of the impotent rage he had felt towards her when she had forced him to abandon his friendship.

"Don't be mad with her. It's just her way." Lucas squeezed his brother's arm, then stood to join a group of boisterous men at their breakfast. Jacob remained where he was, then wandered slowly out to the comparative calm of the parade ground.

An open-topped military car was parked in the shade, the engine still hot, creaking as it began to cool down. He climbed aboard and settled down, enjoying the feel of the soft leather seat. It was a moment of intense quiet. The sharp smell of metal mingled with the scent from the stables, and as he watched two vivid butterflies flicker above the khaki paint, he allowed his mind to drift back to his time as a boy at the seaside, to the boat, and to the events that had led to his separation from Tino. Had he been a coward not to stand up to his mother, or simply too young? He remembered the silent meals, the punishment, how foolish he had felt. If only they had beaten him. That would have been less cruel, he could have taken that. He would have preferred to have been caned than segregated from his only friend.

And he remembered too that final day, sneaking out along the beach in search of a last goodbye, and his sense of self-loathing when at the last he had lost his nerve and turned tail. He had let everyone down. Each guilty step home along the shore had remodelled his rage into melancholy, and in silence he had packed his bags before a curt farewell to the neighbours. And then suddenly the wonder of spotting him – Tino! – running alongside the train! There he was: waving, gurning through the window, laughing. Jacob had ignored his mother and rushed to the open door, leaning out one-handed to brush his outstretched fingers against those of his friend. He had wanted to cry as the figure fell from sight. And that had been the last time they had met. He had returned just once to the family seaside home, but Tino hadn't been there, and the place had seemed empty, boring, the magic gone, and within a few days he'd been ready to get back home to Madrid.

He was suddenly startled from his thoughts by the un-oiled screech of the hangar doors as they slid wide open behind him. A soldier from the motor division was surprised to see him sitting in the car, and was unsure what to do. Seeing his hesitation, Jacob smiled and leapt out.

"All yours," he said, and watched as the man tried to crank the vehicle into life with the starting handle. It didn't fire first time, and the mechanic waited a moment so as not to flood the carburettor. This gave Jacob the chance to glance inside the hangar. There, propped on its stand in the corner, gleaming in the sunlight from the door, stood the Enfield motor bike, clean and oiled after the long journey. Jacob walked to it as though drawn by a magnet, and ran a hand over the polished chrome of the handlebars.

"Is she ready yet?" The words just seemed to jump out of his mouth unplanned.

The man looked surprised. "I guess ... Major Lucas just told me to leave it here for now."

"I know. *My brother* - Major Lucas - told me 11.00 o'clock." He looked at his watch. "You're early. Well done!"

The mechanic stared, then seeing the family resemblance, shrugged his shoulders.

"It's a swap then," the man said, indicating the car with the spanner in his hand. "Hope yours starts better than this old jalopy."

It did start, first time. The engine noise was amplified by the confines of the garage, and the two men grinned at each other across the fumes and heavy bass thud of the pistons.

He had had no intention of taking the bike, it was just that the opportunity seemed too good to miss. Nor had he formed any active thought of trying to see Tino in the prison, yet when he came to the first crossroads he automatically turned towards the city. It was almost as if the bike had a life of its own. He wasn't altogether sure whether it was allowed to visit a captured enemy; the rules were still being written in this strange civil war. It seemed to him more a case of just what you could get away with. He wouldn't want to have to explain himself to his superiors, that much was certain; no one need ever find out. He could just turn up at the jail, have a quiet word with his friend, and be back at the barracks before noon, with no one any the wiser. It was a risk, but worth it. His mother, if ever he were discovered, would be livid, but this thought only spurred him on. As he sped along he considered how he had never fully forgiven her antagonism towards Tino, and this little jaunt was perhaps just a form of innocent revenge.

Jacob turned off onto the small road up to the jail, moving carefully over the cobbled stone, weaving between the sombre-looking pedestrians. Heads turned at the deep rumble of the engine, and as the crowd parted, he realised that he might have reason to be afraid. Women stared at him in open hostility, and men moved from his path with slow, reluctant aggression. Two soldiers were standing guard, craning their necks, wary of the mood, and they beckoned him forward. A third soldier appeared and opened the wooden gates to the perimeter fences, glancing nervously at the grumbling assemblage beyond them.

He stared at the two guards, waiting for them to salute him. They were obviously half-trained recruits, and it took them a second to remember.

"Guard the bike, won't you, boys," he instructed, and thumped hard on the studded iron door, which opened immediately. Inside, he almost faltered. The light was poor, the air soured with disinfectant, and menacing sounds rolled out along the cold stone walls. His voice boomed in his head as he spoke.

He felt as though he were in a play, as if this were happening to someone else, events moving too quickly, beyond his proper control. Within moments he found himself speaking to a clerk, then waited alone in a windowless office. He expected to be questioned, to have his credentials thoroughly checked. Some part of him still hoped that he might be thwarted, that his request be refused, that he could return home with his honour intact, without the need to go through with this reckless errand. He heard a man scream. Was that outside the prison, or inside? He was no longer sure.

Minutes later he found himself marching down a disconcertingly long corridor, accompanied by a stone-faced chaperone. Evidently they had decided that he was a member of an intelligence unit, and were not going to challenge his authority. On each side were rows of sinister, grey steel doors, all closed. There was a low and constant growl of voices; the air was thick with the stench of fear and old sweat, and as his sense of unease increased, he felt certain it was growing colder.

The guard stopped suddenly and fumbled in his pocket for a key. A heavy door swung open, and in the gloom Jacob could just make out the figure of a man sprawled awkwardly on a grey-sheeted cot. A light snapped on above them, and the prisoner yelped.

"Leave us," said Jacob to the guard. "Wait out there."

The guard complied immediately, and Jacob squinted against the brightness of the bulb; the man on the bed kept his eyes closed. Jacob moved closer. He still wasn't sure.

"Tino?" he asked gently. The man didn't move. "Tino? It's me ... Jacob."

As his eyes adjusted, Jacob could see that the prisoner's hands were tied behind his back. His shirt was covered in blood and his bare feet were horribly bruised. Slowly the man struggled to sit up. Beyond the split lip and swollen eye, Jacob recognised the face of the boy who had meant so much to him. He tried hard not to show his shock.

"You came back," was all the man could manage to say. Jacob was sure that there was a faint smile on Tino's face, but suddenly the light left his eyes and he slumped back on to the bed, cracking his head hard against the metal railing. Jacob was distraught.

"He's fainted!" Jacob shouted to the guard in the corridor. "He's unconscious. Fetch me a bowl of warm water. And a glass of cold water. Quick!"

Jacob felt for a pulse. It was still strong; he could see it throbbing in the vein at the temple. That was good. He'd be alright. Perhaps he had tried to sit up too quickly. He'd just taken a damn good beating, that was all. Bastards. With his penknife he cut the rope which held his hands and lifted them gently to his side. As he waited for the man to return Jacob cradled his friend's head in his arms, talking softly, telling him all of the things that he'd been doing, of all the things that they could do together still, about Maria, and about how he had missed him.

He stopped abruptly as the guard returned with the items he had demanded. Leaning in the doorway, he watched in silence as Jacob used his handkerchief to bathe Tino's broken face. Jacob was calmer now. There was nothing else he could do here. As gently as he could he eased Tino's head back on to the bed; his breathing seemed less laboured and the frightening pallor had left his cheeks. He would live, he decided, though no doubt he'd be sore for weeks. He wondered what he had done to provoke such treatment. The rope that had bound him was still on the floor. As he stooped to pick it up he kissed Tino very lightly on the forehead.

"Goodbye, old friend. I'll come back tomorrow to see how you are." There was no answer, but as he turned to look at him one last time he saw that Tino had managed to half raise one arm in a feeble farewell.

In the corridor, Jacob stared hard at the guard who was watching him with a faint smirk. Jacob pulled himself up to his full height, and with barely controlled fury snarled into the man's face.

"What's your name, little man?"

"Martinez, sir," he said, retreating.

"Well listen, *Martinez,* in the presence of an officer you don't lean against a doorway, you fucking stand up straight. Got that? Fifty press ups, now!"

The man hesitated until Jacob raised the hand with the rope as if to strike him.

Jacob heard the man grunt as he began his punishment, then turned and walked quickly down the corridor. He didn't look back.

Chapter Twenty-Five

Toledo, 1937

Jacob found it difficult to sleep that night, and when finally he did drift off, his dreams were infiltrated by confused memories of Tino as a boy and as a prisoner. In the morning he went immediately to Lucas, who surprised him by listening attentively.

"It won't be easy, you know that. I hear this kind of story every day." He looked around and spoke more quietly. "I wonder ... if, at the beginning, we'd really thought it through properly. If we'd known, would we have followed our orders like we did, or bailed out like the navy?" Jacob looked shocked. This was almost rebel talk. "We none of us imagined what civil war really meant. We never thought there'd be so much outright hate, so much poison, that we'd be splitting up families, friends ... I don't know what we thought, to be honest. We just got swept up in all the politics, all the promises and threats of all these big men ... although Franco ..." He looked around the room. "Franco's *tiny*. He addressed us once, on the coast, and I couldn't believe what a midget he is. I mean, he spoke powerfully, and I agree with nearly everything he says, and there's no question that we do need to get rid of all the filthy reds, but it bothers me that we're going to have to pay such a heavy price. It could be generations before all the wounds begin to heal." He stopped to take a deep breath, aware that he might have said too much. "Sorry. I'm on a bit of a downer. And I've got a meeting with the Germans. Did you hear what they did up at that place Guernica? Absolutely flattened it. It's impressive, the firepower that they have, but it's us, the Spanish, who are going to have to put it all back together. If we're not careful we're going to get ourselves squashed between that lot and the Russians and the whole country will end up a heap of Spanish speaking rubble."

Jacob looked at his watch. He needed to get the conversation back on track. Fortunately Lucas took the hint.

"Listen," he said, "it'll be tricky, but not impossible. Find out exactly what he's supposed to have done, and I'll have a word with Father to see if he can lean on someone at the Ministry. I doubt we'll get him off the hook, but maybe we can have him moved to some half-decent civilian prison, and let the warders know that he has a protector. That's the best I can do. Sure he's a good kid, or at least he was, but he's a Commie for God's sake! Don't know why you bother."

Jacob didn't quite know why either. Somehow he had allowed himself to become pulled between loyalty to his own side, and loyalty to a friend he hadn't seen for years. But he would find a way to square it; there was always a way. He decided he would return to the prison straight away, to check on Tino, and to give him the news as a token of hope.

The motorbike was still where he'd left it, beneath a tarpaulin in the corner of the garage. He would miss the old thing, he mused, as he sped away from the barracks towards the prison. This would definitely be the last time that he would be able to use her. He would already have been in trouble had Lucas not pulled a few strings, and besides, if he weren't back on duty by nightfall then he would officially be AWOL, and not even Lucas could help him with that.

In the meantime he would enjoy the ride. The road ahead was quiet, the sun was on his back, and he leaned as far as he dared into the bends, knees all but scraping the rough tarmac as he tilted left and right into each joyous corner. The hills around were deep spring-green, children splashing in a stream by a bridge hollered to him as he passed, and birds, hundreds of them, darted away from the hedgerows at the roar of his approach. He was doing the right thing at last, he decided, the honourable, individual choice, and the thought filled him with a rush of pleasure. He imagined that Maria were there, behind him on the bike, and yelled, then turned the throttle a fraction more, his eyes streaming from the wind on his face.

The bull stood in the middle of the road, invisible behind the bend, and Jacob was travelling too fast, with no chance of stopping. To one side was a drop down to the river, to the other a high stone wall. He saw immediately that the gap to the left was too small, so swerved right. At the last second he closed his eyes, knowing that if the beast moved just a fraction he would be hurled into the wall.

Somehow he made it. He eased the great bike to a halt and looked back, shaking. The bull had moved away and was quietly grazing, heedless of the destruction it had almost caused. That was so close, so stupid. How absurd it would be to die like that, in the middle of a war, and how undignified, how meaningless. He rode on, more slowly this time, determined to take more care, and in his head rehearsed a version of the story for Maria and Lucas which would amuse them.

That day it was quiet outside the prison. He recognised one of the guards who this time saluted him promptly. As the outer door opened he saw too that it was the same clerk behind the desk.

"I've come to see the prisoner I saw yesterday. Faustino Alvarez."

The clerk stared nervously at his desk and refused to look Jacob in the eye.

"Just a moment," he said, glancing at another man who had just entered the room. "Sergeant? Maybe you could deal with this?"

Jacob stared at the man and sensed instantly that something was wrong.

"I'm afraid that there's a problem, sir. See, there was a bit of a struggle this morning. The prisoner tried to make a run for it, and attacked one of the guards. Are you family, sir?"

Jacob shook his head. How could he have attempted to get away? He was half blind and could barely stand, let alone run.

"Seems like the poor chap banged his head as they tried to subdue him. I'm afraid that he's dead, sir."

The room seemed suddenly colder. He could feel an iciness in the pit of his stomach, and his leg had begun to tremble. He tried to hide it: he mustn't let these people know that he was upset. His lips felt impossibly tight as he spoke, and his voice was louder than he had intended.

"You're sure? I mean, where is he? Can I see him?"

"I don't know if that's a good idea, sir."

Jacob took a deep breath, puffed out his cheeks, and blew out hard.

"Sergeant. Let's not mess about. Just take me to him. That's an order."

Reluctantly the sergeant complied and Jacob followed him down the booming corridor, still hoping against hope that there might have been some mistake. After a few minutes they came to a door, outside of which was a hand-painted sign with the word "Mortuary". They entered without knocking. A man in a grubby white coat looked up at them through round, steel-framed spectacles . Behind him, on the floor, lay at least a dozen bodies, spaced neatly apart.

Jacob was horrified. He had seen plenty of corpses, but not like this. The broken ragdoll bodies of the battlefield now seemed somehow more natural, the inevitable consequence of violent struggle. But this futile attempt to bring order and symmetry to death seemed even more grotesque, more cruel.

He could see Tino, or what was left of him, in the middle of the row. Gathering his strength he stepped between the rows until he stood beside him. The corpse was the shade of the worn grey sheet on which it lay. It wore nothing but shorts, which were wet, and smelled of piss. One dead eye stared out, and the tongue protruded through pale blue lips.

Jacob struggled to keep his self control.

"This man ... this man did not die trying to escape. This man did not die of a head wound."

"Sir ... according to my report-"

"Fuck your report! Do you hear? This man was asphyxiated ... He was *garrotted*!" He struggled with the last word; the truth it bore almost too awful for him say aloud. "Garrotted." He forced himself to say it a second time. "This was a crime. Let's not pretend. Don't insult my intelligence. This was murder."

He stared at the sergeant.

"Someone will pay for this!" he hissed, but both men knew that it was an empty threat. Bodies were piling up across the country on both sides. Nuns, doctors, teachers, innocents, even children. Tino's death would be just another tiny footnote to the growing catalogue of malignity and grief, and there was nothing anyone could do about it.

Jacob just couldn't stand it any longer. Beneath his breath he whispered a quick goodbye to Tino and reached for the door. It was all he could do not to run as he went back to the safety of the light. Outside he stood and trembled, so much so that he feared he might not be able to control the motorbike.

Gradually his panic began to dissolve as he wove through the narrow streets to the edge of town. On impulse he followed a track along the river, and came to a halt by a small mud beach. He stripped and swam, despite the cold. A wooden jetty stuck out from the bank; he held onto a strut with one hand, and allowed the current to wash over him, rinsing away the fetor of the morgue and the sense of dread. Keeping his eyes open he forced his head beneath the surface and tried to imagine what it would be like to die in this cold green world, staying under so long that when at last he surfaced black spots slid across his sight. Eventually he let go of the post and drifted on his back, staring at the clouds. It took him almost twenty minutes to fight his way back upstream, and by the time he reached the jetty he was exhausted.

But at least the numbness was gone. He dried himself in the sun, and realised he was hungry. On the way back he stopped at a *venta,* a tavern, and drank a glass of wine with the lentil broth he was offered. The waitress was pretty, and she smiled at him coquettishly as he left.

There would just be time for him to go home before heading back to the barracks. He didn't want to face his mother, but he was desperate to see Maria. He would go in through the tradesmen's' door. He knew they would all be busy because of the reception for the Germans, but he could probably get her to one side, if even just for half an hour. He wondered if he might kiss her, and the thought thrilled him.

The house was in a frenzy. Not even the kindly cook had much time to talk. He slipped up the servants' stairs, hoping to catch Maria in the dining room. She could be anywhere. Suddenly he spotted her through a crack in the door, and without warning felt his viscera give a delicious lurch to one side. The physical effect of seeing her stopped him in his tracks, and he swallowed, as though expecting somehow to taste the electrifying bile which had afflicted him. He watched her; it felt like trespass, but he wanted to drink her in. And then she turned and saw him. For a second a radiant smile illuminated her face and she took two steps towards him. He knew he must be grinning like an idiot. He reached his hands towards her, but at the last moment she turned a second time, and backed away. Still smiling, she muttered some excuse about her work, and opened the door behind her. He called her name. Again she looked at him. He tried to read her expression, but all too soon she was gone.

He blundered back down the stairwell. The cook saw him, and offered him a biscuit, as if that would help. She said briefly that he was not to worry, that it was probably a girl thing; that she knew that lately Maria had been very confused.

Confused! She's not the only one, thought Jacob as he sped alone back to the male solace of the barracks. He revved the bike harder. If this was to be his last ride, he might as well enjoy it.

Chapter Twenty-Six

A party, 1937

On Saturday evening the family had planned to host an informal reception, or soirée, as Jacob's mother had called it, with the embossed invitations promising conversation, cocktails and canapés. Preparations had begun the day before, with the furniture removed from the seldom-used salon, and the connecting doors pushed back either side on to the piano room and adjoining library. The housekeeper had sworn loudly when the tall window shutters were thrown back for the first time in months and revealed a discouraging layer of dust, and had cajoled the rest of the staff to re-double their efforts before this was spotted by the mistress of the house. All day long the premises had been filled with the din of tradespeople as they scurried along with flowers, candles, carpets and cakes. The seamstress from the market was summoned to press the men's outfits; crystal glasses were solemnly unpacked, polished, re-polished; the menfolk emerged shining and pink, one by one, holding blood-speckled towels, from the barber's booth that had been set up in the patio, and from deep in the kitchen came an unremitting growl and clank as the cook, relieved of her duties for the day by the presumptuous patisserie in the town, took out her frustrations by the scouring of her ancient copper-bottomed pans. Lucas, who had tried unsuccessfully to appease her with a smile in his quest for a biscuit, had later told his mother that the family skillets would glow for days like the red-hot mouth of a canon with the patina of her rage.

And throughout the morning Maria fetched and carried, toiling along with the others, trying to appear calm. She was not exhausted as such by her duties, but by the burden of the promise that she would have to keep that evening. It was strange, she reflected: she wasn't particularly daunted by the thought of pilfering letters from some obnoxious soldier, nor had she really thought too much about the consequences should she be caught. What really disturbed her, in fact made her want to urinate whenever she pictured it, was the thought of the moments immediately leading up to the act, those hideous last few seconds when you had to be truly brave. Deep down, she feared she might not have it within her. She tried instead to think of other things, to make an effort to stay light-hearted. As a result, just before lunch, when one of the tradesmen, flirting slightly, made an unfunny joke, she guffawed inappropriately, earning herself a disapproving frown from *la Señora*.

Maria could feel the anger inside her begin to ferment and had to force herself to keep it hidden. As an exercise she began for the first time to examine the possible reasons for her distaste for this woman, for it troubled her at unexplored depths. It wasn't that her employer was a manifestly evil person, and Jacob's filial devotion was plain to see, even if he had begun occasionally to tease her strict, old-fashioned values. Could it be that she, Maria, was trying to invent this sense of loathing in order to self-justify the act of disloyalty she was now planning to commit? It wasn't just her rank, or her bullying of the staff, nor her lack of empathy which so goaded Maria, and surely it wasn't that she was jealous of her wealth or of her beauty. Did she fear her? Was that the reason for this growing rancour? Or was it just her class, and everything that she represented, or was it just that they were all in a state of heightened weariness and tension because of the imminent the visit of these bloody foreigners?

These were the unanswered questions which wove through her head as she sweated her way through the afternoon chores, leaving her ever more vexed and confused.

And then suddenly she saw him through the half open doorway, his intelligent eyes staring at her: a tall, happy, handsome presence conjured out of nowhere. Jacob! Instinctively she took a step towards him, thrilled. But her reaction was short-lived. Caution kicked in a split second later. She couldn't deal with him like this, not here, not now. Instead she dialled down her smile and greeted him formally, trying to ignore the hurt and confusion that suddenly marked his face as clearly as if she'd slapped him.

"It's chaos here," she said by way of explanation. "Your mama is already mad at me and the cook's on the warpath: I've got to run!"

He held out a hand as if to stay her. "Wait, don't worry, I'll deal with them," he said. "I want to … let me …" But already she was turning away from him.

"It's not fair on the others," she said lamely, hating herself. "Let's talk tomorrow?" She fought hard to control her breathing. She strode away from him, and only once she had crossed the room did she feel strong enough to turn and face him, but could hold his gaze for only the briefest of moments.

"Hey," she said as she spun away from him once more, "it's great to see you!" and she thought sadly that this was perhaps the one true and honest thing she had said all day. He mouthed something to her, but she was gone, running for the safety of the stairwell. She stood there alone for a while, gulping in the clean lemon and beeswaxed silence, and gazing upwards at the melting red light that poured in from the stained glass window. Above the family coat-of-arms was a crucifix, and for a moment she was tempted to pray, but tried instead to focus on her rage. Why did he have to turn up like that, complicating everything? Was he not the enemy, or at least in the enemy's clothing? She tried to bury his smile in the rubble of the knowledge that *his people* were at that precise second lobbing shells onto *her people* in the shattered streets of Madrid. She just could not, would not, be a traitor to them.

Someone somewhere was now calling for her. She noticed that she still carried a dust-cloth, which one hand had wound tighter and tighter around the other. As she moved off she observed absently that her fingers were slowly turning blue.

"I'm here!" she yelled. "Just coming." She stepped back inside her strange theatre of deceit, a compliant smile now anchored to her face and saw the steward who glowered at her, though said nothing.

"Maria!" bellowed the cook. "In God's name move these stupid pans!" She waddled into view, flushed, perspiring, as wide as she was tall, and slipped a hot biscuit into Maria's pocket.

"Jacob's here," said the cook as the steward moved away. "Did you see him?"

"Yes. We spoke. He's fine." Even to her own ears Maria's voice sounded shrill and faintly ridiculous. The cook gave her a knowing look.

"Just you be careful, sweetie," she said, pointing a pudgy finger. "Just be bloody careful, alright?" Her cheeks dimpled as she smiled. "And Maria," she added, pretending to cuff her, "just move the bloody pans. Now!"

Maria resumed her work, buoyed by the smile and the biscuit. The

Germans would be there just after 8.00 that evening, the contact had told her. Probably three or four of them. They might not all be wearing full uniform, but would somewhere each display their eagle and swastika insignia, perhaps just on armbands or caps. It was important for her not to confuse them with the Italians, who might also attend, or indeed with officers from the Spanish navy, whose outfits she might not recognise. They would arrive en route to their headquarters on the way back from a ceremony at the Town Hall, where, to much private disgust, the Condor Legion was to receive the formal thanks and benediction of a grateful city.

Unexpectedly, however, a large black car drew up outside the house at least half an hour early . Their colonel, it seemed, had little time for bombastic speeches and was there to help win a war, as he said, and not to listen to tributes, and had with a modicum of courtesy brought the official proceedings to a premature ending. His fine military ambitions, though, were clearly not incompatible with the enjoyment of fine wine, and he and his staff were now making the most of the hospitality on offer, and the air was thick with the smoke of cigars and loud laughter.

Maria can barely breathe. She is outside the scullery which is now being used as a makeshift cloakroom. She is looking through the crack in the door at their coats which are hanging from a pole strung from the inglenook fireplace to the wall opposite. Heavy coats, leather. Earlier, lifting them, all smiles, she'd been astonished that a coat could be so heavy, like armour. From an upstairs window she had seen the Germans emerge from the car, four of them, and had rushed downstairs to make herself useful as they made their entrance. She is suddenly aware just how low the ceiling is, far lower down here for the domestic staff than for the owners upstairs. The confinement adds to her feeling of weight, of being caught in a trap. Caught here cursingin the small room, caught too in the machinations of a drama not of her choosing. What was that word, those puppets in the park, the strings? A marionette, that was it.

This is the agony of indecision which she had so dreaded. She is distantly aware of the low din of conversation and the muffled thwack of heels on the parquet upstairs, but down here her world is hushed. She takes a last look around, hears herself breathe deeply, then, as if observing herself in a mirror, takes two quick steps into the empty room.

Three bags. She picks up the first, rejects it, then bends and opens the second. They haven't told her exactly what to look for. Just to get whatever she can: letters, documents, anything, for all information is precious now. At random she takes four letters from among the pile of many and lays them on the floor beside her. She closes the bag, then on a whim reaches into the third and extracts just one brown envelope from the slim pile within and hides it under her jacket. She replaces the bags, leaves them exactly as they were, picks up the letters from the floor, then crosses the room and deposits them on the hidden ledge inside the chimney breast which is used for drying salt.

It's done, she thinks, it's over, but the pent up sigh that finally escapes her lips turns suddenly to an audible whimper as the dark figure of a man slips silently inside.

She sees the German insignia on his shirt, the black gloves. He's not one of the four, is he? No. Shit. The driver! Of course. Shit. She's shocked, not frightened, and angry at herself as well as him.

He says something she cannot understand, but she sees that he is smiling. She simpers back timorously. He's young, blond and not bad-looking. Excusing herself, she tries to squeeze past him, but still grinning, he tries to put his arm around her waist, so that she has to twist away. As she turns, the envelope that she's forgotten falls from her pocket and glides lazily away, falling with a papery hiss beside his shining boots. With natural courtesy he stoops to pick it up for her, and is about to hand it back but frowns as he notes the seal on the back, with its Eagle and Swastika. As his puzzled eyes move from the letter to her face his confusion is instantly lifted, for guilt is stamped there as indelibly as the black ink of the Reich.

He moves quickly now to grab her by the wrist, shouting. She screams, coiling and jerking in her attempt to pull free, but he is far stronger, and has her pinned against the wall when, attracted by the noise, two Spanish soldiers rush into the room. At first they assume that Maria is the victim here, and stand aggressively close to the German as he flaps the incriminating letter in the air. There is much talking but no comprehension for a while, until one soldier leaves to return with a German-speaking Officer.

His manner is calm, formal, efficient. Maria is taken alone to a room where she will stay until the reception is over. There is to be no embarrassment or disgrace brought upon the household by the actions of a vile little socialist, the officer speaks to her in Spanish. We know there will always be snakes in the grass, he adds chillingly, and we just have to deal with them appropriately, without their ruining our lives.

Maria is soon cold in her windowless room. As time passes she realises she is now anxious rather than terrified, and when Monica, the chamber maid, arrives to tell her that the lady of the house will speak to her soon, she is relieved, for she fears the brutality of men.

Her mis-placed trust is instantly obliterated. She has never seen anyone so completely unhinged with rage. As the door closes behind her, all sense of composure evaporates. La Señora is grey-white with fury. Her lips have all but disappeared and she is shaking, spittle flicking from the thin rouged line of her mouth as she shrieks in

Maria's face.

"Oh you two-faced, traitorous bitch! You whore, you red commie slut!" she yells. "Don't you think I haven't been watching you all this time? Making eyes at my poor Jacob. Trying to seduce him, have his babies, take his money? I know you lot. Scum! Filth."

Her rant continues like this for some while. Maria is stunned by her reaction, by the violence of the harangue. So this is what it's about, is it, she reasons, it's about her and Jacob. Had they been so obvious?

The tirade is reaching some kind of crescendo as Lucas taps on the door and steps inside. His mother is hoarse, panting.

"Mama," he says gently, and with his hand on her shoulder leads her authoritatively outside, turning at the threshold to give a puzzled look to Maria. She is about to speak, but then -

"Bitch," he mouths almost silently. "Oh you fucking stupid, stupid bitch. What have you done?" The force of his words almost knocks her to the ground. The door closes and she hears him striding away down the corridor.

She sits alone in the cold and dark for long, long hours, half-seething, half-weeping, until at last two men of the Guardia Civil barge in without knocking, and she is escorted in silence to the dreaded city barracks.

Chapter Twenty-Seven

Madrid, June 2012

Graffiti. Jess had been looking at the graffiti on the wall when the man had hit her. She's trying to make sense of things. Was it her fault? She remembers she must have bumped into the stranger, and was beginning to apologise as she felt that terrible blow to her upper abdomen. Now she is half-sprawled, half-kneeling on the dirt, dazed, staring wild-eyed at the grazes on her hand, struggling to drag air into her wounded lungs. She sees her comb on the grass next to her, and looks desperately around, scrabbling blindly with her damaged fingers to locate her belongings, aware of a hand on her shoulder, a woman's hand, the smell of perfume, and a mouth speaking incomprehensibly close to her face. Ahead of her, along a tunnel of trees, as if in a film, she is dimly conscious of observing two figures running, and she watches the shocked faces of the bystanders as one by one they spin and gawp as the two men speed past. Suddenly one of the runners falls, the second one, and detachedly she contemplates him as he rolls to a stop. That must have hurt, she thinks automatically.

Now she's sitting on a park bench. Someone has given her a bottle of water, and she watches it tremble as she lifts her hand to drink. She takes little gulps of air; and experiments with trying to inhale more deeply, but the pain is too great. The side of her head hurts too, and fearfully she lifts a hand to her face to check for damage.

"You face is fine, little one, don't worry," says a woman's voice, and she looks up into a small knot of people who have gathered around her. Someone, another woman, sits beside her, and holds her gently by the wrist.

"You okay, sweetheart?" she asks. " I saw it. Bastard. I read there's been a few like that recently. Was there much in it?"

She thinks of the small knapsack she had brought specially for this trip, and tries to remember. Some money, not much. Her notebook. And her phone. Her bloody phone. She feels a seed of anger growing deep down, and tries to stand. But as she rises a man appears in front of her, and she flinches, drops back down and in panic looks to the woman next to her for protection.

"It's okay, love," says the woman, "it wasn't him. This one chased him. I thought he was with you."

Looking up at the man, the woman asks, "Did you get her bag?" but he just shakes his head.

"You're bleeding too!" says the woman, and Jess looks at the grass stains and the hole in his jeans, and the sickly sight of the blood that is beginning to soak into the torn edges on his knees.

"Let's get you cleaned up a bit," says another voice. "Don't worry: I'm a nurse. I just grabbed the First Aid kit from that waiter there at the café. I saw it as I was leaving ... You alright?"

Jess nods. She isn't alright. She really isn't alright, but she doesn't know what else to do. She watches as the woman pours oxygenated water from a sealed bottle, then wipes the grit from the abrasions on her hand. She winces. The woman is efficient and gentle, but still it hurts like hell. Obediently she tracks the woman's fingers as she traces a series of movements in the air, checking for concussion.

"Ach," she tuts. "You'll live. Could've been worse. Now let's have a look at you," and she turns to appraise the damage to the man. "That's a bit messy, sorry. You'll need to take your trousers off, sunshine. Let's go over to the caff." And with that she turns and strides away. "Come on, you two, I've got to get to work!" she yells imperiously over her shoulder, and Jess and the man just look at each other and meekly tag along in her wake.

Jess sits alone as she waits passively for the next development, staring out across the park, trying to get her bearings, to come to terms with what has just happened. After a while the man comes to join her, sitting awkwardly with his leg straight out. She can see the bandage through the hole in his knee.

"She just went away," he says, "our Guardian Angel. Didn't want any thanks, said she had to get back to the clinic." He pauses. "Said to tell you to rest, to keep warm and not to have any caffeine or alcohol."

Jess looks away. She wishes he wasn't there, she needs to be alone to process things, she can't do this when there's a stranger around. She's aware of him looking at her, monitoring her.

"Look," she says, "if you're here to pity me, or to chat me up, then I don't want either, right."

It comes out more harshly than she had intended; the man looks hurt and surprised, and she's annoyed with herself. Just then the waiter arrives, and the man orders water.

"Black coffee," she says, "and a brandy," and looks defiantly at the man. She doesn't understand why she feels this malice, this need for confrontation when he, a total stranger, had just hurt himself in trying to help her.

"It's just ..." she begins, but he holds up his hand to stop her.

"You're in shock, it'll pass. Leave it, okay." He stands to go. "Welcome to Madrid," he says over his shoulder as he limps away.

Appalled at her own bad manners she watches him as he crosses to the bar. He talks to the waiter and she feels a deep sense of guilt and humiliation as for a moment they both turn to stare at her. Suddenly she also feels horribly abandoned, and it is with a sense of loss that she watches his retreating back as he limps out of view behind the long avenue of plane trees. What has she done? She's angry at the world and angry at herself. She doesn't know why she was so ungrateful. He had tried to help her, had been wounded doing so. He had kind eyes and, she supposed, good looks. Why does she react like this. Because he's a man? Because she feels ... vulnerable, exposed, furious?

All of the above, she thinks, not to mention stupid. When the waiter approaches she hopes she won't embarrass herself further. Expressionless, he tells her that because her bag was stolen her friend had paid for her drinks. Also, he had left a telephone number, in case she needed a witness for a police report.

She takes the piece of paper from him, scans it for a second, then ostentatiously screws it into a ball and pushes it into her jeans. But despite her bravura, she pushes it with care, to a pocket from which it can be easily retrieved, when she is alone.

Chapter Twenty-Eight

Madrid, 2012

Befuddled by sleep and the light-proof blinds, Jess looks at her watch and cannot believe she has rested so long. Twelve hours! Joints aching, she limps across the room, remembering and cursing to herself the man who had assaulted her, and soaks for a long time in the hotel bath, until the water is almost cold, and the tips of her waterlogged fingers are corrugated and unfeeling. She almost never slows down like this, she muses, it just isn't her style, and she is perplexed at how much she is enjoying the sense of languor and deceleration. Unbelievably, she realises there is still time for breakfast, and she dresses with slightly more urgency. As she brushes her hair she notices on the table a crumpled piece of paper with a phone number, and stares at it thoughtfully as she irons it out with the flat of her hand.

Later, she retreats to her bedroom with hotel copies of *El Pais* and the New York Times, uncertain now as to how to fill the rest of her day. She tells herself that she is fine, her assurance intact, her determination unquestioned. She had been lucky; it could have been worse. She looks again at the number on the paper. Sooner or later she will have to ring him, the Good Samaritan, to apologise, and it might as well be now, whilst she can use the hotel phone. God, it was going to be so messy here without her mobile; she would have to buy another as soon as she could manage.

Damnit. He doesn't answer and it clicks to the messaging service. She isn't prepared for this and hesitates after the tone. "Hey ... It's Jess ... the idiot in the park who got herself robbed yesterday. Listen, I just wanted to apologise, say sorry, I wasn't grateful, like ... I mean, I was rude ... and I wanted to say thank you. If, if ... if you need to call me I'm in room 624 at the Hotel ... Zenith." Click. Why had she said that? Why would he possibly want to call her?

She tries to settle to the newspapers, turns listlessly to her book, then begins half-heartedly to write the postcards she had bought in the lobby. But by two o'clock the room is oppressive and she is going stir crazy. Outside the sun is coming out; she can feel its creeping heat through the thick glass, luring her outdoors, and she can stand it no more. She brushes her teeth, changes into jeans, and is bending down to look for her shoes in the wardrobe when the phone rings, loud and unfamiliar, startling her. For a second she looks at it, confused, then answers.

"Hola," says a man's voice. "It's Stefan, we erm, we met, briefly, in the park yesterday, you called me ..."

"Wow yes, thank you, I mean sorry, I mean – I just wanted to thank you for your help yesterday. I ... I kind of reacted badly, and took it out on you, you were sort of ..." she searches her memory bank for the Spanish for scapegoat, but gets nowhere. "I just wanted to say thank you, that's all."

"Tranquilo, no problem, really. Are you alright? I mean, do you need to go to the police to make a statement? If you need a witness, I could–"

"No. I won't be going to the police; I don't have insurance. I'm seriously angry about my phone though, and it's going to be so tough here to do what I have to do without one, in fact I'm going out right now to buy another one ..."

"You can't ... not just like that."

"I'll never get the old one back, I need-" She stops mid-sentence. "Eh? What do you mean I can't?"

"Well, you *can,* but only if you have a fixed address. These days, you can't just walk in off the street and buy one like before; ever since the Atocha bombings they've made it more difficult, you need a proof of address, a letter, a ..."

He tails off, maybe realising how he sounds, and there is silence between them as she takes her time to assimilate this news.

"Listen," he says after a while, "maybe I can help you. I know where you are, I mean I know where the Zenith hotel is anyway, it's just a few blocks away from where I am now, let me help. I mean, I could ... if you wanted ... I can be there in 20 minutes. Shall I?"

Jess is drumming her fingers on the table beside the bed, trying to decide, trying to remember what he looked like, the chances of him being some kind of weirdo.

"Ok," she says finally. "20 minutes. In reception. " And just like that she puts the phone down on him. Damnit, why was she so rude? Perhaps her mum was right; maybe she did have a mean spirit. From the outside, her behaviour would have looked unforgivable. Poor man, he was only trying to help her, or at least that's what he claimed.

A short while later she steps outside into the corridor and decides to walk the six floors down, to test her aching leg. Downstairs, the hotel lobby and reception to the side are muted as she opens the door; a sad fountain dribbles onto plastic flowers. The whole place reeks of chemical incense; a faux John Lennon mumbles along to the tune of a muzak *Imagine* and, all in all she decides, it clearly isn't the bijou *fin de siècle* glory hole that is implied on the website. A porter in a threadbare three-piece suit gives her a sidelong glance and decides to ignore her, and just as she reaches the front desk the receptionist darts into an office behind, as if deliberately to annoy her. I'm not the only one round here who's rude, she thinks to herself ruefully. I'd fit right in.

As she turns to scan the room a workman in paint-spattered overalls stands up and makes his way towards her. She's about to make way, but then she sees: it's him! He grins and holds out a hand. They shake and he makes a mock bow, indicating his scruffy clothing.

"I just didn't want to be late, you see," he explains. "I was painting in a friend's house, and I didn't have time to get back home and then here, so …"

"I'm so glad you made the effort," she laughs, and curtsies theatrically.

"Paint painting, that is, white washing, not art painting, I can't pretend I'm an artist or anything like that …"

There is a white splash just beneath his lip, to which she points, then rubs at her own chin to encourage him. It's an oddly intimate gesture, not the kind of thing she would normally do with a virtual stranger.

"So you just walked across town without even looking in a mirror? Dressed like that!"

He shrugs his shoulders, and holds up his hands in that Mediterranean gesture of apology and confusion. "Sorry. I hope you don't mind that I'm so … inelegant. You can walk behind me if you want, so that people won't know we're together."

At first she thinks he might be serious, but the mocking light in his eyes gives him away, and she ushers him out through the slow revolving door.

Once outside on the street she insists on first taking him for coffee. "I owe you, don't forget," she says, "and besides, the coffee in the hotel is lousy, so I need a proper shot before I can concentrate."

There is a bar just around the corner, a good, solid, old-fashioned Madrid joint, with a huge chrome Espresso machine that hisses and burps alarmingly, the racket it makes just adding to the clangs, yells and general vitality of a successful city bar. The coffee is good, and to her the place seems as genuine and alive as her hotel is ersatz. They each have to shout to make themselves understood, and when at last they leave, the busy streets seem calm in comparison.

The instantly recognisable logo of a global phone brand beams down on them from a store halfway down the block.

"This one?" she says, and steps inside without waiting for an answer. In the context of this vast, chic emporium he stands out a mile in his paint-spattered monkey suit, but it does not seem to bother him. They take a ticket and wait until their number is called, and a handsome, uniformed "phone counsellor" explains the virtues of the various models which are available without a contract. Jess makes a provisional choice and the assistant disappears to check if it's in stock.

"What do you think?" asks Jess.

"Erm ... he's hot, I guess, if you like that kind of thing."

"The phone, you brute, not him. Come on, I need some advice."

"Advice? Eat well. Floss, don't spend too much time in the sun, and never trust the singer in a band. That do?"

She sighs loudly, but smiles, nonetheless.

"Honestly," says Stefan, "you're asking the wrong person. It's just a phone to me. Depends if you want to communicate or to show off."

She digests this and compares his answer to that of previous boyfriends, for whom phones were often the source of great reverence.

"Thanks," she answers. "What would I do without you?"

As it turned out, not much, at least not in the phone purchasing department, for as Stefan had prophesised it was necessary to provide identification and a proof of permanent address.

"So technically it's my phone," he reminds her a short time later, "even though you paid for it. Including the 20 euros credit."

They are sitting on a concrete bench in a small plaza, examining the new possession, surrounded by pigeons, skate boarders and harassed parents.

"It also means that when I call you, I'll actually be calling myself." For a second he looks away, mildly panicked. "If I call you, I mean," he adds. They both look down, and there is a slight embarrassed pause, for they both suspect it is a when, not an if.

Suddenly he jumps up. "Shit!" he shouts. "I didn't wash my brushes! They'll all be drying out." He seems genuinely worried. "It's not just the brushes, there's all my kit, the ladder, the paint pots, all the dust covers everywhere. I promised Susanna I'd have it all finished by the time she comes home. She'll kill me. It's for her party tonight."

With that, he says a flustered goodbye, and they exchange an awkward kiss on each cheek. His sudden departure leaves Jess slightly disconcerted, and she feels strangely exposed as she folds up the packaging and puts it in her bag. Susanna, she muses. For some reason she had assumed that the friend whose house he was painting was a man. How odd; did it matter?

Twenty minutes later, just as she gets back to her hotel, her phone vibrates and an unfamiliar ping advises her that she has a new message.

"Hey, English girl," it reads. "Wanna come to a party?"

Does she? She's not sure, and mulls it over carefully as she climbs the six flights of stairs back to her room. She's tired and her hand still hurts. She struggles with the lock then flops heavily on to the bed. The city outside her window stretches enormous and sombre into the distance. How many people lived here, five million, was it? The light was fading quickly to a grey and unlovely gloom, by-passing any attempt at a sunset. It would be easy to stay here, watch a movie. No one would blame her, after all that had happened. She could order room service, or a takeaway pizza. She thinks about his scruffy painter's outfit, and smiles to herself.

"Sí," is all she writes, and presses send.

Chapter Twenty-Nine

Toledo, 1937

Jacob felt the room sway when he walked in and heard the news of Maria's perfidy. On his way over to the house that morning he had stopped to pick wildflowers for her, and they now lay pathetic and broken at his feet as he tried to process the information. *Treacherous. Two-faced. Faithless.* He heard the words as they flew across the room, but couldn't make sense of them. He wanted to put his hands over his ears to drown out the accusations. His mother seemed as jubilant as she was enraged, and her behaviour angered him. He didn't know what to do, or where to put himself. Some foundation had shifted; he needed air. He left as hurriedly as he could, down the servants' stairs, passing the place where last he'd seen her.

The cook came out and blocked his way. He really didn't want to talk to her, but she grabbed his arm.

"She's a good girl, Jacob, a good woman." He tried to shake her off but she tightened her grip. He saw that she had been crying. "A loyal woman, you hear me? Now just you remember that."

He stood outside in the courtyard, alone, waiting. The patio wasn't quite big enough to call itself a garden, but hidden there behind the high wall were plants in enormous clay pots: roses, tulips, jasmine and the first of the year's bougainvillea, just coming into flower. He noticed a nest in the lemon tree, and watched dispassionately as two bright finches flitted from branch to branch, hoping that he would walk on and leave them in peace. Bees hovered over a greasy puddle where someone had been watering, a squirrel spiralled up the cypress tree; a fat grey moth supped on the sap of a cold-split pear, whilst a weary column of ants hauled the carcass of a louse towards the darkness of their lair. All of this he registered, but did not properly perceive. He was aware instead of a sense of disconnection from his surroundings, and of the growing pressure behind his eyelids.

He re-entered the house. It was silent down here. Rather than face his family on the floors above, he walked along the service corridor. The laundry room door stood ajar. Inside it was warm, and filled with the comforting smells of borax, bleach and lye, the scents of cleanliness, and of his childhood. He filled his lungs with happy memories, and sprawled on a heap of woollen blankets which were waiting to be packed away for the summer. He and Maria and the other kids used to play here when they were small.

On a hanger in the corner, sparkling in the half-light, the seamstress had left his dress uniform, brushed and pressed and ready in case he had had time to join the party with the Germans. It was a good job he hadn't been there at the time of the arrest, he thought; he didn't know how he would have reacted.

He leaned on one elbow and stared at it. The shoulders seemed very square on the hanger. How proud he had been when first he'd worn it to the mid-summer ball at the Ritz. He reached out and rubbed the stiff fabric of the sleeve between his fingers, closing his eyes as he felt the officer's gold braid on the cuff. It smelled of camphor.

Was it genuinely elegant, he wondered, or was it just what it represented? The hierarchy, the continuity, the history, the *esprit de corps*. Maria hadn't liked it one bit. He winced at the memory. He'd come home that time with two friends, sleek, debonair and dressed to impress in their new regimental finery, and she – a servant! – had walked out of the room on them. "I don't mind the smell of mothballs," she had told him later. "It's the stink of inequality I can't handle." Stupid girl. Stupid politics.

He lay back and closed his eyes. He needed to think about her, but dared only do so in the past tense. Any thought of what she was doing at that moment was terrifying, and her future too sickening even to contemplate. He tried to picture her there in the laundry, in the dining room, outside in the park, as he'd seen her. He could *just* do it. Just for a vanishing second he could summon her smile, her laugh, could imagine the life in her eyes.

He was so tired; he had slept badly, for each time he had fallen deeply asleep the other thing had taken over. No matter how hard he had tried to banish them, they always slunk back: the nightmares, the loathsome memories, crawling back from their filth, and he had woken sweating and afraid. A shattered horse, a cudgel, an arm in the mud, a blue protruding tongue, and the very worst thing that night, the deep-buried memory of a body washed up on the beach, so long ago.

He stood. He could barely breathe. He felt as if he were drowning and remembered holding his breath in the river the previous day. Going back to his uniform he observed again the ribboning and silver bias. It was splendid, but what did it mean? The precision and faultlessness of the thing made a mockery of what he was feeling. It was as though it were taunting him. With a wail of frustration he lashed out and threw it to the ground. The action shocked him. The uniform lay there on the granite tiles like the body of a wounded soldier. He thought again of the prisoner and the blanket, he thought of Tino, and of Maria. Light was pouring in from the window. Outside, he could still see the darting of the finches, happy now that he had gone. He just had to move. He straightened his shoulders, took a deep breath, and walked towards the sunlight, trampling the uniform beneath the weight of his uncaring army boots.

Chapter Thirty

Prison, 1937

On his way out Jacob stoops by the stand in the hall and picks up his father's swagger stick, a gift from a British officer long before the troubles had started. As a captain it would be unusual though not forbidden for him to carry this in public, but he likes the heft of it, the power it implies.

Toledo is a small city, which since the lifting of the siege of the alcázar the previous autumn has been under Nationalist control, so he ought to feel safe. However, these past few days, following the suspicious deaths of the prisoners, he feels a renewed tension on the city streets, a nervousness, a dangerous, tinderbox energy, and he is wary. Before leaving the house he had taken time to clean and oil his service revolver, which now hangs reassuringly heavily in the holster at his side.

He hails a horse-drawn cab and barks his instruction to the driver to take him to the barracks without delay. He dislikes the tone of his own voice but knows that as things stand he will need every ounce of authority he can muster. The driver is not much older than he is, swarthy, ill-shaven and is for some reason wearing mis-matched boots; in better times the good-natured Jacob would have engaged with such a man, chatted idly about sports or the weather, been affable, but today he stares blankly, jaw set, at the jittery pedestrians, whose numbers begin to thin as they reach the suburbs of the city.

The afternoon sun is surprisingly warm; he's thirsty, and increasingly tormented by the jolts from the pot-holed streets. He's about to speak out, but at last they reach their destination and he is free to dismount.

"Wait here," he commands, and drops more coins than the journey is worth into the wooden box by his seat. The driver does not smile.

The dull grey building is solid, squat, and uncompromisingly joyless. Small iron-grilled windows are aligned in sinister rows, and each corner is guarded by an effective-looking gun turret. Jacob intuits that these are likely to be empty, since this is, after all, no more than a women's prison, and the army here is unbearably stretched, all serious fighting men having been sent to help keep up the offensive on Madrid. The sentries on duty will no doubt be the main force, but this will be largely a show of strength, and no more than that. A charade; at least that is what he tells himself.

A small crowd has gathered anxiously in front of the main gate, their path blocked by four armed guards. Jacob begins to make his way forward, propelled by his height and rank, until he catches the eye of one of the soldiers who instantly orders the throng to give way to allow him passage. They fall back reluctantly, eyes filled with a strange mixture of loathing and hope, and he nods to the soldier as he abandons the sunlight and steps into the gloom of the entrance hall. He smells the familiar reek of bleach and piss. It is strangely quiet. At the desk a soldier is hurriedly getting to his feet, suddenly aware of the presence of an officer. Jacob raps on the table with his stick, harder than necessary, and stares down at the man.

"Stand up straight!" he orders. "Look at your tunic, you scruffy little sod, and do up your buttons!"

With trembling fingers the soldier does as he is told, afraid to look Jacob in the eye. Jacob glares at him, calmer now that his authority is total and unchallenged. The man in front of him has clearly not been long in the army, though long enough to recognise and appreciate the power of a career officer. "Where is everybody?" he asks.

"Lunch, sir, we're always quiet at this time."

"Lunch!" Jacob thunders. "It's half past fucking four! Who's in charge here?"

"I am ... sir," the man mutters, swallowing hard. Jacob breathes deeply, gathering his thoughts. He'd known it would be quiet at this time, but to have no more than a lazy, chicken-hearted corporal to question his motives was more than he could have hoped for. He slowly scans the room, taking in the papers, the litter on the floor, his eyes coming to rest on a half-empty beer bottle at the man's elbow.

"For God's sake," he says with contempt, "what time does your commanding officer arrive?"

"6, sir. 1800h, I mean. Sir!"

Jacob is flooded with relief. "Well you'd better have this pigsty cleaned up by the time I leave," he manages to say, "or I'll have your balls on a plate tonight. Got it?"

The man nods, relieved in turn.

"Now," says Jacob, as he theatrically pulls a notebook from his pocket, "I'm here to question a red spy ... a spy and a thief, it says here. A newbie, name of, erm... Maria Sanchez. Where do I find her? Quick, man!"

The corporal sucks his thumb as he stares at the ledger and pretends to be thinking hard. It's clear he knows exactly where she is. A pretty girl like Maria? She wouldn't have slipped by unnoticed or unimpeded. Jacob, losing patience, grabs the book and turns it towards him, reading quickly. "Cell 14," he says. "Take me there. Now!"

Brusquely he pushes the man ahead of him out of the door and follows him down the corridor. He knows that so far he has done nothing wrong, that his perfect military record remains intact. He is still his father's son. He could still walk out of here head held high. Christ, he doesn't even have a plan. But deep inside him something is changing, something is hatching, and he no longer knows how to resist. It is as if he is acting without thinking, a puppet to someone else's strings. And so they march purposefully, manfully, down the echoing, ill-lit walls, boots clanging, but all the while all he can think of is Maria, and his stomach turns over and over in a hot wave of emotion.

There are around a dozen women incarcerated in each cell. They are sullen, mostly silent, though some hiss or catcall once they have passed. One wolf whistles and the corporal yells at them to keep quiet, prompting an outbreak of sarcastic laughter. Jacob feels the man bristle, and knows that the little brute will expend his humiliation on some other poor soul once he has left. He's about to say something, but the man stops suddenly by cell number thirteen.

"She's at the end there, by herself," he indicates with a pudgy ink-stained finger.

Jacob looks nonplussed. Before he can say anything the man grins, then winks conspiratorially.

"The captain saw her come in last night. Took a fancy to her. He'll be in later tonight, to ... you know, *deal with* her, if you catch my drift... that's why she's on her own. This lot would scratch his eyes out, wouldn't you, darlings?" he leers, laughing at the other women in the cells as he swaggers ahead.

A spasm of nausea and pure fury almost makes Jacob stumble as comprehension dawns, and he is on the point of losing his composure and striking the wretch, when suddenly he sees her.

For a second his world is frozen. A single shaft of sunlight has made it through a chink in the shutters, and the only thing it illuminates is her face, held *chiaroscuro* like the old masters in the Prado, her eyes half-closed, in profile to the intruders. The song of a lark outside makes him appreciate the silence within. Everyone else in the tableau is watching him, watching her. Finally, she turns to him.

"You came back," she says solemnly, holding his gaze, and these three simple, unforeseen words trigger a reaction hidden deep inside him. He stifles a sob and staggers back a little, looks away. How can she possibly know that poor Tino had said exactly that to him? That these were the last words they'd ever spoken to each other, quite possibly the last words Tino had ever spoken to anyone for that matter, for he was a mad, stubborn old bastard, no an *honourable* bastard, and when later Jacob had seen the state of his mutilated body he'd had to run away and had cried himself to sleep that night, thinking of these three fateful words. Yes, old friend, he had come back alright, but then he'd disappeared again, no, *surrendered,* on the pretext of his military duty, and crawled away to sleep the unholy sleep of the coward.

Well no more. This one, this brave girl, he will never let down, not ever. He finally gets it. Here in the misery and the shadows and the gloom he finally acknowledges the true state of things. For years he's been aware of the growls of a nascent sense of revolt, as if ignoring the rumble of a distant storm. But now the storm is here, it's upon him, and he must act.

The guard meanwhile has sensed something odd and is staring open

—mouthed at the scene. Jacob turns to him.

"I'm taking her with me. Give me your weapon," he orders coolly.

"Sir, no..." but in a flash Jacob has grabbed him by the throat and is forcing his pistol into the man's lumpen belly.

"Now!" he insists. "And give me the keys too, or you'll die here, right now." He speaks calmly, and to his surprise he feels calm too. Perhaps it's his military training, he has the time to wonder, or perhaps it's because – finally – he feels in his bones that he's doing the right thing.

He orders the terrified man to unfasten the door himself. Maria steps into the corridor and he bundles the un-protesting corporal inside, shushing him with the pistol to his lips.

Maria has had her gaze trained on him all this time, and at last he allows his eyes to settle on hers, for them to look at each other properly. She raises her hand and traces his cheek and the shock he feels as she touches him is sudden, electrifying, so that he recoils, looking stupidly for a moment at her hand. But he sees that she is smiling slightly as she whispers, "You too, then. Gracias a Dios."

A woman in the neighbouring cell shouts out and the spell is broken. Jacob knows he has to improvise, to move decisively, to exploit his moment of surprise. He turns and looks at the bewildered corporal, who, in an attempt at self-importance had been carrying a thick sheaf of papers, which Jacob now grabs from him.

He gives the keys and a box of matches to Maria, tells her to open all the other prison doors, then instructs her to set light to the papers to start a fire; the bunks inside are flimsy wood with thin straw-packed pallets and catch flame instantly, far quicker than he'd expected. He stuffs a handkerchief into the corporal's mouth then locks him inside. A second later he goes back: he cannot let the fool burn to death, but whispers chillingly in his ear that should he move within the next two minutes then Jacob will come back and slit his throat.

Now he runs down the corridor towards the main entrance. He must get there ahead of the fleeing women, or the guards will shoot them first.

"Fire! Fire!" Jacob yells to the guards at the door. They recognise him at once. "Put down your guns and get water! Those mad bitches have set light to the place! And watch out - your guns will go off in your pockets with the heat. Leave them here. I'll keep this lot back with my pistol." To prove his intent he shoots threateningly above the crowds outside, who cower in confusion.

He's inspired. "And don't hurt any of the prisoners! You know that tall arrogant tramp who came in last week? It's only Franco's fucking niece, mucking him around. I gave her a cigarette and she's set the place ablaze. She's the one I've been sent to fetch. She gets hurt and it's the fucking gallows for all of us!" The guards stare at him, dumbstruck, then turn away.

Smoke is beginning to emerge from inside the building. Abruptly, from the dark maw of the gate, there shoots a crazed swarm of mutinous, light-starved women, running, jostling, hands to soot-torn throats. The people outside begin to panic too, and merge with those coming out to complete a scene of utter chaos. Jacob is engulfed in mayhem. They hear a siren, the sound of shots, the roar of an army vehicle barrelling down the dusty street to meet them.

Frantically he scans the throng. With relief they recognise each other simultaneously. He crosses the street towards her, but she turns, walks away from the disorder, ignores him. She then stops to look interestedly into a dusty shop window. As he reaches her she refuses to turn but he hears her tell him to keep walking, to keep ahead of her. She will turn left at the next street, she whispers, he at the following left. He understands, keeps walking. She, at least, is calm. But then a moment after he steps away he is suddenly, sickeningly, suspicious. Will she be there? Will she deceive him? Dismayed, he breaks into a run.

Breathless, he rounds the corner. She is standing there, triumphant, radiant as any bride in her tattered prison apron. Jacob is too overcome to speak, but instead just gathers her into his arms, and holds her tight, as tight as he dare.

Enclosed within his embrace she is suddenly faint with relief. After so many days of bile and tension and fear she would like to wallow forever in this sense of sanctuary. It's as if she can feel the dread as it leaves her, feel it, she thinks, as it slithers away through the soles of her feet. But a part of her is still alert: there is real danger here, they are too exposed.

She notes a Star of David on the wall next to them, gambles on her instinct, and drags Jacob through the doorway and into a half-lit room. It is a barbershop. The old man with the shears looks at them quizzically for a moment, then resumes his work. The men waiting continue to read their newspapers. It is quiet, and for a while all anyone can hear is the snip snip snip of the old-fashioned barber and the softly muffled sobs of the two strange young people in the corner.

Chapter Thirty-One

1937

From time to time the old barber had glanced at them in the tessellated, fly-blown mirror. "Everything okay?" he had asked her cautiously as he weighed up her prison rags. Throughout his life Jacob's affiliations had always been expressed by his uniform, and he was unused therefore to the shades and subtleties of political recognition, but to Maria the consternation of the older man was obvious. Together they – the civilians – began the wordless, blameless hunt for clues, for certainty. On the low table in front of them there was an overflowing ashtray that partly covered a well-thumbed edition of *Mundo Obrero,* a newspaper reviled by Jacob's family, which Maria now picked up and read ostentatiously. She told Jacob to take off his tie, and as he did so she held the barber's gaze. As the next customer took his place the old man apologised and disappeared through a door in the corner. Nervously she had listened to his tread on the stairs and on the floor above, fearful that she may have misread the signs. As she gathered herself for flight the man had emerged, followed by a stooped and black-clad woman, who had stared unabashed at the young couple.

"I see you've torn your dress," she says eventually. "If you come up here with me I can sew it for you now, *hermana,*" leaning heavily on the last word, hermana, sister. Maria stands and kisses the woman's cheek. "Gracias," she responds. "Gracias, amiga."

Their complicity complete, she follows the old woman to the door, extending the upright flat palm of her hand to Jacob to command him to stay. He is befuddled, the shock and reality of his predicament sinking in slowly. Is she abandoning him again? He hears angry shouts in the streets outside, urgent whispering from behind the door. The two men next to him on the greasy chairs of the waiting room look resolutely at the shorn wisps of hair on the floor in front of them, refusing to engage, even as Jacob puts his hand to his holster to check his gun. He looks around for the baton he'd brought from home. His father will be furious when he finds it missing, he thinks, and despite himself smiles inwardly at the banality of the thought.

Outside the sound of running booted feet grows louder, and Jacob is halfway to the inner door when suddenly it opens and Maria stands there calling to him and waving him within. As it closes behind him the barber strides quickly to the door on the street and looks out, asking what on earth was going on, had there been a fire, was that smoke he could smell? A snarling Guardia Civil shoves his head through the door, and looks around suspiciously. Just as he does so, one of the waiting clients moves his feet and surreptitiously covers the army cap which had fallen from Jacob's lap as he stood; as the policeman leaves the second customer spits noisily into the sawdust on the floor. Neither man looks up.

In the stairwell Maria grabs his hand and together they clatter up the ancient stone steps. It's like one of their old games, he says, and she squeezes his hand harder but does not reply. They fly up three flights of stairs before they emerge breathless onto a tiny rooftop terrace.

They are not alone. Facing them is a bare-chested boy of about fifteen, who holds, improbably to Jacob, a standard-issue army rapier. The boy looks frightened but determined, a combination that Jacob recognises as deadly, and he steps protectively in front of Maria.

"For God's sake put that thing down, Carlos, you can be a hero another day. These two are with us. Your grandma told me to trust them." The disembodied voice come from an alcove in the corner. A woman steps out from the shade, and though she wears the familiar black widow's weeds of the older woman, she is not old, and both Jacob and Maria are struck by her pale beauty. "Running away?" she asks simply, and they nod.

"Couldn't find a better place than this," she says, "this is the heart of the *juderia,* or what's left of it. The Jewish quarter, and it's got more holes than a fucking Swiss cheese." To Jacob's ears she has a strangely refined accent, and the swear-word she chooses leaps out at him. The two stare at each other. She looks like a provocative actress from a black and white movie he'd seen. As she moves he sees the fall of her breast against the thin black fabric of her dress and he has to look away. She points at the boy. "Show them," she commands, "get them out to the east, down past by the barrels, and leave them at the end of the big cave so that they can get down easily to the river." Then she turns to Maria. "Wait till dark, then steal a boat. It's the only way." She hesitates. "And in the name of God get handsome here out of those repulsive Devil-stained clothes." She smiles conspiratorially, walks away, then turns again to face them.

"Soldier boy," she says to Jacob, "were you by any chance at Jarama?" Jacob coughs, nods. "I guess you had to be," she purrs. "That's the way of things. His father," she points at the boy, "that is, my husband, he died there, you see."

And she backs away from them, back into the shadows, but before her pale, expressionless face disappears completely she extends a bare arm and aims a long, whispering kiss in Jacob's direction, a gesture so unexpected that he almost tries to dodge it. "Go with God, you son of a bitch," she murmurs. "Go with any God you please."

Her enigmatic departure leaves a stupefied silence which is broken by the metal clatter of the boy's sword as he lets it drop to the ground. Maria speaks first. "Vamos?" she asks, and the boy, whose face has lost its violence, strides past her and vaults one-handed over the balustrade and on to the ridge of the pantile terracotta roof, beckoning that they should follow.

Silently they pursue the wraith-like boy as he skims along the rooftop, before he opens a tiny trapdoor and they plunge once more into the darkness of a spiral stairwell. His esparto-slippered feet spurt noiselessly along the stone steps, Maria's likewise, though Jacob is hampered by his military hobnail boots which skitter over the hard floor and threaten to send him flying. At the bottom of the stairs there are two doors. The boy opens the one to the left almost without slowing down, and they scamper down the facing corridor. Jacob is reminded once again of the games of chase they had played when they were young. There's a strange half-light, for there are small windows set high on the walls. Maria is surprised for she had imagined they had been running underground, but she realises they are at street level and inside a chamber which runs parallel to the shops and houses outside. The *Juderia*, of course: she'd seen a similar thing in Sevilla.

More doors, at which the boy barely pauses, before the ground starts to slope downhill and they enter what is now an underground tunnel. As the dim light begins to fade behind them they reach a large wrought iron gate which is held shut by pieces of wire. Maria thinks of the prison bars which she had left behind just, what, an hour earlier? She feels she may be dreaming.

"To keep out the foxes and wolves" the boy says in explanation. He has a surprisingly deep voice and Maria realises these are the first words he has spoken. Bending, he takes a flint from his pocket and lights first a wad of tinder, then a candle, which he holds in front of him as they begin to descend, walking slowly now. After a few minutes they begin to see light ahead of them, then a breeze which blows out the candle, and they step out into weak sunlight, squinting down at the silvery line of the river below them.

"We've come right through the hillside," says the boy proudly. "That's the Tagus down there: it goes right out to the ocean, to Lisbon." There is wonder in his voice as he adds, "600 km away, almost. I went there once, to buy cloth." He hesitates, looks at Jacob, then whispers, "with my dad …"

All three of them look down into the valley, unsure of what comes next. Then the boy smiles. "Was it you? Did you two just break out of the jail there with the others? We saw the smoke, the commotion.."

Maria smiles back at him, nodding.

"No shit, that's great, man," he says to Jacob. He peers at his uniform. "You some kind of spy or something?"

"Something like that," Jacob replies, and for a while the two stare at each other, wary brothers-in-arms.

But then, in a flash he turns and darts back into the mouth of the tunnel. The air reverberates to his strange teenage baritone as he yells out three long adios, the last one muffled by his retreat, and then silence.

His absence leaves a vacuum that for a while they find difficult to fill.

"Strange boy," Maria muses. "Strange times; strange, stupid war."

She looks around. It's just the two of them. God, it's beautiful here, she thinks. After even such a brief time in the jailhouse she feels she needs to soak it all up, to treasure the soft air, to come alive again. She runs her fingers through the tufts of grass, savours the background of thyme on the breeze, tilts her face to the sun. Moment by moment she feels herself beginning to relax, to breathe, to fit properly inside her skin again. She hasn't felt like this for such a long, long time, since long before her arrest even.

The previous year she had seen an American film at the picture house in which a cowboy had to save himself from drowning in a whirlpool. She feels like this now; behind her, inside her; she feels the weight of all the dark and ugly ghosts pulling her back down, down, the shock of her arrest, the helplessness of the women in the prison, the dread, the bile, the loathing and despair, the dazed grief of the half-mad widow and all those like her ... and she's still scared, worried sick by the future, she feels responsible and vulnerable, she doesn't yet trust herself to feel comfortable in her freedom, she's afraid of what her dreams will bring. And yet against all this there is now the warmth of the sun on her face, the pureness of the wind, the innocence and physicality of Jacob at her side, reaching down to haul her out, and now something else too, a tiny thing she almost dare not name: a feeble, stupid, slender embryonic sense of hope. She clings to it, and breathes. Suddenly, she understands, here at the mouth of the cave, in a moment of clarity, that doubts and fears, regrets and guilt, these things will not go away, perhaps not ever; these are just a part of the business of being, but that the other things, the good things, these are what matter, what she must fight for.

She glances across at Jacob. She must tell him all of this. Will he understand? They are sitting side by side. Shyly he puts his hand on top of hers. She does not move.

Together they gaze out into the void. Eventually she sighs.

"Is this real?" she murmurs.

"I don't ..." he begins, "I just don't know what to ..." but his voice tails away. Despite his uniform he looks so young, so lost. Their faces are almost touching. She can feel the heat of him.

"What I mean is ..." he begins again, whispering, his lips so close now, unbearably close. "What I mean ..." They both know it is happening. There is a moment of spectacular stillness between them.

"Sshhh," she says softly, and leans in to kiss him.

Night falls, a blaze of gold and orange glory. A long, arrow-headed skein of homesick geese slits the smoking sky, and a cold full moon rises slowly over the blue hills to the east. It is a sunset made for lovers or for poets, and is – quite rightly – a sight to which Jacob and Maria, wrapped tight at last in each other's arms, are utterly immune. In the chilling air they talk and kiss, and laugh, and talk some more, gently easing each other out of the whirlpool, until the great moon sinks beneath a cloud and then it is time, says Maria, for them to steal themselves a boat.

Chapter Thirty-Two

On the Tagus River, Spain, 1937

Lovely though it was, they were no longer gladdened by the presence of the huge full moon, whose brilliance illuminated the night in blue and silver shadow. But they had little choice, and so, as the clock struck midnight, they abandoned the safety of the cave entrance, and carefully made their way down towards the path that ran alongside the river, appalled by the clatter of the stones kicked away by their unseeing feet. Jacob, especially, felt sickeningly exposed, and was unable to stop thinking of how easy it would be for a half-decent rifleman to pick them off from any point along the city wall.

But their luck held, and soon they were standing breathless by the pitch-dark waters of the Tagus, enveloped by the mild, riverside stench of mud and fish. The white backs of resting gulls glowed dimly in the moonlight, and above the silence, they could hear the soft clanking of the wood-hulled skiffs which jostled with each other in the slow current.

Jacob looks at the row of boats, and turns to Maria to ask which one they should choose. But to his horror she is gone. With mounting panic he walks back a few steps, scanning the river and the darkness for any trace of her. The memory of the incident in Galicia forces itself into his mind. Ever since that day he has had a mistrust of boats and deep water, especially at night, and now he feels himself throttled by a paralysing fear. But suddenly, ahead, he catches a glimpse of movement, and in an instant her ghost-like form is beside him.

"Oars," she whispers. "I saw a stack of them back there. Let's go!"

Gulping down his relief, he says nothing, and watches her struggle for a moment with a knot in a rope, before he brings a blade from his pocket to help her, and together they step into a creaking, rocking rowboat. He almost loses an oar which catches in the squelching mud as he reaches behind to push them off, and as he steadies himself, he sees by moonlight that she is laughing. He rows inexpertly, but in the gentle current the boat moves swiftly, and soon the moon is hidden by the soaring cliffs which mark this stretch of the river, and as they melt into the blackness he begins at last to feel more safe.

They glide as much as row for the next few hours. Jacob has no plan beyond flight, and is uneasy at this journey into the unknown. As a soldier he has been trained to think methodically, to consider every step, and now he is quite literally drifting along in the dark; small wonder he is anxious. Yet Maria seems a beacon of calm to him. Inside she is still stunned by the miracle of her escape, and manages slowly to transmit her growing feeling of confidence.

"I know where we are, I think," she says. "There's a fishing village at a bend in the river. If we can get there before daylight, there's a woman who might help us. She's a ... let's just say she doesn't like your side."

A silence rides beside them on the oily current. Jacob is suddenly aware of the stench of the river, and of the cold and damp which are beginning to infuse his tiring legs. "My side?" he asks eventually. Maria knows he is asking the question to himself as much as to her and decides not to answer. They can deal with all that later. Instead she leans forward and puts her hands on his knees, and tries in the darkness to look at him.

"I wish I could still see you," he says. "When I can see you I think that things might be alright. When I can't, I just wonder what the hell I'm doing."

She is about to say more but suddenly there is a bump and they are both knocked sideways. Jacob grips the sides of the boat to steady himself, and realises that the boat has beached itself. Before he has the chance to move he sees that Maria has stepped ashore and is tugging at the boat to secure it properly.

"Pull it up here," she orders. "If we're where I think we are, we'll be safe for now."

He helps her to pull the little boat further inland, then waits as she tries to decide if her guess is correct.

"It's no good," she announces. "We'll need to wait until we can see properly. Shove up; we'll wait here on the riverbank."

They lie on their backs, looking up into the dying night. From time to time Jacob hears noises coming from what he guesses is a patch of woodland just behind them, branches snapping, snuffling, the call of an owl. Do they have wolves there, he wonders, or boar? He tries not to think about it. Nor can he bring himself to think about the last few days which have led him to this mad and perilous position. Instead he thinks just about the heat which emanates from the body lying next to him, and about the black carpet of stars which cover them. He wants to tell her that for some reason he had never felt more conscious, more mindful of these stars, that he'd never felt more fully alive, more aware of his own vital, ecstatic being than he did right then, but as he struggles to find the words he hears the steady rhythm of her breathing and realises that she is asleep. He smiles to himself.

To the east the first faint echo of dawn is pressing into the night, and the first birds are starting to sing. He closes his eyes, yawns, and rolls onto his side. The fury of the last few days is catching up with him. He can allow himself a quick ten minutes before the day breaks.

When he wakes, the sun is bright on his face. And he is alone.

Baffled, he stares at the river. Wisps of morning mist drift over the water, whose flat surface ripples from time to time from the mouths of fish which rise to feed on flies. A statue-like grey heron stands one-legged by their boat, and on the far bank he can see cattle make their slow way down to drink. Behind him are the woods that he had imagined in the night, and suddenly aware of his own visibility, he stands and begins to make a run towards the cover of the trees. He is only halfway there when someone calls out to halt him.

He stands stock still and turns to face the voice. There are three of them, further off than he had expected, but sound carries far in the silence of daybreak. Even with the sun behind them he can tell that it is her, and his heart lifts as he sees her begin to race towards him, a halo of light blazing out behind her as he tries to focus on her face.

"We're safe," she says breathlessly, embracing him. "At least for now. These are friends."

She introduces him to the two middle-aged women who accompanied her, and explains that she had met them when she worked for the barrel maker. They were sisters who ran the waterside tavern, and their husbands were woodsmen who had the rights to fell and season the oaks from the forests on that side of the river. She had guessed correctly that they would be no friends of Franco. Not only that, but the women had already offered to get them to a safe place. Even now, in the middle of the war, a cartload of unwanted, off-cut timber was sent each week to Aranjuez for use as firewood by the town's bakeries. There was one due to depart the next day, and there would be room for a couple of clandestine passengers.

Then what? Jacob wanted to know as they eat and talk all day and night in the attic above the tavern.

"Don't worry," she had explained. "Things are in motion. We lie low. I have a plan."

He wasn't really listening. Only a few short days before on the journey from Seville he had tormented himself in wondering whether he might ever become her *novio,* her man, when she was so special and there was so much to keep them apart. Now, in the heat and the dark of that small attic, and in the passion and the desperation of their needs, all those doubts had evaporated, and he was complete.

Chapter Thirty-Three

Aranjuez, 1937

He'd been at peace when she told him. She found him lying on his side, chewing on a liquorice stick she'd brought him that morning, and gazing out across the shining wet rooftops of Aranjuez to where a stork was adding twigs to a precarious nest on the chimneypots opposite.

"I have to go back," she said. "Back to your house, I mean."

At this he'd turned and looked at her, and she'd laughed aloud at the open-mouthed consternation on his face. He'd thought then that she was joking, and had smiled in response, but his smile died suddenly and he'd felt the awful, battle-dread bubble of panic rising up in his chest as he realised that she was in earnest.

There were documents, she explained, letters, perhaps, she hadn't really had time to examine them, but she had hidden them away in the seconds before she was caught and for all she knew they might still be there. There had been dozens of envelopes in those satchels, she'd taken several at random, and if the soldiers that evening were little more than couriers then they may not even have realised what they were missing. She would have no rest until she knew for certain. She didn't have any choice in the matter, she just had to go back.

Jacob argued that the documents would probably contain meaningless, insignificant reports on uniforms or headlice or pencil-sharpeners. Nothing worth taking any risks over. In fact, chances were the documents weren't still there anyway, and inconsequential besides: he himself had seen thousands of such items, had written them even; it just wasn't worth it.

But in his heart he knew she was right. Anything you knew about the enemy, anything, could prove unexpectedly useful. All information, any information, should be examined carefully, and in the hands of a skilled intelligence corps all kind of deduction and inference could be teased out to help make sense of a bigger picture. All this he had been taught at cadet school, and the message reinforced countless times thereafter.

And he knew too the expression on her face. She was scared, she was torn, but she was determined. He saw that he had little choice. He thought quickly, improvising; together they could maybe manage something. He began to make extempore plans to get them back after dark; he was beginning to see how it could be done.

But at that moment she stepped away from him, shielding him from the falling light at the window, and thrust her hands towards him, palms outspread, controlling, not imploring.

"No," she said. "I'm going alone."

A pause. She could see the muscles in his jaw moving as he sought to gainsay this command. As he began to speak she put down one arm, and came to him, bringing her face close to his, putting a hand to his cheek.

"You can't," she murmured with great gentleness. "You just can't. You stand out, they'd see you. I know you want to help, I know you're brave, but just your being there might make it more difficult for us."

He stiffened. Without his knowing, the hairs on the nape of his neck had risen like the fur of a startled dog.

"Us?" he said.

She broke the contact, inhaled, turned to stare out of the dusty window.

This was the moment he had feared. He knew so little about her. In his innocence had he misread the situation? She's so competent, so pretty, so passionate; it's obvious that there must be someone else somewhere who holds the key to her heart. He should have known all along. Idiot. The brick at the pit of his stomach grew weightier. Still he waited for her to speak, watching a tiny spider on the surface of the fly-blown mirror. The stork, he noticed, has gone. A church bell rang in the far distance, there were children shouting in the street below, a coral sun was setting. Someone somewhere was frying fish in old oil; a repulsive smell, he noted. All these things he took in on the surface of his being. He was properly aware of his surroundings, he absorbed them, but they were irrelevant. The world was moving around him as normal, but he was frozen as he watched her gather her thoughts.

Until at last she spoke. "We ... my group. I'm a communist, you know that, we work together. I've told you so often. And I'm proud of it, it's a part of who I am. And listen: we are an army, Jacob. I may not look or sound like a soldier, but I am. Like you. Most of us don't have uniforms, we don't march up and down and parade, and too few of us have guns, but still we fight, we face danger, we die."

A moment earlier the distance between them had seemed immense, but she crossed the room and reached him in two light steps.

Again she took his face between her two hands. He had the smell of her again, could see tiny beads of perspiration on her top lip, see the white scar of the parting in the raven-black hair.

"But not soon," she soothed, "not this time. This will be easy, you'll see. I just need to go back to tell them exactly where to look. I can't ever go back, but I know someone who can."

They stared into each other's eyes, each softly challenging the other to be the first to look away, then they kissed. Their bodies folded together, pressing, and for a long time they held each other like this, trapped in the stillness and the silence of the threadbare room. Slowly, slowly, the rhythm of Jacob's breathing returned to him, until at last he could take that great deep gulp of air that he'd been waiting for, and as it escaped him, part sigh, part groan, he held her tighter. There is no-one else involved, he knew now, no one waiting for her, it's just him. He was stupid to be jealous, and undignified. But this knowledge and the relief were tempered by something else: all this while he had been thinking selfishly, about himself, about her, about them; ignoble thoughts. But she ... she was still on the high ground, magnanimous, generous, committed to her cause, her movement, her people, and she would put her life in peril for them. He felt diminished, he didn't deserve her; could he ever be so great-hearted?

And so she must go. And that same night they had parted, each of them ham-fistedly enacting a nonchalance and bravura for the benefit of the other.

Three nights. That was what they had calculated. One to go there, one to get into the house, and one to get back.

And that had been five days ago. By now Jacob is frantic, deranged almost. The first three days had passed agonizingly slowly, but that was part of the plan and so had been bearable, just. The walls seem to be closing in on him. The flat hadn't seemed small when there were two of them there; now it felt minute. He had never been much of a reader, but this time, in isolation, he had forced himself to plough through several of the books on the shelf. Secretly, he had actually enjoyed the Flaubert, and he also now knew more than any man strictly needed to know about wheat production in the Soviet Union, but the time for reading was past. Now he stared out of the window, grinding his teeth, mad and unsure, he felt as if he were pawing the ground like the goaded bulls in the ring. In the morning, to his horror he sees that the stork's nest is no longer there, blown down by the wind. Is it an omen? He must go, must strike. But go where, strike whom? He loads and re-loads his gun, cleans it again and again. He can't take this much longer. In the morning he will go and find her.

It had been agreed that the old woman would come each day, tapping on the door exactly after the church bells had struck eleven. She would bring food and fresh water, but he wasn't allowed to talk to her, and was never, ever to open the door to anyone at any other time. There was a strong bolt on the door, and if anyone were to force it, he was to shoot them.

He must have fallen asleep. In his dream he was travelling on a cattle truck, and great horses were bothering him with their kicks to the walls of their stall; he was angry with them. But in a heartbeat he's awake. Someone is knocking on the door. He looks outside to the church clock: just after seven, and almost dark. Shit. Sweet Christ, who was this? He's reaching under the bed, searching for the revolver when he hears a voice. "It's me, Jacob, it's me," and in an instant he's there at the door, scrabbling at the lock, desperate.

He stares at her in disbelief. She's smiling at him as if nothing is wrong, laughing at the hair sticking up on his head and the stubble on his sleep-filled face. Emotions fill him too fast to process, as if he were trying to focus on trees through the small window of a speeding train. Fear has left him, then relief, then momentary rage that she can appear so normal. Then delight, which lingers. Together they stoop to pick up her bag, collide, laugh, skip jinking into the room, talking,

talking as they lock the heavy door behind them.

Piece by piece her story emerges. He has nothing to tell; he decides to play down his anxieties which now seem infantile and unjustified. But he needs to learn every detail of her venture.

She had travelled back to Toledo with "comrades", on this occasion strawberry growers who travelled through the cool of the night to get their produce to market the next day. They were gypsies, who sang all night until they reached the outskirts of the city; she hadn't managed much sleep. From there she had walked to the house of an old workmate, whose loyalties were indisputable. With her help it had been easy to contact their mole, their spy, in Jacob's family's household. At first Jacob was outraged, then incredulous. Was it Edouardo, the houseboy, or Maximino, the old guy who worked in the stables? Neither. One was a half-wit and the other she wouldn't trust if he were the last man alive. She teases him, gives him a clue. Pull back the curtain and look in the closet there, she instructs. Who else has pots like that? Confused, he peers at the burnished copper pans that seem to glimmer in the half-light. She squeals as recognition kindles on his face.

"No way! God, no. Not the cook? Not our cookie? You mean she's one of you?" Then, "One of us?" he adds timorously, trying out the words for the first time.

She was indeed. He's chuckling properly; good old cookie. And the old lady that brought him food? Didn't he know her now? Cook's mother! He could see that now.

It was true, they had people everywhere. "That son-of-a-bitch Mola can brag all he wants about his Fifth Column," she says with fire in her eyes, "but we've got hundreds, thousands of Columns an inch long. We're termite Columns, that's what we are, tiny, invisible, deadly, unkillable termites."

But she'd choked on the word unkillable. She looks down for a moment. "They murdered your cook's brother, you see. The old lady's youngest son. That's why they're with us, why the old girl brings us food."

He takes her hand. And you, he wants to ask, why are you so committed? What foul thing did they do to your family? But he misses the moment; some other time he'll ask her, for by now she's rooting in the pack she had been carrying.

"She's astute, your cookie. Told us to have someone put a brick through the window to make it look like a burglary, then stole all this stuff from your sister's room." She looks at him defiantly. "She's my size. I might need some travelling clothes, some disguise. Like it?" she asks, and swirls across the floor with his sister's coat held in front of her. And stops. "Something else, too: a jewellery box, with a chain and some earrings. I feel a bit bad about that, that's maybe too much. It's in the pack somewhere, you should have that."

But any misgivings she may have had about the theft were lifted the second she withdrew her hand again. "There's this too, she sent you this." And with a flourish she opens up a wax paper package containing a whole *tortilla* and a small bottle of wine.

The tortilla doesn't last long. Later, the old lady comes again with cheese and dried sausage. Jacob looks at her humbly, shakes her hand, tries to read her expression, but she leaves before he can speak.

They are still trapped in their safe house, though unlike the previous days, Jacob hardly notices as the hours slip by. All day they talk and make plans, slowly sipping on the stolen wine.

As night falls, she observes him, half crouching under the eaves of the small canteen at the back of the room, as he begins to put away the plates at the end of their meal.

She goes to him. "Jacob. God help me, I'm so ... so ashamed, but there's something else I need to do," she tells him, and pulls him towards her so that he can stand upright. He raises a questioning eyebrow. He looks worried, though sees the smile in her eyes. "Something I've thought about a lot. Too much, " she says, and with some shyness, reaches up to him and undoes the top three buttons on his shirt, and begins softly to kiss his hairless chest. As she turns to blow out the candle, he trembles slightly in the darkness, enraptured, as her cool fingers go about their work, button after button after button.

Chapter Thirty-Four

Falling into exile, 1937

He had studied her as she put them on carefully, his mouth dry, half incapacitated by love and longing. He'd seen them years before when worn by his sister, had felt their sullen weight in his hand, seen them flicker in the light. But never like this. Now he marvelled as, backlit by the dawn, the earrings caught the sun and shone, accentuating the lines of her long, smooth neck. She has tied up her hair in a black silk scarf, and is smiling indecipherably at her reflection in the mirror, aware of him watching, aware of her beauty. The earrings seem to give her greater poise, confidence. He sees that she is transforming herself, sees that as she discards her old boots and puts on the low-heeled court shoes, that she is becoming something else, a mystery, a new thing, elegant and secret. He wants to tell her this, to describe to her this enigmatic shift, but he feels guileless and clumsy; he senses that he is being left behind somehow. As witness to this sleek metamorphosis, he is at once exalted and disturbed: he's thrilled by her beauty, but she seems suddenly so much more sophisticated, more fully developed than he. Physically he is so much bigger, so much stronger, but he is beginning to feel childlike by comparison.

He struggles maladroitly to find the right words. "They suit you; you look so ... so changed. So ... I don't know, well, like a real, grown-up woman..."

Perplexed, she looks at him for a moment, narrows her eyes and fixes him with her most imperious stare, adopting the look she had seen his mother give to tradesmen, then sticks out her tongue and collapses into giggles.

"Cretin," she laughs, "so what was I before, what was I last night in bed then, if not a grown-up woman, eh?"

But she can see that he is troubled, and that he is trying inexpertly to tell her something, so she speaks again, thoughtful this time.

"It's just a shell I'm wearing, a costume. A disguise. It's me, but it's not me. It's like you and your uniform. You look great in it, more than great, but it's not you, not you really, not who you are. It always frightened me a little when you went away in it, big soldier man, it still does frighten me sometimes, it's what the bloody thing represents, the awful things ... it's, it's ..." She too is struggling for words. "It's just so weird, so ... perverse, that I can hate, just hate, that fucking jacket, yet love the boy inside it." She stops abruptly, looks down, the weight of the words she has just spoken dragging her gaze to the ground.

When a moment later she raises her head, she sees that he is smiling softly: he heard what she said. She's flustered, strangely fearful, but inside, she is smiling too. So she purses her lips to subdue the scarcely bearable joy that all the while has been churning and moiling inside her, and crosses the room to gather her thoughts.

An ancient terracotta pot hangs from a wire to the roof, the water within still delicious and cool from the previous night. She sips from a chipped mug, then picks an apple from the basket, takes a bite, then hands it to Jacob, who has been watching her intently. She makes an effort to avoid his eyes. She's not sure why, but for some reason a tiny voice deep down is urging her to shield the superabundance of affection she is feeling for him. When at last she speaks she sounds petulant, and instantly regrets it, which makes her more cross with herself, and with the situation, and paradoxically with him.

"Look at my hands," she bemoans, and waves them in his face. "All that toil for your ungrateful family, then busted up by your army pals." Two nails are blackened from her mistreatment in the prison, others are cracked, and the skin on her fingers is coarse and red from constant over-work. "How can I dress up as a toff with paws like this?"

Jacob mulls this over, puzzled by the change of mood. "They're not my pals, not anymore," he mutters. Then, "What about gloves?" he asks, hopefully, but as she spins on her heel he realises his suggestion has not gone well with her.

She stands by the window. She's not angry, but tired, and is sad that the special lightness she had been feeling has slipped from the room without her noticing. Her forehead is resting gently on the glass, and she gazes unfocussed on the silent people beyond as they step unimportantly about their daily lives.

And then she sees ... no, it couldn't be. Is it him? Fat. Grey, military hair. Powerful in the black suit he wore. Not again. This hasn't happened for months, not even in the prison. It isn't him after all, a false alarm, but still. She tries to breathe deeply to steady herself, but the deep breath she craves just won't come and she hears the little gasps she is taking, panting almost. She must stop this, she knows, she just can't let Jacob see her, not like this.

Nonplussed, he watches as she moves away from him. Her reaction is unfathomable to him; for all his adult life he has inhabited the hermetic world of the male soldier, whose emotions are not so much suppressed as ignored. This is new territory. He has always been aware of certain complex, tender feelings spinning around inside him, deep down, but his upbringing has always lead him to believe that to allow them to surface is somehow unworthy, weak. But he's certain too that Maria is as gutsy and courageous as any soldier, yet she wears her heart on her sleeve and is as emotionally passionate as anyone he has ever met. What then, if it isn't weakness, but strength? One by one all his rock-solid convictions are being challenged, and he feels adrift. He knows she is upset, but isn't sure if he is the cause, nor how he can help.

She crosses the room, hands held to her abdomen, and sits facing the wall, away from him. The floor is cold and hard, with deep dirt-filled cracks between the red earth tiles, each one chafed and pitted and worn by the booted feet of generations. As she sits, her skirt swishes noisily and a cloud of venerable dust rises into the warm, still air. She settles with her knees pressed to her chest, arms held tight across her shins, absorbing into herself, slowly rocking back and forth to the rhythm of some ancient, unseen pulse.

In the half-light where she sits, Jacob can make out the listless sway of the earrings, whose sparkle has been replaced by a sullen glow. He can feel her slipping, pulling away from him, her absence a bruise, and though she is but a few steps away he feels powerless to go to her.

Her face is pale and she's concentrating hard. It's coming again, she thinks, oh God, no, it's coming again, and there's nothing I can do to stop it. She turns to him, alarmed, breathing faster, trying to control the rising panic. Despite herself, she begins to shake, and as she glances at him again she sees the confusion on his face. Her great, gentle, Jacob, she's got to tell him, he doesn't deserve this. But she can't, simply can't, and when she sees again the fear and the sadness in his eyes, she sobs. He hears her whimper, sees a tear as it's drunk in by the desiccated floor, and moves instinctively to her side.

He's inarticulate, unsure whether he should touch her, but gradually she's warmed by his presence, and forces herself to lean back against him, her breath coming in gasps as she escapes from the rocking that had held her. Tentatively he puts an arm around her, and together they sit in silence as the sun makes its way slowly along the wall.

"I'm sorry," she says eventually. "It just sometimes comes upon me like that, not so often now, but it still happens. Out of nowhere, I get scared, I just panic, I don't know what to do, and I'm so, so embarrassed and …"

She stops. She suddenly realises she isn't embarrassed, not here in the silence, in his arms. She swivels and looks deep into his eyes, kisses him on the cheek, breathes deep. She has to tell him; she can do this.

"You have to know something…"

He stares at her, trusting, saying nothing, until she goes on.

"I'm just so full of anger sometimes. Not just anger, but a black, bitter rage. Like I'm full of hate, full of … madness, I guess."

He nods at her, encouraging, but puzzled.

"It's this … that … a long time ago, well, not that long, I was just a girl, fourteen, and a man came to your house, your family house, and he liked me, he wanted me to work in his house. I didn't want to go, I wanted to stay there, with you, you were my friend, I was happy there, but your dad said I had to go. I was so mad, I didn't even get chance to say goodbye to you, you'd gone away for the summer, and I had to go and … and … and …" she stumbles, sobs, till finally she can say the words. "… and, he took me, Jacob, that bastard raped me … I fought him, scratched, bit, kicked, but he hit me so hard, there was nothing I could do." She squeezes his hand. He is pale, silent. "I swore I'd never go back to them, but then, but then the group said I could help them, that I could hit back, get revenge, but still, still I said I would never, and then it was you, it was you I wanted to see again, get close to, it was for revenge yes, but also it was to see you too, and then the war started, and they told me to steal that stuff that night and it got all serious and …"

Her voice tails off. Jacob is stunned beyond comprehension. He wants to ask questions, wants to know all of it and none of it, and wants, more than anything, to find this man and to hurt him. After the battle of Jarama he'd thought for a while that he'd seen enough of violence, pain, murder, had worried that perhaps he was becoming a pacifist. Another time, in the small hours, in bed after the episode at the bullring when he'd pulled away the Guardia who had kicked the prostrate girl, he had experienced the opposite. He really could have killed that afternoon, and had lain awake that night, appalled by the senselessness and brutality of the man, yet disgusted by his own bloodlust, and the knowledge that he had come so close to losing control and shooting the policeman dead.

But that – the revenge, the justice – all that can come later, he thinks. What he needs to do now, he knows intuitively, is to stay gentle, and to hold and comfort Maria until the panic and the memories subside, and so they sit there, talking quietly from time to time, waiting for calm to return.

Eventually she looks at him through red-rimmed eyes, shrugs, and gives a determined smile. "It's over," she says, "It's done. I might ask you some time, but you must never speak of it to me, that's important for me to know that you won't drag it up. Also, I'll never say his name, never. It's gone now. Usually I try and look on it as just a fight that I lost, that's all; it doesn't matter so much then. He took a bit of my dignity and I took a lot of his hair." She smiles again.

She wants to make light of it. It's almost as if it's her consoling him. She knows at some level that she should stop, but still the words flow out of her. It's strange, she sees from a distance; she's not talking to Jacob as such, it's more that she's musing aloud, and that in his presence the vileness is being exorcised, and her demons cast out.

"For so long I was broken inside. I couldn't talk to anyone about it, I couldn't bear for anyone to touch me. For a while I couldn't go outside some days, they – the attacks, like just now – I'd know one might happen and I'd try and stop it and …" She pauses. "I'm better now, almost better … I swore I'd never tell you, but, you know what, just telling you … just telling you now, it feels like a great stone, a tombstone, has been lifted off my chest and I can breathe again." She holds him tighter. "There were boys. I kissed them, to try really, to see if I could, to see if I was normal; I didn't like them. But … I've been building myself up bit by bit, putting myself back together, bone by bone, do you see that? There was a man too, an older man, my teacher, part of the group, and I was so relieved that I liked him, that I was attracted to him, he talked to me a little, he was Russian, treated me like I was someone, showed me respect, that's all it was, but he's a homosexual, he doesn't like girls, not like that, and he went away, but he was important to me. I miss him, he was a friend, he taught me stuff, and all the time I kept thinking about you, just you, Jacob, about how wrong-headed you were to be in the thick of it with all the army swine, and if only I could tell you and …" she realises that she is rambling, perhaps she's said too much.

She looks sideways at him. The colour has come back to him and she can sense the calm in him returning. She stands abruptly, eases into a long stretch, drinks from the pitcher, then wets her hands and flicks cool water at him, and pulls him to his feet to join her at the window.

They stand there for a while, at peace.

"There's something else," she says after a while.

"Yes?" he says distractedly. She can tell he is concentrating on something outside the window. Then he says the strangest thing. "That bird there, you see it? That stork, it's rebuilding its nest. I'm so glad."

At this she laughs out loud. "It can wait," she says, and pulls him to her.

Chapter Thirty-Five

A long, hot walk, 1937

She knows they are in for a long and dangerous journey across the scalding, arid backways of empty Castille. "*Vaya con Dios,*" the old lady had said to her at daybreak as they left, insisting that they take with them the loaf of grey unleavened bread and a gourd filled with garlic-flavoured chickpeas. "*Go with God.*" And all that day it had seemed to Maria that somehow the Almighty might even be taking a special interest in her at last, even though she was no longer sure if she believed in Him, the certainties of her childhood having been punctured so badly by wretchedness and the atheistic leanings of her left-wing friends. But be that as it may, for whatever reason, this day she felt good, she felt light, and for the first time in ages, she felt hopeful.

Whatever happened they had to keep moving south. Somewhere in the distant port of Adra there were people waiting for them, for whom the contents of the documents she carried were perhaps significant. And they would be safe there, at least for a while. For this reason she was able to call on the help of certain comrades, who, through a clandestine network of sympathisers, had been able to organise the transport in which they now travelled. It was practical, though certainly not comfortable: a converted livestock truck which drove weekly to the city from Manzanares, crammed with fruit-pickers, parcels and hampers of Manchego cheese. It took most of the morning, and by time they arrived they were both thoroughly sick.

The lorry stopped to let them descend at a crossroads just outside the town, since they had to avoid populated places at all costs. They would walk cross-country from here, taking their chances as best they could. They crouched in a ditch out of sight as the vehicle belched onwards, then stood warily. Their caution was unnecessary, for there was not a soul in sight. Maria eyed the low-lying hills to their left as she drank from her flask.

"Suppose we walk two hours that way, see if we can manage it, then stop for a break? You up to that, soldier?"

"You may have to carry me," he says as he tightens the straps on his pack. "You up to that?"

The hills were further than they had imagined, perspective playing tricks on them in the flatness of the landscape, and they are tired by the time they settle to rest for a while. Maria can already feel the journey in the aching of her legs, and her throat is tight from the dust and so much talking, but as she bites into her bread she is exultant.

Along the way they'd found watercress as they crossed the fast-flowing brook, they'd gorged on last year's unpicked almonds, and now their hands are still stained the deep colours of dark wine from the sour sweet juice of the mulberries they had found at noon. Laughing, Jacob had stopped with his finger the blood-red trail that had trickled down her neck as she ate, then moved closer and stopped it again with a kiss, with his tongue. She quivers inside as she remembers the touch of his mouth on her throat; she had known from the look in his eyes that he'd wanted to make love again, right there in the woods, but sensibly she'd hurried them along and back onto the track. There was time enough for that later, all the time in the world. All the same, it had been difficult for her to remain prudent: she could never admit it to anyone, but she has been strangely thrown off balance by the depth of her desire for him.

It is now three o'clock in the afternoon. Jacob, in his drab peasant's rags, keeps his watch in his pocket, concerned that it might draw attention. They are resting for the day on the slopes of a low hill which gives the soldier in him a commanding field of vision. Twice he has wandered around the abandoned farmstead and declares himself satisfied. For an instant Maria wants to challenge his assumed authority, but she sees that he is right, and besides, it is so unbearably hot that all thought of argument leeches from her, so she rolls onto her face in the shade of a time-crippled wall. She considers whether to venture inside the derelict building, but knows it is likely to be infested with fleas, and calls instead for Jacob to lie down beside her.

Beneath them the high meseta of La Mancha stretches out seemingly forever, toasted and smouldering, the stubble in the endless fields a sea of burnt sienna straw. She breathes the heavy scent of thyme, of a summer's worth of dust, of eternity. Bruised by the weight of the omnipotent sun, the unreachable blue mountains to the south are fused together in the shimmering light. Soon she knows they must cross these mountains, but for now they are so, so far away, and meaningless. She takes in the grandeur and timelessness of these great plains, whose uniformity is broken only by the occasional copse of Holm oak, and by the great white sails of the windmills whose eternal job it is to drive water from the wet bowels of the earth far below, sleeping now in the furnace of late afternoon.

There is not a breath of wind. A half-lame ox with a malevolent bloodshot eye walks past without acknowledging their presence, then flops suddenly as if shot, in a cloud of red smut. As the dust settles, even the flies on his emaciated back are stunned to silence by the heat. Now and then they can hear the periodic swish of the rope like tail as he tries half-heartedly to lessen his torment. A khaki-coloured tick, disappointed perhaps by the thinness of his host's blood, squats obscene and only half engorged on the ox's ear. The ox is sprawled within a makeshift palisade in which desiccated branches like the sun-bleached thighbones of giants have been forced into the parched earth as a rudimentary fence. Each branch is spotted with the creamy shells of dozens of edible snails. At least they won't go hungry this night.

The landscape here is disfigured by the presence of man: the pelt of a long dead fox is nailed to what's left of the primitive gate, a stone water trough lays cracked and empty in the corner of the hoof-puckered yard, whilst somnolent horse flies stand sentinel over their domain of shrivelled, sun-crusted cow turds. Yet Maria is blind to the ugliness, deaf to the buzzing of flies. She is alive, fully alive at last, and she is free.

She lies now on her back, a straw between her lips, holding out a hand against the sun so that she can watch a pair of eagles. Jacob meanwhile is watching her in turn, absorbing her profile. "What?" she says finally, grinning, as she feels the pressure of his gaze.

"Nothing," he replies, "just nothing," and smiles before rolling on to his back to watch the birds with her.

"Imagine," he says after a while, "if we could only talk to them. The eagles, I mean; I've often wondered about that."

She looks at him mockingly. "Sure," she says, "we could chat about all sorts …"

"I mean it," he persists. " I mean if they could only tell us what they could see from up there, what's over the next hill, who's about to come marching over that hill, it could change everything. Imagine if a general could know *exactly* where the enemy is hiding, how many extra troops he has in reserve, how many cannon ... imagine in history ... Imagine, say, if Scipio, if the Romans, could have seen Hannibal trooping over the alps like that, there'd be no surprise, no advantage, no victory. A single eagle could have changed the outcome of history."

"A talking eagle, then?" she says, poking him. "But you're right, it's all just information."

"That's how battles are won and lost. You need to know what the other side is doing ..."

They look at each other awkwardly, and then at the bundle of their possessions.

"Those letters," she says at last, "I don't know what they mean, or if they're important or not, but I am going to get them to Adra, or if all else fails, to the English in Gibraltar, no matter what." Her voice trails off. Then, "No matter what," she repeats, softer this time.

He pulls her closer, so that her head is resting on his chest. He can feel the heat in her hair.

"And I'm going with you ... for Tino. Tino and for all the others. And for you."

They stay like this for a while, overpowered by the silence, the scent of scorched soil, and the wistful awareness that they cannot linger.

Suddenly, from the corner of his eye, he spies a shadow speeding towards them, and glancing up sees the outline of an eagle as it hurtles through the air. "Look!" he says, and she just has time to focus before the great bird passes overhead, so close that they hear the whoosh of the wind in its feathers. A split second later they feel a momentary dimness as it blocks out the sun. She shudders. "Touched by the shadow of death, eh?" says Jacob, but she shushes him with her finger and they lay there a while longer, trying to re-capture the moment.

"How many nights before we get to Bailen?" she asks eventually.

"Three, I guess, if we make good time."

She sighs, turns, hooks her leg behind his, presses herself against him, and digs her fingernails into his shoulder, her lips so close he can feel the breath on her as she murmurs, "Four. At least four, please …"

"At least," he agrees, and pushes her face slightly from him. Shamelessly he can now lock his eyes to hers. He sees how her pupils are dilated, and, as the sun finally begins to set, he kisses her, oblivious to the universe beyond.

Chapter Thirty-Six

Another party, Madrid, 2012

"You want to come to a fiesta, English girl?" was all the text had said, and "Si," had been her brief reply.

It was not much of a dialogue, and she was tired, but nonetheless Jess discovered that she was looking forward to the unexpected party, and had dressed carefully. However, as she walked out of the station at La Latina, she had begun to wish that she hadn't been so brave. Despite the attack in the park, she was determined not to allow herself to become afraid of the city, and had chosen to take the metro. But now she wasn't quite sure that this had been a good idea. As a single woman, alone, on a dark street in an unfamiliar city, she suddenly felt vulnerable. It wasn't that she was intimidated by the louche clusters of punks and goths, or unsettled by the swaggering, leather-clad fetishists as they headed out to their clubs, or by the junkies or mean-eyed police; she'd lived in London long enough to be fascinated by this diversity. But she hated to feel exposed, and her bruises were still raw, so it was with a certain feeling of relief that she found the address so easily.

It was a *Corrala,* one of the classic tenement buildings of that part of the city, on the way out to Lavapiès. Stefan had told her that although the area was still chic and bohemian, it was becoming increasingly gentrified, although not quite the gentry that her mother would have recognised, she thought, as she gave way to the two spaced-out grungy weirdos who passed her on the stairwell.

From outside the flat she could hear the thump of loud music. For a second she fought the urge to flee, and was still weighing up her options when the door swung open. Stefan stood there smiling with a bottle of beer in each hand. Before he could speak, a woman pushed in front and squinted at her.

"Doesn't look like a victim. Not to me, anyway," she said, still peering. "Seems alright to me. Must be special. He never comes to parties, you know. You should feel honoured."

Stefan winced. "Jess," Stefan said. "Meet Susanna. She's insane. She's one of our patients. We only let her out at the weekends. Don't pay her any attention unless she actually bites."

The woman smiled. "Come on in," she said. "There are plenty of normal people here too. I'll try and keep this loser away from you."

Jess followed them across the smoky room and into a kitchen at the back where two men were grilling flatbreads on a huge hotplate. Even though it was quieter here they still had to shout. Jess looked around and suddenly realised just how pleased she was to be there. There must have been at least fifty people crammed into the little flat, people of all ages and backgrounds. Susanna drifted around like some warm-hearted earth mother dispensing drinks and bonhomie, shadowed by a tall, good-looking woman in red. Jess guessed they were probably the oldest people in the room. At one point she saw them kiss, and she looked across at Stefan; that was one theory about him she could now discount, she decided. He saw her looking and came over to her side. They danced, like everyone else.

It was two am before people started to leave. Stefan walked with her to find a taxi, the silence outside ringing in her ears as if she'd been to a rock concert. The walls all around were covered in graffiti and street art. A few bars were still open, and outside a 24-hour Asian supermarket they had to step aside to allow a mini garbage lorry to squeeze by.

"This is such a cool neighbourhood," she said. "I love that they manage to keep it so tidy, even at night."

"You should see it tomorrow," he replied, "after the *rastro,* the street market. The biggest in Spain. By the time everyone leaves the place is knee-high in rubbish, not only in all the sweet wrappers and cans but also with the tat and bric-a-brac that the vendors can't even give away." He hesitated. "Do you want to see it?"

"What? The biggest pile of garbage in the country? My, you know how to treat a girl!"

"With chocolate and *churros*?"

"A whole portion? I'm in! What time?"

She felt very differently about the station when she returned the following day. Now, in the bright, bustling daylight she felt at home, swept up by the energy of the crowd, and was privately half-ashamed of her fears from the previous evening.

Pop-up stalls lined every square inch of the pavements. Some were weather-proof booths, others just a sheet of plastic spread out on the floor. It was part Brick Lane, part school jumble sale, part *Antiques Road Show* and part French *Brocante*, but animated by the rambunctious clamour of ten thousand Madridilenos on their ritual sugar and coffee-fuelled Sunday morning high. Everywhere there was the excited whiff of frying food, of impulse buys, bargains, scams and double-dealings, and everyone was there, from women in heels and pearls, to dudes in fake Dior shades and attitude. She watched as two men haggled over a Lladro figurine; one wore a sombre Crombie coat, the other a vest and pierced nipples, and each man handled the piece with equal reverence.

At last they found themselves a seat at a zinc table whose wonky legs were propped by a broken vinyl record, and sat down to watch the world stroll by.

"Trouble with churros," Stefan explained, "is they have this weird tipping point, and no matter what you do, it leaves you feeling bad. Just a few grammes either way is all it takes: either you leave too much on the plate and feel dissatisfied, or you take the extra bit and feel stuffed." They were both looking at the last one; the chocolate in the cup was long gone.

"All yours," she said. "I'm done."

"I'll try it with sugar," he said, and tore open a small white sachet. "Sugar for my bones."

"Hey. That's what Maria always said. About the sugar."

"Maria? Your old lady friend. She sounds great. Was she a sugar lady?"

As the waiter cleared away their table she began to tell him about Maria, and continued as they ambled around the packed streets. As the crowds began to thin she carried on talking, and continued long into their lunch. She filled in details of Maria's life, and tried to second-guess some of her movements and motives as a girl. And then to her surprise she found herself talking about her own father, and of how much she'd learned about grief when he'd died so young, about the failed two years at boarding school, and of the tensions she now experienced with her mum.

And all the time Stefan seemed to listen to her, asking gentle questions here and there, and prompting her for details.

When she looked at her watch she saw that it was almost five o'clock. She felt drained.

"God! I'm so sorry. I've just dumped my life story on you. I didn't mean to."

"Don't you worry," he said seriously. "If I didn't want to listen I would have stopped you. And your story about Maria – it touched me somehow. There's something so heartrending about people who have to withstand that kind of torment for so long, and at that distance, and all without ever knowing the truth."

He looked up at the contemporary glass buildings all around them. "And we're supposed to be a *modern* country ... you know how many people there are still in unmarked graves here? More than a hundred thousand! In the twenty first century. It's a national disgrace. We're so avant-garde in so many ways, and yet still so backward in others. When Franco died nearly everyone accepted the need for the Pacto del Olvido, the Pact of Forgetting; it seemed the only way to handle things. But that was only supposed to last us through the transition to democracy, and look where we are today. How can we possibly learn from our past mistakes if we're told that we have to forget?"

He stopped suddenly.

"Hey," he said. "Sorry. Maybe I just answered my own question. Maybe we just can't talk about it yet because even now we all get so worked up about it. Maybe in another couple of hundred years we'll get over it."

"I knew an Irish girl whose dad used to celebrate the day that Oliver Cromwell died with a special pint of Guinness. People have long memories."

"And when did he die?"

"1658 ... so you've a way to go yet. Mind you, this guy used to have a special pint of Guinness most nights, so that doesn't really count."

Stefan shook his head and laughed.

"Listen, if you're serious about trying to find out about what happened to old Jacob, you should talk to Susanna. She knows everything and everyone. She's a Human Rights Lawyer, and a good one. You might not think it, but she's famous too, and often on the telly. When she lets her hair down, like last night, she comes across as a bit ... alternative, but there'd be no better place to start than with her."

"You're too late," said Jess. "I talked with her last night. She's going to set me up with an appointment at the Military Archives. At least she said she was going to contact them, and arrange for me to see them on Tuesday."

"Impressive. That was fast. She's usually so busy it takes ages."

"To be honest she said she was doing it for you." She smiled again. "She said she'd just deduct it from what she owes you for the painting."

"Typical! I'll talk to my lawyer about that. Hang on, she is my lawyer ..."

They parted soon after, with a promise that Jess would call him. She liked that he'd asked her to call him, rather than the other way around, so that she wouldn't feel hassled. On the bus back to her hotel she tried to analyse him. He wasn't shy, or reserved, or distant, or aloof. He was none of those things. Nor was he flirtatious, not really, or insistent. Other than that she didn't really know that much about him. But he was funny, and he listened to her properly, like a friend.

Chapter Thirty-Seven

Jess searches the military archives, Madrid, 2012

Could it be true? One hundred kilometres of shelving, she was sure that's what he had said. And he certainly didn't look like an archivist, not to her mind, more like a good-looking actor pretending to be one. She had expected a frail, dust-covered kind of chap, blinking in the sunlight as he emerged from the stygian depths of the Archivo Historico de Madrid, within whose sound-cushioned walls she was now standing. But despite whatever surprises that might lay in his looks, as a custodian and detector of army records he was unquestionably proficient.

It really hadn't been difficult to locate the family, he told her, as they had been members of the same regiment as far back at least as the 1870s. Maybe even before that, if she had time to do a little more digging. The search itself was straightforward, although he was a little puzzled as to what had actually happened.

"It looks like it didn't end particularly well for them, did it?" he says. "I guess you knew that."

"Yeah ... we know most of it," Jess lied. "It's more about fleshing out the details."

But details, alas, he was unable to provide. Out of three officers of the same distinguished family, two were marked simply: "Missing. Case Closed."

"It's not that strange, really," he explained. "There was so much confusion then, so much distraction, that there are holes in the records everywhere, especially for the squaddies – the low ranking soldiers, that is. This case is more, shall we say, *incongruous.*" He leans a little closer to her. "Your lot were senior officers. Between you and me, it wouldn't be any surprise at all if they hadn't upset someone higher up …"

He went on to describe how Jacob had been a model young officer, with no real controversy. His final entry in the archives showed him registering a motorbike which had been sequestered in Sevilla. And after that: nothing, which was relatively strange in itself for someone of his background. The case of the father, Carlos, was equally peculiar. Hundreds of pages chronicled a long and illustrious career, but which terminated abruptly with a dispatch from the Ambassador in Argentina.

The circumstances of the elder brother, Lucas, were at least conclusive, but still rather sad. He had been a loyal and able staff officer, fast-tracked to the rank of major, and twice decorated for bravery. And yet at the end of the war he had been transferred out of the army and made governor of a prison near Alicante, where he had died just two years later of typhus fever, along with the majority of the inmates. It was a humble conclusion to what had been such a glittering start, and poor reward for his efforts during the fighting.

"So you'd be excused for thinking that they had somehow made enemies; it would certainly fit the narrative of envy, punishment and exile that's never too far away from any hierarchical system like the army … especially when there's a despot in charge." The archivist had looked over his shoulder and spoken more softly as he added this last part.

Jess nodded thoughtfully. She hadn't known this thing about Lucas. What could he have done to have upset his superiors? And how could it be connected to Jacob? Could Jacob have been one of the prisoners? Her mind was racing, trying to recall any clues that Maria or Kathy might have offered.

The archivist smiled at her sympathetically.

"Look," he says, "the two Missing cases are part-classified. You'd need written permission from my boss to see those. But don't waste your time – a little bird tells me that they're empty, not that you heard it from me. But the other one, the file with the older brother, you can have a look through that. There's a lot of it, mind, and we close in a couple of hours, but the offer's there if you wanted."

She followed him down a corridor to the Research Library, where two elderly men were bent over micro-fiche readers. They barely looked up from their screens. The archivist disappeared for a while, and her heart sank at the sight of the four huge manila folders that he carried on a tray as he returned.

With a sigh she settled to her task, and soon realised that much of the contents were little more than the utterly mundane reporting of a fairly trivial existence. It was all on faded yellow carbon copies, each letter punched in on a mechanical typewriter. She imagined the labour of those fat-fingered clerks and corporals whose job it was to diarise so much dullness. One hundred kilometres of shelves! God help us. Here were the results of an eye test; exam scores; an analysis of his prowess on the rifle range; a reprimand for arriving late for parade; his blood group; a citation for bravery; a recommendation in his own hand for promotion for his groom; chits for expenses; a request for leave of absence, refused; countless dates and times of interviews; a request for an unpaid bill for a barrel of rum.

She got up and walked around the cramped room, wondering yet again if she were wasting her own and everybody else's time. It would be good and dutiful research if she were some PhD student examining the minutiae of 1930s soldiery, that much was true. And in a way it all added to the sense of empathy she already felt for the characters in this little plot, but still, this was all background information, it was all filler, and she wasn't sure if it was leading anywhere.

She looked again at the clock on the wall, and saw with relief that it would soon be time for her to go. Conscientiously she returned to her desk, inhaled the stale perfume of dust and bureaucracy, and opened the final folder, flicking mechanically through the flimsy papers without enthusiasm. At first she didn't see it. But at some level she must have registered the slightly different format, and skipped back two pages to check. Hungrily she scanned the document again, then forced herself to re-read it one more time to be certain.

There it was: Maria Sanchez. For the first time here was a clue, a reference, to link Maria, her Maria, with this strange military family. It wasn't much, just a report written by a subaltern, at the request of Major Lucas, to investigate her disappearance. The report, dated November 1937, indicated that the officer, Lt. Cangas, had ridden specifically to the village of her birth in order to look for her. Regrettably there was no sign of her, and the neighbours said that she had not been seen for at least a year. In a postscript, however, the report indicated that the person concerned had been discovered to have a close relative in Andalucía, to whom it was rumoured she may have travelled. Specifically, to the province of Granada, to a village called Jubar.

Jubar, thought Jess. She knew that name. Maria had mentioned it several times. She was sure it cropped up in one of her letters, too. She would check when she got back to the hotel.

Chapter Thirty-Eight

In which Jess hears more about Stefan, Madrid, 2012

Jess tilted her head to the side and studied the enormous painting. Over the years she had seen so many reproductions and heard so much about *Guernica*, but this was the first time she had actually seen it in person. They were lucky: the Reina Sofia museum was relatively quiet, and she and Stefan had the luxury of sitting on a bench to contemplate the great work.

She wasn't sure what to make of it. Picasso always did that to her. She was overwhelmed at the fact of being there, and at some level understood that she was in the presence of greatness, but knew that she lacked the insight and education to appreciate it properly.

"I'm ashamed of my ignorance," she confessed. "I mean, I know some facts, but I just don't get it, not properly."

"Well you're asking the wrong person," said Stefan modestly. "I might look like a painter, but I sure ain't no expert." He held up his paint spattered hands and she laughed, causing the bored-looking curator to frown at them. They took the hint and moved on.

"I can tell you this much though: it isn't specifically about Guernica, not about that exact raid. It's supposed to represent the horror of all raids. He painted it in Paris not long after, but he could just as well have called it "Durango." That's a town not that far away which the Italians and Germans had bombed about a month previously. Or Almeria, in the south. They did the same there, but from the sea. Parked a huge destroyer in the bay and shot the place to bits. Not quite as savage, and not quite as notorious, but done in the same spirit."

They were walking slowly, keeping step down the marble hallway, and she paused to look at him, smiling, encouraging him to continue.

"It was complicated. Yes, they wanted to help win the war for Franco, and yes, in a sense it was a weapons testing ground, to see what effect the devastation would have on a civilian population – don't forget it was only two years later that they were doing the same thing to you lot in places like London and Coventry. But it was more about jostling for position, to see just how far they could push things, see what they could get away with, the old Great Game of provocation."

"Some game!"

"Quite. I knew this guy in Kosovo, a retired teacher, and he said we were still playing it. The Communist Wars, he called it, beginning with the Russian Revolution in 1916, and taking in the Spanish war, Korea, Vietnam, El Salvador, Nicaragua, even Cuba ... a great, murderous game of political chess between Washington and Moscow. But basically all one war, divided into chapters. I was there for some of the Balkan chapter."

"Kosovo. Yes, the other night someone mentioned that you'd been there. With KFOR, no? The Peace Keepers. Is that something you can talk about?" she asked timidly. "I mean, do you want to? What was it like?"

He shrugged. He clearly didn't talk about it, not usually, but he seemed to be able to talk to her.

"I wasn't actually part of KFOR, they were the proper military people. I was attached as a police observer. I was a bit young for it. They did all the psychological testing on me before and after, but I'm still not quite sure how I got in so young. I think it was because of my English, or because someone else dropped out at the last minute. Or maybe no one else wanted to go, I don't know. It's not as if I have family contacts who could pull a few strings for me."

"No? I was just reading this morning about *enchufismo* – I thought everyone in Spain had family somewhere who can help them. It's one of those things that we dysfunctional Anglo-Saxons are envious of …"

"Not quite everyone. Orphans don't," he said simply.

"God, no" she said, " I didn't know. Sorry … I was just trying to be clever, I'm..

"Actually I'm not one, not technically. But I was brought up in a home. My dad died when I was a baby. A car accident. My mum tried to look after me, but she was falling apart. They'd both done lots of drugs, and she just got carried away, became a junkie. This is what they told me, anyway. She had no money, and well … you know what that leads to, when you're that desperate."

She tried to stop him but he held up a hand.

"It's cool. I can talk about it. It was so long ago that I can't remember anything; it's like I'm talking about somebody else. But, anyway, I got taken in by a Catholic brotherhood and they took care of me."

He looked at her carefully. "And it's not what you think. Whenever anyone hears that, they assume that I was the victim of some kind of abuse. But it wasn't like that, not in my case. I'm not saying it was perfect. I mean, I was sad and lonely, especially at the beginning, and

I wasted so much time on Latin and prayers – well, I assume it was wasted, you never know – but overall it was pretty gentle. And it left me with a deep knowledge of scripture, as well this holy terror of women."

He grinned as he said this. "Really, it was okay. Maybe I was one of the lucky ones. There was this one guy, a teacher, an Irishman in fact, and he kind of took me under his wing. Talked to me about all sorts, taught me English. Every summer they sent me to a school in the north of England; it wasn't until I was leaving that I found out that he – Donat – had paid for it all out of his own pocket. I know that he really hoped that I'd stay on in the seminary, become a priest that is, and it hurt him when I didn't. Couldn't believe it when I joined the police."

By now they had reached the entrance to the café. "You sure you want to hear this? I think we need lunch. You're going to need sustenance if I go on like this."

She did, and she was hungry. "No, please, you go on. You heard all about me on Sunday. I must have spoiled your weekend. You were saying ... about Kosovo?"

"Sure? It's not pretty. I don't come out of it very well."

She smiled encouragingly at him and he gave a little shrug, leading her into the café.

"Well, I'd been there for about four months. I'd seen all sorts of wicked things; nothing really, really awful, but I think the constant tension must have been building up inside me. It was just the constant aggression, the nagging racism, the way the Albanians and the Muslims just seemed to be pushed around, so often cowed, confused, shoved around like cattle. Sometimes the only thing that I thought made any actual difference was when I helped out in the kitchens, doling out the food. Most times people were respectful, and waited in line even when they were super hungry, but sometimes, when a new batch came in there were people who were literally starving, who hadn't eaten for days, then it was chaos, and they genuinely needed us, just to hold them back. It could get quite nasty.

"A lot of people think that a refugee camp is a reason for hope, that it illustrates that humans can make sacrifices for others, that there is a sense of common decency, that there is still humanity in the world. It's partly true, but it's also bullshit. A refugee camp is a place of suffering and misery. All those displaced people with absolutely nothing to their names? Living on the charity of others? Most of them have lost someone, they're waiting, lost, hungry, frightened. They don't have hope, or at least not much; people in the West, at home, we assume that they have hope, but that's just bourgeois self-justification: what they have is not hope, but dread."

She was watching him carefully. He seemed to have entered a slightly altered state, and it was as if he was no longer talking just to her but to a wider audience in an almost stream-of-consciousness monologue.

"Some days there were snipers. Sometimes they wanted to pick off an individual for revenge, but mostly it was to remind us that they were still out there, armed, and to keep up the pressure to get it sorted out. Other times there were mortars, and you heard about the occasional car bomb. We were aware of it, but we had our flak jackets and blue helmets, so I rarely thought of myself as being in any kind of direct danger, but there was this steady drip drip drip of tension. Some people thrived on it, some just couldn't manage it. Me, I thought I was somewhere in the middle, and then it happened."

They were seated now at a table with some bread and a couple bottles of water. He paused to take a sip of his water.

"Are you okay with this? If it's painful ...?" she ventured gently.

"My shrink told me it was good to get it off my chest, to tell people. Am I boring you? Sorry!"

"No, no! Just the opposite."

"It wasn't anything remotely heroic. There was just this.....bomb....it doesn't help to talk about the details, but it happened close to me, and this woman who I'd spoken to only seconds earlier was killed. I actually saw it happen. I was shocked obviously, though I didn't think it would get to me... though in the end it did, apparently. And I just had this episode, let's call it that, so they took me off duty and left me in a luxury hotel on the coast in Croatia. My tour was ending anyway at the end of the month, and they wanted to look after me. I talked to a doctor every day. She gave me Valium, but I threw it down the toilet. After, you know, my mum and all, I have a bit of a thing about drugs, about addiction.

"I'm not sure what they put in my records, but I have a feeling that it wasn't even mentioned, that they glossed over it to protect my career. Thing is, we were volunteers, doing a good thing, and for the very best intentions they don't want anything like that to blot your copybook. They de-briefed me back here in Spain, and I talked to another shrink, but it was mentioned, rather than discussed.

"Then what? Well, you get six weeks off. First, I just chilled here, seeing friends in Madrid, relaxing back into a non-war zone. And I was fine, mostly. Then I went windsurfing to Tarifa with a couple of mates, camping, and that was all fine too, until this thing happened, and I had another panic attack."

"Thing? What happened?"

"I'd gone back out alone for one last session, quite late, well, before sunset, but when most people have gone home and you feel as if you have the whole ocean to yourself. The best time. I was about a kilometre out from the shore. It always feels like more when you're out there, especially in the Atlantic, 'cos you're always aware that there's another six thousand kilometres of ocean behind you. It was pretty windy, high waves, still sunny, the kind of perfect conditions that you dream about when you're into windsurfing. But anyway, as I went into this fast gybe, a downwind turn, that is, and suddenly my fin hits something, under the water. Bam! I'm still convinced it was a whale. A big one, because I just bounced straight up in the air. There wasn't a cracking noise like you'd get if you hit something really solid, something metal, say. No, this was solid, but also, I don't know ... absorbent. It was a really sickening feeling. Even now it makes me shudder.

"My fin broke, of course, and so there I was, stuck out at sea, bobbing around on this tiny board, drifting God knows where, and convinced that I'm about to be eaten by this Moby Dick character that I'd just taken a chunk out of. I couldn't see it. I didn't see a pointy fin, like Jaws. Nothing. But I just knew it was there. That was the worst thing: just to know that it was there, invisible, massive, black, somewhere beneath me, around me, waiting – I thought – just biding its time before it hurt me. And also I was suddenly, horribly aware of the great hideous depth of the water beneath me. I'd never really considered it before – well, you don't if you're into water sports, do you? It was the weirdest sensation, almost more like disgust than terror. And I just lost it completely, and had my own private panic attack. Couldn't catch my breath, heart racing, tunnel vision, sobbing. It was more than pure fear, and then suddenly I could picture the woman's face, the woman who had been blown up, and all the time I had this creeping certainty that something unseen beneath the waves was about to touch me. That was the most grotesque part – not harm me, but just touch me, that would be enough."

"Jesus, I'm not surprised!"

"In the end I was rescued by the Sea Angels. Don't smile, they're actual people, it's what they call themselves, they do it for a living. If you're a windsurfer you pay an insurance premium and they come and haul you back to shore in a Zodiac if someone raises the alarm. I was lucky – my mates tipped them off.

"I couldn't speak on the boat. I was in some kind of shock. With the noise of the wind and the motor you can barely hear anyway, so the crew were none the wiser. They just assumed I was cold and humiliated and sulking because I'd lost some expensive kit. Which was all true, by the way. But there was this other thing, this terror that still had a hold of me.

"I managed to keep it together once we got back to the beach, just about. And all through dinner. Then I told them I had to go to bed early because I was so bloody cold. In the morning I checked out early, before the others woke up. Before my taxi came I walked down to the shore. Even though the sun was still low in the sky it was already warm; there was barely a ripple and the out-going tide had left the tang of wet sea-weed and swept the beach of footprints. It was a world newly made. I was one of those people who with a swim can usually rinse away all the troubles of the universe. All the conditions that morning were perfect ... and I couldn't go in. I just couldn't. And that's the saddest thing. I've never been back in the sea, not once." He looked at her shyly. "And you know what else? You're the first person I've ever told."

She stared at him, wondering if he was having her on.

"Seriously? Why me?" she asked. "Why now?"

He shrugged. "Perhaps it's because we're in the middle of Madrid. I'm far away from the nearest sea, and I feel safe. What else could it be?"

Chapter Thirty-Nine

The high Sierra, above Madrid, 1938

Officer Cadet Ramon Fernandez de Cangas has been given a specific and clandestine order by his superior. He is an obedient and ambitious soldier, and will thus complete that order diligently, without question, and will report back exclusively to that same superior, Major Lucas. He has been provided with a powerful motorbike for the purpose, a Royal Enfield Bullet, and has travelled for more than two hours in order to get to this dusty, God-forsaken hole in the middle of the mountains. His mission is to discover the whereabouts of one Maria S— a former servant of Major Lucas. Thus far it has been a long and fruitless journey. But the grey-faced old crone to whom he is speaking, once she has stopped coughing, at least seems to have most of her wits about her.

"Yes. My husband was the teacher. He's dead. Silly old fool, getting mixed up in all that business, putting his nose where he shouldn't. No matter. And yes, Maria, that Maria, I remember, of course I remember. She must have walked all that way to get here, alone, alone! Aged what, sixteen? This was her mother's village, yes, but she wasn't here. The house was empty; the family had all gone to Barcelona to look for work in the factories. Lots of us did. Her dad had died years before. And here she was again, after all that time. She didn't speak. Not a word, not for about three weeks. No one said anything, but we could guess. It wasn't the first time we'd seen a girl like that. Bastards. No one knew what to do. We fed her. We washed her clothes, tried to talk to her. But then a stroke of luck: an aunt came. What was her name? Let me think ... Carmen, that was it. Anyway, she stayed for about a week, then took her off with her, back south, Andalucía. Granada way, up in the hills, little village, back end of nowhere. The village? Maybe, let me think ... funny name. We got a letter once. Don't look at me like that; course I can read. My old man was a teacher, don't forget. Don't get many letters. Hang on ... here we are ... Jubar. J-U-B-A-R. I don't think she stayed there long. She came back to Madrid, I heard. Can't say I blame her, stuck in the middle of nowhere, all goats and sheep and poverty, I wish I had ... anyway, she must have missed the bright lights and all that. Rotten time to go there, with the war kicking off. Someone said she'd got a job with a barrel maker, something like that, or was it sherry? Bright lass, like her mum. That was the last I heard of her, except that there was a rumour she'd gone back to the family that ... you know, the family that ... But she'd never do that, would she? As I say, bright lass. Pretty too, but scraggy as anything when I saw her, all grey skin and full of poison, know what I mean? She in trouble? You look young to be a policeman ..."

Ramon Fernandez thanks her for her time and ends the interview abruptly. This will have to do; at least he has something. *Jubar.* Old Lucas will have to make do with this. Will he send him there now, to Granada? Or is that Red territory? He observes how the neighbours' tattered curtains twitch as he walks back to his motorbike, and smiles grimly to himself. His visit will have provoked enough gossip and scandal to keep flowing for a month at least. What a shit-hole. It reminds him of home.

Chapter Forty

A short journey by train, 1937

Later – much later – she would look back on those few days with a sense of reverence. Her lips were cracked with thirst, the blisters on her heels had burst, she was exhausted by the effort and by the sun, and she was living in a' state of unbroken fear. And yet everything seemed to make sense then, everything fitted together, she had purpose, she felt burningly alive. And she was sharing it. When she looked at Jacob she could see that he was heartbreakingly tired. He was the stronger of the two, and years of army life had hardened him to the challenges of such a long walk, but even he was drained by the effort of constant watchfulness; she had heard him in the night; her sentinel, pacing, vigilant, afraid.

They had crossed from rebel territory by night and were now in republican lands. It seemed to her miraculous that they should have got this far. Four whole days. Only twice had they been challenged, and each time their story had been accepted. People were mistrustful, but willing to believe a lie if it were well told and attractive to their own convictions. Their narrative of a grieving teacher returning to Almeria escorted by her brother was plausible, but only just so. By being brazen, she had reasoned, they were less likely to arouse suspicion. Thus, when they reached the town of Linares, she had worn his sister's clothes with assurance. From there they were to take the train. Not only would it save them a long and exhausting hundred and fifty kilometres on foot, but, if they were lucky, four hours on the train would probably be safer.

And so far their luck had held. Jacob was emboldened by their success, and assumed that they would stay on the train as far as the city of Guadix. He was standing by the open window, whilst Maria sat with her back to him on a slippery wooden bench. Outside, the scenery rolled past slowly as they trundled south. This was empty country, barren and underpopulated. She recalled the first time she had seen it, travelling aged fifteen at the side of her distant aunt and still stunned by her ordeal at the hands of that evil thug in Madrid. Then, the abandoned countryside had seemed to echo the blankness that she had felt inside, whereas now it's remoteness gave her hope; the fewer people they saw, the better their chances, she concluded.

The woman opposite her smiled, and offered her a piece of the cheese she was eating. Maria was starving, but shook her head, wary of conversation, and kept her gaze out of the window. She must have dozed off, for when she opened her eyes the train had stopped, and in the distance she could see clearly the rugged, snow-covered lines of the Sierra Nevada. It seemed like a mirage. They were getting closer.

A girl sat down next to her, carrying a stinking wooden box. "Piglet," she said by way of explanation, smiling through gap teeth as a sound of squealing emerged.

"It's Grandad's. He's down at the back. He said I'd be better taking this, there's more chance all them soldiers will let me through with it than him."

Maria stiffened. "What soldiers?" she asked, trying to sound calm.

"In Guadix. There are hundreds. There were last week, anyway. Took us ages."

The mountains seemed to be even closer. Maria thought for a while.

"He sounds like a happy pig. Has he done this journey before? Does he know how many more stops there are before we get to Guadix?"

"Just one. Benalua. We'll be there soon. Do you want me to open the box?"

She smiled. "Maybe later. Can I just squeeze past – I need a bit of air. He's a bit smelly, your piglet." She held her nose and the girl giggled as Maria moved past her.

Jacob had been watching, and he nodded as she whispered in his ear. For five minutes he fussed with their few belongings as they drew into the next station. They waited until the whistle blew, and only then, just as the train was about to pull out, did they jump onto the platform. Other than the old man with the whistle, it was empty.

"Guadix?" asked Jacob innocently. The old man looked at him as though he were speaking to an idiot.

"No," he announced, and pointed to the tiny village behind him. "City's that way. This is Benalua." He regarded them without any trace of compassion. "You're going to have to walk." He stared at Maria's city shoes. "Ten kilometres," he said with apparent satisfaction, and turned his back on them.

Maria stifled a laugh. It felt good to be back on solid ground. She pointed first at herself, then to Jacob, then at the mountains, and made an up-and-down gesture with her hands.

"Shall we?" she asked. He kissed her. By his reckoning they would have to walk for a day at least to get to the foot of the mountains where they would find shelter for the night.

All his adult life he had hated walking. Anything - a horse, a car, a motorbike, anything - had been better than travelling on foot. But this was different. He couldn't quite name it, but with her the journey was more than satisfying. It was just who he was now, who they were, what they did; two people travelling constantly, alone and together, and in a vacuum, a cocoon surrounded by fear and warfare. He realised with a shock that despite the fatigue and disquiet, he didn't want it to end, and that wherever they were going, some part of him did not wish to get there.

"That," said Maria, pointing, "is Puerto del Lobo. Wolf's Pass. We should go that way." He followed her finger up to a small indentation on the skyline. "The other Pass at La Ragua is lower, but it will be busier; I bet there'll be patrols there. Over there – look – is the Castle at La Calahora. That's been guarding the pass since Roman times so we need to avoid that too."

He stared doubtfully at the towering peaks. "But there's still snow up there, we're not equipped, we're-"

"Ready? We don't have much choice. And this is the north face – on the south side it will all have melted, you'll see. We can find a shepherd's hut." She tugged at his hand as the little train disappeared into the distance.

"Let's risk this place first. We need food. This might be the last chance we get before Jubar."

Arm in arm they wandered along the unmade road towards the village, where a toothless old man directed them to a house which doubled as the village store, and whose single shelf sat virtually empty. Jacob waited outside whilst Maria bought stale bread, sausage and a rock-hard cheese. As an afterthought she added almonds and a few pieces of fruit which she hid at the bottom of her bag.

At the end of the village stood a recently whitewashed single storey building, with a small perimeter fence and a hand painted sign which read "Escuela Infantil". A teacher somewhere rang a hand bell just as they were passing. It was two o'clock, home time, and from inside came the excited, happy clamour of children. The bell rang again. "Viva la Republica!" sang the strong, clear voice of a woman.

"Viva la Republica!" the children chorused back.

Maria's eyes were shining. "That's the sound of the future," she said. "The sound of hope."

Jacob stopped suddenly. For the very first time he began to consider whether the Republic might actually achieve the victory she so desperately craved. All the while he had been conditioned by his past and his army logic, and had assumed that it was just a question of time before the Republic was crushed by the weight of military superiority. Privately he had thought that he was joining a lost cause, a heroic cause, but one doomed to eventual failure all the same. All this time he and Maria had been running away, and this had merely reinforced this belief. At best he'd been hoping to escape to England, to begin again. But what if she were right? What if there were still hope? Could he somehow still end up as victor, but with Maria at his side? The possibility electrified him.

He pointed to the top of the mountain.

"Race you!" he yelled. "Viva la Republica!"

Chapter Forty-One

Slowly over the mountain, 1937

The seeds were spread like bright red spots of blood across the snow.

Jacob had told her in Toledo that he liked pomegranates, and secretly she had brought one for him to the summit. Then, when he'd gone ahead to scout she'd spent ages trying to extricate the tiny crimson jewels to surprise him, piling them all onto their one tin plate. But then her frozen, cold-clumsy fingers had let her down just as he had arrived back; at first he had laughed at her efforts to pick them all up, before realising that she was genuinely upset.

Now they were sitting with their backs against a sun-warmed rock, away from the ice patch, watching with mixed emotions as a pair of larks tucked into this unexpected feast. Far beneath them they could see the round dome of the castle on the hill, and the faint outline of the long, winding track that they had been forced to follow to avoid the sentries who would be posted there. They had walked since before dawn, marvelling at the purity of a new day as a chrome sun rose slowly to the East, lapping up the warmth it brought them. To the west lay the high mountains, and the trenches and fortifications of the front. They didn't know exactly where, only that it ran roughly from

Motril on the coast to Granada, cutting straight across the high peaks.

"How long could you live here, do you think?" he asks her. " With me, I mean, if we had food and a little place to sleep." He shakes his head in wonder at the thought. "We could have animals ..."

He watches her as she purses her lips in thought. He loves this in her, the way she listens to a question and tries to give a proper answer.

"Nine months," she says decisively. "It's just too cold up here in the winter, you've not seen it, it's bleaker than you can imagine, metres of snow. Nine months, same as a pregnancy. I'd want to see people too, not just you." It's a considered response.

"OK. Nine months, then get away from the snow, I get that. But maybe not people, I've had enough of people. They scare me." He says this with a faint smile, but he means it. " I know it won't last, but right now I'm just so ... jumpy. Feels like I'm a fugitive, on the run from everyone. One side would hang me as a traitor, the other just won't trust me because of my background. I'm pretty screwed, really, when you look at it. It's not as if I can just go home." His voice almost cracks as he finishes.

She knows him well enough to understand that he doesn't show weakness easily, and she's touched by his admission. He looks so young.

"Hey. It's fine to be scared. Scared keeps you wary, scared keeps us alive." She squeezes his hand. "I know it's tough, being on watch all the time, staying alert, but wait till tomorrow when we get to Jubar. They're my people there, we can relax for a day or two, get our breath back. You'll be safe in Jubar."

Jacob goes back to the patch of ice and returns with the tin plate filled with snow, which he begins to thaw above a tiny candle.

"It's not just that," he goes on slowly, "it's that I'm kind of dazed ... I mean, it's fine, no, it's great, when it's just me and you, here, in the moment, alone, that's all so, I don't know, so natural, but when I start to think about things, the past, everything, then it stops making sense and I feel a bit ... lost, I suppose. All my life I've wanted to be a soldier, at least I think I did, and that's what I did. And I did have my doubts, you know that, I could see the unfairness of stuff around me, but I just did what I did. I think in a way that you ... saved me ... don't laugh ... but you did. If it hadn't been for you then I'd just have carried on doing the same things ... being a soldier ... and I still am a soldier, of sorts, but now I don't have anyone to fight for. No one will trust me, no one wants me ... and you know what else? They're right. I don't think I could do it, I don't think I could actually shoot or lob a bomb at the army. They were my comrades, can't you see that? My bloody brother, my dad ... how could I? It's one thing chickening out and running away, it's another to start trying to kill them. I'm just no good to anyone, am I?"

She puts her arm around his shoulders and holds him to her, hard. She had known that this was coming. She pulls back and with both hands she turns his head so that he is forced to look at her.

"*Basta!* Enough! You didn't chicken out, you moron. What you did back there for me in Toledo was tremendously brave. Running away? You call this running away? Risking your life to pass on information, dodging checkpoints, gambling that no one is going to betray you, exposing yourself to danger every second ... this isn't running *away*, it's running *to*. To freedom, to equality, to a better world, and whatever you might say, you are still a soldier, and a soldier who is still fighting. It doesn't mean you have to go after someone with a sword or a cannon, in a uniform even, it just means you're someone who's involved, directly involved, in this massive, international struggle for justice. If you're not a fighter, then what are you? What am I? We're in this together. Jesus! I never saw myself as some kind of warrior, I was just a girl who got swept up in things, but now my whole existence is threatened every day. In fact it's hanging by a single fucking thread most days, and you say we're chickening out …"

She throws herself suddenly onto her back, oblivious to the cold ground, black hair spread heedlessly on the stones and grass. She looks away from him, but speaks more softly now.

"What you have done is far more noble than anything I ever did. I was repressed and wanted to fight back; I was raped and wanted revenge. But you, you were sitting pretty there – posh boy, trapped, cossetted *inside* the crooked, unfair machine, protected and privileged, rich. But still you saw the injustice when others refused to look. And then, not only that, but you had the balls to step outside, to call it for what it is, to do the right thing. And you knew there would be consequences, and there are … this is it, this is where we are, and we'll deal with it, okay."

He moves to be beside her, makes a pillow for her hair with his arm, and they stare together at the swirling clouds.

"It's true," he says, "but only up to a point. I saw bad things and didn't like them, that's all. But when I went to the prison to see you I acted on impulse. In the end it was simple, it was almost as if I didn't have a choice. I just couldn't leave you like that. It was all about you, you see, you were the catalyst. And I'd do the same thing again tomorrow, no question, you need to understand that, because, because … *te quiero.*"

Her breath stops. She could let this pass her by, pretend that she hasn't heard. But these small words are too big to ignore, and she lifts herself up onto straight arms and looks enquiringly into his eyes.

"I know," she says finally. "And I love you too."

They sit for a while, and share sips from the melted snow. There is an extraordinary quality to the light. To the south, beneath them, there are the brown rolling hills of the mythical Alpujarras and beyond that, the Mediterranean. In the far, far distance the tops of the vast ridges of Africa are just visible above a curtain of ethereal cloud; they hear nothing but the gentle susurration of the wind in the bracken, and when this dies they are left with the pure and absolute silence of the mountains. Jacob throws a stone and they hear it clatter far below. In the sanctity of such stillness it feels like sacrilege and he regrets it. He must have disturbed something, for Maria sees something move from the corner of her eye. Her voice seems to boom in her ears as she nudges him and indicates the russet back of a great bird as it hurtles beneath them.

"And another!" says Jacob. "Eagles from above! It feels like flying."

Together they watch in wonder until the birds melt into the background and disappear out of sight. Eventually Jacob's eyes settle on the stone hut on the far ridge, which they are hoping will be empty, and where they can spend the night. They each have wool blankets, though at this altitude he isn't sure whether it will be enough to keep them warm until morning.

"That's our hotel for the night," he says, pointing up and along the slope where the patches of snow grow thicker. "We'd better get going before reception closes."

Chapter Forty-Two

New Friends, 1937

Maria caught the sour, ripe leather scent of the sheep long before she saw them. She dropped to her knees and crawled the last few metres until she could see over the ridge. The sight astonished her. A huge flock, perhaps a thousand or more, wandering slowly over the rocky ground, packed tight together like some enormous pale rug, seeking out what grazing could be found. Behind them walked a shepherd and a young boy, calling out to their charges in a strange, guttural half-language, controlling the dogs who wheeled around them with a series of clicks and whistles.

It dawned on her: of course: the *transhumancia,* the great annual movement of livestock from the lowlands to the richer pickings and pastures of the high sierras. The dogs had spotted them by now, and several came bounding over, all teeth and raised hackles, restrained only by the calls of the shepherds and the threat of the stone in Jacob's hand. Slowly the older man ambled towards them, and as he raised his hand, the dogs grew quiet.

"*Hola, amigos, tranquilos*" he says. "*Que calor*! It's gonna be a hot one today alright," and he sweeps an arm behind him to indicate the cloudless sky, then waits for them to respond. Maria notes the brilliant blue eyes that are sometimes seen there in the south, incongruous against the white, week-old stubble and the corrugated lines of his sun-scorched cheeks.

"I can lead you to water if you want," he says formally, sensing their need. He speaks with the strong, rich tones of deepest andalucia, so that Jacob has to concentrate to understand. "There's water over there, in the next gulley, good water, enough to bathe in."

Jacob can see that Maria's face is caked with the white chalky dust of the high sierra and her lips are beginning to crack; the bottles they had filled earlier are long since empty and he's angry at himself for not having prepared properly.

"Please," Jacob answers. "We've run a bit low."

Together they begin a slow, stately procession across the hillside, their speed conditioned by that of the grazing sheep. Maria asks him about the path and the distance to Jubar, revealing that once she had stayed there for almost two years, and mentions some of the names of the people she recalls.

"I know," he says, " I remember you. There's not much happens in our village, and when new folk come, you tend to remember them, even when you're old, like me." He smiles his old man's smile at her and she grins back in return. She's pleased that she will be remembered, and she likes him. The villagers had told her when she had lived there that the shepherds were always the best looking boys. It's hard to imagine now, she thinks as she studies his venerable features, and then she turns to look hard at the boy by his side.

"Your grandson!" she exclaims suddenly as she spots the resemblance. "I see it! How old is he?"

"Fourteen," the old man says proudly.

"Nearly fifteen, actually," says the boy, and blushes. He's carrying a sling and a kind of bolus, and from time to time he picks up a small rock and flings it expertly at the heels of an errant animal to bring it back into line. Jacob looks at him with respect.

"Bet you couldn't hit that tree," he suggests, pointing to an oak some good distance away. That's a bit unfair, he thinks to himself, it's too far, but then, as he watches the cocksure certainty of the boy as he selects his pebble, he knows he's about to eat his words. They all study him as the boy concentrates, winds back his throwing arm, then uncoils suddenly with effortless power and grace.

"Good shot, sir!" says Jacob as they hear the ping and dying echo of the ricochet, and he holds out a hand to congratulate him. They shake, and the boy turns away, sweetly trying to hide his smile of triumph.

"It's not far, the water. I'll wait here," the old man says. "See the fig tree there? That's where the spring rises. Sergio: go with them and show them the stream."

For some reason Maria thinks he looks sullen.

The boy obliges, and after they climb a low ridge, he watches as they fall to their knees and wallow in the icy snow melt. They splash and shout and gorge themselves, before re-filling their bottles for the journey down, and head back to the shepherd.

"God, that was just lovely," says Jacob laughing. "Thank you so much." He salutes..

The old man glowers at him.

"You taking the piss, sunshine?"

Jacob stares back blankly. "Eh?"

"First you call him *sir,* Good shot, *sir,* and now you come back and *salute* me. And all this with your hoity toity Madrid way of speaking. What the hell's going on?"

Jacob is bewildered. "No, no ... it's just that I'm used to it, I'm a soldier, I mean ... I used to be a soldier, I didn't think, I ..."

Maria steps in. "He's an idiot, that's what he is." She's thinking quickly. They can't hurt her, not these two, and besides, sooner or later they're going to have to tell someone. She decides to trust her instincts. The cautionary words of the Russian ring in her head all the same, and she hesitates. "Can we sit down?" she asks. "Will the sheep be alright for just a moment? We have ham. And bread. Can you keep a secret?"

She sits and the others follow, the old man reluctantly. Briefly she describes the events in Toledo, her imprisonment, the escape. The boy, Sergio, listens open-mouthed, trying to take in every detail. The old man seems less curious, and his eyes stray continuously to his flock.

"You do believe us, don't you?" she implores, adding that they are the first and only people they have told.

"Of course," says the old man with indifference. "Why would we not? Why would you lie to people like us? We don't matter."

"But you do, you do! You matter just as much as anybody else. That's why we're in the state we're in, that's why we have to fight back against this rotten, stupid system, it's why we've had to take up arms against all these sons of bitches who want to keep us down. You're just as good as the rest – better, even, if you ask me – it's just that you were born in a corner, entrapped by a callous political scheme that's so cold-hearted that the lucky sods at the top really don't give a shit whether you live or die ... at least you, that is. Truth is, that in my case they would prefer me to die. Him too."

She's breathless by the time she finishes her outburst, and no one seems quite sure how to follow.

"Your secret's safe with me, lady," says Sergio. " Next year I'm going to the Front to fight as well. *No pasaran!*" He grins at them defiantly, and points an imaginary gun at a bird overhead. His grandfather says nothing, but turns away to peer at the snow-clad peaks; as he does so Maria glimpses on his face an expression of infinite melancholy, and she feels a terrible remorse; somehow she has wronged him. She's about to speak out, but when he turns to face them he seems to have recovered his composure, and the moment passes.

"It's fine. The boy's right: we won't tell." He spits on his hand and offers it to Jacob. They shake hands, comrades now.

Sergio speaks. "They're doing it, Grandad! It's time, they're starting to wheel." He points across the terraces to the sheep, who are forming themselves into a tightly packed circle. As they watch, the sheep do the strangest thing. They each drop their heads and push into the haunches of the beast in front of them, compressing the circle, then stop dead.

"Don't know why," says the old man, anticipating the question on Jacob's lips, "they just do it, that's all, especially when it's hot and still, like now. I think it lets them save energy, or something. Also, the ones in the middle must feel secure, no one can get at them, so perhaps they can relax and sleep properly for a while. It's a mystery. It's good for us too, 'cos we can switch off for a while. Let's eat."

They sit and unpack the food they have with them. The shepherds are thrilled with the bread that Maria carries, for white flour is hard to come by in the high villages, and the cheese they offer in return is incomparable.

"Grandad makes it," the boy says, "I help a bit. Everyone knows that a shepherd makes the best cheese." And he goes on to explain that here, during the long weeks of the transhumance, the only way to keep the ewes' milk is to turn it into cheese, here on the hills. They make fires with the roots of aromatic herbs to simmer the milk in time-worn cauldrons, then, to stop them from sticking together as they dry, they coat them with the leaves of thyme and chopped rosemary, which further infuses them with all the flavours of the mountains.

Jacob nods his head in appreciation. He's happy here, unafraid for a while in the high mountains, with his new friends, this food, and his girl. He looks across at her. God, she's pretty. He could stay here forever. He thinks of all the things that they did to each other in the hot silence of the night, and has to turn away, blushing, when she catches him staring at her, as if she can read his mind.

Sergio lies down with an exaggerated groan of content, and pulls a cap over his face in preparation for his siesta. Maria and Jacob sit side by side on a rock, contemplating the magnificence of the view across to Africa, and the mysteries of the ring of catatonic sheep, who continue in their apparent lifelessness.

"Come," says the shepherd as he materialises beside them, "they will stay like that a while yet. I have something to show you."

Obediently they follow as he strides ahead with his rolling, seagoing gait, struggling to keep up with him across the broken, boulder-strewn terrain.

"Mark that," he demands, pointing to a copse of Holm oak on the horizon. "Turn around. And that." He indicates an outcrop of rock to the north. "See where you are? Good. Remember this." They are on the south-facing flank of the sierra, too high and too steep for terracing. The view to the sea in the far distance is breath-taking, though the air shimmers violently in the heat. A few browning plants cling grimly to life between the rubble and scree, but this is not a world made for plants, this is a world made for lizards, scorpions and snakes, for the creatures of the night, for here in the glare, where metallic rocks bake for months on end in unforgiving heat, the land is cruel to those requiring water. And yet, improbably, just behind where the shepherd is standing, there is a stunted fig tree. And next to this, the small mouth of a cave.

"If ever you get caught out," says the old man, "in a blizzard or a lightning storm, or can't get back because the sun's gone down, then you can shelter in a cave like this. It's always good to have a place for emergencies, just in case. Look for fig trees, they have roots a mile long." He ducks down and disappears from view. Maria and Jacob listen to the muffled noises he makes as he moves around inside, then stoop to join him. It takes a while for their eyes to get used to the gloom, despite the tallow candle that fights a losing battle against the dark.

"No one ever uses this one. It's too far from the village ... and it's supposed to be haunted. I used it a long time ago to store cheese; I was so sure no one else would come here, I thought it would be safe, but the rats ate it all, little bastards."

At the back of the cave is an even smaller chamber, slightly raised, just wide and long enough for a man to lie down.

"I stayed here once, all night. I was only about your age, but that rock is so hard. I hardly slept, and when I did, I had nightmares." He looked around him, as if trying to recollect the dreams more clearly, then shook his head. "Now get yourselves to the village before it gets dark. Antonio and Rafael, two friends, shepherds, good men, are coming up here tonight. There's rumours of wolves, see, though I haven't seen any sign of them myself, no prints, no carcasses. More like two-legged wolves if you ask me, but still ... any ways, it means you can set off with Sergio so you won't get lost. He's a good lad. He can stay in the village tonight, and come back at dawn.

"Listen: You'll need to watch yourselves, be careful. The mood's not great just now. We never really trust strangers, not really. Just watch your backs. Maybe don't tell anyone else what you just told us. I believe you … others might not."

Chapter Forty-Three

Sanctuary, 1937

It was almost dark as they arrived at the village of Jubar. Dogs barked, and their guide Sergio told them to wait hidden in the corner of a goat-shed until he came back. Half an hour later they heard the sound of voices and Jacob drew his gun.

"Put that away, you idiot. These are friends," hissed Maria. Jacob's heart was racing, and in the gloom he made a show of returning it to his kitbag, but hid it in his pocket until she kicked him.

"Amigos," came a voice from outside. "Show yourselves." Maria stepped out, followed by a terrified Jacob. A group of around ten people stood in a knot, their anxious faces ill-lit by lanterns.

"You – girl – come here, step into the light, we can't see you properly," said a voice from the dark.

Maria squeezed Jacob's hand and walked forwards. A woman took a step towards her, and lifted a candle towards her face.

For a second all present all held their collective breath, until -

"Bienvenida, guapa," the woman shouted, and hugged her. "Maria, you lovely thing, you're even more like your mum than you were two years ago."

There followed a relieved moment of laughter and greeting, and Maria had to force herself away to bring in Jacob, who stood lost at the edge of the circle.

"This is Jacob, my *novio,*" she said proudly, "and don't worry: he hates Franco too!"

"Viva la Republica!" shouted someone at the back, a refrain which they all repeated as they walked back towards the centre of the village.

Jacob looked around him. Maria had told him that their intended place of refuge was small, but this seemed tiny. Low, flat-roofed houses lined the unpaved alleys; they were too narrow to call them streets. Iron bars covered the few windows he could see, all glassless. He heard the sound of water running from a fountain somewhere, and the restless stamp of mules' hooves as they settled for the night in their stalls. Everywhere there was the scent of woodsmoke, of cooking, and of horse shit. It reminded him very much of the villages he had seen in the Atlas mountains in Morocco, and he loved it.

The woman who had first stepped forward was named Carmen, and she was a cousin and friend to Maria's mother. By the time they reached her home at the end of the village, most of the small throng who had accompanied them had dispersed. Maria was pleased, for she did not want their arrival to be seen as an event.

As Jacob ducked under the front door he heard the grunting of a pig behind the stable wall and wanted to look, but was pushed in the back by an unseen hand and kept moving. The family obviously lived upstairs, with the livestock beneath. A large inglenook fireplace dominated the living room. Beside it an old lady seemed to be sleeping in a stationary rocking chair, a ball of wool and two knitting needles curled up in her lap. On the low table next to her was the debris of an interrupted meal: a torn loaf of bread, a waxy cheese and the half-dismembered remains of a dried ham, whose bone glowed dull white and grim in the firelight.

Carmen took two small earthenware beakers and filled them with wine from a pitcher, and pushed them towards her two guests, her face aflame with goodwill and curiosity. Without invitation Maria began a summary of their saga which she had rehearsed to herself on the way down the mountain, but to her surprise Carmen held up a hand to restrain her.

"Whoa there," she said, "most of that can wait till morning, and there's a lot I don't want to know, not the war stuff anyway, so tonight, just tell me two things, and then I'll get Paco to take you to a place where you can be alone to sleep. First, are you happy, and also, are you staying long this time?"

Maria was taken aback by the questions, but did not hesitate.

"Yes," she said, "I'm happy. Very happy. I'm shit scared a lot of the time, and exhausted, but I'm happy. And, sorry, but we can't stay long. A week at most, then we need to get going."

Carmen looked at her and smiled. "Good," she said, "I can tell ... you deserve it. Last time you were here, you were so ..." she looks quickly at Jacob, "so *upset* ... and a week! A week isn't long, but it's more than I hoped. I thought you might say you were off in the morning. At least in a week I can feed you up a bit, you look half starved."

Jacob grins at this news. Too polite to help himself until asked, he wolfs down the plate of ham that is now pushed towards him, concentrating hard. When finally he looks up he is confounded to see that Maria has her arms around Carmen's neck, and that the two of them are crying. Maria sees him and smiles through her tears.

"It's fine, Jacob, really, its fine. We're safe here, we're safe for a while."

Safe. That's what they need. And he sits silently for a moment, befuddled by relief.

Soon, the generous and understanding Carmen ushers them out of the house with her husband Paco as their guide. He leads them to a tiny out-building, on the edge of the village by the church. It has one room. The wall to one side is filled with hooks which hold spades, hoes, rakes, axes. The rest of the space is filled with a canvas palliasse, whose horsehair stuffing emerges from the frayed edges; rough russet blankets lay on top, and there is a long tubular pillow.

It's not the most elegant bed he has ever slept in, but it's the most desirable. He blows out the candle and they smile at each other, unseeing, in the darkness. They both assume they are about to make love, but seduced instead by the sudden sense of respite, of heaviness and of calm, they fall modestly asleep in each other's arms. In the morning they make up for it. In the half-light their pale olive bodies move more slowly, deliberately, each more confident and comfortable with the other, more knowing. When Jacob stares at the excited swell of her breasts as they move beneath him, she grabs his face with one hand, forces him to look into her eyes, and then, deliberately, slowly, and kissing him with terrible tenderness, she tells him over and over again that she loves him.

Chapter Forty-Four

Respite, 1937

This was a time of gentleness. That's what she remembered the most. Especially the first few days. After the road and the dread and the horror of their flight from Toledo, this seemed more than a safe harbour. Carmen and Paco doused them in kindness, and in food. The stiffness in her limbs began to ease, blisters subsided, and she and Jacob were able to exist for a while without the pernicious and constant state of alert that had so exhausted her. It was only now, as they stopped, that she became aware of just how truly tired she had been.

Each day they walked together about the flower-filled terraces. On her previous time in Jubar she had recognised the beauty of the landscape. The tiny, manicured meadows, each supported by a defiant stone wall, were alive with trees and plants; innumerable birds flooded the valleys with song; a miraculous line of snow still clung to the tall peaks, and in the distance, cushioned by the long ochre slopes of the foothills, the sea shimmered blue and far beyond reach, as if they were on an island. Even then, two years earlier, in her wounded state, she had noted the beauty. She could see it then, but had been unable to react, unable to feel. Something deep down in her had been dying of thirst to respond, but, she, Tantalus-like, was prevented from tasting it properly. Now, seeing it all with Jacob, the scene was complete, and she luxuriated in it fully.

And yet despite all the kindness and the beauty, they knew full well that their time there was limited. Perhaps that was always part of the charm of it all, she would reflect much later, the fact that they knew, always knew, that their idyll was born to be short-lived.

From time to time, from nowhere, even at the happiest of times, echoes of their duty to continue with their mission would trickle down and haunt them. On the very first morning she had sent a message to their contact Kyriagin in Adra to say that they were close by, and they were now waiting for his response. She didn't quite understand why their approach had to be made this way, but these were her instructions. Their courier was Andreu from the nearby village of Yegen. He was known to be trustworthy, and had been a friend and neighbour of the famous Englishman Gerald Brennan. People joked that he could walk the paths to Almeria with his eyes closed, since he and the *inglès* would travel each month to visit the brothels in the port there, and return blind drunk.

And so the fugitives waited, suspended in a brittle cocoon of elation which they knew must soon shatter.

And the longer they waited, the more tense the situation became. They tried to make themselves useful about the village, fetching and carrying, bringing water, chopping wood. One morning they set off to help with the weeding of a crop of barley, bending low to the ground with a short-handled hoe. To his chagrin, Jacob's back went into spasm after an hour; he was strong, but the contortions required were new to him, and he was unable to continue.

"If that's the best the army can produce then our boys will be home soon," laughed one of the old farmers that night in the square where they had gathered.

"He is one of our boys, you oaf," said Carmen. "He's one of us."

Nevertheless, something had been said aloud, something subversive, that many of the villagers had been thinking all along, even if unconsciously. They *were* different, it was clear: their accents, their manners, they were from the north, from the big city, they were *foresteros*. And in a small, closed place like Jubar, a mountain village where the ghosts of the Inquisitors still flit about the twilight, suspicion lays carpeted over everything like a fine invisible layer of dust. All it takes is a breeze, a breeze borne of controversy, boredom … envy, and the dust begins to stir. To be different meant to be alienated. Maria had a claim: she had a bloodline connection. But Jacob … could they trust him, really, when he'd been in the Nationalist army, an officer as well, no less?

Maria felt this more than Jacob. At some level she understood that as a handsome, love-struck couple they represented a kind of target. It wasn't just intuition. In Madrid she had listened aghast to her teacher when he had explained in his louche, world-weary way that amongst humanity's many sicknesses is an innate and degenerate urge to shoot down our gods: we want to be dazzled by our heroes, we want to touch them, he had said, but at the same time we're perversely keen to see them brought low, to see them suffer.

Maria didn't see herself as a hero, not even as superior. But she was aware that people -some people- might be pleased to see them get their come-uppance. And chief amongst them would be Miguel. She had caught him staring at her, and he had tried to get her alone, to talk. She should have seen it coming, it was her own fault. He was the village *corredor,* the go-between, and saw himself as some kind of self-appointed potentate. She had hoped that he wouldn't be there, that he would have been away in the fighting. He was the right age, he was fit and strong. Why wasn't he there? On her last night in Jubar she had kissed him after the dance. Just a little kiss. It was at a time when she was still coming to terms with her attack, trying experimentally to see how it had affected her, and she had kissed him selfishly. She regretted it now. Surely, after all this time, he couldn't still hold a candle for her? It only added to her growing sense of unease.

She mentioned it to Jacob, who seemed unconcerned. Him? That fat, lazy brute? He's starting to lose his hair. In his mind Jacob weighed men as though he were still in the army, and to himself he predicted that Miguel would make a reluctant corporal at best, and an ugly one at that. This was no rival.

And so it wasn't strictly jealousy that had led him to question Miguel's bookkeeping, but rather the memory of the strawberry pickers. It wasn't even planned: he just happened to be there at dusk when the last of the crates of grapes were being counted. The system was straightforward: the crops were weighed, and Miguel paid each grower there and then, in cash, before taking the crop to market the following day to make his profit. Behind him was a blackboard which he used to work out his sums, and after every calculation he wiped it clean.

"He still owes you two centimos," Jacob said to an old man as he counted his change. "Miguel!" he shouted. "22 kilos at 4 centimos each is 88; you've only given him 86."

Maria could have kicked him. It wasn't that she disapproved of his protecting the interests of their neighbours, but he could have been a bit more subtle, and she knew that Miguel would take it not only as an insult but as a challenge.

"Really?" Miguel said, a humourless smile on his face. "Sorry. An honest mistake; I'm exhausted. Here you are, friend," he called, and threw two small coins to the man.

This wasn't like Miguel at all, thought Maria. Even here in the village they would have to watch their backs, and this doubled her foreboding. At the back of her mind was already the suspicion that something was wrong with her comrades on the coast, for she understood vaguely that there were already schisms in the ranks of those opposing Franco, and that factions had even appeared long before the war had begun. All were united in their determination to fight the fascists, but the internal struggles being waged between the Marxists, the Stalinists, the socialists and the trades unionists were a constant drain on the strength of the coalition. She loathed this lack of unity, and could not bring herself to discuss it even with Jacob, for she felt it was shaming, and a betrayal of the people. But still she was loyal. Her orders were to give the documents in her possession to Kyragin, and to no one else, and this she would do.

And so the wait went on. There was still the sense of respite, still the plentiful food, the loveliness of the hills, the kinship and the long hot nights. But the seeds of doubt that had drifted on the wind were now firmly planted.

And then came the morning when Andreu returned with the news that Kyragin was dead. Andreu spoke to Maria alone, ashen-faced, and told her that her contact had been executed, tied to a tree and shot by another Russian, for he was a traitor to the cause.

Chapter Forty-Five

Betrayal, 1937

As the *corredor*, it wasn't unusual for Miguel to be seen in the old market town of Ugijar. Whilst others broke their backs in the fields, he could be seen drinking and talking with the other middlemen, fixing up deals and generally keeping an ear to the ground in the various taverns. He knew that many of his neighbours resented him, and behind his back called him lazy. Let them. Fools. He knew he had to be more cautious now that the war had started, but he'd been careful to cultivate the proper friendships, to be amongst the most vocal of Socialist supporters, and now his left wing credentials were excellent.

If only they knew, he often thought, as the secret stash of coins continued to fill the box beneath his woodshed. When all this was over he'd be a rich man. And all the while, to hedge his bets, he still had his acquaintances in the army and his cousin who worked in the bishop's palace in Granada. They would protect him if needs be, if in the end the other lot should win.. He didn't care. Whatever the outcome he'd find a way round it; he always did. He was smart; a born survivor.

But he wanted a wife. Someone to come home to, to keep house for him. All successful men had wives, so he deserved one. A good looking one might give him more trouble, but she'd bring him respect. That was why he'd been so pleased when two years earlier little Maria had popped out of nowhere. She was perfect: the right age, penniless and easy on the eye. He had courted her, in his way, and even managed to kiss her after the dance that time. And then she'd just disappeared and cleared off back to Madrid or wherever it was. Silly girl.

He had soon given up on her. In truth he'd been disappointed, but no more than that; it was like being out-bid on a horse at the fair.

But then out of nowhere she had just re-materialised, and if anything was even more pretty than he remembered. Trouble was, she seemed so smitten with that jackass who trooped along after her all day long, the two of them trailing round hand-in-hand and smiling at everyone. It was sickening. And to make matters worse the little shit had caught him cheating, had even called him out in front of the others.

Well, he might live to regret his pathetic little triumph. They said he had been a soldier, that he was a turncoat, a *renegade.* Interesting. Miguel knew people on the coast who would be more than curious to learn more about this renegade, this *spy.* All it would take was a little cunning.

He looked at his watch. There was just time. He'd finish this drink and then amble down to the kiosk to buy pencil and paper. The postman left at 2pm.

Chapter Forty-Six

Paco and the Rifle, 1937

Before his eyesight went, Paco, Carmen's gentle husband, had been a tailor. Once or twice a year, itinerant traders from Granada would make the long trek up the dusty unpaved roads, bolts of cloth from the factories in the north strapped to the sides of their mules. Villagers bought yards of these rough fabrics, and took them to Paco to turn into workaday suits. He had enjoyed it, and built up a small reputation as an honourable and skilful tradesman. But then, to his and everyone else's astonishment, he found one day in 1921 that he had been conscripted, called up to join the ragtag army that was steadily losing the fight to defend colonial Morocco.

There was no way out. He was by then thirty-seven, portly, and with eyes which were beginning to fail him, but the government had drawn a line in the sand and had decided to throw everything at the war in the Rif. Having just lost the remains of their once mighty empire in Asia and the Americas, the Spanish were ineptly intent on expanding their influence in neighbouring Africa. Trouble was, in the Berbers they were up against skilful and warlike tribespeople determined to defend their homelands, and the results, by and large, were predictably catastrophic.

Morale was rock bottom. Officers were not trusted and were often corrupt. At the Battle of Annual the Spanish lost 8000 men in a day, an event which Paco was fortunate to miss. The conscripts went without rations, and to feed themselves would frequently barter their ammunition and weapons at the local markets. And one day a sergeant, an alcoholic pig of a man, slapped Paco's friend in the face in a drunken rage. And so that night, as he slept, they stole his rifle, and deserted like so many others. The rifle was a beauty, a Mauser; Paco was captivated by the elegance of its clean steel German lines, and when finally they parted after their epic journey home, the friend said that he could keep it in exchange for his tailor's shears. He had no real need of a gun, but even less so of shears; by now he was so short-sighted he could no longer make his living cutting cloth. And so he kept the Mauser, almost as a talisman.

All those years he had kept it clean and oiled, he had even managed to acquire a small amount of ammunition from an acquaintance in Motril. He was no great marksman, but from time to time he would take it out to fire at trees in the distance. And when he heard that Franco and the Foreign Legion had landed near Malaga, he placed it carefully in a canvas sack he had made for the purpose, and hid it beneath the straw at the back of the stable.

He was an observant man, and shrewd, and had picked up on the growing tensions in the village almost as quickly as Maria. He had never trusted Miguel, and saw now the way he looked at her, and heard the increasingly poisonous talk in the café. Even before the news reached the village that Kyragin had been killed, he had considered advising them to leave. Now he knew it was urgent. That evening there would be an informal gathering, when Andreu would be expected, in return for his supper, to recount any snippets of news from the coast. As ever, Paco was keen to listen, but first he waited behind as the others made their way out, then took the treasured rifle from its hiding place, and slipped across to Jacob and Maria's room, laying it carefully beneath their bed.

"Those people, those sons of bitches on the coast, they're insane," Andreu was saying as Paco walked back to join the meeting. "In theory they're all still part of the big group, the Central Antifascist Committee, but they're all at each other's throats, all jealous of each other, blaming the others. I tell you, if we lose this war it's not because Franco's strong, it's because we can't stop fighting amongst ourselves."

There is a general murmuring of assent amongst the thirty or so neighbours listening. They are gathered in the church, the only building of any consequence in the village, for it is raining slightly. The building has been stripped of all its decorations, the icons burned or stolen. On the wall behind where the altar once stood they can still see the pale outline of a great oak crucifix, which for centuries had hung there before it was ripped down during that appalling night of terror. That it was still so visible, white against the greying paint around it, had given some small degree of comfort to the priest as they had shot him; and even now, despite everything, many in the village would quietly genuflect if they thought themselves unobserved, at least by their neighbours.

"Just look at poor old Marroto," Andreu goes on, "okay, he's a wildcard, a nutter, but he's got 700 men at the gates of Granada, ready to attack, to take it back, and they – the communists – deliberately, mind, starve him of ammunition, so he has to withdraw. And now they want to lock him up because they say he's a spy! Idiots."

He pauses for breath. "It's the way they can wind everybody up, that's what gets me: it just needs half a dozen of the bastards, all rumours and roaring and madness, and suddenly everyone's with them."

Paco agrees with him, and his mind goes back to the murder of the priest. If it hadn't been for the rabble-rousers who had come up from the town, he would probably still be alive, poor man. He hadn't been a bad man, he was just in the wrong place at the wrong time, and hungry, angry people needed a scapegoat. Give them a cause, an orator, and strong drink to take away their senses, and an otherwise benevolent crowd could be steered towards destruction. Paco had been one of the volunteers to take away the corpse the morning after. He still remembers the sick horror on the faces of his neighbours as they woke to the reality of their crime. He had thought there might be trouble when after much discussion they tolled the bell for him, but none came.

Meanwhile, Andreu is still in full flow.

"... and they're cruel too, you know. The communists are sadists. You know what they did back in November? They horse-whipped all the right-wing politicians, two dozen or more, on the beaches, then tied them back-to-back and put them on a fishing boat, floated them out to sea, and drowned the lot of them. The bodies washed up at Adra a couple of days later; you could see the lash marks on their backs ..."

"Oi! Andreu, basta! Leave it out, mate. We won't sleep tonight."

"Yeah ... whose side you on, anyway?"

Andreu stops suddenly, aware he's said too much. A public outburst like this could see him killed.

To soften the atmosphere, someone mentions the weather, and they all fall to discussing the recent rains, a subject of great joy to those present, for they had faced drought. Andreu says a brief goodnight, and slips out. Paco notices that Miguel comes in at the same moment that Andreu leaves; where the devil has he been?

Slowly the little gathering comes to an end, and people begin to make their way back home. By now the night is clear, and there are many quiet murmurings of disappointment that the rain has eased. Paco and two women, the last to leave, make a half-hearted attempt to tidy up, pushing back a few chairs along the walls. Paco steps outside and lights a cigarette. He watches as the women carefully close the doors. As there is nothing left to steal, the building is no longer kept locked, but they do need to keep out the foxes. As the door swings shut Paco catches the eye of one of the women as she crosses herself, and she looks away guiltily.

"Say one for me," he says as she passes, and winks at her. She smiles back at him, relieved that her secret is safe, and Paco ambles away in the other direction. He has a mission to perform. He's nervous and he wants to run, but he knows that no good will come of being seen to hurry. Instead he walks deliberately towards the hiding place and thinks about his gun. He's passing it on, like a baton in a race. A race to what, he wonders, to where? So often he had studied it and wondered whether it had ever taken a human life, whether a weapon that had done so was somehow cursed, or special. The same question came back to him now as he walked along the silent streets, and for the first time he realised that he didn't want to know the answer. Some things, he thought as he coughed on his rough black tobacco, some things are better not knowing, and this was one of them, even for a curious mind. He spat, and knocked on the door.

Carmen and Jess were holding hands, with Jacob standing some distance apart. They look unusually nervous and Paco can sense that they have come to the same conclusion.

"You have to leave," says Paco simply. "Right now. I don't know what's going on, but there's something bad in the air, and I really don't like the look of things. You need to get up to the high mountains, hide away for a few days, come back when it's calmer."

Carmen hands over a small canvas sack containing a few provisions, and Paco bends down and takes his rifle from its hiding place beneath the bed.

"Just in case …" he says apologetically. "I guess you know how to use it."

Outside they hear the sound of running feet, and they grow silent. It is only children, but it adds to the tension in the room.

"Just go," says Carmen. "Now before I blub, go quickly."

Chapter Forty-Seven

Flight, 1937

It seemed unreal that they had to leave so urgently, but within five minutes their few possessions had been packed away into two rucksacks and they were ready to go.

"They warned me in Madrid that there are subversives," whispered Maria, "that there are factions. Traitors. Listen: things might seem complex. They are. More complex than you could ever believe. You know nothing, and I know very little more. Call it different versions of the same truths ... but these are such dangerous people. In Barcelona the republicans are already fighting amongst themselves. Trust has been ambushed by envy and suspicion, but I'm going to keep my promises. You know what? It's hard to accept that I'm just a pawn within a bigger game, but though the movements of a pawn are limited, in the hands of a skilful player they can have powerful consequences; I've just got to trust my superiors. Kyragin was a senior figure, and if they can kill him, then they won't think twice about killing us."

"But the documents," Jacob began, "they – we – don't even know what's in them. How can they be so important?"

"But they could be," said Maria, "and if the Trotskyists, or whoever they are, now think that we're prepared to take all these chances, to come all this way, then maybe the letters contain some bit of information that's worth knowing."

She paused. "And there's something else: it might not be the message that they're interested in. It might be the messenger ... it could be *us* they want. See, I don't know much, but I do know the identity of my handler in Madrid. Chances are the people in the south don't know who's running things there, and they want to expose him, to use me to flush him out. And so I'm a danger, don't you see. A danger to you and to my boss." She smiles. "Sounds familiar, doesn't it? Hunted by my own side. So now we're both on the run ... from everybody."

Jacob stood, and crossed the room to where she was crouching vigilant by the window.

"Let's go," he said as he pulled her to him, "let's go right now."

They closed the door quietly, but hadn't gone two paces before a voice spoke to them from the darkness.

"Wait there," said a man. "I'm coming with you."

Maria peered into the night and saw that it was the old shepherd, Joachim.

"You can't-" Jacob started.

"It's already arranged," the old man cut him off. "I spoke to Paco. You're coming with me to help with the sheep. At least that's what he'll tell people. You know that my grandson Sergio cleared off last week to join the fighting. I'm all alone. And it means that if everything cools down here then you have an excuse and you can come back for a while. Also, by yourselves you'll get lost in five minutes. And besides, that filth Miguel has been plotting against you and there might be a fight. I might be old but I can still shoot."

Maria looked at Jacob. "He's right," she said. "If you're sure, old man, then please – come with us."

Joachim grunted, tightened the strap on his mule and walked out into the night.

"Doesn't look like we get much choice," said Jacob as they set off behind him.

"When you're true to yourself, then choice is an illusion," she replied mystifyingly and slapped him on the backside like a horse.

They left the sleeping village and climbed steadily, in near silence for four hours, until Joachim stopped by a stone hut and announced that they would rest until daybreak. Daybreak came all too quickly, yet despite the granite tiles on which they had slept so briefly Jacob felt revived and alert.

The old man was outside, shielding his eyes against the rising sun.

"Down there," he said. "Look. Riders coming after us."

Maria and Jacob followed his finger.

"You never know, they might not come far," he said. "They might just climb a while above the village and decide they've had enough. They won't risk horses, not over these rocks."

"Or we could fight them here," said Jacob.

"Not here. We're still too exposed. But up there, that cave I showed you, remember, we could hold off an army."

Jacob and Joachim looked at each other, trying to guess what the other is thinking.

"I could hold them off alone," said the old man, and gave them time to let this sink in.

"But we don't know the way," said Jacob, "and I'm faster. I can deal with them and catch you up in no time. We could separate now, just for a while."

The two men look at Maria.

"Jacob's right," she said after a while. "He's the soldier; let him stay."

She kissed him on the lips.

"Alright?" he asked. "Are you sure?"

"See that hill," the old man interrupted. "That's Lujar. And under it, on the coast, is a town called Gualchos. That's where we're heading. We'll see you there."

By now the sun was fully risen and Maria was hot. As she unwound the scarf from her face, her earring caught in a strand of wool and fell to the ground. Jacob bent to pick it up and was just about to return it when in the distance they heard the sound of the riders calling to each other.

"Look after it for me," she said, and closed her hand around his.

"There's a letter in your bag," he said quickly. "I put it there the other day ... just in case. It's got the names of my cousins in England. If it all goes completely wrong then that's where I'm headed, okay?"

It was all happening too fast.

"It's time," she said. "I need to go now. Gualchos or Gibraltar or England. Whichever one, I'll see you there. Let it not be long. I love you."

"I love you too," he whispered, and kissed her one last time. "Stay safe. Don't look back – like Orpheus."

He watched as they walked away, swallowing hard. This was not the time for emotion. This was a time for action, a time for duty. He swore to himself that whatever it took, no matter what happened, he would keep her safe.

After two minutes she turned, but already he was gone, dissolving into the undergrowth as all his training dictated.

The rifle felt good in his hands. All his life he'd been trained to fight, and the last few months all he'd been doing was running away. He forced himself to breathe in slowly through his nose, then held a hand flat out in front. It was steady. He was in control. If they wanted a fight, he was ready, and he'd fight them on his terms. He noted with satisfaction that all four of the men were now spread out beneath him, coming closer.

This was good: as he'd hoped, they must have assumed that they all were headed due north, and none had followed Maria. He watched as one of the men bent down in triumph, having located the wool jacket that Jacob had left on purpose in his attempt to deceive them. Idiot. For a long moment he held the man in the rifle sights, finger tensed on the trigger. This would be an easy shot. The man shouted to his colleagues, and Jacob felt a familiar power surge through him: if he chose, this would be the last sound the man would ever make.

But not yet, not yet. He'd let them get a little closer, buy Maria and Joachim a bit more time. He wondered if she was cold. He looked across the hills to the saddle on the ridge, to the point at which they would soon be crossing. If his luck held, he would have dealt with his pursuers before noon, when he could stride out and catch them. The old man couldn't move that quickly. Perhaps he might catch them by nightfall. He would much rather catch up with her here in the mountains than look for her in this place Gualchos.

As he glanced at the peaks he saw a lightning bolt flash across the darkling clouds; a summer squall was bearing down on them. She wouldn't like that; he knew she was afraid of storms.

Five more minutes. As the day brightened he could see more broken rock just above him, and he was tempted to move even higher. The rising sun would be in their eyes and they might not see him. But the cave that now held him was perfect, he decided; protected on three sides, with a natural parapet of stone just in front to duck behind. And he didn't want to lose the advantage of surprise. Maybe they didn't even know he had a gun. The way that they were calling to each other suggested that they were not afraid of him. Just kids, easy pickings. Well, they'd see about that.

He looked down. Now he can see only three of them. Where's the fourth? Now he's the idiot, he chastises himself. Keep concentrating. There was a flicker of movement in the trees to his left. *There you are, you bastard.*

It is time to make his presence felt.

By now he can see their faces. As far as he can tell most of them are not local, and their fine horses suggest that they have come from outside. He recognises only Miguel. He is the first one he must kill, since he is a local, and knows the paths. It feels like cold blood. It is the first time he has known the name of his target. It makes no difference. He has trained for this. Kill or be killed. Killing a communist – at last his father would be proud. He allows himself a little smile. How life moves in circles.

He shoots him through the heart and the man goes down in a heap. He sees one of the other men crouching, unsure where the shot has come from. Don't think, shoot, Jacob reminds himself. You can reflect later. Be merciless. As the crouching man turns, Jacob shoots him through the side of the head.

He has revealed his position. A shot rings out and ricochets off a rock, too close for comfort. He tries to focus on where he last saw the third man, scanning around for the fourth. Damnit. *No, I see you*! The next man crumples to the ground.

He hears the thunder of hooves and realises that the terrified horses have broken free. Good. He watches as they surge downhill, away from him. Could a rider stay on like that? Hang on ... how many were there? Too late to count. Could they have brought a spare?

Immediately below him he sees a sudden flash and a splinter of rock explodes above his head. Poor man, thinks Jacob: he must have decided that he can't be seen behind that bush. Jacob ducks and moves three paces to his left in case the fool tries his luck again, then takes careful aim. This is the last one. He squeezes the trigger carefully, and watches the body twitch, then shudder.

At the last instant Jacob rolls to the floor, and lies there trying to catch his breath. She's safe. He has done it.

Chapter Forty-Eight

Gualchos, 1937

An electric jolt shocks her from slumber. She feels as though she has been kicked awake; her heart crashes violently against her ribs and she is panting. Outside she hears footsteps, shouting. Her eyes stare wide, struggling for focus in the gloom of the stable, so that she is dazzled, vulnerable, as the doors are thrown open and a tall silhouette blocks the light. Suddenly she is on her knees, scrabbling in the straw for the blade she had left ready the night before, blind with panic.

"Whoaa! Easy there – it's only me!" says the voice of the silhouette, and she realises it is Manolo, the farmer they had met in the tavern.

"Get out, you fucking weasel! Get out!" she screams, and he backs away, dismayed at the ferocity of her reaction.

She's trembling, flooded with humiliation and relief, her breathing shallow, and so stands upright slowly, tense as a cornered cat. Joachim, who has spent the night in his cot at the far end of the stable, is looking at her, rheumy eyes wrinkled with concern and tenderness.

"It's nothing," he says softly. "You alright?"

"I'm sorry. Sorry," she replies, " I thought … it's …" and she tries to bury the sob that starts way down, ashamed. "I'm fine, fine." But the sob is too strong, too vital, and for a moment she has to look away. She swallows, tries to still her breathing. "I'll be alright. Don't worry ... it's just that sometimes I can't stand this ... this being *this way,* this vigilance, this tension, this ..."

"It's not wrong, you know, to be frightened. I am," whispers Joachim, and she nods.

She does know this, accepts it. But it's not the fear right now, right here, she wants to explain, it's everything: the war, the anxiety, the rage, the sheer constancy of it all. This is where her rage is born, and she is sick, sick of it all, the killing, the secrets, the violence, the whole stupid lack of mercy and understanding, this awful corrosive, undeviating sense of low-level panic that is always there, snapping at her heels. In small doses she could stand it: she'd known pure terror, had had her nights brutalised by the memory of the bowel-weakening screams of the girls in the prison, had wretched at the convulsive death agonies of a bullet-ridden horse; these episodes she could handle, just. And with Jacob it had been terrifying, but different. Yes, she had been aghast at the guns at the prison in Toledo, and petrified beyond reason by the chase afterwards, but she had felt strangely alive; it was an adventure, which had in hindsight a quality of make-believe, like they'd seen themselves in the movies. With Jacob at her side she had felt awash with pure life, and they were invincible.

But this was not the same. This was dark, was poison. Months ago, in the moments leading up to her theft of the satchel at Jacob's home, she had watched through the crack in the door as the German officers came and went, appalled at the imminence of the act she had sworn to commit, horrified at the consequences. She had thought then that she could endure not one second more of this slow mortification, and it was this, this loathing of the moment, that had finally goaded her to action, and which she had promised to herself that she would never,

ever, repeat. But now she felt like this *all of the time,* and she wasn't sure how long she could stand it.

And so in response she was permanently filled with this strange slow-burning fury. She could feel it deep down, heavy, bubbling away, waiting for a vent. Once, years ago, the cook at the Madrid house had shown her a glass ball, clear, like a large marble, that she used to simmer milk to prevent the pan from boiling over. She would often hear it as she walked past, and listen as it clicked, busy and wrathful at the bottom of the copper pot. It was something that had disquieted her, but this was exactly how she saw herself right now: reduced, constantly agitated, simmering with tension, and desperate for peace of some kind. At that moment she really did not know if she would be able to continue, and stood there, cold and indecisive, until Joachim broke the silence.

"You told me it was important to get this stuff to Gibraltar," he says, "and I believed you. Still believe you. But listen, if it's going to break you then I'm going to go on alone. You would be safe here. You can trust them."

This is a long speech from Joachim, clearly prepared, and she is touched. She looks at him for a long moment, and smiles, for she is fond of him. He is shorter than her, despite the tufts of white hair that stand upright, and he is proudly unshaven, one of those men whose grey whiskers make them irredeemably, intrinsically shabby. But as they gaze at each other she sees through and beyond this haggard façade and senses the integrity and purpose that lay beneath, and finds her mood lifting.

"No way, old man. You can't ditch me that easily," she says finally. "I'm going with you, we've come this far and we're sticking together, and that's that."

She inhales deeply, slowly. The soft scent of the straw, and the heat and proximity of the mules in the stable give her comfort. Someone is brewing coffee – coffee! – and somewhere a woodpigeon is cooing, and the man outside in the street with the hammer whistles happily. As she becomes more aware of her immediate surroundings she feels more like a player in this little tableau, rather than an onlooker, and begins, as she calls it, to sink back into her real true self.

The woman from the tavern now beckons her outside, and she steps blinking into the sunlight. She is given milk, honey, a little bread, and eats ravenously, for it has been days since she last ate bread. The woman is staring at her.

"Got to make sure you girls are looked after," she says, and looks pointedly at Maria's belly. "Got to breed us some good little republicans! I saw you last night and I knew. I always know ."

It takes a moment for her to react. "What? No, no ... I'm not ... I'm ..." But the woman has gone. Maria has heard the words, has understood, though refuses to embrace the meaning. But an idea, light as air, has been born, and floats quietly and unstoppably down to the centre of her being, where it waits, untouchable.

She cannot acknowledge it now, dare not, and instead walks down the street towards the square, where a group of men are forcing the driver of a small cart to hand over its contents. It is a familiar sight everywhere these days, this commonplace brigandage disguised as a political act, and she is about to walk on when one of the men calls to her.

"Maria! Come! Just look at what we fine soldiers have just confiscated in the name of the Republic." It's the blond one, the handsome one; they had noticed each other last night, and she turns back to see. To much laughter, four of the men are struggling to lift down a large object, gold at one end. She has no clue as to what it might be.

"It's a harp! A bloody harp. Turns out some old bloke in Granada had taken it out of the music academy for safe-keeping, and accidentally sold it to Pedro here, and we've, well ... we've liberated it for the people. Put it in the church, fellas."

She watches as they carry it less than reverently towards the chapel, and moves on up the hill, aware that the eyes of the blond man are following her.

She and Joachim are to leave after dusk, and take the mule track over the high hills to avoid the busy towns on the coast. All afternoon she has been listless, and at five walks back up to the chapel for want of anything better to do. The door is open, the silence calls to her, and she steps inside and sees the harp standing in the aisle. In the half-light it seems enormous, beautiful. She'd heard one played once, long ago, at one of the free concerts after the feria, and remembers vaguely the gorgeous, unearthly sounds it could make. Dust motes float in the stillness above the gold top-piece, and she runs her fingers absent-mindedly across the strings. The noise is awful, loud, and makes her jump. The strings thrum for a while, then settle again to silence before she lifts a long bare arm and picks at a single string, plucking once, twice.

"It suits you," says a voice, and she turns, startled, to see the blond man grinning at her from the darkness of the pulpit. His name, she has learned, is Victor Perez, and he is the de facto leader of the group.

She is about to reply when the door behind them is flung open and a young man rushes in.

"Come quickly," he says. "There's some guy on the radio saying that Madrid has fallen, and that we're scum and all going to die. It's pretty tense in the bar; there are a few who we still suspect aren't, you know ..." He looks meaningfully at Maria. "I think Pablo is going to hit someone."

The two men stride out together, and Maria follows, eager to get back to Joachim and avoid confrontation. As she passes close to the square she can hear the raised voices, the shouts, the all-too-familiar sense of impending violence. Out of nowhere appears a gang of around six men, loping directly her way, snarling like dogs. Mercifully they pass close by without seeing her, sniffing the air for prey. She turns, and for some reason follows them as they head back up the hill. They are enraged and confused. She stares as they charge into the chapel, and watches fascinated as they push and kick at the harp, which crashes clanging to the stone floor. The men cheer, and one produces a hammer, another an axe, and in a frenzy they attack the instrument, violating the sanctuary of the ancient silence with the monstrous chords of some great dying beast. It seems to her the most repugnant act of brutality she has ever seen. And these, she knows, are the good guys, her comrades, and she begins quietly to weep.

Later, in the gloaming as she steps out with Joachim on the route above the village, she asks herself how she can ever describe to Jacob the sound of a harp breaking. And of how this sound had ruptured something inside her.

A small moon is rising as they set off on the track above the wash-house, outlining the great shards of the mountains they are expecting to cross before dawn. An owl hoots, but otherwise the silence of the hills falls on them like a blanket. As they leave the village the evening air is still thick with jasmine, which as they climb gives way to rosemary and sage. Joachim is in front with the mule, whose sides brush against fennel and wild thyme, and the fragrant dust that this produces adds a strange sensuality to their departure. She reflects that in Madrid she had never really thought much about smells; perhaps it was just that in the city there was simply too much going on, you never had time or space to think about the way things smelled.

And the silence! She loves the thought of being cocooned in this boundless vacuum of sound, though at the same time is unsettled by it. There is a weight, a depth to this quietude that she has never known. It is so profound, so present, that she fancies she can smell it on her clothes. Even the cicadas are stilled. She too is soothed, but when Joachim calls for a halt and the night is suddenly spared even the gentle bump of their own footfall, she becomes fretful, and asks to move on.

The sky is largely clear, and by the light of the stars and the half-grown moon they make their way slowly up the hillside. Ahead she can pick out the flicker of yellow flowers on the gorse, and grasps that the black gash between them is their track. A silvered film of spider web is strung across the heather, glimmering shyly. A stand of tall, tenebrous trees looms up before them then floats away behind as they continue to climb. She does not tire, but is drawn slowly into a trance by the soft rhythm of these ethereal circumstances, at peace at last with the cosmos. Lulled by the symmetry of the moment she allows herself to unbend, and feel again the space between her heartbeats. A priest had long ago wasted his breath, she'd thought, in explaining to her the concept of a State of Grace; but was this perhaps it?

A horizontal teardrop of a cloud collides with the moon. Blackness, and for a moment they must stop. Joachim has told her that he hasn't walked this path for more than five years. How can he possibly know his way?

"I don't," he replies, "I just follow the dog. He sniffs the ground then goes where other men have walked, that's all. Usually."

He looks at her for affirmation of some sort, but she isn't really listening, for she trusts him implicitly, and as the moon re-appears they continue their spectral odyssey in silence. She knows that soon they should reach the gap on the ridge that will allow them to start the track downhill, and she strains her eyes into the night sky, searching for clues in the velvet darkness. Suddenly she is startled as a shooting star fizzes brilliantly across in front of them, so bright she will swear later that she had heard its passing. Reflexively she begins to make a wish, then hesitates. She is about to wish for Jacob's safety, but from nowhere leaps the memory of the lady with the milk and honey, and the look she'd given her belly, and for a split second she havers, wondering whether she should wish on this, and in this case, just what it is she could wish for ... but all of this is too complex, too big, and she wishes instead just that Jacob should be safe. Everything else is irrelevant, she tells herself: she will stay focussed and get to Gibraltar on time, and then, maybe, maybe, allow herself to think of other things. So for now she rides onwards into the blackness of the hills. She is riding one-handed, her other gloved hand pressed hard against her belly, protectively. After a while, in the distance, a wolf howls, and though she is not frightened, she crosses herself for the first time in many years.

The track becomes ever more narrow as they reach the pass, so that they are forced to dismount and lead their mules in single file, the invisible gorse pricking cruelly against their legs. At the top there is a small clearing, where they stop to catch their breath. From here they can see all the way down to the bay, the breaking waves just visible in the pale moonlight. From the far headland comes the recurrent sweep and flash of a lighthouse. Even here, from the land side, its beam is strangely reassuring.

After a pause they resume their journey, moving carefully as the path cuts sideways around a rocky outcrop. Suddenly the dog barks, and at the same time a voice calls out and orders them to halt. Her stomach tightens and in horror she stares beyond Joachim at the faces of two men who are blocking their descent. A noise behind her makes her turn, and she sees to her dismay that two others have stepped out of the shadows, leaving them trapped, ambushed. It is too dark to see whether they wear uniform.

Her heart by now is beating so violently that she thinks she may be sick. A disembodied voice tells them to sit down, to which they agree without objection. From this height she feels even more vulnerable, and this angers her, and her anger gives her a tiny degree of calm. Someone lights a match, then an oil lamp, and the detainees can at last begin to see their captors. She spots at once that they are all young, as scared perhaps as she is, and dangerous.

"Are you ... comrades?" she asks, timorously.

"Comrades! We're all fuckin' comrades in this war!" shouts the nearest one, and the others laugh. "Who the hell are you? What are you doing here? Old man! Tell me before I cut your skinny throat out."

Joachim says nothing. As ever in this conflict there is a terrifying ignorance as to whether their opponents are friend or foe. The truth could kill or save them; a lie could be believed but, if discovered, might have them shot even if they now found themselves in the hands of fellow anti-fascists. Truth. Deceit. It was all the same, really, and Maria is sick of it. She will just have to say something and hope that the morons in front of her are on the side of the angels. Rage tumbles out of her, emboldens her, inspires her, and she stands.

"I'm Victor Perez's girl," she says to her own amazement. "One of his girls. Apparently. Bastard. I'm in trouble and now he doesn't even want to know me. This is Joachim and he's not my granddad, he's my friend, and he took me to Gualchos to see that prick Victor and now we're going home. If you must know we're going now to Malaga to find me a doctor. If you have to shoot someone, shoot me.

Joachim's just a good guy, and me, well, I've had enough ..." Her tears now are real and her legitimate fury is all too plain. There is spittle on her chin and she is trembling. The men all look at each other, shocked, Joachim included.

"I know Victor," says someone at last, "he is a prick. They say he did that to a girl in Motril as well. God knows why they made him a Captain."

Maria puts a hand on the side of a mule to steady herself as relief pours through her. This was not the Guardia Civil after all, and her deception might work. She might have tarnished the reputation of a comrade unfairly, but from what she'd just heard it probably wasn't that far from the truth. God bless the Russian in Madrid who'd told them all so often to note the details, to remember them, to use their intelligence, their wits, since most men were essentially idiots and easily traduced. But at the same time, that anger, that acrimony? That was all too real.

Years later, when she was finally able to look back on events with a trace of dispassion, she would remember this day as pivotal to her small role in the war. It wasn't as if there would be any single momentous episode that would define it, but rather that she became conscious throughout that slow afternoon of the cold, harrowing realisation that she was utterly entrapped by the struggle, and that this was no longer a merely dangerous game, an adventure, but a merciless contest from which there might never be any escape.

She would always be curious as to why, when she recalled the war, her memory would always lead her down this particular lane, to this particular date, when nothing of any great consequence had actually occurred. Perhaps it was just that it was a typical day, emblematic somehow of all of the fear, the confusion, resentment and hatred that would book-end it.

The morning had begun brightly enough. Their young would-be captors had allowed them to continue the previous night, abashed at their own temerity, it seemed to her. As they left them to their naïve vigil, one of them had offered her a bruised apple, of all things, a gesture so guileless it had brought a lump to her throat.

Through waves of semi-wakefulness she had trudged without rest down the winding stony path with Joachim at her side, and had barely observed the shifting greys as night pass soundlessly to dawn. By eight o'clock it was already full light, the poor heat of the sun was warm on her back, and ahead, trapped before a wall of burning pink cloud, was the sea, clean and gentle, drawing them on.

"There'll be a storm later, you watch," says Joachim. She can tell he is pleased, because above all else he is an Andalucían farmer, and in this sun-stricken land the promise of rain is always welcome, especially so after the intensity of this desiccating summer. She suspects that in his heart he'd perhaps sooner see the end of the drought than the end of the war, or perhaps for him it was all the same thing: an endless struggle against the elements, human or otherwise. She notices how he jabs a heel at the ground, intuitively, then kicks out to test the dust he creates, scowling. She realises that he must be anxious about his harvest back home, and appreciates even more the sacrifice he is making on her behalf. She has been too selfish, she thinks, to assume that he will risk so much to help her. She has never really questioned his motives, but assumed that he does so out of a vague notion of solidarity to his humble class. She has respected him, but taken too much for granted, and now, at last, in the quiet calm of the lower valley, she asks him.

"They killed my son," is all he says, finally, and keeps his eyes fixed on the horizon, walking on ahead of her. She is winded by the brutality of his words, his heart-rending mixture of dignity and sorrow, and feels again the coldness rising in her, the wild horse of panic that she fears more than anything, and follows him meekly, swallowing hard.

Later they will stop to rest on the banks of a small stream, where she eats the apple she was given in the night. She takes out the pips and buries them surreptitiously in the damp earth, feeling foolish, but hoping that something might grow in memory of this boy she'd never met.

Chapter Forty-Nine

Arriving at Motril, 1937

"Little Cuba," said Joachim. "That's what they call it. Sugar cane. I worked here when I was younger, in the cutting season; worst job I ever had." With a weatherworn hand he points dismissively to the town laid out ahead of them, Motril, and the lush green hinterland beyond.

"There's a port too, but it's miles away. They put the town inland to protect themselves from raiders. I never really took to it, don't know why. There was a *posada*, a tavern, scruffy kind of place, probably still is ... I've got money ..."

She smiles to herself. There's something about towns, about strangers, that makes him talkative, as if to calm his nerves. In the vastness of the mountains he had seemed a composed and comforting presence; here it was the reverse, and she felt he needed her to guide him. It was about time: she had dawdled too long perhaps in Gualchos, unsettled and anxious; she had sheltered too long beneath the wings of first Jacob, and now the old man. This wasn't like her.

"Let's go then. Let's find your scruffy old posada. I'll go first."

In the heat of late afternoon the streets were almost empty. People who do not know southern Spain may struggle to understand the full, crushing power of the summer sun, but it is a presence, a reality to deal with, as significant as day or night, and daily routines are scheduled accordingly. Now, sombre white houses lie dormant behind louvred shutters, soaked in the scent of jasmine. The very air shimmered. Outside a baking butcher's shop, two dogs competed with the flies over a slick black mess of bone and blood. A drab army truck lumbered slowly past them, with the troops in the back beneath the tarpaulin too sun-dazed even to catcall. At a stone fountain, where they had paused to bathe and to water the mules, Maria helped an old woman fill the terracotta pitcher she was carrying, and asked her the way to the tavern.

At first she thought she was deaf, or ignoring her.

"You're close," the old woman said at last, "two blocks up here, turn left by the post office." And then, pointing a bony finger at the departing army truck, "Just follow those sons-of-bitches."

Would she have dared say this to just anyone, wondered Maria? Could she read some subtle clues as to their allegiances? Or were theirs so blindingly obvious? The thought troubled her as they made their way deeper into town.

"I'm stopping with the mules," Joachim insisted as they got there. "In the stables. I'm not sharing with that lot of snoring, farting heathens."

The tavern was indeed scruffy, and judging by the characters, all men, who sat around in the rank gloom of the bar, he was wise to choose the stable. Maria agreed to share a room with the innkeeper's daughter, a smiley woman of about her age, and that night they talked long enough to establish the beginnings of a friendship. It had been so long, she thought, since she'd had a proper conversation with a woman. The girl – Elene – didn't press her too much on her plans, nor did she give much away. After all, Motril was now firmly under Francoist control; they were both guarded.

The next morning Maria and the old man were to spend the morning in town, to see the lay of the land, as he put it. So far no one had been able to tell them with any certainty whether the coastal road to Malaga, some sixty kilometres to the west, was open, let alone safe. There was a wash house attached to the tavern, and Elene had offered to launder the dust-laden clothes which Maria had worn on the road. She bathed too, emerging pink and scrubbed, then sat in the sun to warm up as Elene brushed her hair for her. It felt good, and as she put on the only other clothes she possessed, those she had stolen in Toledo, she suddenly heard music.

"Jazz!" says Elene. "It's the man next door, he has a phonograph and plays it outside 'cos his wife hates it so much." She takes a few quick steps, pirouettes, then pulls Maria to her feet, and for a while they dance together, beaming and unabashed. For both of them it is a spontaneous, innocent moment of radiance amidst the gloom of the war, which each will come to treasure in the months that follow.

An hour later Maria and the old man step out on to the dusty, shit-spattered streets. There are horses everywhere, pulling carts, pulling carriages, pulling guns; some riderless, others bearing sweating officers with sticks, one a priest. Maria notices a school, a fishmonger, a bank, all open: the place seems to be working normally. They decide to head for the post office to try to gather information, and the old man waits outside as Maria joins the queue. He can see from her face as she emerges that the news isn't good. As they had feared, the coast road to Malaga is said to be impossibly dangerous, especially for women, and they will need to go inland again, over and along the treacherous hills.

Disappointed but not surprised, they make their way back towards the tavern, the old man chuntering to himself about the perils they will face. They notice without interest that a small, curious crowd has gathered at the crossroads, and that the air is filled with a distinctive sweet smoke. Someone tells them that a fire has broken out at the molasses factory, and, trapped by the onlookers, they watch as men struggle to get hoses and water to the blaze.

Suddenly there is a bang, then shouting, and from out of nowhere the crowd seems to be hit by a rising wall of panic. Sparks have ignited the straw in the stables in the brewery next door, and the street is now filled with the screams of terrified horses. Realising what is happening, Maria pulls at the old man's coat and together they try to turn and go back the same way, but it is hopeless. There is wildness and fear in the eyes of the other horses, and men fight to control them with curses and whips, straining in desperation on bridles and halters, losing control. As the gate to the stables bursts open, a team of four terror-stricken dray horses explodes onto the courtyard, and run amok amongst the crowd. The old man shoves Maria violently into a doorway, and tries to shield her with his body. She hears his cry as he loses his grip and is carried away by the wild surge of kicking and confusion.

It's all over in minutes. The horses are gone, and for a moment the world is preternaturally quiet as people try to comprehend just what has happened. Maria walks slowly, shell-shocked down the street. A woman bends over a fallen child; two men are trying to lift a huge wheel from the prone body of a third; Maria's body shudders at the retort of a pistol as a tearful young soldier shoots a broken, dying horse in the head. And then she sees him. The old man lies half-prostrate in the dirt, his head resting against the wall of a shop. Blood runs thickly from a cut above his ear, down under the collar, and one eye is closed. He stirs as she runs to him, and pushes himself up by his arms.

"I'm okay," he says, "I'm grand ... I'll live, don't worry. But this," he adds solemnly as he points to his foot, "this might complicate things for us." Maria stares at the base of his shin, so hairless, so white, that for a moment she thinks it is bone. Wincing with the effort, he lifts himself higher on his elbows, and as he does so she sees the swelling and foul discolouration of an unarguably broken ankle.

She kneels beside him and holds his hand. "Don't worry," she says to his pale, frightened face, "I'll get someone."

Two soldiers, officers, are walking towards them. She stands and blocks their path.

"This man," she says to them with authority, "this man is my friend and I need to get him to a doctor. Will you help me?"

They are good men, and seeing the determination and worry in the face of this pretty woman, they will not deny her.

"Yes ma'am," says the younger of the two, and barks an order at a nearby subordinate. "We can take him to the military hospital. You know it?" She nods untruthfully. "They'll probably make you pay ..." She nods again. "We'll stretcher him there and you can see him tonight. Alright?" The men salute her, and move on. They are cold, but efficient, and their coldness seems to add to the detachment, the unreality of the morning.

Maria buys a bottle of iced water from the bar, and returns to the old man. By the time she gets there, soldiers are already helping him on to a two-pole army gurney.

She can see that he is in much pain, but is stoically smiling through it.

"Not to worry, these boys are looking after me. They're efficient and they're kind ..." She holds his hand again, both of them smiling at the irony of the situation.

He raises a hand in farewell as they begin to trundle him away. Alternate waves of despair and confusion wash over her as she stands alone in the middle of the street, watching until he is almost out of sight. They are kind, she thinks to herself, they are *kind* and they *are* just boys, poor boys probably, by the looks of them, and yet they are my enemies …

Shaking, she stares around her at the damaged street, appalled by the fickleness of things. Life is random enough as it is, she reflects, and curses – not for the first time – the madness, the malevolence, and the sheer perversity of those who want to make it worse. Those utter fuckwits who lead them blindly into war, and those, like her, who follow.

Chapter Fifty

Help, 1937

Back at their lodgings, Elene was at first too jittery to be of any real help. Maria couldn't blame her; it was common sense rather than cowardice. Half the population were either too scared or too confused to decide which horse to back, and were hedging their bets until a winner could be declared.

But later that evening, as they were getting ready for bed, Elene plucked up the courage to mention that possibly, perhaps, she may have heard from someone that the young head teacher at the school may once have been something of a leftie. It may not be true, of course, and he came from good family: his grandfather had been a major in the army. Maria's ears pricked up at this news, and she resolved to go and visit the school in the morning.

She barely slept. She wasn't worried about the old man. He was a survivor, and the hospital would look after him. But she felt trapped, and alone. As far as she was concerned she was now behind enemy lines, and the route to her destination was all but blocked. She thought about trying to make it back to Toledo. But that would mean failure ... and it would mean that she would miss Jacob when he got to

Gibraltar. She had to press on.

Her sense of desperation perhaps made her reckless. Her training and natural caution would otherwise have counselled patience, but when she rose after her fitful night, she chose to follow intuition. She got to the school an hour before classes were to start, hoping that the head teacher would be first to arrive. She had been standing by the gate for no more than a few minutes before the tall silhouette of a man appeared against the outline of the slowly rising sun. Heart pounding, she swallowed in preparation of what she was about to say. He was no more than a few metres away before she saw the cassock, the black *bonete* on his head. A priest! A church school! Of course. She hadn't thought of this ... this might not be such a good idea. But he didn't slow down, didn't even look at her, and her eyes were still fixed on the hill to the east when she heard the jangling of keys behind her.

A youngish man in a worsted grey suit struggled with the lock, and gave a satisfied sigh when finally it clicked open. He stepped back politely to let her go first, and looked at her questioningly. She had nothing to say. She had planned this, but now it all seemed foolish; everything she could think of seems either too dangerously overt or too mysterious.

He looks at her, cocks his head to one side, and raises his eyebrows, perplexed.

"I'm a ... I mean, I used to be ..." She stops, looks over her shoulder, tries again. "I wanted ..."

At that moment a group of mounted soldiers trot down the road towards them. She tries to look calm, but the fear on her face is almost comically plain, and to her surprise the young man takes her elbow and leads her away from them, over towards the school building. She is grateful, but when she looks at him again she sees he is no longer smiling; his mouth is set in a tight grimace.

"Sorry," is all she says, "but I'm desperate. I need help. I'm alone. It's important. Not for me, I mean – for all of us."

Us. The simple pronoun hangs in the air between them like an unwanted smell. Eventually he speaks, decisive now.

"Listen," he says, " I don't know how the hell you found me, or what you're doing here, or who you are. All I know is that we're a danger to each other. Just your being here ... Shit! I'm compromised, I think, they don't trust me."

"Sorry," she says again. And then, after a moment, "It's all dangerous, together or apart, no matter ..."

But he isn't listening. "Leave now," he insists. "Go back the way you came. But tonight, in the port, there's a Chandlers, you know what that is, right? A store, a shop for mariners, for boats, at 7.30pm I'll be there ... and I'll introduce you to someone else, even if we can't speak. Go! Go now!" His voice softens. "Now, *comrade*. Salud."

"Salud," she says in reply, the way of all the republicans. *Adios* – until God – has been banned in many hard-left circles, and the fact of their sharing the more subversive *salud* underlines their sympathies. She turns and nods once more as she leaves. The first of the pupils, the youngest ones, most with mothers attached, are beginning to cluster at the school gates, and she feels conspicuous.

She knows she has brought peril to the life of the teacher, as if there weren't peril enough already. The previous evening Elene had tried to describe the situation in Motril before and after the Nationalists had taken over, without revealing her private loyalties. It seemed the circumstances in this inconsequential little port reflected almost exactly the scene elsewhere. According to Elene, in a sense not much had changed. First, under the republicans, there had been widespread bloodshed. Anyone remotely connected with the ruling classes or the church had been dealt with savagely, and there had been many dozens of vicious killings, barbaric acts of unjustified assassination, execution by kangaroo courts, and general lawlessness, all in the name of the people. And this was *before* Franco came along! Now, under the fascist Rebels, the Falange, the militias, the legionnaires and the regular army were doing roughly the same thing, though this time they were busy murdering unionists and reds, not bankers and priests. In Elene's view they were all bedfellows: same thugs, different uniforms.

It was a bleak conclusion, and Maria could not allow herself to share in it. Of course there was violence, of course there were atrocities: this was war. But her side, her *people*, they *were* different, because what they wanted was change. She had to keep believing this. They had had enough of the old ways, and they wanted – they needed – their world to improve, they needed reform, justice, equality, and for Spain to become a better place, a modern place. She knew this in her heart, just as she had always known it, and the knowledge gave her comfort still.

That afternoon she went to the hospital to see Joachim, and the visit reinforced her courage. He was a fighter. Understated, unassuming and unkempt, he was nonetheless a warrior, a warrior of the right sort. Not one who took pleasure in war, but one who risked himself for what he believed in, for others.

His leg had been set, and a nurse had shaved him. His blue eyes gleamed at her. He was going to be alright, he promised, and she believed him. He beckoned her close and whispered that there was money, gold coin, sewn into the lining of the saddle bag of the mule. She was to take half, she would need it. This was an order, not an offer, and she accepted.

Later that day she used some of the money to buy a rudimentary map of the coast at a bookshop, and tried to come up with a plan. Personal travel was officially prohibited, and, according to the bookseller, who was trying to flirt with her, those roads not manned by the police or the army were infested by rapists, thieves and even worse, communists. She smiled dutifully, and left, imagining all the while how good it would have felt to have slapped his smug, sanctimonious face.

The walk from the town to the port took longer than she had imagined. It felt odd to her, having been so long in the mountains, to be surrounded on all sides by such a flat landscape. She recognised the familiar irrigation channels from the Alpujarra, but the soil here, the vegetation, was quite different: lush, almost tropical, and the sugar cane that grew all around lent a sweetness to the air. In the mountains, by comparison, every square metre of land had been hard won, each micro-terrace tended and repaired, each patch sifted for stones, hand-weeded, composted; each fearful snowfall a peril to the plants. She thought of Paco and the other farmers she had come to know in Jubar. How envious they would be of this soft earth, how comfortable life would be.

Two riders came towards her and she was afraid. Alone in this flat land she was defenceless. They passed her by without pause, but suddenly she felt more vulnerable than ever. They all knew the stories: in some parts of Andalucía, they said, pigs had more legal rights than men; and women had none whatsoever. As she watched the retreating backs of the horsemen, she remembered the tales of the young bloods of the aristocracy. For sport, it was rumoured, instead of hunting boar, they now rode down republican men on their polo ponies. Rage and pride told her not to quicken her pace, though it was difficult.

Despite the richness of the soil inland, the cluster of buildings that made up the port looked destitute. Cranes and derricks stood seemingly idle on the wharves; rusty trawlers rolled gently on the tide, girdled by the oily white backs of gulls; a grey navy ship, a destroyer, lay at anchor, smoke throbbing from a single funnel; there was the rancid smell of old fish, and of the sea.

Maria saw that she was still early, and walked away from the port, along the beach, towards a nest of fishermen's' cottages which she could see in the distance. Upturned boats lay drowsing on the hot sand, paint peeling, lulled by the flux of the waves on the shore. To Maria, a city dweller, it was unbearably pretty. She had hoped she might find food here, but what she found was poverty. A woman with the tell-tale limp of polio clumped into her hovel of a house as she approached. Another turned her face away, but not in time to hide the sores that abused it, and when Jess looked at the woman's hand, she saw that three fingers were missing. Four children lay collapsed, sleeping, on a pile of stinking grey green nets. Each wore a rough white dress cut clumsily from sailcloth.

Maria turned on her heel, the image of the children seared on her mind. Once, when she was a girl, she had sneaked into the park in Madrid, in the cold. It must have been springtime, for there were flowers, and a late fall of snow had crushed the pale white iris, which lay on their sides in their hundreds, all lovely, all broken. That night, as she slept, she would conflate the two memories of the iris and of the children on the nets, and awaken in a state of mild distress that would linger through the day.

Chapter Fifty-One

The long way round, 1937

Maria walked slowly back along the beach towards the port, intimidated by what or whom she might find waiting at the chandlers. A bell tinkled as she opened the door and peered into the gloomy interior. From within rose the deep, rich smells of tar, linseed, turpentine, tallow and beeswax, each familiar to her but the mixture alien now in this new environment. Dimly she saw coils of rope, bales of sailcloth, barrels, nets, items made from brass she could not identify. Her intention had been to ask for a large darning needle such as she thought sailors might use, but her ruse proved unnecessary.

The teacher stands before her, his right fist raised in communist salute. He grins, looking younger and less troubled.

"I watched you walk out to the hamlet on the headland. It's a dump, isn't it. Those women scare me. They should put them on the front line, that would put the wind up the *Regulares*." He stops suddenly, wondering if she might take offence at his light-heartedness, but she smiles in return, relieved that he is there. Trust is not won lightly in this climate, but she feels intuitively that he is genuine.

"Listen," he says, "I'd love to spend more time with you, but we can't be seen together, not round here, there are ... you know ... but there's someone who might be able to help you. She's foreign, English, but she's sound. A priest's wife! Or at least if not a priest then some kind of minister, a Methodist, she says. Don't look so disappointed! Not like our Spanish priests. Lives on a boat, her husband's in Gibraltar. It's tied up near the end of the wharf, she's expecting you."

Just then the shop bell rings again and they spring apart guiltily as the tall silhouette of a man blocks the light in the doorway.

"Go now," the teacher says. "Good luck, comrade."

"Tu tambien," she whispers. "You too." She holds his gaze for a moment then spins on her heel and steps out into the early evening light. She had been with him for no more than a moment, but as she begins her walk down towards the ships in the harbour she feels incomparably abandoned, almost sickened by loneliness, and it is all she could do to stop herself from haring back to the shop to beg him for protection. The white masts of the ships sway silently – eerily – in the gathering darkness. Even the vast, unattended warehouses begin to fade from view, though she can feel the mass, the weight of them bearing down on her, and she holds her shoulders tense against the pressure of the countless unseen eyes which size her up behind the night-blackened panes. There is no one about. She recalls the two riders she had seen earlier in the day, and contemplates the long, lightless walk back towards the town. It would be madness to attempt that now. There would be patrols, drunk soldiers, lawlessness. She wonders if she could sleep on the beach, but instantly recoils at the thought of all the vile and unknown creatures who would rise from the sea to surprise her. She has never felt so isolated, so far from home. She breathes deeply to try to steady herself, and thinks of the courage of the old man who had done so much to help her. Slowly, self-pity turns to indignation at the injustice of her predicament, and a growing sense of fury guides her footsteps further down the wharf.

Ahead of her an oil lamp swings from a boom, and spills yellow, flickering light onto the meniscus of the black and drum-tight sea. There is a laugh, a woman's laugh, and Maria hears the sudden *splosh!* of something dropped into the water. Moths flit about the lamp, and she feels as much as sees the shape of a bat as she stares blindly at the light.

"Is that you?" comes the soft, accented voice of a woman from the darkness, startling her. "The one from the hills? He said you might come. Stay there. Let me help you."

The light trembles, and amongst a confusion of shadow and pale faces a disembodied hand reaches out like some other great moth, slicing through the nebula of insects round the lamp, and encourages her aboard.

Maria stands with her feet widespread, arms half out-stretched, her body trying intuitively to come to terms with the unfamiliar swell of the waters beneath. A woman of her own height peers at her. Considering they are strangers to each other she stands alarmingly close, though Maria can sense no threat here.

"They call me Becky," the woman says at last. They sit down at a small table. "And this is my crew, Andreu and Pablo." Again the same tinkling laugh she had heard from the shore. Two middle-aged men in grubby shirts smile at her sheepishly, and shake her hand with Andalucían solemnity.

"You're hungry," says the woman. "Pablo! Fetch food. And a little rum with water to give us courage!" She reaches forward and holds Maria's hand. It is a tiny gesture, but Maria feels an instant rapport with this woman, and she begins to relax.

They eat, they talk, and drink a little of the rum. Soon after they show Maria to a cot in a small room, a lair, a refuge, a haven for her at last, and she sleeps. In the morning she climbs the steps to the deck to examine the port, but to her bewilderment the land is gone, and all about her rolls the vast blue shining reaches of the sea. Her astonishment is plain, and Becky, beside her now, laughs again. She puts a sheltering arm about her waist, and together they stare at the silver line of the horizon.

"The high seas," marvels Maria. "I can't ... I mean, I never ... it's the most beautiful thing I've ever seen."

Becky disappears for a while as Maria continues to gaze awestruck at the sheer size and flatness of the ocean. When Becky comes back they share strong coffee and dark rye bread. Maria runs suddenly to the side of the ship and vomits.

Becky is staring at her thoughtfully as she returns, stunned and embarrassed.

"That wasn't the sea, was it?" she says, passing her a piece of cloth to wipe her mouth. "You're pregnant."

Maria looks back at her, expressionless. It wasn't a surprise. She had known all along, somewhere, but hadn't had the words, the opportunity, or the courage to admit it, not even to herself, at least her conscious self. She nods.

"Was it ...?" Becky starts tentatively.

Maria stares back at her defiantly. "No," she says, " I wasn't raped." Without realizing it she presses two defensive hands about the soft mound of her belly, and cannot suppress the smile that breaks across her face. She doesn't know that she is crying.

"Oh! My girl, my girl," says Becky, and embraces her in a tight, briny canvas-smelling hug. "No more rum for you, my dear!" She holds up Maria's left hand. "And you'll need the protective charm of a wedding ring. " She smiles again, enigmatic now. "Don't worry I have a small collection."

A priest's wife? That's what the teacher had said. Maria watches as she walks to the far end of the deck, and couldn't help but stare as she pulls off the oilskin to wash her face in the rain barrel stored beneath the mast. She returns and sits by Maria, naked and unashamed beneath a thin cotton smock.

"I heard that your husband is a priest," says Maria; "I didn't know that priests could get married."

"English Methodists can … apparently!" She giggles, squeezing Maria's hand. "That's what I tell everyone. That's my own protective charm. Most people tend to believe it; it confuses them, they can't quite be sure. Nobody wants to harm the wife of a priest. Well, hardly anyone. Don't believe everything you hear."

"So …?"

"I'm old fashioned. Harmless. A loner. A courier, sort of. I move things around for people, discreetly. A bit of cocaine for the English upper classes; artefacts and curios for private museums; opium for the arty Frenchies around Nice; diamonds too, sometimes. I've somehow found myself with this funny little reputation around half the ports in the Mediterranean, someone who the sleazeballs and the crooks can trust, honour amongst thieves and all that. I can't move much – I mean, look at the size of my boat – and I don't move fast, but I get there in the end."

"And people too?" asks Maria.

"Sometimes. For friends."

"Republican friends?"

"I decided a long time ago that I wouldn't get mixed up in all that, in politics I mean. I decided it just wasn't my business. But lately … I don't know, it seems that there is so much fear in the air, not just here in Spain, but everywhere, so much antagonism, so much division

... I think it's reached the point at which you just have to get involved. You can't keep on pretending that you can't hear the alarm bells anymore. We all knew what was coming, what might come next."

Maria stares at her; she has never seen a face with so many freckles.

"And suddenly there's all the Germans and Italians getting themselves entangled, right here on my patch. I've got a bit of a thing about the Germans anyway - they killed my daddy; he died in the trenches in France when I was a little girl, and you never really get over that kind of thing, it stays with you, even if you try. At least for me. And I don't trust them. They want another fight. They claim they're not so active in Spain, but they are, they really are. And they're moving so many guns, so much ammunition from Africa." She laughs. "I should be the last person to criticise trafficking, but this is more than a bit of bootlegging, this is shipping arms on an industrial scale and it scares me. And the French and the British both know it but are too damned chicken to face the facts. Or they hide behind this idea that they ignore it and look the other way because although Hitler and Mussolini might be bad, they're not quite so bad as the Russians. What a mess."

She smiles again, half ashamed by her tirade. Maria is tempted to tell her about the German letters in her bag, but true to her training remains silent. Perhaps later she can tell her.

"I got to know one quite well," Becky continues. "A German, that is, an officer. Arrogant, good looking brute with the eyes of a shark. Told me so many things that he shouldn't have. They've got such plans, and they're so organised it's spooky. He might still be in port when we get there."

"In Gibraltar?" What would the Germans be doing in Gibraltar? That could ruin everything.

"We're not going to Gibraltar," Becky says simply.

"But…"

"Not yet, anyway. All that way, the side West of Motril, to Malaga and beyond is infested with patrols. No place for a smuggler. Don't worry: I'll get you there, but we need to go the long way round."

Maria had gone pale. Could she trust this woman after all? Anxiously she watched as their route was sketched out to her on a nautical chart. At first it meant nothing to her, all meaningless squiggles and dots, but finally she understood that they would first sail south to Tangiers, before heading back on the long side of a triangle, back towards western Spain. She understood too that she had no choice. She might be travelling amongst friends, but was nonetheless a captive, pinned by the bars of the uncaring sea.

The knowledge of her impotence made her paradoxically calm. In a sense it was what she needed: the chance to explore both the reality and mystery of the new life inside her. There was a brass chronometer fixed above a hatch. Dent & Sons, said the lettering. Over the next few days it would be her companion. She stared at it, leaning far back to drag one hand in the water, enjoying the cold, and she and the unborn child together began to examine the cruel slowness of time as though held by a dream.

Chapter Fifty-Two

At sea, 1937

The woman pointed to the pod of dolphins whose sleek silver backs broke the waters to the west.

"If we're lucky they'll follow us for a while."

As she spoke Maria stood suddenly, one hand to her mouth. She had seen something behind them, she was sure; a sinister shadow, the dark, elongated shape of something ploughing silently through the creamy V of the ship's wake.

"Pilot whales," said Becky, laughing. "They're lovely too."

Just then the glistening black head of a whale appeared massively beside the boat, so close that Maria almost screamed. She could see the tiny eyes, the scars on the beast's flanks, and the pale small discs that she would later learn were barnacles. A calf appeared behind it, and then a third whale, bigger, darker. As it came closer they saw the blow-hole open, heard the snorting hiss as the creature exhaled, and for a second the strange effluvium this produced was held iridescent between the air and the sunlight, reeking of old fish and castor oil.

"They're friends, they won't harm us, promise. It's a privilege to see them; I never tire of them."

Nor did Maria. Over the next few hours she gazed captivated at the mysterious surface of the sea, staring so hard that her eyes began to ache in the glare. She saw dolphins, dozens of them, exuberant time after time, leaping and cavorting as though exultant at the joy of their own existence. She clapped her hands in delight at the shimmering flying fish who shot missile-like from nowhere before splashing down fifty, a hundred metres distant, and from far off she spotted the impossibly long grey back of something enormous.

"A humpback. That's the big fella. Just watch."

Together they stared at the seemingly immobile silhouette, until slowly, with astonishing power and grace, the tail began to arch, to breach, until for a brief, tantalising moment it was held almost upright, before sliding languorously, lethargically back beneath the waves. It was a sight of raw, terrible beauty.

"I saw that happen once close up, really close; you could sense the sheer strength of the thing. I was with an Algerian poet. He said it felt like God yawning; I kind of knew what he meant."

God yawning. Maria liked the idea, and spent the rest of the day watching for a repeat. It didn't happen, not that day, but she did spot the great pale form of a moon fish floating just beneath the surface, still and large as a horse.

"The sailors say that when you see those here it means a big change in the weather," said Becky.

"You'll see them cross themselves; let's hope your spotting one is not an omen for us."

Maria was only half listening. By now they could see the coast. "Africa," Maria said softly to herself, as if by tasting the word she might discover something more about this unknown place. It took an age for them to approach; the surge of a strong tide and an offshore wind slowed them significantly, and as finally they reached the mouth of the harbour they had to give way for an hour to the great hulking shape of a battleship which was turning slowly with the aid of two tugs.

"That's the *Canarias*," said Becky. "Trouble. The Nationalists seized it at the start of the insurrection, and it's done massive harm. I saw the shelling of the road out of Malaga. We just happened to be close by, although we fled when the shooting started. Bastards. If there was one ship I could sink it would be that one." She closed one eye and aimed an imaginary rifle at the flat grey hull as it passed.

Their little boat bobbed on its wake, and for a while they were forced to wait their turn amongst the small fleet of trawlers who had likewise been delayed by the departure of the cruiser. Maria kept one hand on the rail as she waved to the row of boys who fished with poles from the harbour wall, smiling in their loose djellaba robes. Already the place seemed wonderfully exotic to her: the guttural unknown shouts that smoked out across the water, the smell of dung, bread ovens, incense, cumin, lamb basting over coals, the city walls shimmering in the heat and scent of a whole new continent. For a while she was over-powered by the newness of it all.

A siren wailed constantly, gulls shrieked, there was the muted roar of potent machines, men yelled. There was the blast of a ship's whistle, the angry clang of heavy things on metal. Becky was saying something to her, pointing. Maria half heard, smiled back at her, but was so enmeshed with the moment that nothing could touch her. The waters had stilled after the passage of the battleship, and now she stood silent, her conscious and unconscious selves absorbing the excitement of this new reality. She saw the vibrancy, the full colour of the place, and for a brief while, for the first time in so long, she felt rich and fully alive, aware of nothing but the uncomplicated joy of being. She breathed the strangely perfumed air, heedless of her hands held pressed against her womb. And suddenly she thought of him, of Jacob. Fear, guilt and anguish all rushed back in to fill her; her thoughts flowed back to him, to Spain, and all she'd left behind, and she spat into the water, consumed by pain and fury.

By the time they docked the spike in her rage had been diluted by curiosity, to be replaced by the slow-burning malaise that she had come to know so well.

"Now what?" she asked sourly.

"Business," said Becky. "Twenty-four hours, that's all. Later – maybe – you can come ashore with me. But if you've got any sense you'll stay here and keep your head down."

Chapter Fifty-Three

Tangiers, 1937

Tangiers. Maria still struggled to absorb the fact of her being there. She was leaning over the side of the boat to watch the silver fish which skittered beneath the keel, the water so still that she could see her own reflection, until the breeze trickled down from the hills and puckered the oily surface, bringing with it the strange warm scents of Africa and the distant chant of the muezzin.

Andreu, the older of the two crewmen, stood on the dockside, inspecting a tired tar rope.

"Is this the Atlantic or the Mediterranean?" she asked him, still staring at the sea.

"Both," he replied. "It's where they shake hands, where they meet. That's why it's always so bloody rough and windy. If either one's out of sorts they start scrapping and keep us sailors locked on dry land."

Maria sat up and looked beyond the port. On the horizon the outline of Spain was clearly visible. The rendezvous of two oceans, and two continents, she mused; what a place. She was about to press Andreu, but then saw the figure of Becky emerge from behind a tall stack of timber. She had left the boat before Maria had woken, and was now striding towards them, burdened with two brown-paper packages, one of which she threw to Maria as she walked across to greet her.

"Catch!" she said. "Wear this. If it's not your colour, too bad; it's the price of lunch." Maria tore open the bag, which smelled of lanolin, and produced a drab brown garment which she held up to inspect.

"It's an *Abaya* and means no one will look twice at us . I'll give you a *Hijab* too, a headscarf. Keep you covered up. Last thing we need is for some moron to follow you home."

Maria giggled as she stepped ashore. "My God! I've gone all wobbly!" she shouted, and put a hand on Becky's shoulders to steady herself.

"Sea legs," said Becky. "Five minutes and you'll have forgotten about it. I remember the first time I went to-"

She stopped mid-sentence. A man on a bicycle was heading straight towards them, wearing an official-looking cap. "Uh-oh. Trouble," whispered Becky. Maria blanched. "Don't worry. Not big trouble – my trouble. I'll deal with it. You wait here." She gave a sigh and took something else from her bag before going over to the man. Maria watched them as they talked; it all seemed very friendly. The two shook hands as they parted, and Becky handed him a small parcel.

"Bloody Customs Officers. That sugar we brought in was legal, that's the problem. They'll have to pay tax on it as they leave the port, and they want me to pay part of it. Me! I don't pay tax. It's a matter of principle! I'm a smuggler, for God's sake." She was laughing. "But they have me stitched up. They buy it themselves, the swine, for themselves, and then tax me on top of it! But anyway, I've sorted it out. That was a *gift* I gave him, not a tax; some silver earrings I picked up in Oran."

They walked on, ignoring the small boys who swarmed around

them. At the top of the hill overlooking the port stood the Hotel Continental, an impressive building that had been opened in the 1870s. Becky walked in confidently, throwing off her *hijab* to allow her long blonde hair to fall over her shoulders. High ceiling fans whirred grudgingly above a haze of blue cigar smoke, whilst two grey-whiskered men stared motionless at a game of chess, oblivious to the clatter of dominos in the background.

"We'd like a table for two over there in the corner, please." She surprised Maria by saying this in English, in a bold, commanding voice. "It's the best way," she explained. "Let them be certain that you're foreign. They expect a better tip, but at least they leave you alone. And this ..." she swept an arm around the ornate dining room, "this is about the only place in town where two women can eat without a chaperone."

Their lunch arrived. Maria had no idea what lay beneath the clay domes of the tajine dishes, and watched warily as the waiter served them. After the first few mouthfuls she began to relax, and even to enjoy herself. By the time that the sweet mint tea was poured, she was happy.

"Those earrings," said Becky at the end of the meal, "the ones I had to offer to the Customs fellow: I was going to give them to you. I saw when you first came on board that you'd lost one."

Maria lifted a hand automatically to one ear. "It's not lost," she said, smiling enigmatically. "Not really. Someone ... someone's looking after it for me." Her companion tilted her head to one side, encouraging her to say more, but Maria gave a sudden little grimace and looked away. Now was not the moment.

Becky gave her a knowing look and excused herself to go to the bathroom. Sitting there alone Maria gazed around her elegant surroundings. Jacob would have loved it here, she thought, he would have fitted in perfectly, this was his world, his people. She began to feel guilty. Perhaps they could come here together some day, when all this were over. If only she could see him here today, see him anywhere; on a beach, a boat, a bed, but just to see him. She began to cry.

An arm appeared around her neck, and Becky settled herself beside her. "Hey. Sorry. Is this my fault? Don't worry, don't be sad."

Maria was embarrassed by her tears and her swift change of mood. Maybe it was the pregnancy after all; they said it did that to you. Suddenly she felt hot, and stifled by the bourgeois atmosphere, and sweeping her friend's arm away she stood and marched to the door.

Becky found her outside, leaning with her back to the restaurant wall, staring down at the port. An enormous cargo vessel had just docked, tall enough to cast a shadow over the men who swarmed along the harbour wall, its bulk and dull metal symmetry incongruous amongst the colourful fleet of fishing ships behind it.

"Fancy a walk?" asked Becky, pointing to the ship. "Let's have a look at our new neighbours."

Arm in arm they strolled back down the hill, picking their way past the beggars and the street vendors, the cobblestones slippery with the detritus of that morning's market. Next to the grey ship a line of grey military vehicles stood ready to embark.

"Thought so," said Becky, pointing to the flag. "Italians. That lot means trouble for someone." She stopped, bent down, and produced something from her bag. "Say cheese!" she said, and Maria heard a click. It was over in a second.

"See those markings on the front funnel? The red, white and black stripes? They're the stripes of neutrality. Yeah, right. Neutrality, my sweet smuggler's arse. God knows what those trucks are doing here. They could be bound for Abyssinia. You know they're at war there, right? That's another lovely place. There's bloody conflict bloody everywhere. On the other hand they could be a gift to Franco." She sighed. "Problem is, there's no middle ground anymore. Everyone's either black or white, communist or fascist, Muslim or Christian or Jew. Nobody talks. Or, that is, they talk, but nobody listens. All these self-important men pulling stunts just to make themselves more popular. And it *is* men. Gorillas. Wonder how long we'll have to wait before women get to lead us?"

"I thought you weren't political?" Maria laughs.

"I'm not! All this isn't politics! Murder and killing aren't politics, they're crimes. And I'm just sick of being dragged along on a rope by a troupe of blasted gorillas! That's the reason I live my life out here on the sea, just to get away from all that. I'm lucky. It's a coward's way out, I guess."

Maria was happy to witness this outburst. The world was changing. Everywhere she went she found this slow-burning rage, this urge to stand up to tyranny, a determination to take no more. And that included Becky: her refusal to submit, her independence; just the simple fact of her flight from conformity was in itself an act of defiance.

"You're no coward. And if there were another ten thousand like you then the world would be a better place."

By now they had reached their boat. Each of them was happy to feel this growing bond of kinship, this sisterhood. They stood for a while and watched the armoured vehicles, which even in the warmth and sunlight of late afternoon exuded a sense of menace. Becky shuddered.

"There's just something so malign in the way they sit there. Waiting ... waiting to kill, to commit evil. They're so lifeless, so passionless, and yet the premeditation, the intent to murder is written all over them. Imagine the poor bastards who are going to be on the receiving end. They scare me, I mean, really scare me." She turned away, as though by doing so she might protect herself from their malevolence, but Maria continued to study them, her mouth set in a tight grimace.

Eventually she stepped onto the boat. She went to her cot, and lay there, thinking. After a while she came back out. There was no sign of the others. A wind had come up from the South, bringing with it the fine white grains of the Sahara which now covered the deck, swirling into piles in the corners. Maria picked up a broom and began to sweep the sand into a heap which she then poured into a sack. It was a thankless task, for no sooner had she cleared one side than the wind brought more, but still it felt good to be doing something, anything. She stopped as the sun began to set. The sack was barely a quarter full, but still she struggled to lift it.

Chapter Fifty-Four

Mischief, 1937

The others had stayed up until late, playing cards and drinking rum, and it wasn't until after midnight that Maria finally heard them crash their way to bed. At first, lulled by the rocking of the boat and their distant conversation, she had feared she might sleep, and had had to force herself to stay awake, but now she felt electrically energised.

The night was cloudy, the darkness almost total. In her bare feet Maria stepped over the rope and across the narrow gangway. The hemp sack was where she'd left it, propped innocently inside a coil of mooring rope. It was even heavier than she imagined. From memory she made her way across to the perimeter fence, and followed it with her fingers down to the seawall. Here she knew that there was a gap in the wire; earlier in the day she'd watched the boy anglers as they sneaked through to fish in the deeper waters of the naval harbour.

She rolled to one side and dragged the sack after her. She cursed as it snagged; the canvas was old and she hoped it wouldn't tear. She listened carefully but could hear nothing above the sucking of the tide, then crept sideways, like a crab, the weight on her shoulders. It was only a hundred metres to the line of vehicles, but in the dark, and with the heavy bag, it felt like more, and when she reached it she had to rest for a minute. Carefully she picked her way along the row of cold, stinking lorries and trailers until she came to her quarry: a half-track fuel carrier. She had watched three men fill it that afternoon from a hose, and knew that the cap was on the very top. It was almost more than she could manage to lift her sack, but desperation gave her strength, and with one final grunt she heaved it onto the smooth metal surface.

The brass cap turned more easily than she could have hoped, and she was enveloped in the thick smell of diesel. From her pocket she lifted a tin cup and a funnel, then untied the sack and began to pour the fine sand into the hole.

It was done. It was absurd, reckless, dangerous, but it was done. They would kill her if she were discovered, no doubt slowly. So be it.

She wiped the loose particles, replaced the cap, slid down and scampered back to the boat.

A cigarette glowed in the darkness.

"I just hope that was worth it," said Becky's voice. She sighed. "Now get yourself to bed, you fool. We'd better leave before dawn breaks ... Comrade."

Maria sensed somehow that she was smiling.

She lay back in her cot. She felt elated, but at the same time guilty. Guilty that she had been swanning around without Jacob all afternoon, and guilty that she had just now endangered Becky and her crew. What had she been thinking? Had she been unfair? It was but one tiny gesture, and quite possibly a useless one at that. In the great scheme of things, would it matter one jot? She didn't care. That's my grain of sand, she thought, in fact more like two hundred thousand grains. She smiled to herself in the darkness.

What was it he had said, her mentor, the Russian? That sometimes they might have to act alone, to show bravery when no one was there to instruct them, with no one there to judge them but their conscience. She remembered his passion as he'd taught them. Courage without witness is the highest form of courage, he had insisted; no single act is futile if it's done in the spirit of the common good. "Even when we are alone, we are many. A thousand pinpricks of light, each separate in the dark, together make a flame to dazzle all injustice." Dutifully she had absorbed and memorised these facts; she hoped that he'd been right.

But it was Jacob, she recalled, not the Russian, who had told her the practical thing, explaining how you could destroy an engine by putting sand in it. Sabotage. It was a despicable act, but she liked the word. Jacob too had told her its origins. In the olden days French workers wore sabots, he'd explained, wooden clogs, which they'd worn to kick down the new machinery in the mills which threatened their livelihoods. She had watched his expression as they lay there in the grass that day, observed the fine hair and sinews on his strong hands, and she'd listened carefully to the words as they flew from those clever lips, waiting for him to stop so that she could kiss them.

In the darkness of the boat, she thought of him.

And then, improbably, impossibly, the night had gone. Daylight streamed in through the small porthole, and someone was banging on the cabin door.

"Oi! Comrade!" came a voice. "Wake up. Dolphins!"

She ran up the ladder expecting to see the port and the hulking shape of the freighter still tied up beside them. Instead, all around was the rolling grey black sea, weighed down by a veil of heavy mist. For the second time she had failed to awaken, to hear either the chains or the motor, or to feel the new pitch of the seas, and they had again weighed anchor without her. Bewildered, she stared into this chimerical curtain of fog, trying to make sense of where they were.

"Not much of a view," said Becky by way of greeting. "We're sailing by compass. Probably better this way. With luck we can sail all the way into the bay without anyone seeing us. Unless we get mown down by a bigger boat, that is."

Maria looked at her wide-eyed. Was she joking?

"I wasn't making it up," said Becky, "about the dolphins. They were there, right in our wake. Keep looking."

Maria gazed about her, quietly terrified, half hypnotised by the roiling wisps of fog. She was cold, despite the heavy coat she wore. She studied the beads of moisture which had formed on the waxen cloth; slowly, her whole world was turning to water.

From time to time Becky cut the engine, to listen out for the sound of other ships. Other than the periodic slosh of the waves on the hull, the silence then was total. The fog seemed thicker here; above them, they could barely see to the top of the mast. It were as if they had floated to some strange, frigid, limbo land, discarded by all humanity. By now Maria was no longer so much afraid as fascinated. Nothing mattered here. It was a place neither welcoming nor hostile. Deracinated, alone in all the world, they drifted on this cold, grey sea, a sea indifferent to their existence

Suddenly Becky shot a hand into the air, ordering quiet. The others strained to hear. And there it was: a long, extraordinary groan. The hair on their necks stiffened in the mist. "The song of a whale," whispered Becky, her face filling with joy. It came again, a low, primeval moan. Maria stared at the others. All three sailors, marooned in the silence, were mesmerised. For Maria too, the song was savage, it was beautiful, it was haunting. And it was the loneliest sound she had ever endured.

Within minutes, as though commanded by the whale, the fog lifted, and ahead loomed the high limestone flanks of the Rock of Gibraltar.

"Bravo, mi capitán," said Andreu. "Impressive."

"More by luck than judgement," she replied modestly. "Let's see if it holds."

Hurriedly she unfurled a Red Ensign. "What?" she said to Maria, who stared at the Union Jack as it was lifted up the mast. "I'm British; I'm allowed to. What do you expect? A Skull and Crossbones?"

The difference in the weather was astonishing. Out here in the sun, Maria had to shield her eyes against the glare as she looked up at the monumental lump that was Gibraltar, whilst behind them she could still see the achromatic wall of fog that screened them from the open sea, pinned there, Becky said, by the cold currents that bled in from the Atlantic. As she watched, a vessel emerged, a tanker of some sort, slowly, a ghost ship sliding out of limbo to the light. That had been her life, she considered, a life lived in the shadows, a life of subterfuge and opacity. Could she adapt to the brightness, or would she now wither and die like a woodlouse caught by a sunbeam? She stood at the prow of the ship, her hands to her belly. She knew the answer.

A man with a megaphone hailed them as they crept into the mouth of the harbour. Becky waved, and followed his directions which he gave by pointing with a white pennant. At the last second she killed the engine, and with a gentle bump the little boat nudged the rubber fender on the quayside. Maria jumped ashore and as instructed began to tie up. To her surprise, when she turned, she saw that Andreu was holding out her small bundle of possessions.

"Here," he said, "take it. And good luck."

"Forgive him," said Becky as she jumped up beside her, "he's a man of few words." Maria was confused. "Listen," said Becky, putting an arm around her. "I didn't really want to tell you out at sea, I thought

... I don't know, I thought you might be worried about the idea of being left alone. Stupid of me. You're strong; gutsier than me. But the thing is, I can't really stick around. I'm kind of *persona non gratis* in these parts, for all kinds of reasons."

Maria squeezed her hand. She had known that this was coming, but now it was happening so fast. She was torn, both desperately sad to say goodbye to this amazing, crazy English woman, but at the same time excited to discover news of Jacob.

"You take this paper to the office over there. When you come out we'll be gone. Seriously. I can't stay. They won't come after us, but there are people here who ... listen, forget it, trust me. I'm going to sail to France, I've got a friend in Toulon."

She put her arms around Maria and hugged her tight. "Bon courage," she whispered, "and good luck with your man. And with this," she added, patting her belly. "And here – take this," she said, handing her an envelope. "Get them to take you to the Governor's Office, and ask for Peter. Make sure to give it to him in person. Say it's from Becky." She smiled coyly. "Maybe you should tell him that when his wife's not around." She put a finger to her lips to shush her. "And give him this, too. Only to Peter. I know I can trust you." In her hand was a tiny, carved wooden box, the kind that Maria had seen everywhere in the souk.

"Don't worry. It's not a love trinket. It's a film." She shrugged, looked deep into Maria's eyes, then laughed again. "My grain of sand, let's call it. Information is power. You know that."

Maria opened her mouth as if to say something, puzzled, but before she could speak Becky kissed her quickly on both cheeks, then jumped back onto the boat. Maria looked one last time at the name painted on the side. She had wanted to ask before. She had to know.

"Hey! What does it mean, *Quite Free*?"

Becky smiled up at her. She shook her head and raised her arms to the sky, palms outstretched.

"Honestly?" she asked. "I still don't know." She let her arms fall to her sides. "I'm still trying to find out."

She ducked beneath the hatchway and disappeared, leaving Maria to walk alone along the wooden pier.

At the end was a small wooden cabin that served as an office. She waited patiently whilst the man read and re-read the paper which Becky had just given her. He wore a tailored uniform, with shorts. Beneath the fine red hairs which covered his knees she could see that he was sun-burned. He drummed his fingers on the table then picked up a telephone. He spoke rapidly in English, then appeared to listen. He sighed.

"Another one," he said. "You wait here. I'll go and get your stuff. Wait in the shade; this sun will fry you." He spoke in Spanish now, a Spanish that mixed the rich rhythms of Andalucía with the faint staccato tones of a foreigner.

Maria followed him outside, then paused. To the east, towards Spain, she could see the *Quite Free* motoring out of the harbour. Maria waved, and Becky, just visible, saluted her. "Goodbye, little boat," she breathed, and blew a last kiss across the water. She watched as it grew smaller, a dot now, until finally it melted into the horizon.

A breeze ruffled her hair, and behind her a door slammed on its hinges. It's time, she thought. Please God, let him be here.

Chapter Fifty-Five

Waiting in Gibraltar, 1937

Nothing. There was no word of Jacob, not even a letter. She had prepared herself for this, and refused to be overwhelmed. She would wait. The authorities in Gibraltar treated her fairly, but no more than that; to them she was just another refugee, one of many, although she at least had the protection of the documents she carried. For three consecutive days she was interviewed by the man Peter. He seemed curious about the information she had delivered, and quizzed her on every detail. On the fourth day he came to the small apartment they had provided for her, accompanied by a woman in uniform who repeated the same questions. And after that they left her alone, simply telling her that things were in progress.

Each day Maria returned at midday to the same beige office to see if there were news of Jacob, and each day her hopes grew fainter. Even at the beginning it was a trial, for she had to cross the barracks and she still detested the sight of men in uniform and the crunch of stomping boots. But at least she had approached those first visits in a spirit of hope. Then, as the weeks wore on, she began to dread the sorrowful shakes of the head, the apologies and kindly smiles, and slowly she came to understand that she was making the short journey not out of expectation, but routine. Not that she could stop herself, and each afternoon she climbed dejectedly to a point on the hill where she could look back over the isthmus to Spain, to leave her tears and whispered prayers decaying on the wind. When she thought no one was watching she talked to them both – to Jacob and to her child – speaking aloud, as if they were there beside her. Was she going mad, she wondered?

Eventually she was told that she was to take a ship to England. Although she was afraid, the news came as something of a relief. Almost anything would be better than this agonizing wait. Jacob's cousins had agreed to sponsor her, and she had been given temporary *laissez-passer* travel credentials. They gave her two days to pack; it took her less than an hour.

Peter came to see her on the eve of her departure. He bought her ice cream and they sat in the cemetery in the centre of town, surrounded by the tombs of the English sailors who had perished at Trafalgar. It meant nothing to Maria.

"This place," he said, "these graves, they leave me chastened somehow. These fellows made history, changed the world and all that. At least that's what they tell us at school. Wonder if we'll ever do that, you and I?"

Ice cream had dripped onto his trousers. He stared at it ruefully then smiled at her. It was a handsome smile, knowingly seductive, the smile of a rake, and Maria was having none of it.

"Maybe start by changing your trousers, then the world," she suggested.

"Let's not get ahead of ourselves." He laughed aloud.

"You're like her, you know, like Becky. And that is meant as a compliment."

Not for the first time Maria asked herself just how involved her friend had been with this flirtatious diplomat.

"She's a force of nature," he went on. "Shrewd, canny, fearless, free-spirited; I've never met anyone who's quite so full of life."

Full of life. The phrase struck a chord. Maria had sensed this in her too. A memory came back to her of them swimming together. Becky had stopped the boat in the middle of the sea for no good reason and just dived in. Uncharacteristically Maria had followed her, equally naked, compelled by the purity of her enthusiasm, and for half an hour they dived and splashed like children. Later, shivering and giggling as they dried in the sun, she had felt almost overcome by the sheer energy of the relative stranger who lay fizzing by her side.

"A bit reckless sometimes," Peter continued. "That's the only thing. I fear for her. I remember a couple of years back, our last job together, I was so worried. A German battleship, the *Admiral Scheer* had docked here in Gibraltar. Caused a bit of a stir. The navy chaps were livid, but the governor wanted to show Herr Hitler on which sides his loyalties lay. Anyway, it gave us a chance to have a little look at her up close, and guess who came up the goods? Still don't quite know how she did it, but she did: sketches, plans, two whole rolls of film … astonishing, really."

Maria had finished her ice cream.

"And that's really why I'm here, chatting to you today."

Here it comes, she thought.

"You see, that information you gave us is really rather useful. Some of it we don't understand, not yet, anyway, and some of it is already old news. But there are some, let's say, *items* that are definitely intriguing. It certainly helps to confirm specific rumours that we've been hearing, and it means we'll be paying special attention to certain people."

He paused for a minute, and looked around the empty graveyard.

"Hendaye," he said mysteriously. "Does that mean anything to you? Ring any bells?"

She shook her head.

"Definitely not something that your boyfriend or his family might have mentioned?"

She racked her brains to remember. "Nothing. Sorry. What is it?"

"Pity. It's a place on the French border. We understand that Franco and Hitler want to meet, clandestinely of course. We don't know when, but we think we know where. Hendaye.* It's mentioned again in one of your documents. Just imagine getting them in the same room! If that information were to get out that news would be …" He searched for the right word.

"Explosive?" she suggested.

"Quite." He looked around the graveyard. He seemed troubled.

"There's something else. The information that you brought to us confirmed something that we've been apprehensive about for a while. Ever heard of Mr Henderson's Railway?"

She shook her head.

"No? Well it's a bit of British track that runs from Ronda to Algeciras, just across the bay there. Now, the funny thing is, the people up at the mines at Rio Tinto have reported a bit of chatter about a plan to strengthen the arches on some of the bridges, which as far as we're concerned isn't necessary unless you were planning to start transporting something very heavy. And even more curious, according to the letters you brought us, is that the Germans have agreed to finance this plan. A bit odd that, don't you think?"

---

* ps. In reality it would be almost 3 years before Franco and Hitler actually got to meet. By all accounts they didn't get on, and the meeting did not go well. The meeting took place, incidentally, in Hendaye

She looked at him blankly, trying to tease from this conversation just what it was he wanted from her.

"Put plainly, it's a threat to us. Our fear is that with stronger bridges the Germans or even Franco could quickly bring down some seriously heavy artillery by train and set it up there on the beaches, in our own back yard, so to speak. And of course we've already made a few preparations: if you look carefully you'll see the new gun emplacements that we've built high up, facing inland. In truth, if it came to a shooting match then we'd probably survive, but there would be a huge number of casualties, and more importantly it would be a major distraction from our main job, which is guarding the Straits. So all in all it would be better not to let that happen, don't you agree?"

Through a gap in the trees she can see the port of Algeciras, not two miles across the bay.

"Makes sense," she says.

"But here's the thing: the hands of His Majesty's Government are somewhat tied just now. We can't act, not officially. For better or for worse, let's say. But having said that, there are still certain people who are ... independent-minded, and who are so concerned in fact that they have decided to forestall the possibility, even if it means, erm, operating outside the law."

"Good for them. Bomb them now whilst they can."

"Absolutely. But it's rather more complicated than that. Any fool can break the law, the trick is not to get caught."

He left this hanging in the air.

"That ship, the one you're booked on for tomorrow," he said, apparently changing the subject. "It will be back here to do the same journey in about ten days." He put his hands together as if in prayer. "Just think: if you were to delay your trip you'd have time to do a little sight-seeing ... to Spain, for example."

"And get myself shot, you mean?"

"Well that's a bit extreme. I shouldn't think so. Look – have you got time for tea? There are some people that I'd like you to meet."

She looked at him suspiciously.

"Coffee," she said. "Tea is for degenerates. And no more than an hour. I'm a busy woman."

They wandered along the leafy lane that lead up to the Governor's residence, and he described in detail their anxiety. Maria remained non-committal. Eventually they turned left into one of the colonial-style villas.

"So you see that it's really to our mutual benefit," he whispered. "Of course you can always say no if you want to be ..."

"A coward?" she hissed. "Is that what you mean?"

"So that's a *yes* then is it?"

She glared at him as a man in uniform saluted them at the door. Before she could speak a woman dressed all in black escorted them to a room upstairs, where there was a piano and enormous billiard table. A group of six men were seated around a long, rectangular desk, and all of them stood at her approach.

"Gentlemen," said Peter, "this is Senorita Sanchez. I think she may have agreed to help us." He cocked his head on one side and grinned at her.

"I didn't have much choice," she said sullenly. "It was emotional blackmail. Your colleague just abused my sense of duty." She gazed around the room at these wealthy men with their tea and their cigars and their power. "Duty to my people, to the proletariat," she almost added, but bit her tongue; her point would have been lost on them.

"Jolly good. So you'll do it then, will you? Better to be ahead of the game. *Semper paratus* and what have you." The voice came from behind her; she hadn't realised that there was anyone else in the room.

When she turned she saw that it was the Governor.

"Glad you're here, I must say. Shows that our little network is still alive, that chappie beavering away in Madrid … oh? Should I not mention that?" He looked startled. "Anyway, fact is," he continued, "we do need a little help with this. Sow doubt in the enemy's minds, chuck 'em a decoy and so on. I know it's a bit underhand, a bit … caddish, but if the British Parliament ever got wind there'd be no end of trouble. Sit down, won't you. Let me explain."

The plan itself was rudimentary. British undercover agents working at one of the more famous sherry houses in Jerez would blow up the bridges covertly, employing fuses with a time delay to give them chance to get away. That part was easy. The trick then was not just to avoid detection, but to deflect blame onto the shoulders of a third party, in this case Russian-led Spanish communists.

"It's not entirely fair, is it," she argued, "to play dirty and then have another government take the rap?"

"But Russia is already *involved,* don't you see?"

"Yes, and if you do this then you too are *involved,* as you put it. You need to be brave! All this means is that Mr Stalin has got bigger *cojones* than your Mr Chamberlain."

There was an embarrassed silence and someone coughed.

"You've got to admit it," said one of the men, holding up a slim tin tube. "These little things are ingenious. Dare say we'll be making them ourselves some day."

He handed it to Maria. It seemed fragile. "Don't worry: it's fairly strong."

She held it up to the light.

"Russian pencil fuse. You just break the seal, and over time the two acids eat away at the copper plug dividing them until they meet, and when they do meet, they react, and ignite those crystals there. Rather brilliant, actually."

This was part of the ploy, to plant evidence of Russian interference – this and a handful of forged correspondence from a supposed puppet master.

"Sign it Konstantin Kyragin," Maria told them on a whim. He was dead now and it could do no damage.

"Any reason?" Peter asked hopefully.

"Just do it." She would give them nothing more. Already she felt disloyal. It was one thing sleeping with the Devil for the greater good, but that didn't mean she had to bring him his breakfast. The only reason that she had agreed to this charade was that by harming the bridge she was harming Franco, and that it might give pause to the fascists to think that a pocket of communist resistance should remain so deep behind the front line. That and the thought, kept secret and close to her heart, that for a short while at least she would be back in Spain, and closer, perhaps, to Jacob.

Two days later, the big Rolls Royce drove punctually across the frontier at ten o'clock. If asked, Maria was to play the role of the Argentinian wife of the British Ambassador to Buenos Aires, and she was on her way to lunch in Ronda. Her would-be husband sat beside her, in reality a middle-ranking diplomat en-route to his new posting in Alexandria. She wore a copy of a gown recently made famous by Greta Garbo; two tailors had worked all the previous day to make it perfect, and her bulge barely showed. In the bag between them were her ordinary clothes, neatly folded.

They made good time. Maria was both appalled and astonished by the speed and opulence of their progress, and tried to imagine what Carmen would say if she could see her travelling in such style. In what to her seemed no time at all they had reached the agreed spot just north of the little town of Almoraima, and the great car eased to a stop beneath a canopy of oak trees. As far as they could see, there was no one about.

The two men stepped outside and walked a little way from the car. Both were armed, she noticed, and for the first time her mood lurched from excitement to fear. Quickly she tore off her fine dress, put on her old clothes, grabbed the battered canvas bag from the seat and followed them into the woods.

"Four o'clock" said the chauffeur. "Don't be late."

A minute later she heard the engine fade as it roared away into the distance. It took her a full minute to absorb the fact that she was alone again, and back in Spain. She took a huge breath to give her courage, and turned to walk back towards the village.

She walked for an hour, passing no one, until she met up with an old couple struggling with a sack full of onions. She helped as best she could until the old lady prodded her belly and told her to stop.

"I used to have a mule," Maria said, "until that madman Franco took it." She waited for a reaction but the old folk kept their eyes firmly to the ground. "Never mind," she added as they parted, "when we win this war, maybe the communists will give it back to me. Hope so."
There was still no reaction, but she knew that the message had been received.

She went into a butcher's shop and had a similar conversation. Then a bakery. The baker stared at her defiantly.

"You want to watch your dirty mouth, missy. There are people round here who might want to wash it for you."

Maria was unnerved but pressed on. "And there are people out there who might want to stop them," she added, and ran out quickly, pleased that those in the queue behind her had heard the exchange. Her heart was beating fast, and she was more circumspect when she reached the marketplace. It would be foolish to be too overt.

At midday she went into the small civic office which served as a library, and allowed herself to be drawn into a petty argument with the large middle-aged woman behind the counter. Nothing too outrageous, just enough for the woman to guess on whose side her sympathies lay. Before she left she made her way to the bathroom, and taking a red lipstick from her pocket, wrote "Viva la Revolución" and drew a careful hammer and sickle on the cracked mirror. As an afterthought she added her name, then Jacob's. She looked at her reflection. What a way to win a war. A woman was waiting patiently outside the door when she emerged, and they smiled at each other. It crossed Maria's mind that she was the first attractive woman she had seen all day, and hoped she wouldn't be held responsible for her graffiti.

Finally she went to the tavern by the church, and pushed the bag she had been carrying beneath the bench. In addition to her falsified documents, it contained three copies of a communist pamphlet and two letters with cryptic messages, signed Kyriagin, in her own hand. Crucially, at the very bottom, was the pencil fuse. This was simpler than she'd imagined; could they really be fooled so easily?

A split second later her assurance turned to dismay, for when she glanced up she saw that two men from the Guardia Civil were standing in the doorway, staring at her. Next to them was the baker, and when he too looked at her she thought that her heart was going to leap from her chest. She'd been too obvious, too cocky. Now what?

She looked down and tried to busy herself with the things in her bag for as long as she dared. In desperation she turned to her neighbour on the bench, a priest, who was busy scribbling in a notebook. A familiar choking sense of panic began to grip her. Why hadn't she accepted Peter's offer of a gun?

Suddenly a hand gripped her roughly on the collar and she turned in pure fright. It was the woman from outside the bathroom in the library. She was pale and smiling frantically, holding her face just inches from her own.

"It's Maria, isn't it?" she said. "I read some of your work in the library this morning. Tell me about Jacob." She stared into her eyes. "It's okay," whispered the woman. "You can trust me."

It wasn't as though she had much choice.

"Walk out with me. You go first. They won't touch us."

Maria did as she was told, and pushed her way between the baker and the policeman. In the street outside she could feel their eyes on her back as they walked away. It was all she could do to stop herself from running.

"I saw them following you, so I followed them" said the woman. "I'm Marti, by the way. Let's go back to the office; I virtually live there these days."

Maria's heart rate was beginning to slow, though she realised that she was still terrified. She thought of her baby, and tried with an act of will to calm herself.

The building was less than a minute away. Marti opened a side door carefully, and closed it as soon as Maria entered.

"Don't want these to blow away," she said, and indicated a table on which rested a collection of wildflowers, a magnifying glass and a set of watercolours.

"I've got two weeks to finish them. Then it's the Big Day. I'm marrying the son of the chief of police. That's why the coppers out there wouldn't bother you."

"But why help me?" asked Maria. "Are you a comrade?"

The woman shook her head. "Let's just say we swim in the same direction. The war here is lost; you have to keep your head down or you'll lose it. I'm a realist, not an activist. When all this is over we want to go to the States. My fiancé is a scientist ..."

Maria interrupted her. "You know you probably saved my life back there. Our lives," she added, patting her tummy. "That took courage. You were scared too; I could see it."

"Not really. Not much compared to you."

Maria reached for her hand, and the two women stared into each other's eyes.

"Hey. I've got to go. Really. Good luck. And thank you." She put her hand on the door.

"Your pictures are beautiful, by the way. I should have said so before. That flower there, the blue one, I know that one: what is it?"

"*Myosotis sylvatica*. Forget-me-not."

They smiled at each other one last time.

"Go!" said Marti, and pushed her gently into the street.

Outside it was quiet, with no sign of the police, and Maria walked quickly towards the road out of town. Only then, when she was back under the protection of the trees which sheltered the ancient road, did she begin to relax. She drank cool water from the spring, listened to the callings of the birds in the trees, and was back at the rendezvous with an hour to spare. As she waited she gathered wild strawberries, walnuts and a russet apple, which she ate seated on the sun-warmed stump of an oak, surrounded by butterflies and the flitting of wrens and finches. She croaked back at a toad who sang to her from a nearby pond. There were worse ways to wage war, she decided as the big car drove back into view, and for the first time she smiled properly at the man who was pretending to be her husband.

Their little cameo was re-played, with the two men standing gallantly at some distance as she changed back into her fashionable dress. She had the curious feeling that the diplomat was suddenly more attentive to her. Was it her costume, she wondered, or the fact that she had paid him some attention? Either way it didn't really matter, for within five minutes she was sound asleep.

At three o'clock that night Marti and her fiancé were sharing a cigarette on the rooftop terrace of his parents' house long after everyone else had gone to bed. They had just made love, and in gentle whispers were planning out their lives together. Suddenly, in the far distance they heard a series of bangs, and then a deep, thunder-like rumble.

"What the heck was that?" he asked dreamily. "Sounded like explosives."

She squeezed her eyes tight shut, and put her arms around him. So, there is still some hope, she thought, smiling to herself in the darkness.

Her breathing became more measured; she was barely awake. "Myosotis sylvatica," she said softly under her breath as she drifted off to sleep on his arm.

Chapter Fifty-Six

At sea, 1937

The ship had called at Lisbon, then at Porto. The weather stayed fair, and Maria walked all day about the open decks, looking for her friends the dolphins, until, as they rounded Cape Finisterre and entered the Bay of Biscay, the wind began to blow. Cupboards rattled, objects slid from tables, the outer doors were closed, as all the while the passengers laughed nervously amongst themselves. Outside, the howl of the gale increased. The vessel began to pitch and yaw, so that people teetered drunkenly from side to side as they made their way down the corridors. From time to time the whole ship gave a horrifying shudder along its whole length, and from deep within the bowels came the dissonant clang of iron on iron as heavy things slipped about the hold, and the inevitable, contagious sounds and smells of vomit stalked the decks like smoke.

Maria was becoming frightened and decided to return to the cabin which she shared with three other women, trying to remember the things that Becky had told her. These people, these sailors, they knew what they were doing, there was nothing to be afraid of; Becky would probably have even enjoyed this storm. She thought of her as she waited for the people beneath her to make their way down the stairs – the companionway, as Becky had taught her to call it.

She was halfway down when something hit her from behind. Hard. There was nothing she could do; she didn't even have time to cry out. The handrail was wrenched from her grip, and she was hurled into the man in front of her. As the poor ship tilted yet higher on the wave, more people fell from above, leaving her pinned beneath a mound of terrified passengers.

She couldn't breathe. Her head seemed to be trapped between a pair of women's shoes, and something, a fist, a leg, a knee, was rammed viciously hard into her abdomen. For a minute she thought she was going to die. She closed her eyes.

At last something moved above her. A face appeared and she was lifted upwards, cradled in the arms of a bearded stranger who carried her back up the stairs and laid her gently on the carpeted floor. The ship heaved, people screamed; she thought she might puke.

She rolled to one side. Something was wrong with her, she knew it. With a huge effort she managed to get to her hands and knees. She had to find a doctor. If necessary she would crawl there. A man's face appeared at her side and he helped her to stand. At first she felt dizzy and was unable to focus properly, but after a minute she was able to take a few tentative steps and they moved slowly down the corridor.

She had begun to bleed even before they got to the ship's infirmary. She could sense it, could picture the growing red stain black against her dress, she could feel it, but refused to look, unable to face the reality of what she already knew to be true. She held out a hand as the door opened, and fainted, falling into the arms of a nurse.

Later, she couldn't quite count the hours that she spent drifting in and out of consciousness. She was aware of voices, faces, people messing with her body, waking for moments, remembering, half-remembering, falling back to the oblivion of sleep. When finally she came to her full senses she found herself looking into the face of a young woman who was bent over her, struggling to undo the cleat on one of the straps that pinned her to the bed.

"We had to tie you in, sweetheart. Sorry about that, but you'd have been thrown out again if we hadn't. You alright? God, that was a rough one. Talk about a storm. There are injured people all over the place; it's a right mess. We've had to call in here at Nantes to get some of the worst ones off the ship. A car flipped in the hold, there was a fire and a couple of the boys in the engine room got burned." She pulled a face. "You were one of the lucky ones."

Maria struggled to sit up, put her hands to her abdomen, and began to cry.

"Sorry, love. That was harsh. I didn't mean that, really I didn't. It's awful, what's happened to you, just awful." She picked up one of Maria's hands. "I know," she continued, "I've been there. It happened to me when I was twenty. I've got two boys now, but when I miscarried that first time I thought I'd never get over it …" she trailed off. They both knew there was nothing more she could say. This was not something that Maria would ever get over. The grief would stay with her forever; it was a part of her now. There is a common misconception that grief gets smaller over time, but it doesn't, the nurse knew. All she could do was hope that one day she might grow around it.

The ship stayed in port for three days as the storm continued to roar out in the open sea, and all this time Maria stayed in bed, struggling to adjust. The two over-worked nurses were kind to her, and she got to know another patient, Mr Edmonds, who had banged his head and broken his wrist in a fall, and his wife Hillary who came to visit. He was a businessman who spent a lot of time in Gibraltar, and they made this trip twice a year. They both swore that this was by far the worst gale they had ever seen. They were gentle with her, and eventually were able to persuade her to walk around the deck, so that the three of them stood together, hanging on to each other as the ship sailed out of harbour.

She was strong, but this was harrowing. Just to keep going was the hardest thing she had ever been asked to do. She was overwhelmed, stunned by the loss. She tried to think of the courage of the old man, Joachim, in the hospital, hiding the pain of his smashed leg and of the wounds he had nursed in silence for his dead son. Sometimes she tried telling herself that amidst all this killing she could not let herself be brought low by the loss of just one unborn child. Her conscious brave mind repeated this over and over again, but still the kernel of her body moaned, and at night this non-controllable other self kept screaming at her that she had failed them all, and stabbed at her with blades of shame and guilt. She dreamed of the reaming tool, the device the cooper used to widen the stopper on the barrels, and woke howling, convinced her sheets were shavings, the fear in her so real that even the wise old night nurse was distraught.

Behind her back the older couple looked at her with confused sympathy. The woman especially could see the impossible weight of the trauma she was trying so hard to mask, and when she saw how Maria unknowingly pressed hopeful fingers to the mound that was no longer there, she had to run inside to hide her tears.

But as the land slipped out of sight Maria made herself a promise. She would get over this, she kept telling herself, for she was a warrior. No matter what, she had to stop feeling sorry for herself. There was war and fighting everywhere, and Jacob, the father of her child, was wrapped up in the middle of it all. She had always thought self-pity unattractive, but right now, in her circumstances, it was contemptible, and she just would not accept it.

Chapter Fifty-Seven

A new life, 1937

A mile from Portsmouth, the English wind was cold and angry, ripping unclean spume from the tops of the breaking waves. It blew off-shore, back towards Spain, as if to warn her away; even the seagulls struggled. She watched them as they flew down close to the water, before being wheeled around in great shrieking arcs as the gale took hold and flung them back seawards.

The ship ploughed on, aided now by two tugs whose propellers chewed the water to a seething brown foam. Maria stood defiantly, holding on tight to the rails, steeling herself for whatever challenges this inhospitable-looking island might throw at her. Her hair streamed horizontally behind, her coat tails whipped against her legs, her eyes red raw from the weeping and the wind. She would endure this. By now she did not know whether the pain in her womb was real or imagined, but it was there alright: a weight and an absence combined, a void and a cannonball glued to her insides. She would endure this too.

She jumped when without warning the ship gave a great blast on its funnel, then another. People around her cheered. Ahead she could now pick out the cranes and derricks of the dockyard, and behind them, tiers and tiers of tiny, grey-roofed houses. There was a lighthouse, church steeples, more ships, more grey. She felt a tapping at her elbow and turned. It was Mr Edmonds.

"We're going to wait in the lounge, dear. It's too cold out here!" The wind was so strong that he had to shout into her ear. Up close, he smelled of cigars and peppermint. "Perhaps you should come with us? We don't want to lose sight of you now, not after all this." Maria noted that he had asked her, not told her. He was a kind man. She was accustomed to being ordered about by men of his age, and she took his arm willingly.

It was almost dark as they finally made their way down the gangway, and she was relieved that she had the Edmonds for company. Later she would examine just why it was that she had never really questioned her reliance on the kindness of these relative strangers, but she would remain forever grateful.

"Come on, come with us, please," Hillary had begged. "We've got this great big house, and with the children all away there's lots of space. We won't bother you." She spoke Spanish with the singsong lilt of the Canary Islands, where she had been educated many years earlier by her shipping-merchant father. The accent seemed mildly out of kilter with her dress and English mannerisms, and to Maria's ears the effect was completely charming. She accepted the invitation with all the grace that she could muster.

The house was like a library, with books in every room. The Edmonds had a daughter, married and living in Scotland, and a son, a doctor in India who they hadn't seen for five years. Five years! They talked about him as if they'd only seen him yesterday, and Maria took comfort from the thought that it was a mere five months since she had last seen Jacob.

In the end it was two weeks before Hillary decided that Maria was strong enough to continue with her journey to the Midlands. She had been in telephone contact with Jacob's cousins and everything was arranged. They protected her, cossetted her and even taught her a few words of English. Their kindness extended beyond her departure, with Hillary sending her off with a pile of ham and mustard sandwiches that she had prepared herself, and Mr Edmonds insisted that he go all the way to London with her, just to put her on the right train to Birmingham.

"It's really not out of my way. I need to go up to town anyway, to see my chap at Coutts. It just so happens that Middlesex are playing Surrey, which means that if the weather holds we might even get to spend the afternoon at Lords."

She had no idea what he was talking about, but she suspected it was just an excuse to mask his kindness. He even walked all the way across the station at Marylebone and escorted her to her seat before making a formal goodbye. She watched him walk away along the platform with a lump in her throat, for she had grown genuinely fond of him, and he and his wife had shown her that people could be both affluent and generous-hearted at the same time, two states of being which until then she had considered incompatible. When she had first set foot in their large house she had felt as though she were stepping into enemy territory. These were bourgeois capitalists, the people she had been taught to hate, and yet they were both kind and charitable. The boundaries that she had set herself were shifting underfoot. First Jacob had opened the door and proved to her that an honourable individual could move from one camp to another, and now these two gentle souls had suggested that not all rich folk were inherently evil. Perhaps the two camps were less distant than she had supposed, perhaps there was enough middle ground to be able to live together after all.

She would share this thought with Jacob; he would be thrilled to think that her hard-line dreams were perhaps less inflexible than she had imagined. Perhaps! She thought of him now as the train gave a lurch and pulled out of the station. His young eyes had seen this very country. What had he made of it all?

At the next station a bespectacled soldier pushed his way in behind a huge canvas kitbag, almost falling to the floor beneath its weight. He blushed when he realised he was alone in the carriage with her. Later, timorously, he offered her some of his sandwich. She wasn't hungry, but took some anyway for his sake. He spoke not a word of Spanish, but by showing her his textbook, and much pointing, he was able to explain to her that he was leaving the army, which he had never wanted to join, and that he was studying to become a vet. As he got off the train at Oxford she realised that this was the first communication she had managed in English, and to her surprise she had enjoyed the challenge. *Goodbye*, she practised to herself, *good luck.*

As instructed she descended from the train at Warwick. The handful of other passengers soon melted away and she stood alone on the empty platform, squinting at the sign and wondering how she should pronounce it. She heard footsteps behind her and turned to see two young women, one blonde, one dark.

"Maria?" said the blonde one. She reached out and held on gently to the fabric of her coat.

"Yes," she managed to whisper, keeping her eyes down. She felt intimidated by the scrutiny of the two cousins who continued to stare at her as though considering the purchase of a new dress.

"My God! No wonder little Jacob fell so hard for you: you're lovely," said the dark one. "I'm Philippa, and this is Olivia, and we're going to take care of you. Come on!" With that they picked up her bags, linked arms and almost frog-marched her down the platform, each talking happily over the other in animated Spanish.

A chauffeured car was waiting for them in the road outside, and the two women instantly began a small fight over who should sit in the middle seat. Maria caught the driver's eye, and he shrugged as if to suggest he was used to this. Over the following weeks she would come to realise that the sisters were close, but squabbled over everything. Shoes, films, men, politics. Conflict was the modus operandi of their relationship. Just like their cousins, in fact. Perhaps it was in the blood. At least it made her feel at home.

The big car moved slowly across the venerable town, waiting patiently as it crossed the market square where vendors were still busy taking down their stalls and packing the unsold wares onto carts. Maria stared at the neatly ordered houses, their exposed timber frameworks projecting an antiquity which she recognised from Toledo. And she recognised too the tired expressions of the shoppers, the toil of the two men who heaved a huge cheese onto a barrow. She saw the familiar sanctimonious smirk of a priest who nodded to the car, the red raw hands of a girl washing windows, and the gurnings of a boy who pulled faces behind the teacher's back. Just people, she thought, busy being people.

As they reached the edge of town Philippa asked if they could stop.

"Just look at that," she said.

Beyond a vast striped lawn sat the dreamy sight of Warwick Castle, all battlements and turrets, a child's King Arthur vision of a fortress. In the foreground was an elegant bridge whose arches were reflected in the smooth waters of the canal to form a perfect ring. Maria watched spellbound as a swan sailed through the circle to complete the fairy-tale image.

"Byron says it's the fairest sight in all England," said Philippa proudly.

Maria looked at the driver. Was he Byron, she wondered?

"Yes. And you know how they paid for it, don't you? Hostages. A King's ransom. All those French princes kept there until their families coughed up. You've got to see the pain behind the beauty, and all the war and dishonesty that goes with it."

The sisters continued to bicker quietly as Maria gazed at the building.

Warwick castle. A beautiful prison for foreigners, a dungeon with an open sky.

Was that to be a metaphor for her time in England?

Chapter Fifty-Eight

Madrid, 2012

They had both been busy and Jess hadn't spoken to Stefan since the day they had been to the museum together. At his suggestion they were now sitting side by side at a new co-working office near Chamartín; it felt more like a business meeting than a date, but that, after all, was exactly what it was, she kept reminding herself.

"You're serious, aren't you?" he asked her. "About pursuing this thing. And this place Jubar ... where is it precisely?"

"Granada. Province of. Somewhere in the mountains."

He drummed his fingers on the table and reached for her phone. "Can I?" he asked. "You got Google Maps?" She pushed it towards him and waited whilst he studied it.

"Thing is, I got some news too," he said after a while. "Remember I told you about the Jesuit brother, Donat, the one who mentored me, and paid for all my trips to Ampleforth? We still keep in contact and chat about once a year. Well, he called me to say that he's in the desert this week on a winter golfing holiday."

"A golfing monk in the sand," she said. "Why do I find that funny? Does he play out of Habit?"

"Yeah right, funny. And he was a priest, not a monk, you bloody heathen. But no, he left the Order a couple of years after I did, went back to Dublin. He works like a dog these days, a proper job he calls it, working with MSF- *Medcins Sans Frontières* – as some kind of manager helping refugees. He told me that as a priest he'd always thought he was following a higher calling, but that this is a step up."

"And this means ..."

"Well, he wants to see me. Kind of urgently. This week ..."

She raised an eyebrow. "And?"

"And he means the Andalucían desert. The Desert Springs Almeria Golf Resort, to be precise. Which according to your Google Maps is only two hours from Jubar."

"Interesting ..."

He watched her nervously as she peered at her phone.

"Can I finish my coffee first?" she asked.

He smiled at her. "Be my guest. Can your splendid new phone make a reservation for a hire car too?"

Things were clicking into place suspiciously easily, Jess thought to herself as she made her way back to the hotel. Had she always been this spontaneous? It was easier to follow your intuition when you had a bit of money, she decided. Hire car? Sure, no problem. Hotel room? Yeah, whatever.

But it certainly felt good to be speeding the next day down the almost empty motorways that lead out of the city, and across the even more empty hills of Castille. She was happy: she had a clue, an inkling, and already an idea was forming which she dare not yet put into words.

Her companion seemed almost gloomy by comparison. She knew that at the back of his mind there was the fear that his friend Donat might have bad news for him; why else would he not discuss it on the phone? For this reason she did most of the talking in an effort to distract him.

"Hey, but guess what? I went to see one of Jacob's distant relatives, an old man in a nursing home whose mind is still sharp as a pin. He actually knew Jacob's mother when she was much older, and he told me that towards the end of her life all these super-lucid stories kept pouring out from her almost like a confession, and that other people had corroborated them. It turns out that she wasn't quite the frigid old bird that I'd imagined. She might have been like that when Maria knew her, but as a young woman she was quite the rebel. As far as I can make out, when she was about eighteen she stepped outside the rigid confines of her orthodox Catholic childhood and got her fingers badly burned in the process. Basically she had this huge crush on a theatre Impresario from Malaga almost twice her age, and allowed herself to be seduced by all his classic lies and hype. She was a great beauty by all accounts, and for her this was the great love story of the ages, but of course he was just using her and he disappeared long before the promised wedding could ever take place. What was worse was that she found out soon after that he'd been making similar promises to another poor girl in Cadiz. It goes without saying that she was totally broken by the experience, and apparently suffered this almighty fall from grace and could barely show her face amongst the smart set that she had been used to. Her own father didn't speak to her for six months, until out of the blue this other suitor turned up, Jacob's dad this is, and offered to take her off the old man's hands.

"It sounds like they couldn't wait to offload her; she was real damaged goods and yet for some reason this gallant son of an established military family was suggesting not only marriage but instant social redemption. It was too good to be true, at least from her parents' perspective, and within the year they were marching her down the aisle."

"Not exactly a whirlwind romance then ..."

"No, but the thing is, it worked. It wasn't so much an arranged marriage as a re-arranged one, but they stuck at it. It was as though she had learned her lesson, and almost overnight became this ultra-orthodox figure who committed herself a hundred per cent and more to the values and traditions of the damned Regiment. No wonder she flipped when Jacob followed her example and jumped ship. Not only was he a renegade to the army, but he'd also done for love what she'd been unable to manage herself."

"And unwittingly turning his mama into an embittered, emotional outcast."

"Well, yes, kind of. She would never allow his name to be mentioned in her presence, refused to acknowledge him. He'd been her favourite and he'd let her down. Then not long after he disappeared his sister died in childbirth; that was obviously nothing to do with Jacob, and yet she blamed him, I think, for bringing bad luck on the family. And then his brother Lucas somehow blotted his copybook and instead of going on to have a glorious military career he became the governor of a prison in Alicante and died of typhoid."

"So she ended up with no children, the family reputation once again in tatters, and still married to the man who was evidently not the love of her life."

"Yes, but not for long. Ultimately Jacob's father was equally destroyed by the whole saga and went off on a mission to South America with the Germans, and just never came home. According to his great-niece, who I met in Paris, he became this middle-age philanderer and died just five years later, a burned out junkie."

"Cool guy. You can see why this might have made her a bit

resentful."

"And why she wouldn't even open Maria's desperate letters. It's a wonder she didn't destroy them."

Stefan announced that he needed a break and they stopped for a while at a roadside café. Afterwards they drove in silence for a while.

"You okay?" asked Stefan.

She hesitated. "Sure," she said. "It's just that I was thinking about what you called your *episode* in Kosovo. You never really told me what triggered it all. And I'm not even sure that I should ask you about it."

He paused to gather his thoughts. "Ask away. It's supposed to be better to get it all off my chest. I just don't want to unburden myself on you, that's all. Perhaps I'm scared that you'll judge me."

"Too late for that," she said, and smiled at him.

He pulled a face.

"I told you. In a sense it was nothing. I wasn't hurt, I did nothing heroic. It was simple. They used to do checks, and those lucky enough to still have passports or some kind of identification papers had to be processed in these huts. It wasn't our role, but we just used to do it to help out. So one day there I was, and I'd been talking to this young Albanian woman with a baby in her arms who had waited all morning in the queue. We used to help photocopy any documents they had, and fill in as many details as we could in these great ledgers. There wasn't much choice, you had to identify everyone – there were infiltrators, people traffickers, frauds, you name it, but this one woman was genuine, you could just tell. She was in transit, waiting for her husband who was supposed to arrive any day. But anyway, the photocopier was jammed, so I told her to wait there and I wandered off to a cabin across the track, where the main office was.

And I was just opening the machine when there was this huge explosion and all the glass came flying out of the windows. Lucky I was facing the other way. I wasn't hurt at all. But when we staggered outside, the checkpoint where I'd been standing just before wasn't there anymore. Just a crater, and when the dust settled you could see all these body parts, and blood, people screaming. It was a mortar, a stray mortar, they said, that some evil swine had lobbed over for no reason. There were three people killed, and it felt like ... felt like she had swapped places with me, had taken my place, and that I'd betrayed her.

"The medics came and took me away, checked to see if I was alright. And I was, really. I had bad dreams in the night, and someone had to wake me up a couple of times before I yelled the place down, but other than that I felt more or less alright. I knew that logically it wasn't my fault, that I couldn't have saved the poor woman and her child, so I just kept going. You do, you see: you're supposed to be there as a helper, for humanitarian purposes, so you just bottle it up and soldier on, quite literally. To be fair to the people in charge, they kept trying to monitor me, but I just waved them off and told them not to mollycoddle me. And they told me a million times to talk to someone if I was feeling the pressure. It's funny, I heard them, I heard the words, but unless you're ready for them, they're just words, just sounds, not really ideas that you can connect with."

He paused to concentrate as they overtook a slow-moving lorry.

"They were right, of course. I should have sought more help. In retrospect it's easy to say that, but I didn't want to let anyone down. Even now it's not easy to talk about it. It's like showing someone a wound. It's humiliating. I used to think that it was harder for a man, a young man especially, to discuss these things, but it's just the same for women, for everyone, we're no different. I'm not just saying that for you, by the way.

"For days I just felt guilty. All around there were people far worse off than I was, people genuinely suffering. Not just the refugees, but my colleagues too. We were all under the same pressures, but some of us – well, me, anyway – were not handling it very well, but at the time I just didn't know it. I knew I was a bit stressed, a bit edgy, a bit frightened, but that was normal, or so I thought. And then ... and then something cracked."

He looked sideways at Jess. She smiled at him, and nodded again, not wanting to interrupt this intimate recitation.

"In a Land Cruiser. Hardly heroic. We had parked in the middle of this huge loading bay next to some warehouses. There were four of us, and three got out, leaving me to guard the vehicle as we had guns in the back that the local warlords would likely try to steal from us. It was a grey, cold day. The car park was grey, the buildings grey. At first there were lorries and cars parked all around me, but as time passed they all began to move off one by one. Eventually it was just me there, parked all by myself in the middle of this massive grey car park. I got cold and walked around a bit. The others were late, much later than we'd planned, and I was beginning to get a bit anxious. It started to rain then, so I got back into the car, and just sat there with the wipers on. I can remember feeling very exposed, sitting there alone in the middle of all that space, like the bullseye on a target. I don't think I was scared, no more so than normal anyway, more just, I don't know ... dismal. And after that I honestly don't know what happened. The others came back and found me sobbing and shaking on the back seat, not making any sense. I wasn't crazy, or biting or foaming at the mouth or anything like that, but I was sweating despite the cold and my heart was racing. They thought at first I might have been poisoned, but there was this French guy who'd seen it before, and named it for what it was: a panic attack."

"Jesus. You say it was nothing, but that was awful. And you say it wasn't heroic, but it was, you know. Just being there was bloody heroic. I wouldn't have the courage. You should be proud to be able to tell me about it, not ashamed. I mean ... respect, seriously."

He struggled to suppress a smile.

"Does that mean I'm in your good books?"

"Maybe ... why?"

"Nothing. Our stop-over tonight ... you'll see."

She looked at him suspiciously as the uninhabited landscape flew by on either side. It was warm, and she was tired, and despite herself she felt her eyes beginning to close, and finally she fell asleep somewhere near Murcia. When she awoke, they were almost at their destination, the little town of Palomares.

"Why here?" she asked him.

"It's near enough to the resort, and I'd just always wanted to see it, that's all. You do know the story, don't you? That in 1966 an American B-52 dropped a stick of atom bombs that miraculously didn't go off. It's about the biggest cover-up there ever was. The Yanks said there was no radiation, but even so they ended up taking more than two thousand tons-worth of topsoil back to the States. Seriously. It's amazing what you can get away with when you mix Cold War with a bankrupt dictatorship."

"Gee thanks. I think I told you before: you do know how to treat a girl."

She had only just woken up and wasn't sure whether to believe him, but she was able to confirm it at dinner that night. She ate alone, with her guidebook. Stefan still suspected that his friend might need to reveal some bad news and preferred to keep their appointment intimate. She had understood, and didn't press it.

They met again at breakfast and she looked at him anxiously, trying to gauge his mood.

"He offered me a job!" he announced, unable to keep the smile from his face. "I can't believe it. It's only three days a week, and with a minimal salary, but they want me to coordinate the fund-raising with Médecins sans Frontières, at the MFS office in Madrid. He wanted to tell me in person."

"Hey! Man! Well done. High five!"

He was bubbling with excitement and struggling to suppress the grin that kept reappearing. She was genuinely pleased for him.

"Jess, I can't tell you how ... overjoyed I am to be able to get something like this. It's humanitarian, ethical, non-profit, it's an honour to be asked, and I get to stay in Madrid, and with luck I'll be able to study at the same time. I mean ... Wow!"

He suddenly seemed to remember himself.

"Erm, sorry. How was your night?"

"Well, you know, I took a little walk, tripped over a few unstable atomic nucleii, took in a bit of radiation, just all the regular tourist stuff that people do here. I learned something too: that *Pu* is the chemical symbol for plutonium, so the evening wasn't entirely wasted." She smiled at him. "Hey, but listen, I'm really pleased for you, okay. Really. And by the way, I've been looking at the map: you can compensate for abandoning me in this radioactive dump by taking me to see the National Park at Cabo de Gata, the place with all the volcanoes are. It's on the way to Jubar ... kind of."

He looked at her. She was serious. She was a force of nature with a guide book in her hand: it wasn't worth arguing.

Chapter Fifty-Nine

A slight difficulty, 2012

The little car twisted along the lanes between the dead volcanoes, raising a cloud of dust that forced them to keep the windows closed.

"There's no water here, no topsoil, no monetary value," said Stefan. "That's why no one has ever lived or built here. It's how the Mediterranean should be, just as Homer saw it."

"Homer Simpson?"

He scowled at her as he parked by the sea's edge on a cliff overlooking an almost deserted cove. What little cloud cover there was had been swept away by the stiffening breeze; white horses were beginning to form beyond the cover of the bay. Stefan showed her the deeper blue of the wind-line out to sea; it would be rough out there, he said. They scampered down the rough volcanic rocks which gave such amazing grip.

"It's like walking on Velcro," he says. "I feel like a gecko." He bends down to examine the crabs and small fish that are trapped in the many pools. Jess listens to the crump of a wave as it slaps against the rocks, brilliant white against the blue, hissing as it hit the sun-scorched basalt flats.

They take off their shoes and begin to walk across the horseshoe beach to the opposite headland. The sand is almost black, and fine as talc, so hot they had to sprint to the sea to cool their burning feet.

"Swim?" she asks, regretting it as soon as she remembers. He shakes his head comically, embarrassed.

"I've been dreading this bit," he confesses. "But I don't mind if you do."

"Another day, maybe."

In an effort to change the subject he explains how difficult it would be to windsurf there, with the angle of the wind and the current and the big breaking waves all working together to keep you on the beach.

"You could just about do it here; you'd just have to keep waiting until a big set of waves ends, and hope the wind doesn't drop."

"The Seventh wave. Isn't that the big one, or is that a myth?"

"It's not quite as simple as that. I wish it were. The basic rule seems to be that the big wave comes when you're least expecting it." He looks thoughtful.

"And the tide is off shore here. Did you see that Lilo earlier? It's dangerous. The only good thing it does is blow the jellyfish away from the beaches, and the litter."

Just then Jess notices one of the two little boys that they had seen earlier. She wonders then where the parents were. Where's the other one, she asked herself, but then she sees a swimmer out to sea, perhaps a bit too far out to be comfortable. Stefan had seen it too.

"Is that your brother?" she asks the boy.

"He's gone to get our ball," he says. "He's been ages."

Together they climb up onto a higher rock to get a better view. At first Jess is relieved to see that he had turned towards land, but he didn't seem to be making any progress. They watch for five more minutes.

"He's caught in the current," says Jess. "He's not strong enough."

She sees that Stefan has gone pale, and that he's holding his head in his hands, panting slightly.

"Jess! I can't, I can't ... the water, the deep, the, I ..."

He looks up to see her pulling off her shirt and shorts.

"I'm a better swimmer than you," she says. She has no idea whether this is true, or quite why she says it, but she leans out as far as she dare from the rocky ledge, waits a moment for the incoming wave, then hurls herself into the foaming water, knees tucked tight to her chest. The water is so rough that he doesn't even see the splash, but in that single instant Stefan seems to come to his senses and by force of will takes control of the panic that had threatened to overwhelm him. As she disappears beneath the confusion of spume and surf that batter the land, he stares stupidly after her, as if into a hole which he expects to re-open. He counts slowly, convinced she must have struck some unseen object. But then suddenly, there! He sees her re-emerge a good ten metres away, her arm rising from the waves and signalling a diver's "O" with thumb and finger to show that she's okay.

He calculates that to have travelled so far so quickly she must already be in the stream of the rip tide, taking her out quickly towards the boy. Her polished crawl is strong and rhythmic. As the two come closer Stefan sees how every few strokes she has to stop to look around; the waves out there must be larger than they seem, for she obviously cannot see her quarry, who is now right by her. For a second he thinks she may have over-shot, but then the two dots merge to become one, and he can begin to relax.

As he stands up Stefan notices that his shins are bleeding, scratched on the unforgiving rock. He realises he must have been on his hands and knees as she went out, like a dog, like a pathetic cur, he thinks miserably; what must she think of him? He shields his eyes with his hand and tries to focus on the two swimmers. Despite their efforts they don't seem to be making much progress. Will she be mad with him, he wonders? The swimmers have turned over and are trying back-stroke, he notices. She'll never respect him, that's for sure. For a full five minutes he watches as they struggle, concerned more with her reaction than with their plight.

Then suddenly it hits him. They cannot fight it. They cannot fight the rip tide. You have to go with it, out to sea, to follow it out, out to deep water, and wait for rescue. *You moron, Stefan! A rip tide like this is just too strong; fight it and it will drown you.* He knows that; every surfer, windsurfer, every sailor knows that. Does she know? Or is her clever mind so clotted now with cold and dread that she has panicked and forgotten? Will she fight and tire and die on the tide like so many others? Dear God, someone has got to get to her. He thinks of the depths of the sea, of the blue that fades to black beneath the waves, of the huge, hollow deepening fall to the ocean floor, and of the vile and ancient things that lurk there, dark, like fear.

Meanwhile, a hundred metres out to sea, Jess is wrestling to keep the boy afloat. Each time she turns toward the shore the wind and the current conjoin to fill his face with water; his lips are turning blue and he barely has the sense or strength to keep his mouth closed.

"Kick!" she yells at him and turns them both onto their backs, but his feeble efforts stumble after just a few seconds and the faint twitches in his legs now terrify her as much the tide. He'd been so relieved to see her. He was so young, what twelve? She could feel the frailness in those slim ribs as she held him, could see the fear in his fawn's eyes. It isn't fair. She would not leave him now, she swears, she would not let him go. She could feel the cramping in her foot. As she bends to squeeze it another wave surprises her and she sucks yet more loathsome, salted water into her tiring lungs, losing buoyancy as she coughs so that for a second her head drops below the surface.

She kicks again. And again. For a brief while she thought she was moving closer at last to the shore, the beloved shore. But then she feels again the tug of the tide; it seems to cling to the length of her, drawing her back to the open sea, back to the coldness and the deep. It seems to want to part her from the boy whose head she held in tiring hands; she glances at him. Oh God, his eyes are closed. She will not leave him.

But suddenly he's there beside her. Brown arms pull her to him. He's calm. She can feel the strength in those shoulders. "Turn round," he says. "Follow me, trust me. I've got the boy. We go out, not in. Do you understand?"

She feels the lightness enter her as she releases the weight of the child and swims and floats with the current, riding it, not fighting. *Stefan*, she thinks, *you came.*

The boat arrives moments later. Another family had moored their speed boat in the shelter of the bay and had been alerted to the boy's predicament by an ornithologist who was camped by the gulls' nests on the cliff.

The boy, who recovered quickly, is met by a mixture of relief and fury from his anxious parents. But everything is ok. No police, no reports, and all the life sucked out of the drama.

Jess desperately needs quiet, and heads out to walk alone along the beach. Once the panic and agitation have abandoned her, she returns to him.

"You took your fucking time, Batman."

He smiles at her.

"I needed to finish my Sudoku. It was a hard one."

She sits down next to him and squeezes his hand.

"Hey," she says. "That was tough. That took courage. Thanks. I mean it."

"You too. You're the brave one; you started it."

They sit close, side by side, trembling with a mixture of cold and adrenaline, elated to be alive, and confused by their connection.

Chapter Sixty

Jubar, 2012

Jess trailed her hand along the wall of the church at Jubar, as if to read with her fingertips the stories which she felt must pour from the ancient stones. She was standing beneath an Islamic arch, for it had originally been built as a mosque, and yet above her on the tower were both a crucifix and a Star of David.

"It's a good idea to have all your bases covered," said Stefan approvingly. "Although it doesn't look like it gets much use these days, does it?"

"Hardly surprising: it says here they killed 193 priests in the war, just in this tiny part of the Alpujarras. 'Immolated by Marxism,', to quote. That's a lot of dead priests ..."

She stopped, remembering too late that it was only the previous day that Stefan had been with his friend.

"Sounds like a bit of papist exaggeration to me," he said. "How many people here do you think had any kind of political education in 1936? Most of them wouldn't have known a Marxist from a turnip. Lots of priests were murdered, that's for sure, whether they were good men or bad, but that's because they were seen as the face of a hostile system, and seen by angry, hungry people. To call them Marxists is deliberately divisive."

She wanted to ask him more, but he had turned his back on her and was walking towards the cemetery. She joined him and began to tour the despondent rows of graves.

"Hey," she said after a while. "Look at this." She pointed to four tombstones. Only two had names, but all four shared the same date.

"Busy day for the undertaker," said Stefan. "And?"

"Well it's two days after Maria last saw Jacob. July 14th 1937. I remember that she told me the French Bastille celebrations always made her sad."

"So this could be him then … let's have a look at the parish register."

The church was locked but it wasn't difficult to find a villager with a key. Six villages now shared a priest, the old lady told them, and he wouldn't be there until Tuesday, but she also had the key to the vestry. Unfortunately, she explained solemnly, she could allow them twenty minutes and no more because the bread van was arriving at noon.

"She couldn't have sounded more serious if she'd announced that the Messiah was arriving at noon," said Stefan as she left them, and he began to leaf through one of the heavy books.

Twenty minutes was more than enough.

"You're sure?" she asked. "He's definitely not here?"

He shook his head. "Not unless they changed his name. Maybe he got away?"

Jess looked crestfallen. "Let's ask the Oracle at the Bread Van," she said. "Maybe if there was a battle or something then people might remember it."

The women in the queue for bread were anxious to please, and loudly so, but were unable to shed any light on what might have happened.

"Too bad. Nice people," said Stefan. "I love the way that what they lack in knowledge they make up for in volume."

"And repetition." She smiled. "At least the croissants are good."

They sat in the warmth of the sun to consider their next move. A cat appeared with two kittens to beg for crumbs, the water gurgled in the fountain and from the church tower came the soft cooing of pigeons. Nothing else moved.

"You can see why the bread van is an event here, anyway; you wouldn't want to miss that. Otherwise this place would be boring …"

As he spoke an old lady turned a corner and walked slowly towards them.

"I heard your question," she said. "At least I heard that name. Jacob. It's only just come back to me, but when we were young we used to scare ourselves with tales about Jacob's cave. I never really thought about it before, it was just a thing we said. But go and see El Francès. He knows more about it. He said he went there once."

With that she turned away from them. Stefan tried to question her but it was clear that she had no more to say.

Stefan and Jess looked at each other. She just shrugged, stood up and banged hard on the nearest door. Eventually it opened. El Francès, they soon learned, lived in the big house above the village; if they listened they could hear his tractor.

They followed the noise of the engine, and arrived just as the driver was reaching the end of a long, straight furrow. He switched off the motor and looked at them suspiciously.

"Eh?" he breathed. "Thank Christ for that: I thought you were from the National Parks again. You look, you know …" His voice tailed away.

"Official?" asked Jess. "Well we're not that. We just want to hear anything you can tell us about Jacob."

"Not police either then? Promise?"

They followed him into the house and waited as he washed his hands. The walls of the room were covered in sepia photographs.

"Jacob's Cave? I've heard of it yes," he said cagily. "Why do you want to know now, after all these years? How do I know you're not investigators or bounty hunters or something? You know what? When I saw you arrive I hoped you weren't officials, but now I wish that you were. You're going to have to come back with some paperwork."

Stefan could see that this was going nowhere. He was about to speak to Jess who was studying the photos on the wall when suddenly he heard her gasp.

"It's her! Look – Maria. And Jacob."

Both men turned to stare at her.

"May I?" she asked, but without waiting for an answer she reached up, lifted the picture from the wall and wiped the dust from the glass with her sleeve.

"That's my dad, and my granddad," said the man.

He held the picture up to the light, and put on a pair of reading glasses. He looked at it more closely.

"I recognise the couple. I remember now. My dad told me. But he also said that no one else knew." His mistrust returned and he glared at them. "So how come you …?"

Jess opened her bag and fished out a copy of the faded images which had lain for so long in the drawer by the bed in Wimbledon.

"Because she was my friend," she said simply, and held up a copy for his inspection.

For a moment the man looked as if he might cry.

"And my dad was her friend. Imagine that. He said he'd only known her for about a month but that she was his inspiration, and that poor old Jacob was the real reason that he'd been able to escape."

He made them sit down. "My name's Jorge, by the way, though everyone calls me El Francès." He sipped at a beer bottle as he gathered his thoughts.

"My dad – Sergio – knew that there was a body in a cave up in the hills. He never knew for certain if it was Jacob, because he'd sneaked away to front line just before Jacob and Maria left, even though he was only fifteen. His older brother had been killed by the fascists and he wanted revenge. Somehow he escaped from where he'd been fighting in Almeria and came home just as the war was coming to an end. This would be about two years after Maria and Jacob had been here, you follow? Anyway, more or less at the same time two soldiers came sniffing round Jubar – a bit like you are now – and asked about Jacob, because he was the brother of some big shot Officer. So my dad is forced at gun point to show them the cave. They saw the body whilst he waited outside, and after a while they all went down to fetch a coffin from the next village, Mairena."

Jorge paused again to drink. "So, by now my dad thinks something really fishy is happening, and he's seen enough killings and kangaroo courts and general mayhem to know that his life as a republican is in real danger. Besides, by now he has no family left, so he steals these soldiers' horses and just walks away. It's almost unbelievable how lucky he was. It took him two months but he walked and rode all the way to France. He'd been a shepherd all his life and so was at home in the mountains, but even so … it was a bit of a miracle.

"And his luck held. He spent the next war lying low in the Pyrenees, and earned some kind of medal for helping Allied soldiers over the border back towards Spain. He said he knew what it felt like to be alone and on the run, and that it was better to help men than to kill them."

"And still his luck held. He met my mama, who was a farmer's daughter. She and my grandfather ran this piss-poor, good-for-nothing farm up in the high, high mountains, and they were only just able to keep things together when I was a baby. But then another miracle happened when these crazy people came and bought out the place to turn it into a ski station. It was more money than he had ever dreamed of, and with it he bought a better farm further down the valley.

"And all this time he couldn't or wouldn't come back to Spain, not whilst it was still a dictatorship. Until 1975, that is, when Franco finally died. The following summer we all came here, to Jubar, and the first thing he did was to drag me up the mountain to see the cave where the body was. It was still there alright, just a plain wooden coffin, and he refused to open it. He thought it was probably Jacob, but my guess is that he just couldn't bear to know the truth. And there was no choice but to leave it where it was, so the next day we went back with a mule and a couple of sacks of plaster and walled it into the corner.

"I can't imagine that anyone has ever been near it. It's all a National Park up there now, so not even the hunters go that far. I bet it's just as we left it. Every year that passes I promise myself that I'll go and check it out, but somehow I never get round to it. I want to, it's just that … I don't know …"

"How about tomorrow?" asked Jess.

"Tomorrow?" He looked shocked.

For a long time he stared at the photo in his hands, and then at Jess.

"Yes," he said at last. "Midday, by the fountain. I'll bring tools."

Chapter Sixty-One

Jubar, 2012

"How you feeling?" Stefan asked Jess by the water fountain as they waited for Jorge to arrive. She could see that he wanted a proper answer; it wasn't just a ritual greeting, and she paused to consider.

"I'm not sure," she replied truthfully, and tried to explain the complex jumble of thoughts that had kept her awake that night. Sure, she was excited, a little scared even, that they might be caught, and at the same time fearful that they might be disappointed if they didn't find anything at all. Also, she felt an odd sense of what, of *trespass*, that they should be meddling with other peoples' past; it was an almost superstitious foreboding, which was strange since she wasn't at all superstitious. Meanwhile she had a niggling anxiety that they might find something just too hideous to look upon, and what her reaction might then be. And she was, of course, obsessively curious as to how this was all going to end. She could have added that she was curious too to discover the direction in which their own relationship was heading, but chose not to reveal this. Instead, as Jorge's old 4x4 drove up into the village square, she tried desperately to summarise.

"I don't know ... I'm *agitated*. That's what Maria used to say."

"Agitated?" he thinks for a moment. "Yes," he says, "that will do. Agitated. Me too."

They climb aboard the hot car and set off up the pot-holed, unpaved path that leads to the mountains. Jorge, they discover, is one of those drivers who will happily turn to face his passengers on the back seat as he talks to them, heedless of the yawning drop to the side, and they are relieved when after a few miles he parks the car and announces that they can drive no further.

"Cross-country from here," he says. "On foot, up there," and he points vaguely to the peaks in the far distance. "It's not far," he adds encouragingly, "not really," and hoists on a heavy-looking rucksack. He turns and begins to make his way along a barely discernible footpath. "And watch out for snakes!" he adds cheerily over his shoulder. Stefan and Jess pick up their bags and follow.

It takes them some time to get into the rhythm of the walk. Jess can feel the tightness in her calves, a slight shortness of breath; gorse scratches annoyingly above her boots and she can feel the prickle of sweat as it runs down her neck. But despite this she is happy. She knows she has the reserves of energy to keep going, and when she looks around she is awestruck yet again by the scale and beauty of her surroundings.

They stop for a moment to admire the flight of a pair of eagles who seem to race each other across an otherwise unscarred sky. After a while the great birds begin a slow circle overhead, a movement which is at once languid and threatening. Jess has never seen a golden eagle, not this close, not in the wild. Suddenly one draws back its wings and stoops; Jess can imagine the swoosh of the wind in its feathers as it cuts at such speed through the thin mountain air. It disappears behind a low line of bush and re-emerges seconds later, struggling with the weight of its kill. Jess feels like she ought to applaud.

Everywhere there is the deep, soporific thrum of the bees; otherwise it is silent. No breeze stirs the flowers or grasses. When they pause they feel the dead weight of the afternoon heat on their backs. To her Northern European sensibilities the hillside is alive with the seductive fragrance of the Mediterranean: thyme, rosemary, lavender; all the soft sweet scents of Spain that remind Jess so much of her holidays as a girl, and of her father.

As they walk on, Stefan puts his foot too close to the nest of a partridge, which detonates into the air in an explosion of whirring feathered outrage, making him cry out.

Jorge laughs. "They don't half make you jump when they do that, little buggers; it's as if you've stepped on a mine."

Stefan smiles briefly and says nothing, though Jess can see plainly that he has paled, and the tight line that has formed around his lips

When they look back they can see the white villages disappearing far below them in the valleys. Above them the high peaks brood stark and tree-less, their flanks still covered in the last, yellowing snows of Spring. A slippage of stone ahead of them rattles suddenly in the silence, and when she looks up Jess sees a herd of ibex, the wild mountain goats, skipping away from them, the colour of the rocks, visible only as they move.

Slowly, as they climb higher, all sign of human activity is eradicated. They pause again, to drink and to catch their breath, for the air is thin enough here for them to tire quickly.

"If ever you wanted to be reminded of your own insignificance," says Stefan, gazing around, "then this is the place to be."

Jess smiles at him, and thinks back to her ex, and to the time that they had climbed Snowdon together. All he'd ever wanted to know was how far it was to the pub; they had split up shortly after that trip.

Jorge tightens the straps on his rucksack and they move on. Gradually the clumps of bushes that they pass begin to grow taller, small trees appear, and these eventually merge, so that they find themselves standing at the bottom edge of an ever-thickening woods. The shade provided by the foliage above them is a mercy, though they are assailed now by tiny black insects.

Jorge is cheerful. "Back then," he says, "all this would have been open country, pasture. So many sheep, goats ... they kept it all cropped close to the ground. The transhumancia ... they, the shepherds, were up here for weeks, with their flocks, all this was ... well, not exactly managed, but contained. But they've all died now, moved on, got jobs in the cities, you know, constant depopulation ... year by year the *Encina,* the oak trees, are reclaiming it for themselves, turning it back into woodland. These days no one ever comes up here, no one at all. I love it."

He stops again without warning, and it isn't until he sets down his bag that Jess and Stefan realise that they must have arrived. Through the filmy, grey green light they see enormous boulders stacked together one upon the other, with giant ferns springing up between the cracks as if to hide them. A huge slab of rock lays tilted on its side, propped on one of the boulders, giving the impression of a triangular doorway.

"That's it," says Jorge. "Have a look."

Moss sprouts over the stones at the mouth of the cave. A fig tree the colour and texture of an elephant's leg grows defiantly up from the darkness, as if to guard it. Nettles and fierce brambles have in turn wrapped themselves around this tree, and climb upwards to the light, meshing with the ivy on a neighbouring oak. Jorge points a torch and whistles softly.

"Seriously," he says, "it wouldn't surprise me if me and my dad weren't the last people to come up here, more than forty years ago."

From his rucksack he produces a pair of shears, an axe and a pruning saw. "This might work up a bit of a sweat," he grins, and after handing them each a pair of leather gloves, he begins to hack at the tangle of vegetation.

Jess and Stefan do their best to pull away the debris that he produces, mindful of the sharp spikes and insect life that they are disturbing. Progress is slow and Jess at first is daunted.

"Don't worry, this should be the worst bit," Jorge encourages her. "The brambles only live here at the entrance, where there's light. Inside, as long as it's still dry, it should be clear."

His optimism is rewarded. Within half an hour they have cut away enough of the natural barricade to be able to pass through without it tearing at them.

The two men go first. Before she follows them, Jess looks up at the sky between the branches high above, and thinks of Maria. She hopes she is doing the right thing.

Inside the cave she is stunned to discover that she can stand. With her torch she sees that small stones cover the floor, which is flat and free of vegetation. Short white stalactites line the roof, just beyond her reach. The space is roughly rectangular, with the entrance on one of the shorter sides. The side walls lean heavily inwards, jagged and rough to the touch. Jorge is standing at the far side, staring at a relatively smooth piece of wall.

"It's still here," he says, marvelling. "This is what my dad did. Amazing." He turns to them, his headtorch dazzling them for a second so they cannot see his face. "I'll get my stuff," he announces and squeezes his way back outside.

Stefan and Jess try to read each other's thoughts in the half-light.

"We can't ..." he begins, but Jess cuts him off.

"We haven't come all this way for nothing," she insists. "At least I haven't."

"But ..." he insists, but before he can finish his sentence Jorge reappears, a chisel in one hand, a mallet in the other.

He looks at them happily. She loves this in him, in people like him. He's been given a task, and he'll complete it; no need to complicate things, just get on with the job.

"It should be easy," he explains, "it's just a layer of sun-baked brick, and a really weak mortar chucked on to disguise it a bit."

He places the chisel at the centre of the wall and raises the hammer. As his arm comes down, Jess sees in the corner of her eye that Stefan is still shaking his head.

It takes only a few sharp blows. As he had predicted, the wall is weak, but there is so much dust that they have to run out coughing to let it settle. No one speaks as they wait outside, each alone with their thoughts. After the darkness of the cave even the half-light of the forest seems bright.

"I feel like Indiana Jones," says Jorge. "Vamos."

They follow him in and are drawn magnetically to the shattered wall. Dust still swirls like smoke as high as the roof. All three crouch now, silent, by the newly made entrance, which reveals a low ledge of stone. On it sits an oblong box. This moment for Jess is frozen in time. For some reason she imagines someone painting them like this from behind, from the cave entrance; one of the old masters, Vermeer, say, or Poussin, with every detail, every fold, recorded on canvas, of three enigmatic backs bent over an unknown tomb.

"Poplar wood," says Jorge. "It'll last for years if it's dry. And those are hand-made nails."

He speaks to fill the vacuum, for none of them know how to react.

Stefan reaches forward and pulls on a leather strap, which comes away in his hand. Undismayed, he crawls halfway into the opening, almost laying on the lid of the box, until he can reach a hand behind it, and pulls. Slowly, with Jorge pulling from the front, they manoeuvre it forward. It seems less heavy than either of them had imagined. Stefan has to wriggle to extricate himself from the gap, and as he does so the coffin tilts, and from within there comes a sickening, unmistakeable rattle. Jess steps back, hand over her mouth, as the two men recover their composure and lift it gently to the middle of the floor.

They all try to speak at once, but then stop, leaving a void of embarrassed silence. At last Jorge shrugs his shoulders and retrieves a crowbar from his bag.

"Shall we?" he asks. "It's what we came here for."

He forces the heavy steel tool into a tiny gap by one of the square-headed nails, and leans his weight to lever it upwards. The nail screams as it's pulled from the wood, the terrible shrill sound bouncing off the walls of the cave. Jorge looks up at them questioningly. Jess puts her hands to her ears.

"Go on," she says, and watches in horrified fascination as one by one the nails which have secured the lid for so long are prised from their sockets.

Jorge steps back. For a second they look at each other, then Stefan moves forward decisively, pushes the lid away, and peers inside.

"It's just bones," is all he says. "Mostly bones."

Together they stand and stare into the box, the whiteness of the bones exaggerated in the lamplight. Jorge examines the lid on both sides, looking for a nameplate, a clue, anything, whilst the others, without touching anything, scrutinise the contents. There must be a dog-tag, a plaque, something.

"If you're right, Jess," says Jorge, "and I'm sure you are, when his brother Lucas sent someone here a couple of years later, to identify him, to find out what had happened, then he might not have had time to fix up a proper burial, even if he'd wanted to, not actually during the war. Once he knew where his brother was, there would have been no need for identification ... in fact as a renegade it could have made it worse. And most likely he'd have taken any personal stuff, a watch say, or a chain that he recognised."

Jess nods her head. "That's exactly what happened. That's what he wrote to his cousin, that he would come here after the war ended to sort things out properly, to try to patch things up with their mother. Leave the body here in the meantime. I mean, there were bodies buried everywhere, there still are, even today, it's just what people did."

"And that's the problem," says Stefan. "Bodies everywhere; caves too, no doubt. This could be anyone. We can't be sure that this is the one you're looking for. The authorities could do the DNA, but they'd never let us do that. Better we just send an anonymous tip-off to the police, tell them we came across it by accident."

Jess looks at him sadly.

"He's right, you know," says Jorge. "It could be anyone ..."

They sit in silence for a few minutes, tired and deflated.

Jess sighs. "I guess so," she says eventually. "Put the lid back on. I need air."

She stands, and takes one last look at the pathetic skeletal remains.

And then she sees it, just a glimpse. "Stop!" she shouts. "Wait!"

She searches in the zipped pocket of her bag, frantic in the dark, and pulls out a small dark case. This she opens, keeping its contents locked in her left hand. With the other, she reaches down now into the coffin, between the bones, the bare white ribs, the strips of fabric and the dust. Her teeth are clenched, she can barely breathe. At last her busy fingers find what they know must be there, and hold the thing tight.

The two men look on as she withdraws her arm, sits upright and brings her hands together. She stays like this for a long moment. Eventually she opens one palm, then the other. The pale beam from her headtorch reveals two pearl earrings, which seem to glow from within in the cold electric light. The earrings match.

"Jacob!" she says in a voice not her own, and to her own surprise bursts into uncontrollable tears.

Chapter Sixty-Two

El Ejido, Southern Spain, 2012

They had left the chest containing Jacob's remains in Jorge's garage in Jubar, concealed beneath a pile of olive nets. It had felt a cold and distant thing to do, but at this stage Jess was determined not to be overwhelmed by their emotional significance; all that could come later. At this point she was just astonished by their own audacity and good luck. The more she examined her behaviour, the more foolish she felt. In her head she rehearsed how the re-telling of the saga might sound to one of her friends back in London, or to her mother. It might be compelling, but likewise ludicrous, and she made a promise to herself to leave the accounting until later. It was already difficult enough to persuade Stefan. That evening they had quarrelled when Jess announced her intention to have the bones cremated.

"I only went along with bringing him out from the cave because I assumed we would give him a decent burial. A Christian burial. He must have been a Christian right? A headstone and all that. But this … this is mad."

But he could see that her mind was set, and that it would be futile to argue. Reluctantly he conceded that having come this far it would leave her more than dissatisfied to abandon her plan, and that morning he had begun the journey with good grace. But his spirits sank lower the more they descended towards sea level, as if his mood were changing with the scenery.

"If the beauty of the Alpujarras conjures up a vision of Eden," he said, reading from the guidebook, "then the shoreline to the south is surely its antithesis." At least they had been warned. As far as they could see the coastal plain was disfigured by the hideous grey plastic of the poly-tunnels, tens of thousands of them, squat, industrial and unremittingly ugly. At first Jess mistook their dull shine for the sea. Eventually a whispered "Jesus" was about all she could manage as the scale and grimness of the landscape began to dawn on her, and they drove in near silence to their destination, crushed by the degradation which surrounded them.

The crematorium was easy to find, not least because of the huge silver hearse which lead a slow cavalcade of the bereaved down the poplar-lined boulevard.

"Looks like they were expecting us," said Stefan cheerfully, "they've brought out the welcome party."

At this Jess laughed louder than was necessary, relieved that he sounded happier, for she knew that her nerve might easily fail without his support.

They parked the car in the shade provided by a row of dusty wind-bent trees, and sat with the windows down until the last of the mourners had shuffled away. When all was quiet they walked across the hot tarmac and waited self-consciously in a room marked: Reception.

"What must it be like to work in a place like this?" wondered Stefan aloud as a little man in a sombre suit sidled up to them, his face a mixture of professional sympathy and deference. The suit had seen better days, and he wrung his hands theatrically as if from the air itself he could squeeze a portion of true compassion. Although they were less than a mile from the Mediterranean, the skin of his gaunt cheeks was as white as the dandruff that speckled his shoulders.

"A delicate matter, you say, madame? A delicate matter indeed. Perhaps we could step this way to the comfort of my office?"

His fawning does not seem to elicit much empathy, at least from Jess. "Vampire?" she whispers to Stefan as they follow him down the corridor. There is a faint tang of disinfectant, which reminds her of school.

Jess has decided to be direct and gets straight to the point.

"Well yes, the law certainly does allow for exhumation, and we can send specialists to take care of things, provided that you have all the necessary documentation.

"Ah ... well there's the thing. You see, we won't need any help with the exhumation. That's already taken care of." She looks at him levelly, and decides to take the risk. "And we don't have the paperwork." The man is about to interrupt but she holds up her hand. "You see, my parents fled to England. You can tell by my accent. But we already have the remains. Old bones. Very old. My Great Grandfather, who died in the Civil War."

"Madame, there is quite a lot of paperwork involved, quite a ..."

"We know," she says impatiently, "and we are also aware that it takes a long time. We know too that we might never be able to get it. Old family tensions, shall we say. Even now, after so long, it's a sensitive issue, as I'm sure you know."

"Well, yes, quite, but even so ..."

"Look. He's been there, in the basement, for God knows, sixty years or more. In a box. He was more than just an atheist; he was violently anti-Catholic, and his wife refused to let him be buried in the churchyard. Everyone knew about it, even as kids we knew, but now he" – and with her thumb she indicates a nonplussed Stefan – "he says that after the wedding he won't move in, not with a body in the house. He's a scaredy cat really, a bit superstitious, and he just refuses, don't you, honey?"

Stefan nods meekly but Jess can see he is furious. He didn't want to be doing this.

"So basically what's happened is that I've inherited this great big house," she continues, relieved at last that she can mention something truthful, "which means that I'm now fairly well off. Rich, you might say." She pauses for this to sink in. "Which also means that I'd be more than happy to make a charitable donation to the crematorium." Again she waits. "In cash, of course. And I wouldn't need a receipt."

The two men in the room are equally flummoxed.

"We thought around three thousand euros, isn't that what we agreed, honey?"

The man swallows.

"Well?" says Jess. She can see him thinking.

"What you're asking is very irregular, it's ..."

"Four thousand. With flowers, a bouquet, carnations, whatever you want. That's your lot. Any more and I'll just find myself a trawlerman and chuck Great Grandad into the sea, like he says." She points again at Stefan. "Come on, you. Let's go. I've had enough of this. And you, sir, I'll call you tomorrow, okay."

She stands, and turns towards the door. The man clears his throat.

"Cash, you say?"

Jess nods.

"Maybe, maybe we can some to some arrangement. Could I call you tomorrow, perhaps?"

In embarrassed silence they exchange telephone numbers, and say their cursory goodbyes, each in their own way desperate to escape.

Outside, as they return to the car, Jess is half-triumphant, half-appalled at what has just transpired, whilst Stefan is simply astonished.

"Wow!" she says, widening her eyes and theatrically dropping her jaw. "I've never spent four thousand euros on anything in my life, and now I've just offered it to some random guy to cremate someone I've never even met! This time last year I was making eight euros an hour. Am I going mad? Is this real?" She laughs aloud. "Money talks! Shit, I'm shaking like a leaf! Are you okay?" She squeezes his hand on the gearstick. "You're not angry, are you? It's just a little ... bribe, that's all. He's not rich, you can tell that. Did you see his shoes? I can afford it. He can have some fun, and Maria and Jacob can be buried together. That's my plan. Did I tell you that? I did it for her, for them. And yeah, I guess it might satisfy something in me as well."

"You might have told me," begins Stefan, but he trails off.

"Come on, Stefan. What's the worst that can happen?"

He bites his lip. "I could end up with a criminal record that would prevent me from ever working with MSF ..." he trails off again, as if he's pondering how much that really matters to him anymore.

"That went well, I thought," she said. "Easy. I think we have him hooked. A ninety kilo undertaker-fish." She's so happy, so relieved, that she realises she must have been more anxious than she realised. Let's see what he says tomorrow."

Chapter Sixty-Three

2012

Stefan blew out his cheeks and smiled to himself. Even now he still could not quite believe the nerve, the audacity, the criminality and the sheer good fortune that had allowed them to get away with it.

Jess was still in England, and he was sitting cross-legged on the shingle, looking out at the other sails as they scudded across the white-topped bay. He had to move: his wetsuit was too tight and the harness was digging into his midriff. But even this was a bloody miracle. He had really thought that he'd never be able to windsurf again.

He looked back to the car, which for security he'd parked as close as he could to the surf shop. In the boot were Jacob's ashes; it would be beyond tragi-comic to lose them now.

God, this felt good. Mid-week on a windy, sunlit beach, deserted save for the other lucky sailors. In his head he applauded as his new friend Victor steamed into an immaculate carve gybe right in front; it took another windsurfer to appreciate the skill and guts it took to pull that off, and the satisfaction it bred.

He wondered once again whether he would have agreed to her

suggestion had it not been windy the previous week. On such details whole kingdoms were lost, people said. After leaving the crematorium they had driven the short distance to the coast, and he had still been vaguely angry that she had strung him along so easily. But old habits die hard, and like a cartoon rat to a lump of cheese he'd been drawn to the windsurf shop, and was soon babbling away to the owner. He'd looked enviously at the surfers out on the water. The cold of Madrid seemed a world away; it might well be wintertime, but here in the deep south the sea was a rich blue, and the sun held enough warmth to plate the sands in a quivering haze.

Jess meanwhile had entered the boutique next door, and had bought herself a new bikini. He could tell that she was a little self-conscious, but there was no question that she looked stunning; heads turned as she walked down to the water's edge. It was like a challenge. If she could swim in this cold, then he could bloody well windsurf again.

And he had! At the last moment he'd almost flunked it, but a combination of her enthusiasm and his pride had forced him the last few steps across the shore break, and suddenly he was up and flying. He hadn't gone far out, not that first time, but when he got back to the beach he'd been utterly elated.

"Jess. You have no idea just how overjoyed I am!"

"I think I might have some idea," she replied. "If your smile gets any wider you might break your jaw."

When he returned an hour later, exhausted and ecstatic, she had told him of her plan. Or perhaps more truthfully, she had given him his instructions.

"I've just checked with your pals there – this *Levante* wind is forecast to blow for another three days. How about staying here, in a hotel? I'll pay."

A beautiful woman, asking him to pick up a sport he loved, but which he thought he'd lost forever; it wasn't hard to obey.

"Alone," she finished

"Ah ... so there's a catch."

"A little one. But it's not complicated. I fly back to London to get Maria's ashes, and you go back up to Jubar, then do the business at the crematorium, and then we meet back in Madrid. Easy, no?"

And she'd been right. It had been easy, scandalously so. He had gone back up to the village, said his goodbyes to Jorge, picked up the wooden crate that he had made for the purpose, and called in at a Western Union branch to collect what he still thought of as a fortune in cash. He'd been nervous at the crematorium, but no more than that, and had returned that very morning, once the thing was cold, to collect the casket.

In between he had sailed, alone, and couldn't believe his luck.

Just one more go, he said to himself. It might be a while before he saw the sea again.

Chapter Sixty-Four

2012

"I think this is a good place," says Stefan softly.

She looks cautiously around the hillside, listens, tries somehow to taste the atmosphere of the low valley, then nods. She's pleased he's taken the lead, for she had been anxious that it would fall to her to choose, that they would spend the morning tormented by her indecision. And she can see that he is right: it is a good place.

According to their map they are around fifteen miles north of Manzanares. Earlier they had abandoned the new, European Union-sponsored highway which cuts clean across the countryside, and picked their way between the potholes of the discontinued road which it was built to replace. They had then stopped for a while by the cadaverous shell of a long-derelict building. Time and termites had melted the beams in the roof, and rainwater had devoured much of the mortar, so that in parts, only the dressed cornerstones remained. It stood at a rudimentary crossroads, at the axis of what Stefan had called a *Cañada,* a sheep drover's trail, and as she ran her fingers across the lichen-spotted bones of a window frame, trying to imagine the lives of the builders of such a place, they had heard the lonely bleating of sheep in the far distance, and she was touched by this continuity between past and present.

For a while longer they had clanked south along the age-old dirt track until they agreed that the suspension of the poor hire car could take no more. This was it.

He takes a deep breath and stares absently through the dusty windscreen. Jess steps out first, walks round to his side and yanks open the door.

"You ready?" she asks. "Vamos! All of you!" She wants to make light of things since she is determined not to be dominated by the solemnity of the occasion. She thinks of the wakes she has seen with her cousins in the north, feisty, irreverent affairs. To make the point she has left a bottle of cava in the boot of the car, which she now brandishes, half afraid that he might be offended by her profanity. She needn't have worried.

"A toast! Just what we need! Libation to the Gods! Me too, look!" And from his coat pocket he produces a miniature brandy bottle . "Well, I'm Spanish, after all," he laughs. "We see things differently, we know how to grieve and to party at the same time, pretty much all our lives, not like you uptight Anglo Saxons" She can see that he's teasing.. "I knew this Columbian guy in Kosovo; that lot are worse than us; he used to say this thing: *Los muertos al cajón y los vivos al fiestón.* Corpse to the coffin, the living to the revelry, something like that."

She looks shrewdly at his bottle. "You nicked that from the hotel mini bar, didn't you! You coming over to the dark side, Anakin?"

"Ahhh. But I have the high ground," he replies, and she laughs aloud.

"Shall we?" she asks, and together they each hoist one of the two caskets, and shuffle down the precarious embankment beneath them, following a faint goat track that makes its way through the thicket towards a desiccated stream in the distance. She is glad of the moment of levity that they had just shared, but each step that takes them further from the car punches a hole in her good humour, and she hugs the casket protectively to her chest.

The winter sunlight is exquisite, but it lacks the kick to outdo the cold, and she can see her breath. As she inhales she feels the burn inside her nostrils; it's England cold, the cold she knew as a schoolgirl walking the frost-white streets of Kent on her way to class. Out of nowhere a memory of her father's car leaps out at her, the old blue Jaguar that he'd loved so much; he would come to collect her sometimes after school if it was raining, she would look for him through the gates and pray that he'd be there, even after it all went wrong. But no: she won't think of him, not here, not now, and she tries instead to focus on the stillness of her surroundings.

Ahead, the bleak skeleton of a lifeless chestnut tree stands black and tall against the skyline, its deadness italicised by the exuberant pale pink blossom of the almonds that besiege it. There are tiny flowers beneath her feet too, pushing against the odds through the stony ground, orchids, maybe. She studies the thousands of alabaster snails which stick like barnacles to the abandoned fence posts. She wonders idly if you can eat them. The weight of her foot snaps a twig, and the morning hush explodes, spooking a hare which bounds terrified up the slope opposite. Then, most wondrous of all, she watches a stork as it sails unconcernedly above them, so close she swears she hears the rhythmic hissing skirl of its wings.

She listens carefully as he begins then to tell her quietly about another enigmatic Spanish concept. His voice is soothing. The idea of the *Querencia,* he explains, originally comes from the bullring. For some unknown reason the bull will adopt an invisible spot to which he will always return, and it is the job of the *toreador* to discern precisely where this is, for as soon as the bull is goaded from it, he will want to rush back. And the notion can be extended to people.

"We all have our special places, you see, our personal asylums that we can retreat to in the mind, the places we go to when we're in the dentist's chair, or waiting for results outside the exam room, a kind of virtual sanctuary. There's no reason why it should be any particular place, it's just where at some point in your life you've felt that all was right with the world. It's a bit arcane, I know, but it's just that feeling …"

She knows just what he means. She knows too that he's watching her as she considers privately what her own might be, and she's strangely consoled when he doesn't press her; it's not that she is embarrassed by the places that come to mind; it's more that she likes it that he's not pushy.

"It's a cool idea," she says. "Could this be one? For Jacob and Maria, I mean?"

He shrugs, and contemplates their location. The silence about them is palpable, and she strains her ears for the least infinitesimal sound.

"You never know," he suggests, "the mystic might say that it always has been … that it is they who have brought us to their special place … that they've come back at last …"

She smiles at him. "I like it. Their querencia. Cool. But, Jesus, here, now, for all time …" She shudders.

An old orange tree has somehow survived the neglect; in the cool she can just discern the exoticism of its scent. The most gentle of breezes stirs its evergreen leaves and small birds alight on the branches above them; when she listens now she can hear the deep thrum of bees. There's life here after all, she thinks. The breeze picks up for a moment, and as the orange tree trembles she watches transfixed as hundreds of tiny white petals flutter earthwards.

"Look!" she exclaims. "Told you it was a wedding, not a funeral! Confetti! God's confetti!"

He smiles, relieved that she does not seem too dismayed, since he wasn't sure if he had it in him this strange morning to console and comfort her. This is not my war, he kept thinking, this is not my crusade, my grief. He hadn't even known either of the victims, he wasn't involved, he reminds himself. Yet at the same time, deep down, he's beginning to recognise that this is the shallow, simplified version of the narrative. Despite everything, despite whatever efforts at denial he might make, he cannot escape the notion that he is implicated. Not responsible, not damned, but nonetheless entangled by his knowledge of the circumstances, by the bloodthirsty actions of his recent forebears, and by the simple fact of his presence as witness there that winter morning. He knows that the imminent humble ceremony is perhaps only symbolic, but understands too that symbols are potent. He gets this, he really does, the power of semiotics. Could he tell her any of this, he wonders to himself? Could he tell her that sometimes at night he can still feel the horror and relief as the novice's dog collar was torn from him by a livid, foul-breathed priest; that he recalls the unexpected lump in the throat he had felt when the Colonel in the blue helmets had pinned the medal to his chest; or that he remembers the disgust he had felt as his companions in the Guardia Civil had pissed on a Catalan flag after the riots that night?

"You okay?" he hears her ask, and turns to smile at her in reassurance.

"I'm okay. You?"

She nods. "You're right. It is a good place. It feels ... I don't know ... appropriate. There are worse places to spend eternity, I guess."

She takes one last look around, her face warmed now by the

strengthening sun. She watches as a faint wind announces its arrival as it bends the flax coloured grasses on the high plains opposite, and as it reaches them, she licks her lips as if to savour the herb-rich fragrance it carries. She is ready.

"Let's put them there," she announces, pointing to a moss-covered stone bridge. "An arch like that will last forever. I like it here; it smells of Spanish hay."

They had decided earlier that they would neither bury them, nor mark the remains with a cairn. Instead, simply, side by side, they pour out two bleak cones of grey-black ash. It is done. They stand back wordlessly, and watch as the breeze begins to stir the dust, the two small piles mingling with each other and with the world around.

"Flowers," is all Jess says, and swivels away from him. As she turns he sees clearly the tears that bisect her pale face.

By the time she returns only moments later with a spray of lavender and rosemary, the cones of ashes are already almost gone.

Stefan crouches to lay one of these tiny, aromatic wreathes, and under his breath she hears him whisper his farewell. "*Vaya con Dios*," he says, and she knows this absolutely to be the right thing to say. "*Vaya con Dios*," she repeats, and for a while they stand there, the ashes spiralling in the wind.

"Let's go," she says at last, then adds mysteriously, "Don't look back!" and in silence they begin to make their way up to the track.

When he swallows Stefan notices how his throat is sore with the effort of not weeping. He stumbles as they get to the steep embankment, steadies himself, then turns to pull Jess up behind him. It is only as they reach the car that she realises they are still holding hands.

Chapter Sixty-Five

Back to Madrid, 2012

At first Jess had felt self-conscious as they got back into the hire car, and had reached for the distraction of the radio. They listened for a moment to the opening bars of Bohemian Rhapsody, before Stefan leaned over to turn down the volume.

"You know what? This was in the charts the year that Franco died. Seriously. I learned that only recently. Funny thing, it seems an old song, but not like, *really* old. It kind of reminds me that old Franco was around not all that long ago ..." He trails off, and she looks at him, amused, shakes her head, and turns the volume back up.

"I know, Maria told me. Mama! Oooh-oooh ooh ... didn't mean to make you cry!" she sings along, and together they belt out the rest of the song as they weave between the potholes, the tyres creating a huge dust cloud that settles on the olive saplings either side of the track. He's driving quickly, enjoying the speed, the freedom.

"You always drive this fast?" she asks.

"Yeah," he says. "You know me, the reckless sort."

She grins at his mocking self-knowledge. But he slows down as they reach the main road, and sedately they make their way north.

Gradually, as she stares out across the vast fertile fields, trying to focus on one of the iconic white sails of a windmill, they begin to chat, an enthralling, untroubled chat. It's odd, she reflects, that she should want to listen to him, and at the same time to want to tell him so much too; it makes for effortless conversation.

They pause to buy water at a roadside shop, and as she waits for him in the car she feels a deep, almost unnerving sense of calm. She's managed it, she's done what she set out to achieve. Mission accomplished, she thinks, and sighs. It feels to her as if she's entered the rest period, the *Shavasana* at the end of a good yoga session, or as her friend had described it mischievously, the *petite mort* of Ashtanga. Would she dare share this observation with Stefan, she wonders, as he opens the door, startling her slightly. Another time, maybe.

They stop for lunch in Toledo, whose walls look Tolkienesque and forbidding, she decides, as they wander up the side streets towards the old town. Dutifully they pay their tourist dues to see the church where El Greco is said to be buried, and for a while she cosies up to a pod of Americans whose guide rattles off a series of modestly entertaining facts about the great man's life. She sees Stefan staring intently through the half-light at a small painting in the corner, and goes to stand behind him, close enough to smell his after-shave above the church incense.

"I was hoping to impress you by showing you a detail," he says.

"And?"

"Nada," he laughs. "I can't remember. Let's eat," and with that they step out into the street.

Over a thick lentil broth and delicious country loaf he tells her the story of the castle, of the Alcázar of Toledo in the war. In the summer of 1936 it was surrounded and besieged by an army of increasingly enraged Republicans, all desperate to reach the defenders inside. At one point the son of the besieged leader was captured by the attackers, who threaten to execute him if his father fails to surrender.

"They let him speak on the phone to his dad. Know what he said? *Commend your soul to God, my son, and die like a patriot.*"

"And then they shot him?"

He nods. "It was a great propaganda coup for the Fascists. The defenders held on by the skin of their teeth until Franco and the Army of Africa arrived to save them, and two days later Franco was declared the Caudillo, the Great Leader. This story references an earlier myth, of course, centuries ago, in Tarifa, when the local King, King Guzman, did a similar thing to his own poor son when besieged by the Nazrids. Only this time, even worse, he actually chucked a knife over the walls to them to do it … and you know what we call him today? Guzman el Bueno, Guzman the Good! The *Good*." He shakes his head. "Shall we see it?" he asks her.

"You're kidding! No way. Not after all that! Call me old-fashioned, but I just want a stroll and a coffee. And cake. Good cake. *Actually* good, as in not like your mate Guzman."

And so they wander down and along the ancient winding alleys of the *Juderia*, the Jewish quarter, into whose narrow streets the light can barely penetrate. A numbing cold clings to the wasted stonework, and as they come across a small patio, lined with gnarled oak doors and tiny, wrought-iron windows, she glances skywards, to the sunshine, casting about for warmth.

"She's okay, look," she says, and motions upwards. There, high above them, on a third floor balcony which even at this hour still catches the sun, he sees a decrepit old lady dressed in black. As they gaze at her she turns arthritically to reveal a withered forearm, pale and slender as the legs of the venerable bamboo chair in which she sits. For a second Stefan thinks that she's pointing at him, and he looks quickly away, discomfited.

The growing chill of late afternoon forces them to abandon the hunt for cake, and they settle instead for roast chestnuts bought warm and aromatic from a vendor in the park. Idly they watch two small boys struggle numb-fingered to undo the knots on a kite string; a flushed jogger pants past in unflattering pink Lycra; a frock-coated terrier chases something of great fascination beneath the piles of fallen leaves, and a fat priest shouts animatedly into his phone. Just an ordinary day, she muses, just a regular day in the park.

The journey back to Madrid passed quickly, despite the traffic, with more music, more free-flowing conversation. He had booked a hotel in the centre, and after a quick change they were headed out to see the city.

"Don't know about you," he had said, "but I'm exhausted! How about we just wander round the Plaza Mayor, grab a beer or two, then dinner?"

She wasn't going to argue; it sounded perfect. She was hungry, her feet ached, but she was full of a wonderful, celebratory energy. The streets were packed, far busier than she had imagined, and she picked up quickly on the verve and intensity of the people around her as they disappeared into the effervescent crowd. It was quieter by the time they reached the Plaza Mayor, whose stately arches held a number of small bars, with outdoor terraces warmed by hissing space heaters, and the beer was good.

Close by was the Casa Botin, the would-be oldest restaurant in the world, if they were to believe the Guinness Book of Records. It sounded cheesy and probably over-priced, she thought, but in the end proved surprisingly fun. There were more arches, linen tablecloths, and an improbable amount of meat. And they talked the whole time.

He filled in some of the details about his time with the Peace Keepers in Kosovo, and she told him more about her parents. She felt guilty discussing this when she knew he'd been abandoned so young, but he pressed her to continue, listening carefully; it was the first time she'd talked so freely about this in years, and it felt good.

The restaurant had grown busier, and noisier. As Stefan stood up to pay, Jess watched as a group of girls on a night out, a hen night by the looks of things, cackled as they checked him out unapologetically. One squealed as her friend elbowed her and whispered something in her ear, causing him to turn around and smile, blushing slightly. Behind his back the pretty girl gave Jess a leery thumbs up, and she returned a kind of embarrassed half wave in recognition. He certainly is a clean-cut, good-looking boy, Jess thinks; just why does she keep denying it to herself?

At almost seven hundred metres Madrid is a high city, and when they step outside the air coming down from the mountains is glacial. They walk quickly. The crowds that had slowed their progress earlier are long since gone, and soon they are back at the hotel. As they approach, she realises that for the first time that day she is a little unsure of herself.

What sense of precaution, of decorum, she asked herself later, had led him to book rooms several floors apart? She should take the high one, he had insisted, for the view. They said good night in the lift, his foot pressed firm against the door to prevent it from closing, and she had held him close as she scanned his tired face.

"Thank you," was all she could manage, and had hugged him tight again before he kissed her on the cheeks.

She studied herself now in the mirror as the lift went up without him. Was there some enigmatic Spanish word, she wondered, to describe this feeling of simultaneous relief at something not happening, and yet huge disappointment that it hadn't? She would ask him.

Her room is large, functional and over-heated, and she crosses straightaway to the window, struggling to open it to a permitted hand's width. The view is breath-taking, and as she gulps down the freezing fresh air she gazes out over the brilliant city, all towers and headlights and sirens beneath her. She stays there for a long time. She doesn't know it, but Stefan stares out at the same scene, separated from her by six floors of steel and concrete. If you could have been standing opposite, on the roof, say, of the Post Office building, you would have seen them both there, silhouetted against the amber lights of their rooms, two tall dark figures each sending out their silent, complicated thoughts into the cold night skies.

Chapter Sixty-Six

Madrid, 2012

That night she had dreamed of rebuilding the old house, the ruin they had seen the previous morning. As she struggles to wakefulness the dream fades and vanishes as she fights to capture it, to pin it down and take it apart, leaving her with an odd sense of loss.

She shades her eyes against the sun as she peers through the hotel blinds. The city is as gorgeous and dramatic by daylight as it had been last night. She fills the small kettle by her bed, and as she waits for it to boil, begins absently to scan an old copy of *El Pais*. She is reading out of habit, disinterestedly, as a way of kicking her brain into gear until the instant coffee can spark her fully back to life. Her eye is drawn to an image of a group of young people, students, an advert for one of the universities. It's the third time she has seen this advert, and she lingers on it until she hears the click of the switch on the kettle. An idea is beginning to form.

She realises she has been singing to herself in the shower; always a good sign, she thinks, and hopes no one could have heard her in the room next door. It's nine o'clock and she has a few hours until her flight. She is both excited and sad to be leaving. *Saudade*, she remembers. She sends a text to her friend Naomi to remind her that she had offered to meet her at Heathrow, trying to imagine what it will be like to be back, how she will respond to her friend's questions.

"Stefan? What's he like? Well, you know, depends on your perspective really. On the one hand he's a failed would-be priest, an ex-cop given to the odd panic attack, and a moody, penniless Latin to boot ... what could possibly go wrong? On the other hand he's an honourable, intelligent, sensitive, good- looking war hero who just took a job with a refugee charity ... take your pick!"

She is interrupted from her reverie by a knock at the door. Stefan asks self-consciously if she would like to join him for breakfast.

"Give me five minutes," she yells to him. "See you in reception!"

She scrambles to find her clothes. She brushes her hair carefully, and studies herself in profile. Then, as she purses her lips in the mirror, she imagines the inquisitive, knowing, eyebrows-raised look her mother would have given her if she could have seen her applying make-up at this time of the morning. "Darling! Lipstick before breakfast! That's daring of you ... anyone we know?"

She'll ring her mum as soon as she gets back, she promises herself, then closes the door and skips down the corridor to join him.

There are more steps than she had imagined, and halfway down she begins to regret her decision to avoid the lift, and she is breathless as she reaches the ground floor. She sees him in profile, facing the lift doors, waiting, and for a moment she thinks he looks angry, but as he turns to her his face softens and breaks into an enormous film star smile.

"Coffee?" she asks after they hug their hello. He smells of hotel soap.

"You bet. But not here – I had one earlier and it tastes like ..." His voice tails off but she gets the message. "There's a proper bar just round the corner, let's go there."

They walk together through the revolving door and she's tempted to take his arm, but holds back. She's tempted too to shock him, to tell him just how much she wants to sleep with him, that she hasn't felt this way before, and that she just doesn't know why she's so confused, or so reticent. She wants to tell him that he makes her laugh, that she's inspired by the goodness in him, and that when she's not with him she thinks about him all the time. She wants to tell him that it's an utter mystery to her – a tragedy – that she hasn't even kissed him. She wants to say all that and more. She wants to tell him that they have unfinished business, that the door on their adventure does not need to close. Why is she so timid?

He seems restless. Is he angry with her? No, he's just not good at farewells, that's all, he tells her. He looks so sad.

The coffee is bitter, the conversation fragmented.

And both their tongues are tied.

Chapter Sixty-Seven

Au revoir, Madrid, 2012

It was a flat and ordinary winter day. The smoked glass of the optimistic modern buildings flickered in the sunlight, taxis blared, and exhaust smoke rose noxious and blue in the thin cold air. People shouted and laughed on the pavements. But in the car on the way to airport the two passengers were quiet, subdued, sitting alone and apart on the back seat of the old Mercedes. It exuded the spice of worn leather and decades of tobacco and seemed impossibly wide; there was more than distance between them Stefan felt, and the further they got from the city, the worse the strange tightness in his chest. They hadn't quarrelled, they hadn't fought, but the absence of their togetherness had shattered him. She was going away and that was that. He almost panicked as he had that day on the beach, and could imagine this overpowering sadness as a physical blockage that was literally choking the life force out of him.

He forced himself to concentrate and to breathe deeply as his yoga teacher had taught him. He turned and looked at her in profile. Her hair was down and the black tee shirt she wore accentuated the pale glow of her skin. She was wearing Maria's earrings. As she gazed out of the window he had time to watch her properly; he wanted so much to take in this moment, to not forget the fine structure of her cheekbones, the curve of her lips. *O Dios mio*, she was lovely; there was a lightness to her somehow, a fragility and a gentleness, and it was this, the deep, deep awareness of her gentleness that tipped him over the edge.

He couldn't help it. This wasn't panic, but sadness pure and simple. He cried quietly. Cried for Jacob, for his father, for all of stupid Spain, for all the thuggery and ignorance of the past; he cried for her and for himself and for all the days they'd had and never would have, and he cried for not having the words to tell her what he felt. He was unmanned, unfit. Humiliated.

And then the strangest, kindest thing. She turned to face him, reached for his hand and just looked at him, quizzically almost, with an inexpressible tenderness that tore his heart and soothed him all at once. Silently she stroked his hand and it was almost as if she was *allowing* him to see her properly, to see that she shared and understood . It was the most intimate, enigmatic moment of his life. He was so out of his depth.

He looked away, guilty, and in turning missed the tears in her own eyes.

How could he find a way to tell her that it was only in her presence that he felt himself truly coming alive? He opened his mouth to speak, but words drifted from him. He lifted his hands, as if that might help. It was like catching smoke. And suddenly they were there, and this other him was paying the taxi driver and picking up her case, and helping her, escorting her away and out of his life. What was he thinking?

The airport terminal was busy. Like an automaton he walked past the security staff, immune to the excitement and energy of everyone around him.

Time was running out. There was so much he wanted to explain to her, important things, but in his whole life he had never felt less articulate. He could no longer even formulate the ideas, let alone the words. Everything was happening too quickly. What was that poem she had mentioned? *Le bateau ivre.*

She put down her bags and looked him full in the face. He tried to tell her; it was no good.

"It's like I'm back in the rip-tide in Cabo de Gata," he said miserably. "Dragging me away with nothing to hold on to."

She smiled her Mona Lisa smile. "You know what to do. You told me yourself. Let go ... go with it."

Stepping forward he hugged her with all the strength he had left, then kissed her left cheek. To his dying day he would never know for sure whether their lips had actually touched, had accidentally grazed as he moved to the right, but they were breath-takingly, dangerously close and he quivered. She moved back slowly, smiling and light, and with one quick gesture pulled off one of the earrings.

"Here," she said, "for you. Just one."

"No," he mumbled, "after all this they belong together."

"I know," she whispered. "Look after it for me. Just for a while."

She turned and waved and walked away whilst Stefan reeled, for his whole world had just tilted with the weight of a few grammes of gold.

Chapter Sixty-Eight

Adieu, 1937

Jacob couldn't quite be certain. At the very last second, just as he had looked up after shooting the last man on the ridge below, he thought perhaps that he had seen movement across to his left, and had thrown himself to the floor. A fifth man? Could that be possible? Had there been five horses? He waited, and watched, letting his panic subside. He still had the high ground. If the man moved, he would shoot him. If he didn't move it meant the man was trained, and dangerous. Better to wait it out until dark. He could wait all day if that was what it took. He had food, he had water, he had discipline.

The man spread motionless on the hillside opposite was a Russian. A sniper, an expert, veteran of the October Revolution and the battles in the east. Twice he had been wounded, and twice decorated. He had been sent to Spain with the others to ensure that Kyriagin was murdered. A less emotional man might have baulked at the task, for they were old comrades, having served together on the Black Sea. But those were his orders, and now he was required to kill these people from Madrid; he knew better than to ask the reason why.

All day he lay still, the dull muzzle of his rifle invisible amongst the bracken. This was nothing: at the siege of Vladivostock he had waited immobile for almost two days, so long that he'd had to piss his trousers, the cold so intense that he'd almost frozen to death. He got his man in the end though; he always did. Now these same fingers that had shaken the hand of Lenin were still, the index finger crooked patiently round the trigger, waiting for the moment. He knew he'd only have one shot: the man in the cave was good, he'd seen just how fast and accurate he was in the morning when he had despatched the other four. And canny too, and the sniper admired the way that he'd kept himself hidden for so long. He preferred it this way. It was better to have some respect for your enemy before you killed him. And so he waited. It was just a question of time.

Throughout the long day Jacob considered his choices. He talked himself through it yet again. He could still go home to Toledo. The front line here in Andalucía was porous, everyone knew that. He could sneak through again at night and be in Granada by the weekend. He'd talk to the military governor, get him to send a telegram to Lucas and to his dad. There'd be hell to pay but they would sort it out somehow. He'd probably lose his commission, but he could earn it back. He hadn't caused the fire in the prison, the women had, it was just coincidence that he was there. And then he'd panicked. Everyone does, once in a while, even generals, and so he had run away. He was still so young, they would forgive him.

Who was he kidding? The only way he could resurrect himself with the army would be through deceit, betrayal and influence: the very things he had learned to despise. He could never live with himself. He smiled sadly. And he could never live without Maria.

All day he remained vigilant. When the sun was at its highest it found him and its heat added layers to the fatigue building up behind his eyes. Still he would not sleep. Sleep would bring danger to Maria,